"Kill him! And then kill his master!"

There was a cry from the door. Both men whipped around. They saw an old man standing there, his mouth agape, his eyes wide in horror.

"Pirem!" Dejanus shouted.

Pirem snapped out of the terrible shock that had frozen him in place. He backed away from the door.

"Kill him, Dejanus!" Orkid cried. "And then kill his master!"

Dejanus lunged forward, but his feet slipped on the pool of Berayma's blood and he fell heavily to his knees. He looked up in time to see the servant flee like an old rat with a cat after it. He jumped up, but before he could set off in pursuit, Orkid grabbed his arm.

"No, wait! There is a better way! All the pieces are in place, we only have to keep to our roles." He took Lynan's training knife from Dejanus' hand and dropped it on the floor near the body of the dead king. "Put the bodies of the sentries back in their place, then call out the Royal Guards." He could not help staring at Berayma's corpse. "The king has been murdered by Prince Lynan and his protectors, the constable and Pirem. What a pity they were slain trying to escape the palace."

The Keys of Power

INHERITANCE

FIRE AND SWORD*

SOVEREIGN*

*Coming soon from DAW

INHERITANCE

Book One of *Keys of Power*

SIMON BROWN

DAW BOOKS, INC.

DONALD A. WOLLHEIM, FOUNDER

375 Hudson Street, New York, NY 10014

ELIZABETH R. WOLLHEIM
SHEILA E. GILBERT
PUBLISHERS

http://www.dawbooks.com

First Printing, October 2003
1 2 3 4 5 6 7 8 9 10

DAW TRADEMARK REGISTERED
U.S. PAT. OFF. AND FOREIGN COUNTRIES
—MARCA REGISTRADA
HECHO EN U.S.A.

PRINTED IN THE U.S.A.

This book is dedicated with much love to my nephews and nieces—Alice, Amy, Andrew, Ben, Bennett, Billy, Caleb, Christopher, Daniel, James, Jane, Kea, Kylie, Lachlan, Louise, Nate, Phillip, Rebecca, Tara and Thomas.

ACKNOWLEDGMENTS

I would like to thank Alison Tokley, Sean Williams, Jack Dann and Sara Douglass for all their advice and support during the writing of this book. I would also like to thank the wonderful work done on my behalf by Stephanie Smith, Julia Stiles, Garth Nix, Russ Galen, Betsy Wollheim and Debra Euler.

Kingdoms are but cares,
  State is devoid of stay,
Riches are ready snares,
  And hasten to decay.

Pleasure is a privy prick
  Which vice doth still provoke;
Pomp, imprompt; and fame, a flame;
  Power, a smouldering smoke.

Who meanth to remove the rock
  Owt of the slimy mud,
Shall mire himself, and hardly scape
  The swelling of the flood.

   —King Henry VI of England
   (1421–1471)

1

A GER, still not forty, crippled by war and itinerant by
nature, had sat down for a quiet drink in the visitor's
room in the Lost Sailor Tavern. He fidgeted in his seat, trying to ease the pain in his crookback but without avail; the
ax blow that had cut tendons and bone all those years ago
had been too deep to ever fully repair. He took a sip of his
drink, a strange, sweet, and warm brew that tickled all the
way down his gullet, and took in his surroundings.

The room was busy, but not crowded. Aproned staff wandered between tables, taking orders and delivering drinks.
The guests were a mixed lot of merchants, sailors, off-duty
soldiers, local dock workers, and a handful of whores. A couple of the women had thrown him glances when he first entered the room, but on seeing his misshapen back and his one
eye had quickly turned away. He did not care. He had not
slept with a woman for fifteen years, and sex was more a
memory than a desire these days.

Suddenly the seat opposite his was taken. He looked up
and saw a youth dressed in farming gear of woolen pants and
shirt and a dirt-stained coat; his round face was arse-smooth,
his eyes brown, his gaze intent. The youth nodded a greeting

and Ager returned the favor, noting there were plenty of vacant tables around.

"You were a soldier," the youth said bluntly. "I can tell. I have seen wounds like those before."

"There's nothing special about losing an eye," Ager replied calmly, "and many are born with a crookback."

"The injuries are rarely seen together. An arrow in the eye, perhaps? And a halberd or spear in the back?"

"Right about the eye, wrong about the back."

"Judging from your age, sir, I would guess these happened during the Slaver War."

Ager found himself increasingly curious about this strange young man. "And what would you know about the Slaver War?"

"I'm interested in everything about it," the youth replied with surprising earnestness. "In what battle did you receive your wounds? Or were they inflicted in different battles?"

"The battle at Deep River," Ager told him.

The youth's reaction surprised him. His eyes seem to light up like lanterns, and he said in a subdued voice, "I have searched for you for many years."

"Me?"

The youth shook his head. "No, no. I mean, someone who was at Deep River."

Ager leaned forward across the wooden table, moving aside the cup he had been drinking from, and said, "What did you say your name was?"

"I didn't," the youth replied levelly. "It's Pirem."

Ager nodded, trying to recall whether he knew the name. A distant memory sparked. "I knew a Pirem once," he said quietly. "A long time ago."

"There are many Pirems in Theare," the youth said reasonably.

"This one was a soldier. He was in my company during the Slaver War."

"He fought with you in the battle at Deep River?"

The man shook his head, then looked away. His single eye, as gray as a winter sky, looked as if it was searching for a memory in the drifting blue smoke that wafted from the kitchen through the common room.

"No; he died before then. Caught a sniffle that traveled to his lungs. He died in a delirium, thinking he was back with his wife and children."

He returned his gaze to the youth. "Most of our losses during the war were to disease and not battle. Did you know that?"

Pirem blinked. "I remember reading something about it."

"You read?" Ager asked loudly, clearly impressed. The skill of reading was rare enough to hint there was more to this boy than suggested by his farmer's clothes. He tried to study the youth's hands, but there was not enough light to catch that much detail.

"No more difficult a skill than ploughing," Pirem said, keeping his voice low. The veteran's exclamation had drawn attention to their table. "And talking of names, I don't know yours yet."

"Ah, now, names are not things you should pass on so easily." He smiled easily. "Pirem."

"I trust you."

The statement was made with such direct simplicity that Ager was flattered. "Ager, and don't worry about my last name. Why are you so interested in the Slaver War?"

"My father fought in the war."

"Many fathers fought in the war." Ager's eye blinked. "And sons and brothers." He rested back in his chair and a brief spasm of pain flickered across his face. Pirem looked concerned, but Ager waved a hand in dismissal.

"My father died while I was still a baby," Pirem added.

"He fought at Deep River?"

"Yes. He fought in almost every battle of the war."

Ager heard something like anger in Pirem's voice. "He didn't survive?" Pirem shook his head. "What was his name?" Pirem hesitated. "If you trust me with your name, you can trust me with that of your dead father's. Maybe I knew him."

Pirem opened his mouth to speak but closed it quickly. Ager waited, emptying his cup and catching the attention of one of the tavern's bustling staff to indicate he wanted a refill.

"His name was Pirem, too."

"God, the world is truly filled with your namesakes, isn't it?"

Before Pirem could reply, a thin boy wearing a white apron streaked with dirty handprints was by their table and filling Ager's cup with a warm brew, smelling of clove, different than his first drink. He tried an experimental sip and decided he liked it even more.

"An' who's payin' for it?" the boy demanded, holding out his hand. Pirem handed over a coin before Ager could dig out any coppers from his purse.

"Bugger me!" the boy cried. "That's a whole penny! I can't change that, sir. I've only got three eighths on me . . ."

"Keep his cup filled during the night," Pirem ordered, clearly concerned at the attention their table was getting once again.

The boy disappeared with a smile as wide as the city walls; there was no way the cripple would ever drink through a whole penny in one night, and he would pocket the remainder.

"You don't have to ply me with drink to talk," Ager said gruffly. "I'm no pisspot babbler. If you really want to know about the war, I'll talk until winter." His face darkened. "No one wants to remember it anymore."

"I want to know about Deep River," Pirem said. "None of the books I've read can tell me much about it, and there weren't that many . . . many . . ."

"Survivors?" Ager laughed harshly. "No, there weren't

many of us. But there were none left of the other side. None at all."

"Was it an ambush? The histories say different things, as if no one can make up their minds about it."

"That's because no one will ever know, now that Elynd Chisal is dead." Ager's voice caught, and he gulped quickly from his cup. "Only General Chisal knew what was really happening during that bloody war. He was the best soldier Kendra ever produced."

Pirem leaned forward eagerly. "Please. Tell me everything you can."

Ager settled in on himself and closed his good eye; the empty socket, a shallow bowl of skin furrowed with scars, stared vacantly at Pirem.

"The general had learned of a Slaver camp on the other side of Deep River. He decided to go after it before they got news of us. He was always like that, taking the battle to them. It was hot, dry as a priest's mouth. My section was in the vanguard. We scrambled down the ravine and waited for the rest of the division to catch up. General Chisal himself was with the second regiment, his own Red Shields, followed by a squadron of dismounted Hume cavalry, pissed off at having to leave their mounts behind; but they were horse archers and it never hurts to have a few bows around to sweep the enemy's ranks before you hit him with sword and spear. Last in the line was a militia regiment, all huff and bluff, but green as baby shit through and through. When we were all down, we started up the other side. We hadn't gone more than a hundred steps when it started."

"The Slavers attacked?"

Ager nodded. "Oh, yes. First arrows, and then boulders. Their shooting wasn't that accurate, and the boulders were easy enough to dodge, but with so many of us stuck on the slope some had to be unlucky."

"So the general was caught by surprise? It *was* an ambush?"

Ager shook his head. "No, I don't think so. He knew the enemy scouts would have to be asleep to miss us scrambling down the ravine, and would have plenty of time to organize some kind of defense. I think he counted on them not being able to shift their whole force to the river in time to stop us getting up the other side." He smiled grimly. "And he was right."

"What happened then?" Pirem urged.

"The general ordered the archers to keep down the Slavers while the rest of us scrambled up as quickly as we could. We had almost reached level ground, but then two companies of Slaver mercenaries charged down slope. That shook us, I can tell you. We were exhausted, and the archers had to stop shooting because we were hand-to-hand. It was hard fighting them back up the slope, but we outnumbered them." Ager grinned then. "And my company beat the Red Shields to the top."

"But that wasn't the end of it, was it?"

Ager's grin melted away. He shook his head. "No. That's when the real battle started, and when I got my wounds." He drank another mouthful and opened his mouth to resume when a shadow fell across the table. He glanced up to see who it was, and then all thought froze in his brain.

Pirem turned as well, and let out a low groan. "Oh, God, not again," he muttered.

A giant of a man glared down at the pair. His flat blonde hair, starting to gray, was cut close to his scalp, a short salt-and-pepper beard covered most of his face, and his eyes were narrowed to slits. He wore a long cloak, but there was no disguising the shape of the long sword that hung from his waist.

"Damn," Ager said, but softly and without anger.

The stranger placed his large hands on Pirem's shoulders. "You'd better come back with me."

"But, Kumul, I've finally found someone who fought at Deep River!"

The one called Kumul briefly lifted his gaze to Ager. "You're being fed chicken shit by someone desperate for company and a night's drinking. Only a handful survived that battle, and you'll find none of them in this place."

Pirem turned back to Ager, his eyes pleading for him to refute the words, but the look was lost on him. The crookback could not take his own eyes off the giant man. "It *is* you, isn't it?"

Kumul frowned. "Now that's an asinine question."

"Captain Alarn," Ager said. "Captain Kumul Alarn, of the Red Shields."

Kumul flinched, and Pirem took one of his hands. "You see? This man knows you! He must have fought during the war!"

"Many men know me," Kumul said levelly, "and how do you know which side *he* fought on?" He stared accusingly at Ager, but the man could say no more for the moment—his skin had gone the color of limestone. Kumul grabbed the youth's coat in both hands and lifted him to his feet. "Let's not waste any more time here," he said.

Ager stirred suddenly. "No! Wait!" But Kumul ignored him, half-dragging and half-carrying Pirem along with him. Bundling the youth past one of the servants, he exchanged a nod with her. Pirem caught the signal.

"One of your informers, Kumul?" Pirem demanded. "Or one of your whores?"

Kumul grunted, gave another tug that almost had the youth in the air. They had reached the exit when Ager, struggling hard against his crookback, caught up with them.

"Captain Alarn! Wait!"

Again, Kumul ignored him. He used a shoulder to barge open the heavy wooden door and pulled Pirem after him. Ager was not put off and followed them onto the crowded street. He bumped into a passerby, mumbled an apology, lurched forward, and managed to catch the tail of Kumul's cloak.

"Oh, for God's sake!" Kumul cried, and spun around, one hand still on Pirem and the other pulling free his cloak from Ager's grasp, showing the design on his jerkin and exposing his sword. "Do you recognize the livery, man? I am no longer Captain Alarn of the Red Shields. They are gone and forgotten! I am Kumul Alarn, *Constable* of the Royal Guards. Now leave us alone or I'll arrest you!"

"And I am no longer Captain Ager Parmer of the Kendra Spears," Ager shouted back defiantly. "I am now Ager Crookback or Ager One-Eye, or just plain Ager the Cripple. Look at me, Kumul! Look at my face!"

Kumul stopped short, pulling Pirem back with him, and put his face close to Ager's. "Ager Parmer?"

Ager slouched, the effect of his rush finally catching up with him. The slouch turned into a slump, his left shoulder lifting to be level with his neck. He nodded wearily.

"I thought you were dead," Kumul said quietly.

"No, not dead, but as good as. It took two years for the wound in my back to stop weeping."

"But that was fifteen years ago. Why didn't you find me?"

"The war was over, my friend. I wanted peace and quiet." Ager swallowed. "But I could never find it. No one at home wanted me around. I've been wandering ever since, picking up work where I could find it."

"What kind of work?" Pirem asked, then blushed. "I didn't mean . . ."

"I'm not offended," Ager said quickly. "I have some learning. I can read and write, and know my numbers. Officers in Kendra's army must know these things. I work as a clerk, usually for merchants, who care little one way or the other about my deformities. I earn some spending money and my passage from port to port. As with you, Pirem, there is more to me than shows."

Kumul looked at the youth, raising his eyebrows. "Pirem?" The youth shrugged.

"Your name isn't Pirem?"

"No," Kumul answered before the youth could open his mouth. "Pirem is the name of his servant."

"Servant? Then what *is* your name?"

Kumul laughed. "Since I could not recognize you, I should not be surprised that you cannot recognize this one."

Ager peered closer at the youth's face. After a moment he pulled back as if something had stung him on the nose. "He couldn't be," he said to Kumul.

"He is," Kumul replied smugly.

Before the conversation could continue, there was a scuffle among the crowd of passersby and someone cried out. All three turned to see what the commotion was about. A tall, thin woman was bent over picking up fruit that had spilled from a basket and was at the same time cursing the clumsy dolt who had tripped over her long legs. The offender, still scrabbling to his feet, his face red with anger, ignored her. As he stood, there was a glint of steel in his hand. He looked up to see he was being observed by the giant man and his two companions, one a cripple, and the other . . .

He cursed and charged toward them, now holding his long knife out in front of him.

Kumul pushed the youth behind him with his left hand and with his right drew out his sword. He smiled tightly, silently thankful their assailant's clumsiness had given him away. What he did not see was a second man behind him, stepping quickly and silently toward the youth, a knife raised above his head for a single killing blow. The crowd around him fell into frightened silence.

Something in the sudden stillness made Ager turn. Seeing the new threat, he moved without thinking to sandwich the youth between himself and Kumul. The second attacker shook his head—the cripple would slow him down but never stop him. He waited until he was three steps from the crookback before playing the trick that in so many vicious street fights had given him victory. He threw the knife from his right hand to his left and lunged. He was so sure of his advantage that the sudden rasp of metal against scabbard barely registered in his mind, nor the flash of a bright short sword swinging up to impale itself in his body.

Out of the corner of his eye, Kumul had seen Ager shift position and knew what it must mean, but only had time to hope that Ager's injuries had not ruined his skill with a sword before his own attacker was upon him, slashing wildly with his weapon. Kumul easily deflected it downward with his blade and then flickered the tip up and into the man's throat, the man's own impetus driving the point a finger's length through muscle and artery and into his spine.

The assailant spasmed once and dropped to the ground, dead. Kumul tugged his sword free and spun around, using his left arm to keep his charge behind him. Relief flooded through him when he saw the second assailant on the ground, Ager on top of him, blade sunk deep into his heart and lungs.

"Well done, old friend," Kumul said, then noticed how still the crookback was. He moved forward and placed a hand on Ager's twisted shoulder. "Are you all right?"

Ager coughed, turning his head so he could see Kumul with his one eye. "The bastard shifted his knife to his left hand," he said weakly. "Too late for me to change my grip." His head slumped and his eye closed as he lost consciousness.

Kumul bent down and saw that a knife had been driven into Ager's right side to a third of its length. Blood was flowing freely. The youth knelt down next to Kumul.

"That is a serious wound," he said. "We must get him to the palace."

Kumul nodded. "I'll carry him. You take his sword." Leaving the blade in for fear of doing more damage, Kumul lifted Ager gently as if he weighed no more than a child.

The youth jerked the short sword out of the dead man. "I'll run ahead to wake Dr. Trion."

"God!" shouted Kumul. "Behind you, boy!"

The youth spun on his heel and saw a third attacker almost upon him. Obviously undeterred by the fate of his two companions, he had seen his chance to strike when the giant had taken up his burden.

"My friend," the youth said quietly, "that was a mistake."

The assassin saw his target move forward to meet him. Surprised, he had no time to slow his charge. Instinctively, he raised the knife's point to deflect as best as possible any swing toward his neck or head. It was the last mistake he would ever make. He saw the youth take a step sideways and crouch. Before he could react, a sword sliced upward into his belly and ripped out as he stumbled forward. He gasped in pain, felt the earth rise to smash against his head, and lost consciousness before the blade fell against his neck, almost severing it through.

The youth stood, washed in blood, his eyes alight for a moment and then suddenly as dull as coal. His sword hand dropped limply to his side. The crowd started talking excitedly as if the fight had been put on for their benefit.

"Quickly, Lynan! We have to go. There may be others!"

Roused by the use of his real name, Lynan looked up at Kumul. "It's . . . it's not what I thought it would be like."

"Later! We have to go. Now!"

The two hurried off. Ager, still unconscious in Kumul's arms, moaned in pain.

"I fear we will be too late," Kumul said grimly.

"He will live," Lynan replied fiercely.

"If God is calling him, no one can hold back his ghost."

"He *will* live," Lynan insisted. He looked up at Kumul, tears welling in his eyes. "He knew my father."

2

AGER slipped in and out of consciousness, at times the feeling in his side a gnawing pain and then nothing more than a dull, persistent throbbing. At one point he thought he was floating in air, but he managed to open his eye and realized Kumul was carrying him. He had a vague memory of Kumul doing this once before, but then remembered the memory was of Kumul carrying a friend of his from the battlefield. Dimly it occurred to him that his friend had died, and he wondered whether that would be his fate, though whether he died or not did not seem terribly important to him this moment. Another time he caught a glimpse of a figure of a man floating in the air beside him, his face young and then surprisingly older, and he knew that face, knew it almost as well as his own. *It's his ghost,* he thought. *He's come back to take me with him.* But then the face was young again, and none of it made any sense to him.

After a while, the feeling in Ager's side was gnawing more than throbbing, and in his clearer moments he understood it meant he was still alive and unfortunately coming out of whatever delirium had held him. He tried to say something, but Kumul told him to shut up. On reflection, that seemed like a good idea, so he did. Then, just as the pain was becoming too much for him, he was carried through a huge gate. Kumul shouted orders and soldiers scurried away to do the constable's bidding. He knew he was coming to the end of his journey, and knew that meant some bastard with small hooks and cutters would soon be slicing into him to dig out whatever it was that was causing the hurt.

Kumul was carrying him up a flight of stairs now, and the man's jolting stride sent spasms of pain through his body and, absurdly, made his empty eye socket itch. He moaned involuntarily, and felt humiliated. He tried apologizing, but Kumul again told him to shut up. Eventually they entered the most luxurious room Ager had ever seen. One wall was hidden by a tapestry of dazzling color. Opposite, a hearth was aglow with a blazing fire. Kumul finally laid him down on something he assumed must have been a proper woolen mattress, for it made him feel as if he was floating. He could hear Kumul and the young man talking earnestly with each other, but for some reason he could make out only a few words, and they made no sense at all.

Despite the warmth from the fire, Ager was beginning to shake. He concentrated on trying to keep his limbs and jaw still, but to no avail. To make things worse, the pain in his side was almost unbearable. He wanted to cry out, but the only sound he could make was another moan. He reached for the source of the pain, but felt something hard there instead of his own flesh. Perhaps he was shaking so much Kumul had had to pin him to the bed. The thought made him want to laugh.

And then Ager was aware of a new presence—a short, bearded man with a clipped monotone of a voice that only added to the room's background hum. What distinguished him from the other two was a smell that was strangely comforting, and after a moment he realized it was the smell of the sword bush. The realization alarmed him.

Oh, no, he thought. *It's a surgeon. I'm going to hate this man, I know it.*

The doctor placed a gentle hand against his forehead. Kind brown eyes looked down into his single gray one, then the hand moved to his side and took hold of the thing sticking into him. The doctor did not move it, as Ager had been afraid he would do, but he retreated and talked to the other two again. A second later he was back. Ager heard him say, "This will hurt like nothing you've ever felt before."

"I've had a fucking ax in my back," Ager tried to say, but could make only a hissing sound. "Nothing can hurt more that."

Then Kumul was leaning over him. The giant gave a lopsided smile and held Ager by the shoulders, pinning him down. He felt the young one doing the same with his knees.

And then agony. The surgeon was right. It did hurt more than anything he had ever felt before. He screamed. His body arched into the air. He screamed again. A great, swallowing abyss opened beneath him and he fell away from the earth.

The surgeon Trion left the room shaking his head. "I don't know, Kumul. I just don't know."

"He saved my life," Lynan told Kumul.

"He saved both our lives," Kumul replied, not lifting his gaze from the crookback. "You were lucky tonight." Lynan said nothing. "You must not do this again."

"Do what?"

Kumul turned to face him. "You know my meaning," he said, anger creeping into his voice.

"I've been leaving the palace—"

"Sneaking out of the palace," Kumul corrected him.

"—*sneaking* out of the palace most nights for over a year now. Nothing like this has happened before."

"You know I put up with these expeditions because I

think you deserve some leeway—you're a young man now—but I warned you to stop last month."

"For no reason."

"No reason!" Kumul barked, then glanced anxiously at Ager, guilty about raising his voice. "You know as well as I do the *reason*." He grabbed Lynan by the shoulders and looked him straight in the eye. "Your mother the queen is dying. Her ghost may stay with her for another week, or another month, or even another year, but it may just as easily flee her body tonight. Things are starting to happen in Kendra. Forces are aligning themselves for the succession, including the Twenty Houses."

"The Twenty Houses have no reason to hate me," Lynan said weakly, knowing the lie even as he spoke it. "My mother is Usharna, Queen of Kendra. I am one of them."

"And your father was a commoner made general, and *his* mother was a Chett slave. The Twenty Houses have every reason to want to see you put out of the way before the queen dies."

Lynan turned away, not wanting to hear. Kumul sighed heavily and leaned over Ager to check his bandages.

"He is still bleeding a little. And that fire is dying. I will get more wood."

"I hope this wound doesn't weep for two years like his last one," Lynan said. As soon as he had spoken the words, he regretted them. He had not meant to sound so callous. But it was too late. Kumul stared angrily at him.

"Have the courtesy to watch him for me while I'm gone," he ordered, and left.

Unreasonably angry himself, Lynan tried standing on his royal dignity, but alone and with no one to be arrogant with, he slipped back to reality. What did he think he was doing? Kumul deserved better than that from him. And who did he think he was fooling? He had all the royal dignity of a midden, unlike his older half-siblings, all true bloods and sired from Usharna's first two noble-born husbands. Kumul was right: he had the form but not the substance of the court's respect. His own mother, the queen herself, did her best to ignore him. He knew, too, that this was why he so desperately wanted to know more about his father, whose blood apparently flowed thicker through his veins than his mother's. But General Elynd Chisal was not even a memory for him. He was made up of tales and anecdotes, history lessons and hearsay. "Kendra's greatest soldier," Ager had said of him.

Lynan remembered the crookback then with a strange mixture of gratitude and unexpected affection. He checked Ager's breathing—shallow but blessedly regular—and laid the palm of his hand on the man's forehead to test his fever. He heard someone come in the room, and turned, expecting to see Kumul.

"That was quick . . ." he began, but stopped when he saw a small, slightly built young man with a mop of hair on his round head that did not seem to know which way to sit.

"Olio!"

"Good evening, b–b–brother," said Olio, and hesitantly approached the bed. "Is this the one?"

"The one?"

"I met Kumul rushing down the p–p–passageway. I asked him where he was going and he shouted something about a wounded m–m–man." Olio looked with real concern at the hapless Ager. Of all Lynan's siblings, Olio was the only one who had ever had time for him, and his gentle nature made it easy for Lynan to like him despite his noble father. Even when he was a child, it had been only Olio among the royal family who seemed to acknowledge him as a member.

"Yes. He saved my . . . I mean . . . Kumul's life tonight." Lynan did not want the whole court to know he had been out of the palace. The last thing he needed was to be kept under close supervision by a nervous Royal Guard. Being tagged by its constable was bad enough.

Olio's eyes widened in surprise. "And he is wounded b–b–badly?"

Lynan nodded. "Trion seemed doubtful he would live," he said, but added quickly, "I think he will."

"He is a friend of yours?"

"No. Yes. I mean, I hope so." He groaned inside.

Olio simply nodded, as if he understood exactly what Lynan was trying to say, and of what he was trying not to say. Olio was eerily empathic like that. "Then I will p–p–pray for him." He turned to leave.

"You would pray for him if he was your worst enemy," Lynan said without sarcasm.

Olio inclined his head as if he was seriously considering the remark. "P–p–probably," he admitted. "And b–b–by the way, I would change your clothing if I were you."

Lynan looked down at himself. His clothes were covered in dried blood.

Before Olio reached the door, Kumul returned, followed by a male servant carrying a basket filled with firewood. They both bowed briefly to Olio, who waved an informal dismissal and moved out of their way.

As the servant started stacking the firewood by the hearth, Kumul mumbled to Lynan, "Prepare yourself."

"What are you muttering—?"

Lynan never got to finish his question. He heard the sound of heavy feet coming from the corridor and Dejanus appeared, dressed in the full regalia of the queen's own Life Guard, his mace of office held erect in one hand. He was an even bigger man than Kumul, and filled the doorway. He saw Lynan and offered one of the quizzical smiles he was famous for, then stepped aside. Behind him, standing with what seemed impatient frustration, was Usharna, the queen herself.

She was fully dressed for office, with a heavy linen gown bejeweled with emeralds and rubies, and a black velvet cloak sweeping behind her that shone in the firelight like still water under a full moon. Around her neck hung the four Keys of Power, the ultimate symbols of royal authority in the kingdom of Grenda Lear and all its subject realms. Their weight seemed to drag her head down, and the muscles of her neck and shoulders were taut with the strain of carrying them. Already small in size, the tangible burden of office, together with her illness, made her appear like a frail clay doll. Her white hair was pulled up on top of her head and kept down with a gold tiara decorated with an engraving of her family crest, the black silhouette of a kestrel against a gold field. Fine hands like china nested together under her heart, and her pale brown eyes tiredly surveyed those before her.

"Your Majesty!" Lynan called out in surprise. All in the room bowed stiffly from the waist.

Usharna snorted her satisfaction and allowed Olio and Lynan to come forward and each kiss a cheek. "Well, it's nice to see you at home, however late," she said to Lynan, looking disapprovingly at his bloody dress. Without waiting for a reply, she went to Ager and peered at him closely. "This is the one?" The question was directed to Kumul.

"Yes, your Majesty."

"Where is my physician?" she called out, and Trion seemed to appear from thin air. Lynan caught a glimpse of the crowd waiting in the corridor; it looked as if the queen's entire entourage had followed her down.

"Your assessment?" she asked Trion.

"He is seriously wounded, your Majesty. If he survives the night, he may live, but I do not think he will see another dawn."

The queen stood deep in thought for a long time. Lynan had never seen her looking so frail. He wanted to go to her and hold her arm, take some of her burden on himself, but he stayed where he was, made immobile by her aloofness. *Always so far from me,* Lynan thought.

"I wish to be alone with this man," she said at last, but Lynan thought her expression suggested she would rather be anywhere else than alone with Ager.

Dejanus looked as if he was about to object, but Usharna raised one hand and he bowed deferentially. Everyone filed out obediently, Dejanus shutting the door behind him and standing guard over it. Lynan, squeezed between Kumul and a courtier whose violet scent made him feel queasy, wondered why Usharna should worry about a cripple injured in a street fight—he looked at Kumul out of the corner of his eye—unless someone was indiscreet enough to let on about the night's events and their role in them.

Was she going to wake up the poor man and interrogate him? The hair on the nape of his neck started to rise and he tried to ignore it. Trion was saying something to one of his aides, an attractive young woman dressed in the latest fashion of fine linen layered with strips of colored felt. She was only recently attached to the court from one of the outlying realms, and her dark golden skin told Lynan she was either a Chett or an Amanite. Probably the latter; by all accounts the Chetts did not take well to lots of clothing. The thought made him smile. The woman saw it and thought he was smiling at her. Appealingly, she returned the favor. Lynan's heart skipped a beat. Most of Usharna's courtiers, while making some show of bowing to him if cornered, would not look at him sideways under normal circumstances. They haven't gotten to her yet, he decided, and the thought saddened him.

He was aware that the hairs on his arms were starting to rise, and the skin on his face seemed tight and irritated. He saw the blond hairs on Kumul's massive forearms beginning to stand as well, and realized that whatever was affecting him was affecting everybody in the corridor. Some of the courtiers were starting to look distressed.

"What's going on?" he asked Kumul in a hushed voice. Kumul refused to answer him, his blue eyes locked forward and his body rigid as a board.

One of the courtiers fainted. Lynan recognized the very round Edaytor Fanhow, Kendra's magicker prelate, his ceremonial robes folding around him like the wings of a giant moth. Someone knelt down to make sure he was all right. Lynan felt sorry for the prelate, then decided his time would be better spent feeling sorry for himself. His stomach had started roiling, and he was afraid he would pass out as well. And then it occurred to him that the prelate was by no means the largest or oldest in Usharna's entourage. So why did he pass out so quickly?

The answer shook him. He stiffened, his breathing became shallow, and a cold wave passed through his body despite the close, hot confines. Edaytor fainted because among those present he was the most sensitive to magic. Usharna was using one of the Keys of Power. It must be the Key of the Heart, the one sometimes called the Healing Key. He had never, in all his years, seen Usharna employ the power inherent in the royal symbols. He had been told stories about their strength, but he had cynically believed they were nothing but legends created to give the throne more authority through their possession, just like King Thebald's Sword of State, an overly ornate and utterly impractical weapon held by new monarchs during their crowning. It was not that he doubted the existence of magic—he had seen members of the five Theurgia employ it—but the fact that his own mother could wield it disturbed him greatly. And to wield magic of such strength!

Lynan's chest was tightening; he let out his breath in a long hiss, but it did not seem to ease the pressure at all. Now other people started to pass out. First, an old dame who was lucky enough to be caught by her son, and then—of all people!—Trion. Just when Lynan thought he could no longer hold on, and that he, too, would faint, he found himself taking in air in great, heavy gasps. The pressure around his chest had simply disappeared as if it had never been, and so had the queasiness in his stomach.

"It's over?" he asked Kumul, his own voice sounding distant to him.

Kumul, himself as pale as a sheet, nodded once and immediately approached the door. Dejanus, still recovering himself, made a vague effort to block his way.

"The queen has finished whatever she was doing," Kumul told him. "Let me in."

"Not until she opens the door herself," the Life Guard wheezed.

Kumul lowered his mouth to the guard's ear. Lynan heard him say, "And what if she is unconscious? You felt the energy emanating from that room. You know better than anyone how frail she is."

Dejanus still hesitated. Lynan did not know what made him step up at that moment, but the same concern, the same sudden anger, must have struck Olio as well. They stood on either side of Kumul and together ordered the door be opened, Olio even managing not to stutter. Against the commands of two princes, and with no sign from Usharna, even Dejanus had to give way.

They rushed into the room, but the sight that greeted them stopped them in their tracks. The room's sandstone walls seemed to be aglow; even the fire in the hearth seemed dim in comparison. Shimmering blue threads coruscated in the air and then died, leaving behind trails of ash that hung suspended before slowly drifting to the floor. By the bed, standing more erect than anyone had seen her for years, was Usharna, arms wide, surrounded by a soft halo of white energy that pulsed with her rapid breathing. More people crowded into the room, their mouths open in surprise. Trion and Edaytor, the latter flushed and moist with perspiration, came up beside Lynan.

"I never imagined . . ." Edaytor began, but ran out of words to describe his astonishment.

Even as they watched, the energy in the room dissipated like mist burned away by the morning sun, and the halo around Usharna faded away into nothing. The fire flared once, brilliantly, and then settled down to produce a steady, warming flame. Usharna looked at her court, the merest hint of a smile on her face, then slumped forward.

Kumul and Dejanus were there before she reached the hard floor and together supported her weight.

Trion hurried over and quickly checked her pulse and breathing. "She is all right. Her heart still beats strongly." He turned to the crowd. "She is exhausted, nothing more." The collective sigh of relief sounded like a prayer.

Kumul helped Dejanus scoop up the queen into his arms. Then the Life Guard hurried out of the room to take her to her own chambers, Trion and most of the courtiers following close behind. Kumul closed the door and went to Ager.

Edaytor Fanhow joined him, moving like a supplicant approaching a holy relic, his hands held out before him.

"There is a great deal of magic residue," he said, more to himself than the others. He touched one of the walls, gingerly at first, but then placed his palm flat against a single sandstone block. "Still warm," he muttered. "Utterly incredible."

"It was certainly a p–p–performance," Olio said in a hushed tone.

"Did you know our mother could do that?" Lynan asked him.

Olio shook his head. "Well, in theory, of course, b–b–but I've never seen the Keys used b–b–before, except as decoration around the queen's throat." His brow furrowed in thought. "I wonder what the other Keys m–m–might be capable of."

"How is Ager?" Lynan asked Kumul.

"His breathing is almost normal," Kumul said with obvious relief. "And see, the bleeding has stopped altogether."

"It is a wondrous thing the queen has done," Edaytor said.

"The queen would do anything for Kumul," Lynan said.

"Which shows how little you know about your own mother," Kumul replied sharply.

3

KUMUL woke with a start, almost falling off his stool. He had fallen asleep with his head resting at an odd angle against the wall and now had a painful crick in his neck. Standing up, he went to Ager's bed. The man was still asleep, but it seemed to be the sleep of the peaceful and not of the dying. The crookback's face seemed very old and careworn for someone who could not have been older than forty years of age, and his long hair, mostly gray, was lanky and thin.

Although the fire in the hearth had long gone out and the room was cool, Kumul felt the need for fresh air. He went to the room's only window and eased open the wooden shutters. The city of Kendra slept in the darkness. A faint light broached its eastern walls. He could make out on the water just beyond the harbor entrance the phosphorescent glimmer of the wakes of fishing boats returning to the city's wharves, although the boats themselves, and even their sails, were still lost against the black expanse of sea.

He returned to Ager and, once again, carefully studied the man's face, trying to remember what it had been like all those years ago when they were both comparatively young, filled with an energy that had long since been dissipated by war and injury and the loss of their beloved general.

Kumul had not seen Ager for over fifteen years and had assumed he was dead; but last night, against all expectation, they had met again, only for Ager almost to die in his arms. He felt bitter at that last twist of fate.

The sharpness of his feelings surprised him. He had lost friends before, and his friendship with Ager during the Slaver War largely had been largely professional, not personal. Yet now it seemed to him that the friendship, stretched across a war with as many defeats as victories, had inherited the weight of years of vacant peace during which Kumul had slowly learned he had few real friends left in this world.

A sound rose from the great courtyard outside, the clattering of hooves on cobblestone, the challenge of the guards. He heard the sentries stamp to attention, something they only did for members of the royal family. It must be Berayma, Usharna's eldest child, returning from his mission to Queen Charion of Hume, one of Usharna's less predictable and more outspoken subjects. The mission had been a sensitive one, and Kumul prayed that Berayma, severe as a winter wind, had been up to it.

Kumul looked again at Ager's face, calm in sleep but carrying with it all the scars of war earned in the service of Queen Usharna. He had a premonition then, a warning of some danger, distant but closing in. He tried to wish it away, but it hung at the back of his mind, formless and brooding.

Gasping, Areava broke away from the shreds of her sleep. She looked around wildly, pulling the sheets about her. It took her a few seconds to recognize her own chambers, and when she did, she collapsed back against the bedhead, shivering in the predawn stillness.

The black wings of the nightmare that had roused her still

beat in her memory. She had dreamed of the sea rising up over Kendra and the peninsula it was built upon, washing over the great defensive walls, flooding through its narrow streets, surging against the palace itself, and still rising. She had seen her mother Usharna struggling against the waters, the weight of her clothes and the Keys of Power dragging her down relentlessly, and then her half-brother Berayma had appeared, holding out his hand to the queen, their fingers locking. For a moment it had seemed that Berayma would drag her free of the flood, but the pull of the sea was too great and his grip weakened. Areava saw the strain on her brother's face as he tried to hold on to the queen's hand, and then her fingers, and then the tearing sleeve of her gown . . .

"Oh, God." Areava wrapped her arms around her knees, hugging herself tightly. A sob broke from her and she could not help the tears that came. She felt ashamed of her weakness, but the dream had been so terrible, so frightening.

She steadied her breathing, made herself stop crying, then slipped out of bed. She stirred the dying embers in the hearth, added a few small logs. Slowly the fire restarted; with the increasing warmth the last shreds of the dream seemed to evaporate from her mind, leaving behind nothing but a vague disquiet about the future. But Princess Areava of Kendra did not believe in premonitions or prophecies. Putting aside the uneasiness, she started dressing, wondering what had woken her. She remembered the sound of riders cantering into the forecourt. Had it been part of the dream? She went to the narrow door that led to her balcony and opened it. She looked over the railing to the forecourt below and saw several horses being led to the stables. So that part was real. A thought, unbidden, came to her that perhaps all of it had been real, and a shiver went down her spine.

* * *

The sun was already well above the horizon when Lynan was roused by Pirem. His servant gave no greeting, simply held out his clothes for him as he dressed and helped put on his belt with its small dress knife.

Lynan checked himself in the mirror. He liked what he saw. If not as tall as his siblings, he was as wide, and he did not object to a face which, if not handsome, was not so bad it would scare the ghosts out of children. His focus shifted and he smiled at the reflection of Pirem, whose face would scare the ghost out of a seasoned warrior. He was as short as Lynan, thin as a fencing blade, with a head made up of more sharp points than a knife box. Pirem's lips were sealed tight.

"Not talking this morning, Pirem?"

"No."

"Did you have a particularly heavy night on the drink?"

"Not as heavy as you, your Highness," Pirem said pointedly.

"Ah. I see. You are angry with me."

"Angry with you, your Highness? Me? What right has a lowly servant to be angry with the boy he has raised almost singlehandedly when that boy goes off an' almost gets hisself skewered by the likes of street thugs? I ask you, Your Highness, what right do I have?"

"You've been talking with Kumul."

"Someone had to carry fresh water and sheets up to the room where that poor man who got hisself skewered on your behalf now lies on his deathbed."

"Don't exaggerate, Pirem. Ager is not on his deathbed."

"Pirem, is it?" He cocked his head as if listening to the sound of his own name. "I thought that was a moniker used by a certain lad who's got not enough sense to do as he's told when what he's told is for his own health and happiness."

"Oh, for God's sake, Pirem, give your tongue a rest."

"An' here I was thinkin' you were concerned 'cause I wasn't sayin' enough. Silly me."

Lynan turned away from the mirror and confronted the servant. "All right, Pirem, have it out. Give me your lecture."

"Oh, far be it from me to lecture your Highness, who knows so much already about the ways of the world he doesn't bother listenin' to the advice of his seniors . . ."

"Forget it!" Lynan said abruptly, his irritation turning to anger. "I've had enough, Pirem. I had all the lectures I needed last night from Kumul, and I don't need any more from you."

Pirem could take no more. His voice broke as he cried out: "God's sake, lad, you almost got yourself killed straight dead!"

Lynan's anger melted away. Pirem was almost in tears. "Really, I was in no danger. Kumul was there—"

"Kumul? Kumul's lucky to be alive, too. He should've taken me. Someone's gotta watch his back. It's too damned big for hisself to watch it. You're both careless, you both think blades will turn on your hide, and you're both as ox-headed as the general . . ."

Pirem stopped suddenly and turned away, but not before Lynan saw the tears start to flow. Lynan felt ashamed. There were few certainties in his life, but one of them was the love he knew Pirem held for him, and the love Pirem had held for his father, General Chisal. Pirem had never recovered from failing to stop the assassin's knife that struck down Elynd Chisal. The fact that he was able to slay the assassin before he could get away had never been any comfort for him.

Lynan reached out to put his hands on his servant's slim shoulders, but pulled back. "I am sorry," he said quietly. "I promise to be more careful."

Pirem, his face still averted, nodded. "Being careful may not be enough anymore."

Lynan sighed. "I will not leave the palace again. At least, not by myself."

Pirem looked at Lynan over his shoulders. "You'll take Kumul with you?"

"I'll even take you along, as well."

Pirem sniffed and straightened. "Well, good enough is good enough," he said, his voice still subdued, and carefully examined his charge. "Pretty enough to frighten the queen's horse. Get on, then. You're expected in court this morning."

"Me?"

"Your brother's back from Hume. The queen wants the rest of the family to welcome him."

Lynan groaned. "I hate these sorts of things."

"Berayma's your brother, like it or not. You've got to stick with him. He'll be king one day. One day soon, maybe."

"Not much difference to me. Though at least Berayma will be no worse than my own mother."

Pirem glared at him. "You've got no sense, sometimes. You don't know when people are doin' you good or evil. Her Majesty may have her faults, but not as many as you. Keep that in mind. An' keep in mind your father loved her above all else, and he was no fool. An' keep in mind that you are her son, an' that she's never forgotten it, even if you have."

Lynan was taken aback by Pirem's fierceness. "When has she ever shown me a kindness?"

Pirem shook his head. "It would take all day and the next night to tell you, and you're in no mood to listen right now. So go or you'll be late, an' there's no point in makin' her even more angry with you than she already is."

Usharna gripped the armrests of her chair as exhaustion overcame her. She tried to force away the nausea by concentrating on the words being spoken by Orkid Gravespear, chancellor of the realm of Grenda Lear, as he strode about the queen's study like a tamed bear. One of her ladies-in-waiting approached, but she waved her away.

She had known last night when she had used the Keys of Power to save the life of that poor cripple how exhausted it would make her. The Keys held great magic but the cost of using them was also great. She was barely sixty years of age, yet she felt as if she inhabited the body of someone twenty years older again, thanks to the number of times she'd used the Keys during the Slaver War. Until last night she had not used them since the end of that terrible conflict, but she could not let the man die after he had so valiantly saved the life of her son.

Oh, Lynan, she thought, *despite everything I have done to protect you, my enemies still get through.*

Or maybe, she conceded, not her enemies but those of her last husband, Lynan's father. Elynd Chisal had been a great man and a great soldier, but common born. His skills as a general had earned him the enmity of the Slavers and their backers, and her marriage to him had earned him the enmity of the noble houses.

Usharna had tried to keep Lynan safe by keeping him out of the court as much as possible, by feigning indifference to him, by not letting him hold those minor offices her other children used to practice their royal responsibilities. But all to no avail. Her enemies and Elynd Chisal's enemies were now her son's enemies as well. She thought it bitterly ironic that the offspring between her and the only husband she had ever truly loved should have so many in the kingdom set against him, that her love should generate so much hate.

Her thoughts were interrupted by the chancellor's rumbling voice.

"And as you predicted, your Majesty, Queen Charion of Hume has agreed to allow Berayma to tour her lands in an official capacity early in the new year." The chancellor grinned inside his thick, dark beard. "And in so doing has once again conceded your son's right as your successor to be her overlord."

He glanced at Usharna, noticed how white she had suddenly become. "Your Majesty. . . ?"

Usharna waved one hand. "Just more of the same, Orkid. Don't concern yourself." She smiled at him with genuine affection. "I try not to," she added dryly.

Orkid, unconvinced, nodded anyway, and continued. "The gift that accompanied our proposal gave her a way to accept the tour without losing face."

"Always best to let them think they have the better of you."

"Charion is too proud."

"Which knowledge we work to our advantage. Hume is a border realm, traditionally independent and aligned with the kingdom of Haxus, our oldest foe. Charion, and her father before her, are the only rulers from Hume to have ever owed allegiance to another crown. Hume must be treated with patience and every courtesy."

"She takes advantage of you."

"And we *own* her, Orkid, her and her kingdom. Never mistake the fortress for its stones." She closed her eyes, conserving the little energy she had left. "When did you see Berayma?"

"Early this morning, as soon as he arrived. He gave his report—succinctly—handed over his papers, and went to get a couple of hours' sleep before coming to see you. He should be here any moment."

"When I am gone—"

"You shouldn't say such things, your Majesty."

"When I am gone," Usharna persisted, "Berayma will look to you for wise counsel. Serve him as you've served me."

Orkid bowed stiffly, a concession lost on Usharna, whose eyes were still closed. "Yes, of course, your Majesty."

"You did not tell me how he took to reporting to you in the first instance. Did it rankle his pride?"

Orkid allowed himself a smile. "Stirred it a little, I think."

"He must learn to trust you and take your advice." Orkid returned the compliment with another unseen bow. "And you must learn to flatter and cajole him, as you flatter and cajole me."

The chancellor was genuinely shocked. "Your Majesty!"

"Oh, Orkid, you have been my chancellor now for fifteen years. You are my right arm, so do not dress up our relationship in clothes that do not fit it. You needle, old blackbeard, until you have your way."

"Or until you tell me to leave well enough alone," he rebutted.

Usharna actually laughed. "As you say. We make a fine pair, you and I, and Grenda Lear should be grateful to us for its prosperity and peace. I want you to forge the same relationship with my son. There is nothing in creation as dangerous as a new king ready to try his wings for the first time."

"Nothing so dangerous?" Orkid teased. "Not even a new queen?"

Usharna laughed for the second time that morning, a rarity even on her best days. Orkid felt absurdly pleased with himself. "Well, in my day, new queens had a great deal to prove. New kings will only repeat the mistakes of their predecessors because they are taught to emulate them."

"He could do worse than emulate you."

"Now you're buttering me up, and I don't like it. He will be his own man, but he must also be king of Grenda Lear, and the two may not always sit easily together. It will be your job to ensure his throne is big enough to fit, but not so big he slips off."

"I will do my best," Orkid said humbly.

"I know. You always do your best." She breathed deeply, telling herself she should go to bed as soon as the morning's official functions were over, then admitted to herself that she would do no such thing; no successful monarch ever ruled from the bedchamber.

There was a knock, and the double doors to the Usharna's study opened wide. Dejanus announced Berayma, then stepped out and closed the doors behind him.

Berayma went to the queen's side and gently placed a hand on one of hers. He looked at Orkid. "Is she asleep?"

"The ruler of Grenda Lear never sleeps," Usharna said, opening her eyes. "That is another trick you must learn, Berayma."

"There is time—"

"Not much more."

"I don't want you to go," Berayma said fiercely.

"Die, you mean." Usharna shook her head. "You can't even say the word."

"I don't want the throne, mother."

Usharna looked at him in astonishment. "You think I wanted it when my turn had come? To lose my freedom, and in return gain nothing but a life of drudgery, problems, and sleepless nights, with no release except through death?" She looked at him carefully. "You have been coddled and protected all your life, and now it is time you faced your responsibilities."

Berayma looked hurt. "I already help administer the kingdom for you."

Usharna looked sternly at her son. "The Kingdom of Grenda Lear and all its realms comprises eleven states, six million people, and a host of lesser kings and queens, princes, and dukes. It spans almost the entire continent, contains forest and jungle, plain and mountain; half of the kingdom can be in drought while the other half is in flood.

"Over the last year, you have spoken for me—on instruction—on some councils, acted as my representative when meeting the odd dignitary or two, delivered a speech in my name at the occasional official banquet, and you have just completed your first ambassadorial mission. This is not administration. I still rule this kingdom and its people."

Berayma looked abashed. "Is that all I have been? Your mouthpiece?"

Usharna sighed. "No. You are training to be king. But never think you have learned all the lessons. The time will come, soon enough, when you truly will be administering the kingdom and will have to make decisions on behalf of Grenda Lear by yourself." She glanced quickly at Orkid. "In consultation with your court, of course."

"I will face my responsibilities, you know that."

"Yes, I know you will. But don't worry needlessly. The task before you will not be as great as you think."

"What do you mean?"

"You will see soon enough." She waved Orkid closer. "Now, my chancellor and I have things to discuss before we all meet in the throne room."

"Perhaps I should stay," he ventured in a whisper, glancing at Orkid warily.

"You are not king yet, my son. Leave us. I will see you again later this morning."

"What is left to discuss, your Majesty?" Orkid asked after Berayma had left. "My report is finished."

"The Keys of Power. You still disagree with my intentions."

"A foolhardy tradition is not worth following. "

"Foolhardy or not, it is the only way," she said wearily.

Orkid forbore arguing. The queen was tired, and that would make her more stubborn.

The official court reception for Berayma was held at midmorning in the throne room. It was a court event, and anybody who had or sought influence there was present.

In her simple basalt throne, balanced on a cushion, sat

Usharna herself, her robes of state flowing down the royal dais. On her left hand side stood Chancellor Orkid Gravespear, and behind her stood Dejanus with his ceremonial mace. On the dais' first step, to the right, was the royal family, presently Areava, Olio, and Lynan. To the left were the kingdom's senior officials and members of the queen's executive council, together with Usharna's ladies-in-waiting.

The group looked out over the palace's single largest enclosed space, considered quite a wonder in the world when first built some centuries before, and still a matter of some awe for strangers to Kendra. Two rows each of thirty twisting stone pillars, painted gold and black, divided the space into three long sections. The middle section formed the concourse, and a thin gold carpet stretched along it from the dais to the throne room's entrance. The areas on either side were used by the members of the court to survey any visitors as they made the long and intimidating walk along the concourse, or to wait in silence as the queen delivered speeches, passed judgments, and made declarations.

A hundred arched, stained-glass windows set in polished granite walls let in so much light that it was almost possible to believe the throne room had no roof, but high above the court curved headseed beams supporting thousands of sharrok pine shingles set in patterns that suggested waves lapping against a calm shore. Standing to attention before each of the pillars was one of the Royal Guards, under the eye of their constable standing only a few steps from the dais; next to Kumul was Usharna's private secretary, Harnan Beresard, sitting behind his small writing desk.

Lynan always felt out of place among the august group occupying the dais. Shorter than most, dressed less finely, and without the haughty demeanor that usually came with rank or blood, he thought of himself as an interloper who at any moment would be exposed and escorted out of the palace. The rest of the court, bigger now than it had ever been before, peered up at them with eager, envious, and often spiteful eyes. The back of Lynan's neck ached with all the long stares boring through it. He risked turning his head to look behind him, but the faces there were all directed toward Usharna herself, looking splendid and pale on her black throne. Of course no one would bother noticing him. He was only the fourth son of the monarch, half noble and half commoner, and since it was the half-commoner part that obviously counted in the palace, why should anyone pay him any attention at all?

Because I am Elynd Chisal's son, that's why! he roared at them in his mind. *Because I am the son of the best soldier who ever came from Kendra, the soldier who saved the queen from defeat during the Slaver War, because . . .*

He ran out of reasons, embarrassed by his own anger. There were many more reasons, he was sure, but here and now they did not seem to matter. At least not to the court. He looked over his shoulder again, got some idea of just how many there were behind him, and then did the same for those along the opposite wall. Kumul was right. The crows were gathering for the feast, all hoping it would come sooner rather than later. He wondered how many of them sided with the Twenty Houses, and how many of them with Usharna. How far would the aristocracy go to reclaim the power it had lost to the queen? The only certainty was that no move would be made against the queen herself, such was the love and respect held for her by the common people. But after her death? Where would Lynan stand then, and what chance would he have against the scavengers?

There was a great metal clanging from the other end of the throne room. The wide bronze doors swung open and the court sergeant stood there with his heavy black spear. With great solemnity and grace he made his way up the concourse to the foot of the dais.

"Berayma Kolls, son of Queen Usharna Rosetheme, son

of her consort Milgrom Kolls, Prince of the Kingdom of Kendra and all its Realms, returns from an embassy to her Majesty's realm of Hume."

"Then let him come to me," Usharna answered formally.

The sergeant returned to the entrance and called out Berayma's name and title. Usharna's eldest son appeared at the entrance. Tall and wide-shouldered, dark-haired, stern-faced, and erect, he looked splendid in his fine woolen clothes and fur coat. He started the long walk, led by the sergeant and followed by the small retinue he had taken with him to Hume. When he reached the dais, he and his followers bowed low.

"Your Majesty, I bring word from your loyal subject, Queen Charion of Hume. She sends her greetings and devotion."

"I am much pleased to hear it," Usharna replied. "And much pleased to see you safely returned. Take your place, my son."

Berayma bowed again and mounted the dais, taking a position on the queen's right-hand side, above his siblings. His retinue dispersed.

"Court Sergeant, do I have any other visitors?"

"Two applicants, your Majesty, awaiting your pleasure."

"Then let them come to me."

For the next hour, the queen and her court listened to the appeals of two applicants, the first a minor nobleman asking for the return of some land taken from his father during the Slaver War for taking sides against the throne. The queen asked what else his father had lost.

"His head, your Majesty," the son replied.

"And who holds this land?" she asked.

"Yourself, your Majesty."

The queen asked Harnan the secretary if any wrongs had been recorded against the son, and being told there were none, announced that the nobleman should not inherit the crimes of his father, and returned the land. Harnan officially recorded the decision. The nobleman thanked the queen for her wisdom and generosity, and quickly departed.

The second applicant was a merchant from Aman, who declared in a longwinded speech that some of Usharna's officials were blocking his trade from reaching the city of Kendra.

"On what grounds?" Usharna asked.

"On the grounds that I am an Amanite, your Majesty," he replied.

The queen looked sideways at her Amanite chancellor, but Orkid was stonefaced. The queen promised that she would look into the matter, declaring that every member of the kingdom, whether from Kendra or Aman or distant Hume, had equal access to the capital's markets, and again nodded to Harnan Beresard.

The queen ended the session by rising from the throne. The formalities over, everyone visibly relaxed and started to mingle and talk. The throne room was instantly filled with the low and incessant babble of a hundred, gossiping voices.

Berayma approached the queen and said in a low, urgent voice: "I have been told that you used one of the Keys of Power last night."

"You are well informed," Usharna said.

"Everyone is talking about it!" Berayma declared.

"I was being gently sarcastic, my son. I wish to God you would develop a sense of humor."

"There is nothing funny about what happened, your Majesty. You are old and weak and—"

Usharna glared at him. "Too old and weak to rule, you mean?"

There was a hush among those on the dais. All eyes were on Berayma. His face flushed. "No! That is not what I meant at all, but that if you use the Keys, you will exhaust yourself—"

"Enough, Berayma," Usharna said harshly. "I am the queen, and the Keys of Power are my instruments, to be used at the right time and in the right place and for the right purpose. If I did not use them thus, I would not deserve to wear my crown."

"But, mother, to save the life of a drunk cripple!"

It was Usharna's turn to flush, but in anger. "This man you speak of was captain of the Kendra Spears during the Slaver War. He served me faithfully and paid dearly for it. He was dying from a wound inflicted on him by doing me another great service . . ."

Berayma turned on Lynan. "By saving *him* from petty bandits—"

"By saving your brother's life, and that of my constable."

Berayma said no more; he recognized the tone in his mother's voice, that sharp edge of righteous anger that always made nobles, courtiers, soldiers, husbands, and children shut their mouths against any argument with their queen.

Usharna looked around at the others gathered by the dais, including Orkid and Dejanus. "Any one else volunteering to comment on my actions last night?" Some shook their heads, most just dropped their gaze. "Then the day's business is over." She beckoned to Harnan. "Meet me in my sitting room. We have correspondence to complete."

The secretary, a thin reedy man who looked barely strong enough to support his own weight, nodded, packed up his papers and pens, and followed Usharna and her ladies-in-waiting as they left the throne room. Dejanus brought up the rear. All talk stopped as the court, acting as one, bowed out the queen.

When she was gone, Berayma strode to Kumul. "It is your fault, Constable. I have been told that you allowed my brother to leave the palace at night and stroll around taverns and hotels at his own discretion, inviting the very sort of attack visited on him last night!"

Kumul said nothing. He knew better than to answer back to one of the royal family, especially Berayma who was such a stickler for court protocol.

"How can we trust the man in charge of the Royal Guards to protect the palace if he cannot even protect one small, irresponsible youth?" Berayma pressed.

Kumul, impassive, stared straight ahead.

Lynan, who was almost as afraid of Berayma as he was of the queen, wanted to speak up in Kumul's defense, but his tongue seemed glued to the roof of his mouth.

Berayma, however, had finished his public dressing down of the constable and stalked off to join a group of his friends from the Twenty Houses who were loitering nearby and enjoying the show. Lynan thought they looked ridiculous in their silk tights and decorated codpieces, a fashion only lately come to the court from Haxus in the north.

Lynan was about to move to Kumul, to apologize, when he was confronted by his sister Areava. "Is this true?" she demanded.

"Sister?"

"Don't feign ignorance, Lynan, I know you far too well." Almost as tall as Berayma, but with the golden hair their mother had once possessed, Areava made an imposing spectacle, and when her face was pinched in fury as it was now, she reminded Lynan of stories of the beautiful mountain witches who ate the faces of lost travelers.

Before he could answer, Olio joined them and said to his sister: "It is unfair to b–b–blame Lynan for the actions of thieves, Areava. It was not his fault. And as our m–m–mother said, the cripple she helped last night was owed something b–b–by this family for p–p–previous service."

"I do not question our mother's actions, but Lynan's," she

said to Olio, but not harshly, since she loved him above all others. She glared again at Lynan. "Well?" she insisted.

"I did not mean to place anyone in danger, least of all the queen," he said meekly.

"You are a thoughtless boy, Lynan. One day someone will pay for your self-centeredness."

"I am sure you are right." Lynan could not help himself; before he could catch the words, they were out.

Areava acted as if she had been slapped across the face. She looked at her half-brother almost with distaste. "You assume too much from your position," she said tightly and stormed off.

"What did she mean by that?" Lynan asked Olio.

Olio shrugged. "I had b–b–better follow her and calm her down b–b–before she insults some visiting dignitary."

Left alone, Lynan felt he had come off badly from the morning's events, not unusual in his experience of court life. He remembered Kumul and went to him.

"I'm sorry for what Berayma said to you. It was all my fault, not yours or Ager's or the queen's."

"Berayma was only demonstrating his concern for Her Majesty," Kumul replied, his face as impassive as it had been when he was being publicly berated. He looked around the room. "Do you see them all, Lynan?"

"See all the what?"

"All the newcomers. See, over there, new staff for Aman's commission in Kendra." Lynan saw a trio of heavily bearded gentlemen wearing long hide coats. They looked like smaller versions of Orkid. "And over there, old Duke Petra, back from his retirement on the Lurisia coast. Next to him are representatives of Hume's merchant navy; they came with Berayma." Kumul pointed to a group of men and women dressed in leather jerkins and breeches. "Mercenary commanders, from all over the kingdom, come to sell their services as bodyguards, or worse."

"This is what you were talking about last night," Lynan said. "About the scavengers gathering for the feast."

Kumul nodded. "They can hardly wait for the queen to pass on so that they can press their claims with a new and untried king."

"Berayma will not be so easily swayed, I think."

"No. He has made his friends within the Twenty Houses. The old aristocracy welcomes him with open arms. Milgrom Kolls was, after all, one of them, and pushed on the queen in exchange for their support in the early days of her reign."

As the son of the man the members of the Twenty Houses hated so much, and now a victim of their spite as well, Lynan sympathized with Kumul's concerns. "They would have applauded last night if those thieves had been successful."

"Thieves?" Kumul looked at him in wonder. "Even you could not be so naïve."

Lynan felt a twinge of anger. Surely no one, not even among those in the Twenty Houses who hated him the most, would arrange for him to be killed. The risks of being found out would be too great. He looked around the room again. Perhaps the risk might be worth it if there would soon be a succession.

"Are you certain?" Lynan could not help the tingle that traveled down his spine, and he glanced nervously over one shoulder and then the other.

"Not yet. I have my people working on it. But there are others who would see you out of the way, even if they hold no personal animosity toward you. Assassinating a prince, even a prince as lowly as yourself, must unsettle your mother, and that would serve to unsettle the kingdom. This is why you must not leave the palace at night by yourself. Whoever tried to have you killed last evening may try again."

*   *   *

As soon as the throne room had cleared, the members of the court returning to their offices, guild halls, or commissions, Kumul returned to his quarters to check on Ager's progress.

The crookback was sitting up in bed and gulping broth from a huge mug. Kumul was surprised to see how well his friend looked. Ager put down the mug and offered him a huge smile, his single gray eye twinkling.

"I did not expect to see you awake so soon," Kumul said.

"And last night I did not expect to ever wake up again," Ager replied. He turned aside and lifted the nightshirt to show Kumul his wound. It was nothing more than a raised white scar. "How did this happen?"

"The queen herself performed this service for you."

Ager swallowed. "Usharna? Here, in this room with me?" Kumul nodded. "What did she do?"

"She used the Key of the Heart," Kumul said, his voice subdued.

"On me? But why?"

"Have you already forgotten the youth who was the cause of all our trouble last night?"

Ager frowned in thought. "Of course I remember him. He was asking all those questions about the battle of Deep River . . ." His voice faded away, and his gaze lifted to Kumul. "There was something about him . . . I dreamed it last night in my fever. His face turned into the general's face, and I thought . . ."

"You still haven't put it together, have you?"

Ager's frown grew deeper. "I thought I had, but I can barely remember all that happened after I was knifed. The youth was called Pirem—no, that was his servant's name. I heard you call him Lynan, and . . . my God, that was the name of the general's son!"

Kumul nodded. "So now you understand the queen's interest."

Ager's mouth dropped. "A prince of the realm bought me a drink? Chatted to me like a young soldier talking to an old sergeant?"

"Is all the pain gone?"

Ager laughed. "Gone? Not only do I not feel the wound, but it is the first time in fifteen years I've felt no pain at all, not even in my back. And my empty eye socket doesn't itch anymore. I feel like a new man."

"Well, your shoulder is still raised, I'm afraid. It would take more than even the queen's power to rid you of that."

Ager shrugged. "I got used to being a one-eyed crook-back, but I never got used to the pain."

"I've been thinking about what to do with you."

Ager looked suspiciously at Kumul. "Do with me? I'm no beggar, Kumul. I can make my own way in the world."

"I've no doubt about that. But I need your services."

Ager still looked suspicious. "My services? You need my experience as a bookkeeper?"

Kumul smiled. "No. I need your experience as a soldier. Most of my troops are too young to have fought in the Slaver War. Since then, Kendra has been at peace, thank God and the wise head of Queen Usharna. But I need old blood as well as new in the Royal Guards. I'd like you to take over my training duties."

"What's the pay like?"

"Captain's pay. Keep and board, and tenpence a day."

Ager looked impressed. "Better than I ever got in the Kendra Spears."

"You'll work for it, mind. The Royal Guards are the best Kendra has."

"As good as the Red Shields?"

Kumul snorted. "No regiment will ever be as good as the Red Shields. We had the general back then. Well, what do you say?"

"I'll need time to think about it, Kumul. I've been a wanderer for thirteen years. It will be hard to give that up."

"How much time?"

The crookback paused in thought. After a minute he said: "That was plenty of time. I actually hate the roving life. Do you think you can get a uniform to fit over my hump?"

4

THE summer dragged on in Kendra like a slow ox ploughing a field of clay. On the hottest days the city entered a great torpor. Sailors rested over hawsers and stared at the blue waters of the harbor, dock workers lounged in the shade of unmoved bales of hay and kegs of grain, soldiers drooped over their spears, and craft workers and stall owners did their best to ply their trade with minimum effort. Stray dogs lay in whatever shade they could find and panted desperately. Even in the palace, where work only became more urgent the longer it was left unattended, members of the court moved with sullen obstinacy, and the queen and her bureaucracy struggled through the mountain of appeals and offers, trading licenses and administrative minutiae. And on those few days that were relatively cool, the people spent their time recovering their energy and enthusiasm, and then husbanding it against the next heat wave.

Just after midday on one of the hottest days of the year, tucked into the corner of the second floor in a low stone building not far from the docks, Jenrosa Alucar slammed shut the book she had been reading—ignoring the clump of dust that geysered into the air—and stood up from her desk.

The Magister Instruction of the Theurgia of Stars, a long

strip of a man wizened by age and alcohol, looked up in surprise. The other four students in the room kept their noses down but their ears pricked open.

"Student Alucar? Is there a problem?"

Jenrosa actually seemed to consider the question, an event rare in the Magister's experience, and finally nodded. "Yes."

"Is it something I can help you with?"

"I doubt it," she said flatly.

"I see. Is it something, perhaps, that the maleficum himself could help you with?"

"I do not think either you or the head of our order can help me."

It was the magister's turn to pause in consideration. With something like exasperation he regarded the young woman with the sandy hair and spray of freckles across her too-short nose. She stood with legs apart as if steadying herself in expectation of trouble. She looked as pugnacious as she really was.

A bad sign, the magister told himself. Always a bad sign. And she possessed such a promising mind. . . .

"If it is the text you are presently studying, we could rearrange your schedule," he offered.

"You mean give me yet another book on interpreting the movement of the stars," she said, her hazel eyes seeming to spark with frustration.

"You are in your third year of study, Student Alucar, and interpreting the movement of the stars is the prescribed course. Without it, how could you go on in your fourth year to study interpreting the movement of the planets?"

Jenrosa picked up the book she had been reading and waved it at the magister. "But the summaries of interpretations included here directly contradict many of the summaries in the book we had to read last term."

The magister shrugged. "That, regrettably, is one of the

great conundrums of our art. We hope, through constant observation and analysis, to explain away those very contradictions. And yet, without being aware of those
contradictions, how would we know where to direct our efforts?"

Jenrosa nodded wearily. "I know the argument, Magister.
I just do not see the sense in it. We have been observing and
analyzing now for hundreds of years but have managed to
do no more than collate even more contradictions. We now
have more contradictions than there are stars in the sky.
Why don't they have these problems in any of the other
theurgia?"

"Dealing with the vagaries of the soil and of metals, even
of rain and the sea, are straightforward compared to the vast-
ness of the Continuum. If it takes a magicker in the Theurgia of Fire, for example, a decade to discover that certain
chants and routines produce a harder steel, then how much
more time is needed to discover the secrets of those bodies
that traverse the night sky and their influence on our lives?"

"But I don't . . ." Jenrosa bit off the sentence.

"But you don't have centuries in which to make great dis-
coveries?" the magister guessed.

Jenrosa blushed, making her freckles stand out more
brightly. "I am sorry. I know that reveals abominable pride
on my part."

The magister sighed deeply. "Perhaps it is the heat as
much as your frustration that irks you so. But the frustration
is something you will have to learn to deal with. As for the
heat, even those in the Theurgia of Air have little control
over it in summer. You may go. Take the rest of the day off.
Do not read any more summaries. Clear your head and come
back tomorrow, refreshed." The other students now looked
up eagerly. "Jenrosa alone," he continued. "The rest of you,
obviously less befuddled by contradiction, may continue
with your study."

Jenrosa left the school and found herself on an almost empty street. A woman carrying a basket of bread on her head walked by, the sun's heat adding to her burden. A dozen steps away a street vendor, sweating and swearing at the lack of customers, was packing away his stall. Air shimmered above buildings and stone pavings, and the harbor was aflame with reflected light.

Jenrosa put her hand in her tunic pocket and jingled a few loose farthings. She decided to make for a local tavern that promised shade and a beer, but when she got there, she discovered the tavern was filled with other refugees from the summer sun. After buying her drink, she ended up sitting on the street under the shade of the tavern's eaves.

She had intended not to dwell on the incident at the school and instead think about the cooling swim she would have in the local baths west of the docks once the sun was down, but her frustration at having lost her temper thwarted her intentions. She knew the magister had let her off easily this time, but another outburst could see her brought before the maleficum, and that could result in her dismissal from the Theurgia of Stars. And where would she be then? The theurgia gave her a place to sleep at night, fed her twice a day, trained her for a lucrative career, and paid her a modest stipend that allowed her to buy the occasional beer and go out with her friends every few days.

She took a swig of her drink and promised to do better. She would work harder at study, work harder at trying to comprehend the conflicting paradigms nesting within the Theurgia. She must not lose her position. The theurgia was home . . . and more. She never regretted the time and effort spent actually learning as opposed to simply memorizing. She yearned to discover new ways of doing things, to find links between the magic of the different theurgia. But the magic guilds were increasingly stratified and stultified, increasingly separated from each other.

She dribbled some of the beer from her mug onto the ground and concentrated. The puddle divided into droplets that started moving around one another. She saw a tuft of grass growing out of a crack in the tavern's wall, pulled out some of its shoots, and carefully placed them vertically in the droplets. They whirled around like skinny dancers. She muttered a few words and the tips of the shoots changed color.

Jenrosa laughed at the absurd spectacle. *No,* she told herself, *not absurd.* No one else could perform magic so easily from different disciplines and make it work together, and only as a student within the theurgia would she have the opportunity to learn all that she wanted.

And, she reminded herself again, she had no other home. She had been six when the magicker with his entourage of students and guards had come to her village. She had been outside the house she shared with four siblings and a mother who cared more about getting her next flagon of wine than looking after her children, when she had noticed the procession of strangers. She was feeding scraps to the pig—her family's only asset—when she saw the man who led the way was wearing the stiff-collared tunic of a magicker. As Jenrosa watched, he made his way through the village, looking neither right nor left, but walking with determined precision as if he was following someone else's footsteps. When he finally came abreast of Jenrosa he stopped and turned to stare at her with eyes as blue as the sky.

"What is your name?" he asked gently.

Jenrosa was not used to being spoken to by adults, and she hesitated. The magicker smiled at her and made a sign in the air. A white mist seemed to follow his finger, forming a sign that raised goosebumps on her skin. Without knowing how or why she did it, she copied the sign, and the mist disappeared. The magicker was watching her keenly now, and came closer. He bent over and drew a second sign, this time on the ground. There was no mist or magic this time, except that again she was compelled to copy him. As soon as she had finished it, a small whirl of air formed above them, spraying dust into her eyes. She blinked the dust away and saw that both signs had gone. The magicker pulled a bracelet off his wrist and said something in a language she did not understand. The bracelet seemed to melt and re-form before her eyes, taking on the shape of a silvery snake. She touched it and the snake immediately re-formed into the bracelet. The members of the magicker's entourage started talking excitedly among themselves. One of them came forward and handed the magicker a simple wooden drinking bowl, poured water into it from a flask, and stepped back. The magicker made a sign again, tracing it in the water. Before Jenrosa's eyes, the water seemed to change, become greener and deeper somehow. She thought she saw fish swimming in it, and other creatures she did not recognize; it seemed to her she was looking down into an ocean from a great height. She placed her palm over the bowl, closed her eyes, then took her palm away. The bowl held just normal well water again, clear and untroubled. The magicker stood up. He looked ready to laugh out loud.

"One more test," he told her in his gentle voice, and pointed above his head. Without any control over her own actions she looked up, and even though it was a clear day she saw a group of stars set against the blue sky. She stared at them for a long time before anything happened, but then they started to whirl about a central point, like dancers around a spring tree. Some of the entourage clapped at the performance. Jenrosa pointed at the stars and they blazed briefly in a glorious light and then disappeared.

"What is your name?" the magicker asked again, but before she could reply, her mother appeared, curious about the eruption of noise on the street. When her mother saw the magicker, she took a step back into the house.

"I hope my daughter's done nothing to offend you, sir?" she asked in a whining voice.

The magicker shook his head. "What is her name?"

"Jenrosa."

"Jenrosa is to come with me."

Her mother considered the words for a moment, and then a smile creased her face. "That would come with a fee, sir?"

The magicker nodded. "Of course. You will receive an annual award as determined by the queen. What is her family name?"

"My husband is dead, sir, and so she inherits mine. Alucar."

Jenrosa tried to let go of the memory, and returned her attention to her beer, but not before acknowledging with some bitterness that her name was the only thing her mother had ever given her, and she would do anything to avoid returning to her.

And what if there were contradictions in her studies? she asked herself. Magic itself was a contradiction, a way of viewing and manipulating the world that broached common sense and was out of reach of the vast majority of people. Some were lucky enough to be born with the ability to take advantage of that contradiction, to influence the way clouds formed and rain fell, or the way metal changed in a furnace, or the way water ran down a hill, or the way crops grew.

Or the way the stars influenced the lives of all the mere mortals trudging the common earth beneath their gaze. Maybe.

Jenrosa shook her head. She knew all the other theurgia—those of Air, Fire, Water and Earth—performed real magic, but she was yet to discover anything magical at all about the stars. Or rather, she had not learned a single magical thing. What she did know was what she had picked up from observation, and from questioning sailors in taverns just like the one she was now outside. She knew that if you kept the prow of a ship in line with the star Leurtas, the last point of the constellation known as the Bow Wave, you would eventually reach the pack ice that lay far south of Theare; or, conversely, if you kept the constellation dead on the stern, you would head north into the Sea Between, eventually hitting the reefs and shoals that guarded the waters around Haxus. She knew that all the constellations spun around the very point of Leurtas, moving in a slow graceful dance, and that, as you sailed north, new constellations came into view even as the familiar ones disappeared behind you. And yet, as far as anyone in the Theurgia of Stars knew, there was no formula, no sign, that could make the stars bend to human will or human desire. Jenrosa knew there had been great sages in the past who could use the stars to predict momentous events, but the last of those had died decades ago, and no one alive today could replicate their achievements, although many within the theurgia tried. As far as Jenrosa could tell, the real stars obeyed only their own rules. She sighed heavily and finished off her beer. Despite her misgivings, if she wished eventually to earn her own keep, to gain even a modest independence, she would have to keep her doubts to herself and accept—contradictions and summaries and conundrums included—what the theurgia instructed her to accept, and in that way survive.

The problem, as Lynan told himself afterward, was the sun. Or rather, his position in relation to it. When he was sent sprawling by the guard's side-stepping maneuver and sweeping foot, he found himself staring straight up into the glaring orb.

So he never saw the point coming.

Lynan felt a sudden jarring impact just below his throat's hollow that sent his head crashing again into the dirt. Kumul called out "Kill!" so loudly that everyone in Kendra, let alone the palace, must have heard.

Cursing under his breath, Lynan stood up a little groggily, massaging the point where the head of the guard's wooden spear had marked him. He knew there would be a bruise there as wide as a bread plate before nightfall, and that it would trouble him for days.

The guard helped steady Lynan, and he mumbled some thanks.

Kumul appeared in front of him. "You're lucky Jemma didn't aim higher, Your Highness, or the palace surgeon would now be on his way to straighten out your larynx."

"I was lucky to catch him like that, Constable," Jemma said generously.

"Nonsense. You were too quick for him." Kumul glared at Lynan. "Or *he* was too slow for you. Either way, the prince loses the bout." Kumul's tone became theatrically deferential. "Does his Highness have anything to say in his defense?"

"Well, the sun—" Lynan began.

"Other than the fact he fell for one of the oldest feints in the book."

Lynan blushed. "No, nothing."

Kumul nodded. "Well, at least you've learned *something* from this fiasco. Let's see another round . . ." Kumul bent closer to Lynan's ear ". . . and for God's sake, boy, this time watch your feet."

Lynan nodded, raising his wooden sword as Kumul withdrew. The guard raised his spear and they resumed their training.

In the shadow of the arena's entrance stood two figures, paid due deference by those nearby but unseen by the dueling pair not forty steps from them.

The Lord Galen Amptra, son of Duke Holo Amptra, had watched Lynan's humbling with keen interest. "Your half-brother quite happily prepares to make a fool of himself a second time," he observed to his cousin, Prince Berayma.

"Even you would have to admit that takes courage," Berayma said.

"Arrogance, rather. The arrogance of his commoner father." Galen sighed deeply. "He shames us all. Your mother's blood runs diluted in his veins."

Berayma eyed Galen warily, but said nothing.

Galen licked his lips, continuing cautiously. "Everyone accepts that new monarchs must make their mark on the world, it's a sign of their authority. No one will be sorry to see you rid Kendra of Lynan. I hear the merchants of Lurisia have been pleading for the queen to appoint a representative from the royal family to attend permanently their Great Council Hall in Arkort."

Berayma's voice betrayed his rising anger. "Don't speak so lightly of my ascension to the throne. That cannot be achieved before my mother's death—"

"For God's sake, Berayma, she's at death's door now! You have to consider the future."

"This is not the time or place. You should know better."

Galen bit back a reply. He understood his cousin's ire, yet felt frustrated that Berayma would not acknowledge reality as he and other members of the Twenty Houses had learned to do. His devotion to the queen, if not as strong as Berayma's, was genuine, but he recognized that the time for planning for the succession was overdue. Berayma, however, would countenance no talk about his ascension, and there were some who found this attitude not only unwise but also an unsettling portent for his reign.

Nevertheless, Berayma was his cousin, and he cared for him a great deal. He sighed in resignation and gently placed a hand on Berayma's shoulder. "As you say. Not here, and not now."

* * *

Stung by Kumul's sarcasm and his own loss of face, Lynan fought much harder the second time. He attacked at every opportunity instead of waiting for the guard to come to him, slowly forcing his opponent back until he was ready for a killing stroke. He rested on the heel of his back foot for a split second as if he was about to lunge. His opponent spread his feet and brought round his spear to parry the expected thrust, but Lynan moved one step sideways and then quickly brought forward his back foot. As the guard shifted the position of his spear to counter the new angle of attack, Lynan struck, the tip of his sword pushing deep into the flesh just beneath the guard's rib cage. If the tip had been steel instead of wood, it would have ruptured blood vessels and a lung.

Lynan started to smile, but just then he heard the sound of someone running toward him from behind. He spun around and saw a second guard bearing a wooden trident bearing down on him. Lynan charged his new attacker, diving low and tackling him below the knees. The pair rolled once in the dust of the arena. The moment Lynan was on top, he used one knee to stop himself from turning while he rammed the other into the side of his opponent. The man gasped as the air was driven from his lungs, then wheezed in pain when Lynan brought down his sword on the back of the hand carrying the trident. The guard let go his weapon and rolled away, holding up his good hand to concede defeat.

Lynan remembered the first guard. He turned just in time to deflect a thrusting spear. His attacker had been too confident of success and his momentum carried him forward. Lynan's foot stuck out and his opponent went flying. The prince stood over him, sword pointed at his throat.

"Enough, your Highness," Kumul said.

Lynan stood back and lowered his weapon. "Was this one of your tricks, Constable?"

"You have made up in part for your earlier mistakes."

Kumul was being sarcastic. Lynan's last maneuver had been similar to the one that had brought him low in the first bout. Kumul waved his hand, and the two guards picked themselves up and hobbled away. As Lynan watched them leave, he saw two shadows lurking in the entrance and recognized them immediately.

"I had an audience," he said to Kumul matter-of-factly.

"You are a prince of the royal blood, Lynan. Do you think there is ever a time when you are not watched?"

"That attack was unusually ruthless, even for Kumul," Berayma observed.

"We've had as tough," Galen said, somewhat subdued.

"You think so?" Berayma turned to leave. He wanted to see his mother. Since her use of one of the Keys of Power earlier in the summer, her illness had grown worse. Every day was filled with anxiety for his mother and the fear that he would soon inherit the job he had been groomed for since childhood.

She'd made sure he was well trained. He could outride and outfight virtually anyone in the empire—or outside it. He had been given the best teachers and instructors, all in preparation for a job he didn't even want.

But his sister and brothers? What purpose lay behind their training? What had his mother planned for them?

His thoughts turned to Lynan as he left the arena. He had no particular affection for his half-brother, but he certainly felt no malice toward him. His disinterest stemmed largely from his mother's own. She had barely spent any time with Lynan since his birth, and afforded him no great courtesy or allowance beyond the bare minimum demanded by his rank as a royal prince.

Galen ran his fingers through his thinning hair and watched him leave, wishing he could find the words that would make him come to terms with the future they both knew was imminent and yet which Berayma refused to accept. The queen was in death's grip, and nothing could free her from it. The ship of state that was Kendra needed a firm hand to keep it on an even keel, to balance the competing demands of its member states. The last thing Berayma should do was defer a decision about what was to be done with his half-brother Lynan. A new king could not afford to offend the most powerful families in his kingdom for the sake of a wastrel.

Galen shook his head. This was a problem with many solutions but no prince ready to implement them.

From a balcony above the arena, Areava also had been watching Lynan at practice. She did not know it, but her thoughts, mixed with the feeling of shame she felt about her half-brother, mirrored those of Galen. The fact that the queen had imperiled her life for Lynan's injured acquaintance had only confirmed for her Lynan's ignorant selfishness, proof of the tainted blood that ran in his veins. She, Berayma, and Olio, true and pure scions of the Twenty Houses, understood it was selflessness, not selfishness, that marked the nobility. They were born to rule for their people, not to take advantage of their position. Anger boiled within her. What could be done about him?

She left the balcony for her own quarters. She was so absorbed in her thoughts she did not hear or see the greetings and salutations offered her by passersby. Most of them shrugged and continued on, used to her fierce concentration. One, however, turned on his heel and pursued her, tugging playfully on her elbow as he caught up.

"Who in God's name. . . !" she started, but swallowed her anger as soon as she saw Olio striding beside her, a grin on his face that stretched from one ear to the other.

"Hello, sister! You're looking p–p–particularly formidable this m–m–morning."

Areava frowned. "I am?"

"Oh, yes. You're m–m–moving north through the p–p–palace like a storm front. Black clouds p–p–precede you, lightning illuminates the roof. *Very* formidable."

Areava snorted, then smiled. "I don't mean to come across so threatening."

"Everyone knows that, which is why they p–p–put up with it. What p–p–particular ache is souring you this m–m–morning?"

"The usual."

Olio sighed. "Let m–m–me guess. Lynan."

"As always. There was no guessing involved on your part."

Olio stopped Areava with a hand on her sleeve. "Slow down, sister. It is impossible to talk with you at this speed." Areava faced her brother, her hands on her hips. "And don't come high and m–m–mighty with me. You m–m–may be m–m–my senior, but not b–b–by enough to warrant your anger."

Areava drew in a deep breath. "Say your piece, then."

"What happens after our m–m–mother dies is B–B–Berayma's affair, not yours. He will be king, we will remain p–p–princess and p–p–prince. If he needs us to do any worrying for him, he'll let us know. Do not take on responsibilities that are not yours."

"We are members of the royal family, Olio, the first of the Twenty Houses. We are responsible for the good administration and safety of this kingdom, whether we like it or not. It is our duty to worry."

"Not without the m–m–monarch's leave. And remember, Lynan shares our inheritance."

Areava's face pinched. "He knows nothing about being a prince of the blood. He has spent his whole life as a wagging tail. His father's blood and his natural laziness makes him unsuitable to rule his own life, let alone any part of Kendra."

"You do not know him as well as you think."

"I see people for who they really are."

"Do you hate him so m–m–much?"

Areava seemed shocked. "I don't hate Lynan! I don't even dislike him."

"Are you sure? Have you ever forgiven Lynan for b–b–being the son of the m–m–man who replaced our father as the queen's consort?"

Areava shook off her brother's hand and walked away from him. "You go too far, brother!" she cried, her voice filling the hallway. "You go too far!"

Lynan wiped the sweat from his forehead and adjusted the quilt padding around his body. Under the heavy, lead-lined roof of the fencing stalls, part of the palace armory, he felt twice as hot as he had in the open arena. He nodded to Dejanus, his opponent in this session of real weapon fencing. Lynan enjoyed his practice sessions against the Life Guard; the man was as fast as a whip, and Lynan was already two points down.

"Ready, your Highness?"

In reply, Lynan pulled down his visor. Dejanus did the same. Kumul, standing on the sideline, called "Start!" Lynan flicked his blade against that of Dejanus, who brought his own weapon across to defend his body. Before the Life Guard could react, Lynan swept the blade underneath and over, and lunged. His sword point sank into the padding over Dejanus' chest.

"Wound!" Kumul shouted. "That's two counts for the prince, three for Dejanus." The pair separated. "Start!" Kumul said.

Lynan tried the same maneuver, but Dejanus foiled it simply by stepping back as he brought his sword across. Lynan lunged, but his point was short of the target by a finger's length. His opponent overreached, Dejanus quickly took one step forward and lunged in return. Lynan knew he was in trouble halfway through his attack, and brought his sword down and perpendicular to the line of his body, catching Dejanus' thrust just in time. He brought his sword up, forcing Dejanus' weapon across from his right to his left and lunged a second time. Dejanus parried easily by copying Lynan's tactic, and the two blades slid against each other. Both men stood erect and each retreated a step, their weapons held out in guard, their tips touching ever so lightly. Lynan tapped, Dejanus held steady. Dejanus feinted to Lynan's right, but the prince moved his sword only enough to parry it. They carefully watched each other's eyes, not the weapons. Lynan smiled slightly, Dejanus responded. Lynan stamped his foot, lunged, but kept his blade in guard. Dejanus hastily retreated a step and parried the strike that never came. Lynan used his back leg to send him into a second lunge and this time sent his point in to the padding over Dejanus' heart.

"Kill!" Kumul shouted.

Dejanus slung his sword under his arm so its hilt was showing to the prince. "Excellent point, your Highness."

"Don't feed his pride," Kumul said lightly, but he, too, had been impressed by the maneuver. It was not one he had taught the prince.

Dejanus laughed and held out his left hand. Lynan took it and thanked him for the exercise. "You are at the point now when you could take on the constable himself."

Lynan blushed. Coming from such an experienced swordsman as Dejanus, it was high praise indeed.

"That would be an interesting bout," said Ager, entering the stalls. The crookback, who was now a captain in the Royal Guards and spent his days training the troops, often watched the young royals at their own training, which was still personally supervised by Kumul. He paid special attention to Lynan.

"Even more interesting would be a bout between you and the prince," Kumul said to Ager.

"Now that would be something to see!" Dejanus declared. He had trained several times with Ager and had learned to respect the crookback's fighting skills. Since joining the Royal Guards, he had seemed to grow in stature. Partly that was due to the better diet combined with the real exercise he now enjoyed while training recruits, the latter something the crookback would have found impossible before Usharna had worked her magic on his wounds. Mostly, though, it was his renewed pride that most changed him and his appearance. His hair was close-cropped to a gray fuzz and his manner had become more confident. Ager Parmer was a new man.

"I'm willing to try my hand against the captain," Lynan said, eager to show off his skills to Ager.

Ager glanced at Kumul, who nodded back. "Very well. But my choice of weapons."

"Of course," Lynan agreed readily, confident after his win against Dejanus.

Ager went to a basket of blades standing in one corner. He withdrew a short sword and hefted it for weight. Lynan groaned inside. The short sword was one weapon he did not enjoy using, and his skill with it did not match his skill with the long sword or knife, or even the bow.

Ager saw Lynan's expression. "Don't worry, your Highness. You can keep your longer blade."

Lynan blinked in astonishment. "But I outreach you already, Ager."

The crookback smiled at Lynan, cutting air with his sword. "I worked my way up the ranks of the Kendra Spears, Your Highness. I became captain through years of hard work and surviving battles." His eye seemed to look far away, seeing memories. "What hard work and how did I survive so many battles?" he asked rhetorically.

Lynan shook his head.

"One of the first things I learned as a new soldier in the queen's employ all those many years ago is that a spearman without a spear is as useful as a prick without a bladder. Unless, of course, the spearman actually knows how to use the short sword he is issued with. All us recruits trained with it but barely enough to know which end to grasp. But I *really* trained with it. I practiced every day until I knew the weapon like my own mother, God bless her gentle ghost, and it saved my life on more than a dozen occasions. I reckon I use the short sword with more skill than anyone I have ever met. Indeed, I reckon I use it with more skill than you use your long sword."

Ager took up the ready position.

"What about padding?" Lynan asked.

"None fits me," Ager answered. "And I'll not need any."

Lynan shrugged and raised the point of his sword. He took a step forward and made half an effort to thrust, afraid of hurting his opponent. Ager suddenly leaped forward, and the next thing Lynan knew he was on his back with the tip of Ager's short sword resting over his heart. He heard Kumul and Dejanus laughing.

"Foolish move, your Highness," Ager said. "Take advantage of your reach if you've a long sword. Don't approach any closer than you have to." He put out a hand and helped the prince to his feet. "Let's try that again."

Lynan, still with the breath knocked out of him, retreated a few steps and went to guard. Ager stood back, seeming to consider his position. "Well?" Lynan urged.

"Well what, your Highness? You don't think I'm going to come at you with that bloody great thing pointing at me, do you?"

"But you told me to take advantage of my reach . . ."

"True, but now you're so far away you could use a bow. I thought you knew how to use that thing."

Embarrassment and anger made Lynan blush. "Right," he said determinedly, and carefully edged forward three steps, holding his sword in front of him.

"Right," Ager said, and took three steps back.

"Oh, this is ridiculous!" Lynan cried, turning to Kumul in appeal. Out of the corner of his eye he saw the crookback move faster than he would have believed possible. Before he could do anything, he was on his back again, the tip of the short sword once more resting over his heart.

"You're used to fencing with those who follow the same rules as you, your Highness," Ager said. "But those rules don't apply in a real battle."

Lynan scrambled to his feet. "Again!" he ordered fiercely, and attacked before Ager was ready, forcing him back at the very first. Lynan's attack was furious, but Ager had the skill to deflect every strike and blow. Nevertheless, the crookback gave ground until his back was against a wall and he could retreat no farther. Lynan redoubled his efforts, again and again almost finding an opening for his point. Though Ager kept up with him at first, eventually he started to tire.

"Your Highness!" Kumul called. "Enough!"

Lynan felt as if cold water had been poured over him. He dropped his point and stood back, his face white as a sheet. "Ager . . . I . . . I . . ."

Ager was actually grinning. "Don't apologize. I as good as told you not to play by the rules. I've rarely met an attack with such ferocity behind it."

Lynan nodded numbly. That his anger had so overwhelmed him made him feel nauseous. "Nevertheless, Kumul has always told me never to lose control of my emotions in a fight."

Ager nodded, glanced at Kumul. "Good advice, but sometimes—just sometimes—it pays to forget that rule as well." He returned his short sword to the basket and asked to see Lynan's. Lynan handed it over, and Ager inspected it carefully. "I thought I'd seen this blade before. Most wonderful work." Ager handed it back.

"It is all my father left me," Lynan said simply.

"You are very skilled with it."

"It is the only skill at the prince's command," Kumul said. "He has no time for any study except that of killing and war."

Lynan looked offended. "I am fair at geography."

"Like I'm fair at making pots," Kumul replied. "You will be late for your other lessons if you don't hurry."

Lynan sighed and handed the sword together with its belt and matching dagger to Dejanus, who took it to the special cabinets reserved for the war gear of Usharna's children and returned with Lynan's dress knife.

Before he left, Lynan turned to Ager and said, "I'd appreciate a lesson with the short sword sometime."

Ager seemed flattered. "I would be honored."

5

ORKID Gravespear was leaving the daily meeting of the queen's executive council when he was intercepted by a messenger boy with the news that two visitors were waiting for him in his office. He thanked the boy and gave him a small coin for his trouble.

Instead of heading directly to greet his visitors, he paused in the hallway and looked out over the palace's main courtyard. He was deeply troubled. It seemed to him that day by day the queen was losing her grip on life. The skin on her face was taut around her bony cheeks and high forehead, and her hands trembled so much she had trouble signing any document placed before her. He had served Usharna for almost half of his life and had grown to love and respect her. More than that, he knew that on her death certain events, long planned, would start almost of their own accord and with such momentum that nothing would divert their course. Plans he had been putting in place for over twenty years; plans the Twenty Houses had been putting in place for even longer. As chancellor, he enjoyed almost more power in the kingdom than any other mortal except the queen herself, and yet in the face of such momentous change he knew his authority—even his own life—could be cut short as easily as a rope severed by a sword.

He remembered he had visitors and shook his head to clear it. He entered his rooms, passed by his secretaries without a word, mumbled apologies to the two men waiting in his office, then stopped short. His mouth dropped open, and he went to one knee.

"Your Highness! I'm sorry I kept you waiting. I wasn't expecting—"

"Stand up, Orkid," said a gentle voice, and the chancellor obeyed. "There was never any such formality between us before, Uncle, and I do not expect it to start now."

Orkid looked in wonder at the young man standing before him, as tall as himself, slender with youth, clean-shaven, wide-eyed and grinning. "You've grown, Prince Sendarus."

"It happens, Uncle. And my father sends his warmest greetings."

"How is the King of Aman?"

"Well when I last saw him, but looking forward to the day when he may see his brother once again."

The two men looked at one another for another moment and then embraced suddenly and fiercely. When they parted, Orkid held him by the shoulders. "I was not expecting you for another month, but I am glad you are here," he said.

"And no greeting for his mentor?" asked the second man.

Orkid glanced at the second visitor and received his second shock of the morning. "Lord of the Mountain! Amemun, you old vulture!"

Amemun, round and red-faced, his mound of hair and beard white with age, frowned at Orkid. "Must you always take the Lord's name so lightly?"

"Only in your presence, faithful teacher," Orkid replied, raising a smile in the old man. They clasped hands warmly.

"Now, sit down, both of you," Orkid told them. "You must be exhausted after your journey."

"True. These bones are not used to such a long expedition," Amemun said, easing himself into a seat, "although the voyage from Nunwa was uneventful."

"Unlike the last time you made it," Orkid added. "I remember it like yesterday when you first brought me to Kendra as part of Aman's tribute."

"A terrible day for me," Amemun admitted. "I felt like I was losing a son."

"And I a father," Orkid added.

"Well, I could have done with a little adventure on this trip," Sendarus said. "I was bored from the moment we left Pila. I couldn't wait to leave my father's palace and see more of the world. Instead, all I saw was the highway to Nunwa, and then leagues of empty ocean until last night when we could make out Kendra's lights on the shore."

"How is your new pupil shaping up?" Orkid asked Amemun.

"New? It's been ten years since the king placed his Highness under my tutelage." He regarded the prince with a skeptical gaze. "Impetuous, perhaps, but a quick learner. His head is filled with romantic notions and what he calls 'noble' ideals. Other than that, he makes a passable student."

"Passable?" Sendarus exclaimed. "The Lord of the Mountain himself would struggle to meet your standards."

Amemun's eyes rolled in his head. "You are here less than five minutes and already you blaspheme as readily as your uncle."

"Just as well," Orkid said, suddenly serious. "You are in the heart of the kingdom, now, and the Kendrans do not like being reminded other gods are worshiped in their realms. They are so certain in their power they believe their own deity is the single, true creator."

"They do not let you pray to the Lord of the Mountain?" Amemun asked.

"As long as I refer to him as God, and by no other title, they are pleased to turn a blind eye to my worship, pretending that I have conformed."

Amemun nodded, but his expression showed his displeasure. He had little time for such self-righteousness. "Then you must learn the trick," he told Sendarus.

"Surely we will not be staying long enough for it to matter," Sendarus said lightly, making nothing of the glance exchanged between Orkid and Amemun.

"You must be tired," Orkid told the prince. "My secretary will show you to a room where you can rest, and in the meantime I will arrange for proper chambers to be prepared and notify the queen's private secretary that you have arrived."

Sendarus was about to object, not feeling the slightest bit tired and eager to see something of the kingdom's capital, the greatest city in the world, but he saw Amemun looking at him with his grave brown eyes and knew the sights and sounds of Kendra would have to wait.

"As you say, Uncle."

"Where are your servants and baggage?"

"Still with our ship."

Orkid called in his secretaries and gave instructions. Two of them bustled out to collect his guests' retinue and belongings. The third led Sendarus to Orkid's own chambers to rest.

"So Marin had decided that his own son should be unaware of his part in Kendra's future?" Orkid asked Amemun after all had left.

Amemun refused to meet Orkid's gaze. "The future is so uncertain, Orkid. The king did not want Sendarus' hopes raised."

Orkid sighed deeply. "Old friend, I know when you are

lying. You cannot meet me in the eye, and you sound apologetic."

"I never sound apologetic!" Amemun declared hotly, and having declared it lost all his huff in an instant. "Well, when I'm apologizing for others, perhaps I do," he conceded.

"So what is the truth?"

"When I said earlier that the prince's head is full of foolish notions, I was not being sarcastic. Marin is afraid his son would refuse a role he felt was dishonorable in any fashion."

"We can't let nature take its course. If Aman's dreams are to be realized, we must all take our part whether or not it brings us honor."

"The king has no intention of letting nature take its course. He wants you to dig a furrow for it."

"Ah." Orkid stood up and went to his window. He beckoned Amemun to join him. "Do you see the size of this palace? Its population almost equals that of Pila itself. I can dig a hundred furrows, but in Usharna's court they would be no more than scratches on the surface."

"Nevertheless, the king does not want Sendarus told of his part in our plans."

"Then the sooner we introduce him to the queen and her family the better," Orkid said.

"How much time do we have?"

"Before the queen dies? It could be tonight or next week, or next month. She is the strongest person I have ever known, but she is very ill."

"And how long after her death before the first part of the plan is put into effect?"

"As soon as possible."

"The pieces are all in place?"

Orkid nodded. "Assuming nothing unexpected happens between now and then."

Amemun looked alarmed. "What do you mean? Surely the opposition would not move before the queen's death?"

"Against the queen herself? Of course not. But against us or those perceived as our allies? It has already happened. Disaster was averted only by good fortune, and that none of my doing. You must understand, Amemun, now is the most dangerous time for the plan, not what comes after the queen's death—that is only when it is most dangerous to us."

Areava felt listless. She wandered about the palace like a ghost, through its great halls and rooms, its balconies and towers, its gardens and enclosures. At every window she paused to look out, seeing the great city spread out before the palace like a tapestry, catching glimpses of the harbor or Kestrel Bay beyond it, or seeing the craggy heights of Ebrius Ridge or even sometimes seeing the mountains of distant Aman.

Of their own accord, her feet led her eventually to the courtyard, and from there to the palace's west wing, now the priory for the Church of the Righteous God. Priests bowed to her as she walked by, but knew from her expression not to talk to her. She passed sleeping cells and the royal chapel, confessionals and the refectory. Eventually her journey ended in the church library.

This place and not the chapel is closest to God, Areava thought. She was surrounded by ranks of books and manuscripts, old wooden shelves and reading desks, the smell of ancient dust and earnest study. Here she felt a part of the quest for knowledge, a quest more holy than any other she could imagine because it implied a quest for truth irrespective of its beauty or desirability. She could feel peace in the chapel, contentment in the palace gardens, but here, among all this gathered learning, she felt most alive and in the presence of something sacred.

Areava selected a tall, thin book from a shelf and sat down in one of the study cubicles to read it. It was an atlas and geographical commentary compiled over a hundred years before by Brother Agostin, one of the church's most famous missionaries. Her finger traced the outline of the continent of Theare, from its northern shores around the nation of Haxus, and then along the east coast past Hume and Chandra and the Horn of Lear—where sat Kendra—down to the swollen belly of Lurisia in the south, and then west along the desert plains of the Southern Chetts before heading north past the Oceans of Grass—the home of the Northern Chetts—and back to Haxus. In the top right corner of the page was the unfinished outline of the Far Kingdom, a place of mystery and danger, never visited by any from Grenda Lear. The Sea Between was too wild and unknown for anyone to cross it, and any who were foolish enough to try disappeared without a trace. The coastline in the atlas was conjecture only, shaped by rumor and legend.

She wished she could absorb all the knowledge of the book by touching it like this, and so in her own lifetime read every volume within the library. She sighed. The things she wanted most were never possible.

"I thought I would find you here," said a light voice behind her.

Areava did not turn, but smiled and said: "You have never had any trouble finding me, even when I did not know where I was myself. You know me better than I do."

Father Giros Northam, Primate of the Church of the Righteous God, pulled over a chair and sat down next to the princess. He craned his long, wattled neck to see what book she had out. "Agostin! How wonderful! I read him often. I have always hoped that one of my brethren would fancy taking up his walking staff and traveling his road. The map could do with more detail, and the commentary undoubtedly needs updating. Alas, these days the brethren are all too spiritual for such a mundane and secular task. They prefer chanting in the chapel and preaching in the pulpit."

"I wish I could take up the task," Areava said. She touched the map again, imagining herself on the road without responsibility or care.

"Perhaps one day you will," Father Northam said gently. He was a large man, big-boned, with the largest feet and hands Areava had ever seen on any man. Grey eyes regarded her affectionately.

Areava shook her head. "No. No, I don't think so."

"I suppose every book you read takes you on a journey of some kind." Areava said nothing. "Why are you here now?"

"To read your books, Father."

"Perhaps. But sometimes you come here because you are troubled. This is your refuge and your confessional. What is troubling you?" Areava shook her head. "If you do not tell me, I cannot help you."

"I cannot lie to you."

"That is not an answer."

Areava stood up and replaced the atlas on its shelf. "It's the only one I can give you."

Before she could leave, Father Northam caught her arm. "When you were only five years old, I found you here. Your father had died, and instead of mourning with the rest of your family you came here to hide away from the world, and you looked as if you carried all its troubles on your young shoulders. I look at you now and see that five-year-old girl again. You know you can tell me what is wrong. I have always been your friend, Areava, and never your confessor."

"Perhaps it is a confessor I need. But Father Powl would not understand either."

"My secretary is a very understanding man, Areava. That is why I assigned him to you."

"You know more about me than you do about your own secretary. Father Powl is a great scholar, but as a confessor he listens too little and holds forth too much."

The priest looked bemused. "For God's sake, child, what is it you think you have done?"

"It is what I have not done, and am afraid to do, that is my sin."

"You cannot sin through omission. God the Righteous understands us well enough to forgive our desires and condemn only our actions."

Areava gently eased the priest's hand from her arm. "It is a sin I may still commit. We who are born to rule must sometimes carry out mean actions to achieve great things. It is our privilege and our curse."

"That was glib coming from you." Areava breathed in sharply. He had never spoken so hard to her before. "Forgive me, your Highness, but we read many of the same books. Those were not your words, but those of your grandfather. Old Duke Amptra held convenient opinions about right and wrong but thankfully was never in a position to put them into practice. Do not make the mistake of thinking that his noble rank gave him a noble mind. Look instead to your mother, the queen, for your model."

Areava blanched, as if she had been slapped. The priest's words struck deeper than he knew. Her grandfather may never have had an opportunity to put his ideas into practice, but his son Tafe—her father—did. No one ever talked to her or Olio about their father except in the most general and cautious terms, but through the books she had read, through the gossip and careless remarks she had overheard and by diligently applying her intelligence to the mystery, she had slowly discovered the dark truth. In that terrible civil war between the throne and the Slavers, her father had played one side against the other to further the interests of his family. When his duplicity was discovered, Usharna confronted him and forced his confession using the Keys of Power. By the time she had finished with him, he was nothing more than a smoking, burned-out hulk. Two immediate results had been the dramatic reduction in the influence of the Twenty Houses, which the Amptra family led, and soon after Usharna's marriage to Lynan's father, Elynd Chisal.

"Ah, I see now." Father Northam's words broke her reverie. He smiled sadly. "You are afraid of losing Usharna. That is why you have come to the library today. Here you can enter all the worlds in these books, all the histories and all the legends, and in none of them must you ever confront the mortality of your own mother."

Areava laughed bitterly. "Her mortality? It is her heritage that makes me afraid, Father. She leaves behind a kingdom that is entirely loyal to her but not to the throne."

Father Northam looked at her blankly. Areava shook her head in frustration. "When she dies, she takes with her all the goodwill owed her, Father. The merchants and generals and magickers and even the church will not know where they stand when Berayma becomes king. Nor will any of the kings and queens who come under Kendra. Only the Twenty Houses will be sure of their position, for Berayma has made clear where at least some of his sympathies lie."

"But, Areava, why should anyone want things to change? There is peace in the kingdom now, and there will be peace in the kingdom after Usharna. Berayma will not change the good administration she established. You know he will rule fairly."

Areava shook her head. "For the kingdom's wisest man, you understand so little of the real world. With a new ruler, everyone will try to maneuver closer to the throne, to benefit themselves and their friends. Queen Charion will try to take trade from King Tomar, the merchant guilds will try and reduce the influence of the theurgia, Haxus will try and take a bite from our northern territory . . ."

"Your mother went through the same turmoil when she first ascended the throne, and came through it," Father

Northam argued. "So will Berayma. The people will not want to destroy the prosperity they enjoy."

"There will always be those disgruntled with the share they receive. When my mother became queen, she was forced to marry into the Twenty Houses. There was no center of resistance, no rallying point. But this time there will be. This time there will be Lynan."

"Lynan?" Father Northam said, obviously surprised. "This is about *Lynan*?"

"Am I the only one who can see how destabilizing it will be for Berayma to have Lynan at a loose end, an heir to the throne whose father was a commoner and a soldier? Lynan will become the focus of every disgruntled citizen and every conspiracy."

"He is so young, so . . . so *uninterested* in being the center of anything, let alone a conspiracy against the throne."

"It does not need his compliance. His very existence is enough."

"But, Areava, you said yourself that his father was a commoner. The people won't follow him, or pay attention to anyone else trying to raise him up."

Areava sighed deeply. "Do you know what will happen to the Keys of Power on Berayma's succession?"

"He will inherit them with the throne—"

Areava shook her head. "Your Father Powl could tell you. He understands the politics of the palace far better than you."

"I am not Prelate because I understand politics—" he started to reply.

"Exactly. That is why my mother allows you to hold the office. She does not want a prelate who plays at politics as well as religion."

Father Northam opened his mouth to object, but stopped himself before he made the lie. Of course that was why Usharna had given him her support. He had known this ever since the queen had allowed the church to base itself within the palace walls, but it was a truth he hid behind what he believed was the greater worth of his faith, their work among the poorest of Kendra's people, and their quest for knowledge from all corners of the queen's kingdom.

"My confessor would tell you that Usharna was an only child—"

"I knew *that*, Areava—"

"Which is why she inherited all the Keys."

The primate's eyes widened with sudden understanding that came from a memory from his own youth. "Only the ruler inherits the Key of the Scepter, the 'Monarch's Key.' The ruler's siblings inherit the other, lesser Keys."

"And this time the queen has four children, so each will receive one," Areava said.

"You mean Lynan will possess one of the Keys of Power?" He was genuinely surprised. "Which one?"

Areava shrugged. "That is for the queen to decide, and if she dies before she makes known her will it will be for Berayma to decide."

"But surely the tradition can be changed?"

"The queen could do so, but only at the risk of destabilizing the kingdom just as Berayma is about to inherit it. The Twenty Houses were the queen's opponents for so long because she received all the Keys. That is why they twice forced her to marry within their ranks. It was only after she had been ruler for nearly twenty years that she could marry without their blessing, and when my father died, she chose that trooper-made-general, Chisal. Usharna would not risk alienating the Twenty Houses now when she is too weak to isolate them. And if the decision is Berayma's, who is a friend of the Twenty Houses, Lynan will still get his Key. Now do you understand why I am afraid of him? Common blood or not, as a holder of one of the Keys he becomes a symbol beyond his own birthright."

6

CAPTAIN Ager Parmer of the Royal Guards studied himself in the reflection of one of the tall windows that illuminated the Long Walk, the palace's chief promenade, connecting the throne room to the queen's private rooms and offices. He could not believe how well the uniform had been made to fit. That dark, wire-haired woman Kumul had found to measure up Ager and then sew and stitch the blue jerkin and pants was a miracle worker. He spun on his heel and admired himself in left profile, but his high shoulder spoiled the view. *Ah, well,* he told himself, *not everyone can be Kumul's size and shape.*

The wide double doors to the throne room opened wide. The queen appeared, followed by her entourage and a bustle of guests. Ager shouted a command, and his own detachment of guards formed in front of the party and led the way down the Long Walk to the official dining room, a long space filled with the biggest table Ager had ever seen. Despite the room's name, the queen herself ate there only if she had a large number of guests, preferring her own sitting room for most meals. Ager and his men spaced themselves evenly along the wall and stood at attention, the blades of their long spears glistening a foot above their heads.

Ager watched Usharna sweep by, looking frail but still regal and completely in charge. She was followed by her family and chief officials, then her special guests—some nobleman and his party from one of the provinces, Ager had gathered—and finally by representatives of Kendra itself, such as the mayor and heads of the major merchant guilds. Attendants, polite and bowing, made sure everyone sat exactly where they were supposed to and then brought in large platters and bowls which they set on the table between the guests.

The nobleman, Ager could now see from his long formal coat, was from Aman. Seated between his countryman, Orkid Gravespear, and the Princess Areava, Ager thought he was a pleasant-looking youth with a quick smile and an open face. He noticed that several of the guests, relatives of the royal family from the Twenty Houses and including Berayma's cousin and friend Galen Amptra and his father the duke, were looking with some displeasure at the visitor and the easy familiarity he was showing toward Areava. The princess, for her part, seemed to enjoy the attention of the foreign prince, talking with him animatedly and occasionally even laughing softly, something Ager had never heard her do before.

Perhaps she is just a good actress, Ager thought. Kumul had told him that, unlike Berayma, Areava held a great antipathy toward the Twenty Houses; so, knowing their dislike of commoners, provincials of any class, and clerics, she might be paying special attention to the Amanite prince simply to irk them. If that was the case, it was working. *And good for you, Your Highness,* he thought. *Anything to put a burr under the seat of a nobleman.*

As the meal progressed, Ager noticed that some of the Twenty House nobles were glancing at him and whispering comments to one another. The queen noticed it as well. She gently tapped the table with a knife and immediately got everyone's attention.

"I notice, Duke Amptra, that you and your accomplices are whispering between yourselves. Is it something we should know about?"

The duke, an overweight man who suffered from gout and, Ager would bet, a few varieties of pox, looked in surprise at the queen. He was not used to being addressed like a schoolboy, and the word "accomplices" suggested the matter was something decidedly underhanded.

"Your Majesty, merely small talk, chitchat, asides of no consequence . . ." His voice trailed off and his double chin wobbled.

His son leaped into the breach. "Your Majesty, we were merely discussing the splendid uniforms of your Royal Guards."

"Really?" She took time to survey the uniforms herself. "I notice nothing different about them, my Lord Galen; as far as I can tell, they are the same uniform worn by the guards in my father's time."

Galen swallowed hard. "True, but it is often the way with everyday things that suddenly you will notice their special . . . umm . . . qualities?" He ended his statement as a question, and knew it was a mistake.

"Qualities," the queen said, carefully chewing over the word. "Such as?"

"The color, your Majesty," Galen said quickly.

"Like the sea that surrounds Kendra," his father added.

"Ah, the color." The queen nodded.

Then, satisfied that a lesson had been taught, she turned to the visiting prince from Aman to ask a question when another voice, sniggering, said: "And their shape!"

There was the sound of muffled laughter. Usharna's head snapped up, and her angry gaze returned to the representatives from the Twenty Houses. She noticed that Duke Holo

Amptra and his son looked hideously embarrassed. Next to them, Minan Protas, who had only recently succeeded to his family's dukedom, was desperately trying to swallow a giggle.

"Duke Protas, you are referring to something in particular?" Usharna asked, her voice so cold that Berayma and Orkid, sitting on either side of her, edged away.

Protas was counted a bluff, arrogant fool even among his own kind. He pointed to Ager, who was standing as erect as possible and looking straight ahead at an invisible point on the opposite wall, and said: "Not something, Your Majesty, but some*one*." No longer able to contain his mirth, Protas broke out in a strangled guffaw.

No laughter joined the duke's. The queen silently waited for him to finish. Finally, Protas realized no one else was enjoying the joke and brought himself up with a wheeze.

"Duke Protas, how old are you?" Usharna asked solicitously.

"How old, your Majesty? Let me see. I would be over forty. Yes, I would own to that." He smiled at the queen.

"Shall we say forty-five?"

Protas considered the number for a moment and nodded. "Close enough."

"Then you would have been thirty when the Slaver War ended."

Everyone watched Protas do the math in his head. After a long pause he nodded again. "Yes, your Majesty, that's about right."

"With what regiment did you fight?"

Where there was silence before, there was now a dread and expectant hush.

"Umm, no regiment, your Majesty. I had onerous duties to perform under my father, the late duke."

"Tending the vineyards in your estates in Chandra?"

"My father's estates, your Majesty. Well, mine now, of course—"

"So while men of Kendra such as Captain Parmer over there risked their lives in ridding Grenda Lear of the vile curse of slavery, you watched grapes grow?"

Protas blinked and the color drained from his face. Even he realized his patriotism and manliness had just been brought publicly into question by his queen. He felt the mixed emotions of shame and rage. He opened his mouth to curse the woman, but something in the look of the crook-back Captain Parmer—who now stared at him directly—and the restraining hand of Duke Amptra on his arm, told him to leave well enough alone. He had been ambushed. In shock, he settled back in his seat and bowed his head.

Usharna turned again to Prince Sendarus and, as if on cue, everyone else resumed their conversations as well.

Ager, staring straight ahead again, could not help swelling his chest just that extra bit further, filling up his blue guard's uniform, and almost forgetting he was a crook-back at all.

Sendarus had watched the public humiliation of one of the kingdom's premier nobles with amazement. His own father, the first among equals among the Amanite aristocracy, would never have dared even to attempt such a thing. In Aman, kings could still be challenged to combat for a personal slight. Apparently, things were different here in Kendra. He wondered whether or not that was a good thing.

When it was all over, Usharna had turned to him and asked if he enjoyed hunting. For an instant, Sendarus thought she was alluding to her humiliation of the duke, but he gathered his senses in time to reply: "In the mountains around Pila, your Majesty, I often hunt the great bear. I have two heads hanging from the walls of my father's meeting hall."

Usharna was impressed. She realized she had underestimated the strength and skill of this young man. In many ways, in his build, in his manner of speech, and in his readiness to smile, he reminded her of Olio. She decided she liked him. "Did you know that many years ago, in the time of your grandfather, Aman sent several great bear to Kendra. We released them in the woods of the Ebrius Ridge just north of here, and now hunt them ourselves. They provide a greater challenge than the boar and wild dog my ancestors used to hunt."

"We could go on a hunt tomorrow!" Areava said excitedly, her brown eyes sparkling.

Sendarus greeted the idea enthusiastically. The queen agreed, and promised she would arrange a party to accompany them.

"Your Majesty, do you think it wise to let them hunt at this time of the year?" Orkid asked, clearly concerned. "The great bear is most dangerous at the end of summer when the males are fighting for a sow."

"But it is also the most exciting time to hunt the beast!" Areava countered.

The queen nodded. "Indeed, and I wish I had the strength to come with you. If you are so concerned, Orkid, you can pull yourself away from your duties for a day and accompany them. I know you used to enjoy the sport as much as me."

"I will gladly go with them," Orkid conceded. "But I should warn the prince that hunting the great bear here is different from hunting it back home. In Aman, the beast has learned to retreat into the heights when harried, but here they have learned to use the woods to keep themselves hidden. They enjoy ambushing unwary hunters and travelers, and have acquired a taste for horse meat."

"The greater the challenge, the greater the victory," Sendarus said without conceit.

"Ah, the courage of youth," Usharna said. "But Orkid is right, this is a dangerous time of the year for hunting the bear. I will send some of the guards with you."

"What a magnificent woman!" Amemun said for the third time in an hour.

Orkid, riding by his side, smiled to himself and nodded. There were some things he despised about Kendra and its suzerainty over his homeland, but Usharna made up for almost all of it. Twenty years ago, when he had been Sendarus' age and the younger brother of Aman's new king, he had been sent to Kendra as part of his home's tribute. More hostage than guest, he had hated everything about the city then, but he worked hard—and according to the plan he and Marin had worked out together—to place himself in a position of trust with the kingdom's new ruler. Back then, Usharna was not only a sole child but a woman, and her ascension to the throne had not been a sure thing. The fact that her father had himself passed on to her the Keys of Power, and the fact that in Kendra's dim past it had been ruled by another queen, gave her the opportunity to prove herself. And prove herself she did. And Orkid had helped her, first as a minor court official and then as chancellor. But, brutally honest with himself, he knew she would have flourished with or without his assistance. She had the ability to choose good men and women for positions of power, either on her executive council or as leaders of the various organizations tied to her, such as the church, the merchant guilds and the theurgia. Regrettably, she had been less fortunate with her husbands.

"I never thought I'd live to see a monarch—a woman, no less!—thrash a nobleman like that," Amemun continued. "I can see why you are so devoted to her, my friend."

Orkid heard something crash through the brush up ahead, and looked around anxiously for any sign of danger. It turned out only to be an outrider rejoining the hunt trail. He exhaled in relief and relaxed the grip on his bear spear. It had been a long time since he had been on a hunt, and the tension was getting to him.

"Are you equally devoted to the daughter?" Amemun asked suddenly.

"What do you mean by that?" Orkid asked.

"I mean, do you see Usharna in Areava?"

Orkid frowned. He was not sure he liked the line of questioning. It sounded like something Marin would ask, not his old tutor. He laughed aloud then. Of course, it *was* Marin asking him. Amemun was acting as messenger again.

"I see Areava as the key to our plans in Kendra."

Amemun nodded, apparently satisfied with the answer.

There was a "Haroo!" from up ahead, and the sounds of horses being kicked into a canter.

"That's it!" Orkid cried to Amemun. "They've found our quarry! Hurry, or we'll be left behind!"

The two men dug in their heels and their mounts surged up the trail. The low brush gave way to scattered conifers that towered over them, reaching for the sky. They caught up with the main group, now scattering among the trees to take up flanking positions on either side of the royal party. Somewhere ahead, one of the outriders had seen or smelled one of the great bears and given the call.

Orkid and Amemun reined in their horses to a walk and hefted their spears under their arms, the blades pointed toward the ground in front of them. They eased up next to Sendarus and Areava. Orkid stole a glance at the princess, and had to admit she reminded him of the young Usharna. In her youth, the queen had possessed the same long hair the color of summer corn and the wiry frame that held surprising strength and speed. Areava was taller, more angular, but he knew as she got older she would lose height and become rounder, and so be the mirror image of her mother.

Perhaps Marin had been right to worry about Orkid's feelings toward Areava. He shook his head. No, that would never happen. His devotion to Aman came above all else, including the queen's children.

The woods became more dense, and low branches slapped the riders' faces. They reached a shallow, fast-flowing stream along a narrow ford that continued the trail. Areava gave the order to dismount. Two of the guards remained behind to hold the reins; the rest held their spears in two hands and went on. They crossed the stream and continued up the slope, now so steep it was getting difficult for the hunters to keep their weapons steady.

They climbed for several minutes before there was another "Haroo!" from up ahead, closer this time, and more frantic. The party heard something coming toward them, thrashing the underbrush, but there was no sign of any beast. The conifers now crowded around them.

"It could be anywhere," one of the guards said.

Areava ordered him to keep quiet. Everyone was listening so intently for any sound that would give away the position of their prey that when it actually came they all jumped. They heard the voice of an outrider cry "It's here! It's here!" and then the words were cut off with a scream.

"God's death," Areava breathed, and rushed up the slope with such agility that all but Sendarus had trouble keeping up with her. The scream died to an agonized whimper and a sound of breaking bone, then silence. A moment later the party burst into a small clearing. At first, they thought the clearing was empty, then Sendarus saw and pointed to the head of the outrider in a silver leaf bush. A long trail of blood led them to the rest of the man, his body gutted.

Areava was the first to pick up its spore. "Here."

"Lord of the Mountain!" Sendarus cried. "It's heading downslope, toward the horses!"

Areava ordered four of the guards to follow the beast's

trail, then the rest of the party headed directly back toward the horses, shouting warnings to the guards left behind with their mounts. But they were too late. They all heard the screams of the horses and men, the sounds echoing around in the woods like the calls of lost ghosts. Areava shouted her family's war cry, a long ululating shout, and rushed down the slope, heedless of branches and jutting roots. Sendarus kept up with her, his blood rushing in his ears.

Orkid called for them to wait for the rest of the party, but his cautioning words went unheeded. He ran as quickly as he could, but he was too stiff and too old to make any more speed. Amemun, puffing like a woman giving birth, was falling farther and farther behind.

Areava and Sendarus reached the stream to find the bear on its hind legs, the claws on its forelegs sunk deep into the chest of one of the horses, its terrible jaws clamped around the horse's neck. Another horse lay dead on the ground, its throat slashed open, its blood pouring into the stream and turning it red. One of the guards was dead, opened up from neck to crotch, and the other lay in a heap nearby, his head bleeding heavily from a deep gash. They could hear the other horses galloping away down the ridge, heedless of falling, frantic to escape.

Areava leaped across the stream and charged the bear, using all her strength to drive her spear into the hollow between its shoulders. The beast spun around with such force that the head of the horse was torn loose, its body collapsing. Blood fountained over Areava. She tried to retreat, but her feet slipped and she crashed to the ground. The bear swiped the air where Areava had just been, overbalanced, and dropped to all fours, Areava's spear wobbling in its back.

Before it could turn around to finish her off, Sendarus was by the princess' side. He drove upward with his spear, catching the bear in its open maw. The beast made a horrible gargling sound and lurched up and back, its front paws scrabbling at the blade impaled in the roof of its mouth. Sendarus grabbed Areava by the arm and pulled her to her feet. They retreated, keeping the bear in sight as it thrashed on the ground. Both spear hafts snapped, but the blades remained embedded.

A guard appeared. He saw his princess covered in blood. Shouting in anger, he jumped the stream and lunged at the bear, but the animal's movements were so frantic, he only caught it a glancing blow on one shoulder. The bear dug into the ground with the claws of its rear feet and swung around to meet the challenge, knocking the guard's spear out of his hands. It lurched forward and cuffed the guard with one paw, raking him across the skull. The man screamed, falling to his knees. The bear stood to its full height, roared in anger and pain, and picked up the guard between its front legs.

"No!" Areava screamed. Before Sendarus could stop her, she rushed forward, retrieved the guard's spear, and slashed at the bear's face.

The bear dropped the guard and twisted around to face this new threat. For one instant it exposed its throat, and Areava did not hesitate. With a great shout, she hurled the spear into the exposed muscles and tendons, severing the animal's jugular. Its forelegs pinwheeled uselessly in the air as it fell backward to the ground. There was a sickening crunch as the blade of Areava's first spear was driven into the bear's spine and snapped.

The rest of the party arrived in time to watch the creature thrash around one last time and then fall still.

Orkid saw Areava and gasped in horror. He rushed to her, but she fended him off gently. "I am all right. It is not my blood."

"My God, what were you thinking?"

"I was thinking of saving the guards!" she replied angrily, but then her eyes dimmed. "We were too slow for some." Shock was setting in; her limbs were trembling.

Amemun appeared, saw what must be done, and tore a strip of cloth from his cloak. He wet it in the stream and started cleaning Areava's face and hands. The guard whose life she had saved knelt down before her and thanked her.

Areava put her hand on his shoulder. "You tried to save mine. How could I do less for you?"

"This one is still alive!" Sendarus cried. He was bending over the body of one of the men left behind with the horses. "The head wound is horrendous, but he still breathes."

While some of the guards left to recover the surviving horses and Orkid directed the others to making a stretcher from tree limbs and his own coat, Areava went to the stream to clean off the rest of the blood.

"If I don't get this off before I return to the palace, I'll give my mother a terrible fright," Areava told Sendarus. He sat on the edge of the stream and watched her. "We killed a male, you realize. Maybe one of the biggest ever taken. Would you like a new prize for your father's meeting hall?"

Sendarus shook his head. "It is your kill, Your Highness. Besides, it would put my other trophies to shame. Our bears are kept small by the harsh terrain, but here they seem to flourish. You were magnificent, by the way."

Areava stopped her washing and looked up, surprised. Compliments were common enough from members of the court who thought they could curry favor through flattery, but Sendarus sounded so genuine she was embarrassed and did not know what to say.

Some guards returned with the horses they had managed to catch, including Areava's. She retrieved a long coat from one of the saddle packs and pulled it over her. "There, that should stop the queen from thinking I've been disemboweled."

Sendarus cupped his hands to help her mount, but she

shook her head. "We've only recovered four horses, and we'll need two of them to pull the stretchers for our wounded. One can carry the bodies of the two we lost, and the last can carry the head of our bear."

"You are very generous toward your guards," Sendarus remarked.

"I am a princess of Grenda Lear, Prince Sendarus," she said. "My duty lies with serving my people."

Amemun and Orkid were close enough to hear her. "She takes her responsibilities *that* seriously?" Orkid nodded in reply. "And I thought Sendarus was an idealist."

"She is generous to all but her half-brother."

"Berayma?"

"Oh, no. She loves Berayma dearly. It's Lynan she has little time for."

"Why is that?"

"Because of the accidents of prejudice and history. Her father, Usharna's second husband, betrayed Kendra—"

"I know all that," Amemun said impatiently.

"Leaving Usharna free to marry Elynd Chisal. The queen was over forty years old. No one expected her to fall pregnant a fourth time."

Orkid fell silent a moment, reliving the past.

"Go on," Amemun urged. "What has this to do with Areava's dislike for Lynan?"

"Areava discovered what her father had done. I was there when she confronted Usharna over the matter. Not only was she distressed that her father had betrayed the kingdom, but also that the fact of it had been kept secret from her. Areava felt that meant no one trusted her because of her father's sins. It was a terrible time between the queen and her daughter, and it took many years for the two to become reconciled."

Amemun shook his head in frustration. "What has all of this to do with Lynan?"

"Don't you see? Her father had destroyed the natural order by betraying his queen, his wife, the mother of their two children. He had betrayed his own country and his own nobility. Then Usharna compounded the act by marrying a commoner, by raising to royal status someone who was basely born. The product of all these tumultuous events was Lynan. He exists only because the natural order was destroyed by her own father, and while Lynan lives, that natural order can never be restored. Tafe Amptra and Lynan Rosetheme give lie to the universe she believes in."

"Which explains her hatred of the Twenty Houses," Amemun said, almost to himself. He looked at Orkid. "But does she actually *hate* Lynan?"

Orkid shrugged. "She claims not to, and probably believes that is true, but it is hard to credit when you hear her mention his name."

Amemun asked no more questions. It seemed ironic to him that Usharna's family was the kingdom's greatest strength and at the same time its greatest weakness, a weakness his own people would soon exploit. The knowledge gave him a grim satisfaction, but no joy.

The sun had been down for two hours and Queen Usharna's maids-in-waiting had finished dressing her for bed. She was exhausted, and the pain in her chest was worse than it had been this morning. She stood before her bedroom's single large window, which gave her a view out over great Kendra and the placid expanse of Kestrel Bay, wondering if she would see another dawn. She angrily closed off the thought. In her reign of nearly a quarter of a century she had worked diligently on behalf of her kingdom and its people, allowing herself no time for self-pity or the enjoyment of those luxuries that were hers by right, and she would not start indulging in them now.

But still, I could do with more time. There is so much left to be done. Usharna laughed softly at herself. *There will never be enough time, you old fool. Kendra is far too harsh and demanding a mistress.*

She told herself that no one was indispensable, and even a ruler could be replaced as easily as an old gown. Then the truth awoke in her again that she was being dangerously immodest. After a quarter century of stable, prosperous and, with the exception of the Slaver War, relatively peaceful rule, she did not know if Grenda Lear was ready for her successor. For that matter, she wondered if he was ready for Grenda Lear.

Perhaps, she told herself, Berayma would never be ready.

Thinking of him filled Usharna with sadness. Nearly thirty years of age, a large and powerful man with a generous heart and a disciplined mind, he was a hard-working king-in-waiting; but also he was stern, too slow to make up his mind, too inflexible once his mind was made up and, worst of all, he was an ally of the Twenty Houses. The nobility had been the queen's most steadfast foe in all the years of her reign, and it had taken her more than half of that to build up the support she needed to keep their demands and strictures at bay, to keep the Twenty Houses under her control. Usharna loved Berayma dearly, but she was afraid he would never rule with the decisiveness and agility Grenda Lear required. Her greatest fear was that he would allow the Twenty Houses to destroy the kingdom, unless the kingdom destroyed him first.

A sharp pain stabbed into her heart and her breathing stopped. "Not now!" she cried. "Not now!" She clutched the four Keys of Power that hung around her neck, and felt new strength surge through her. With immense relief she felt the pain disappear as quickly as it had come, and her lungs sucked in air.

Tonight, she thought. *It must be done tonight.*

Usharna raised her head slowly and again looked out the

bedroom window. South of the bay, in the distance, she could just make out the coastline of the subject kingdom of Lurisia, the empire's wealthiest and most economically important domain, and the first conquered by the armies and navies of Kendra all those centuries ago. Keeping Lurisia's merchant captains happy was one of her most arduous tasks, and one example of how the Twenty Houses could trip up her son with their stupid prejudices and petty hatreds.

A sound from below distracted her. She looked down at the palace's main courtyard and saw Areava returning with her hunting party. Seeing that horses carried wounded and dead, she desperately searched for her daughter. At first, she could not see her in the poor light, but to her great relief recognized the coat she was wearing. The party was bedraggled, without enough mounts to carry them, but they carried with them a trophy, a head so large Usharna could see it even in the dark. And she saw, too, that Areava was deep in conversation with the visiting Amanite prince.

Hmm, not a bad thing, she thought. *He is an intelligent and likable fellow. Areava could do worse.* She laughed bitterly. God, she herself had done worse twice over, not finding true love and a worthy companion for her endeavors until she married Elynd Chisal. Tears came to her eyes as she remembered her third husband, a man who was frank to the point of rudeness, with a vocabulary that scandalized the court, and a propensity to wear the plainest of clothes. But she had loved him more than she had loved anyone except her own children. Thinking of Elynd made her think of Lynan.

A son she never thought she would have. She grimaced. A son to whom she should have shown more kindness, but for his own good and for his own protection she had kept him distant and apart not only from herself but from his siblings as well. It had been, she realized now so late in her life, a wrong decision, and she desperately wished there was someway she could make up for it.

But there was not enough time, and now upon Lynan's young shoulders would fall an unexpected and unfair burden. She closed her eyes briefly, automatically murmured a prayer to a God she had never been sure she believed in, and grasped the Keys even tighter.

The pain in her chest started again, and this time would not go away.

7

LYNAN was woken by someone gently shaking his shoulder. He sat up and rubbed sleep from his eyes.

"Hurry, your Highness," said Pirem's voice. "It's the queen, she's callin' for you. She's callin' for all of you."

Standing next to Lynan's bed, Pirem was holding out Lynan's tunic and breeches. "You haven't much time, Your Highness. The others are already gathering like vultures."

Lynan looked as sternly as possible at the old man. "Is that how you see us, Pirem, as vultures?"

"Not you, Lynan, no." Pirem tried smiling, but the effort was too much for him and he grimaced instead. "Nor your siblings. But many in her court are as ruthless as you are easygoin'. If you don't hurry, your mother will be dead before you can get there an' you'll not even receive her blessin', an' if that happens, your life won't be worth a handful of bird shit, pardon the expression. Now hurry!"

Lynan hurried out of bed, his sleep-befuddled senses at last comprehending Pirem's message. His mother might not live to see morning, and she was calling all her children to her side to publicly declare who could rightfully claim descent from her. He tugged on his breeches, found his boots under his bed, and pulled them on. He scurried out of his

room and down the cold stone hallway to the other side of
the palace and the queen's apartments. Pirem scuttled behind, handing him his tunic, then his belt, and finally his
dress knife, his gasps for air rattling in his old throat.

When they reached the royal quarters, Lynan waved
Pirem back, slowed to a quick walk, and straightened his
tunic. As he turned the last corner to Usharna's bedroom, he
met a section of the guard. They stood swiftly to attention,
dipping their spears slightly as Lynan passed. He stopped at
the entrance, caught his breath, and pushed aside the heavy
doors.

It was a large room, with the head of the queen's huge
four-poster bed set against the west wall. Built into the east
wall was a fireplace which was always kept burning. Rough
wool tapestries covered the cold stone, and exposed pine
rafters in the ceiling gave off a sweet fragrance.

Berayma's long, dark body was bent over his mother, his
face showing great pain and grief. Lynan knew, as did everyone else in the kingdom, that Berayma cared for little in this
world and what love he carried in his heart was reserved almost entirely for his mother. Lynan felt a pang of guilt that
he did not feel the same way about the old woman, but then
he reminded himself she had showed him scant affection in
his seventeen years of life.

Standing at the end of the huge bed was Areava, tall and
as fair as Berayma was dark. She had her mother's face and
eyes, but while her hair glowed like sun-ripened wheat, the
queen's was colder than a winter moon. Next to Areava, de-
mure and slight, awkward in the presence of his mother,
stood Olio. Olio looked up when Lynan entered and offered
him a sad nod.

The queen was propped into a sitting position, several
pillows between her and the bedhead. Her skin was gray and
dry, her eyes sunken, and her long white hair fell loosely
over her shoulders like a mantle of snow. Lynan had never

seen his mother's hair let down before, and he could not help staring at it.

"Did you think I was bald, child?" the queen asked suddenly, noticing his presence and the direction of his gaze.

"I did not know it was so beautiful," he answered honestly, and then blushed. He knew his mother did not like blandishments, but this time she surprised him by smiling, making him blush even more.

Usharna looked closely at each of her children, then rested her head back and closed her eyes.

"Mother?" Berayma asked, taking one of her hands in his. "Are you in pain?"

She opened her eyes and shook her head. "No. Just tired. More tired than I have ever been before. I am tired of living."

"Don't say that, your Majesty," said Orkid's deep voice. He appeared from the room's shadows to stand behind Lynan. "Your devoted subjects don't want you to leave them."

The chancellor brushed past Lynan and took up Usharna's other hand.

Orkid tried to make his patriarchal face, with its full black beard and beaked nose, look as sympathetic as possible, but he could not help glowering at the dying woman. "No more talk of being too tired for life."

"If it was up to you, Orkid, I'd outlive my own children," she remonstrated. "Fortunately, nature has been kind enough to let me avoid that disaster." Orkid opened his mouth to reply, but Usharna lifted her hand in a command of silence. "I have little time left, and there's much to be said."

She drew in a deep breath and her eyelids fluttered with weariness. "Bring me the Keys," she ordered.

Harnan Beresard came to the queen, a wooden casket in his hands. He opened the lid and gently placed the casket on the queen's lap. Usharna reached into it and retrieved the four glimmering, golden Keys of Power, each on its own thick silver chain.

She glanced up to make sure she had everyone's attention. "Now is the time custom insists I declare my successor. Let it be known that on my death, my firstborn, Berayma, will take my place on the throne, and his descendants will rule after him."

Those in the room gave an audible, collective sigh of relief. It was done. Such a public declaration guaranteed a peaceful succession, something the entire kingdom prayed for near the end of a monarch's life. The number of witnesses present guaranteed the succession would not come into dispute.

"I have four children," Usharna began, "all accomplished, and the kingdom can ill afford to lose so much talent. Against the advice of some, who would have me pass on all the Keys to my successor as I received all the Keys from my father, I will maintain the tradition of our family and pass them on to all my children. Accepting a Key implies swearing fealty to Berayma as head of the family and as the rightful ruler of Kendra.

"The Key will remain with the bearers until their deaths, when they will be returned to Berayma, or until the death of Berayma, when his successor will determine their possession."

Usharna paused to catch her breath, her eyes red with exhaustion.

"You must sleep, Mother," Berayma insisted, patting her hand. "We will come back in the morning."

She feebly shook her head. "No time, my son. My past is catching up with me. I had the good fortune to enjoy the pleasure and company of three husbands, but the poor judgment to outlive them all."

Her bony hands scrabbled at the Keys, and she looked at Berayma. "As king, you must have the Monarch's Key," she said, and gave him a star-shaped piece with a thick rod fixed in its center. "The Key of the Scepter," she intoned, her voice seeming to gather sudden strength.

Berayma seemed unsure what to do with it. "Put it on, Berayma," Usharna insisted. He slipped the silver chain over his head, the Key resting against his broad chest. "That's fine," she said, and patted his shoulder.

She took hold of a second Key, a square with two crossed swords pierced by a single spear. She handed it to Areava. "My secondborn, you will have the Key of the Sword. Grenda Lear will look to you for protection against our enemies." Areava bowed and stepped back a pace.

"Olio," the queen continued, waving him forward, "you are the gentlest of your siblings, and perhaps the least understood. You will have the Healing Key, the Key of the Heart." There was a quiet murmur in the room, which Usharna silenced by looking up sharply. "It is said that this Key holds the greatest magic of all. Perhaps it is true, but if so its power is one of creation, not coercion." She handed the Key, a triangle holding the design of a heart, to Olio. He stepped away from the bed, fingering his gift curiously.

Usharna now looked back at Lynan, and her eyes seemed to soften. Lynan swallowed hard and resisted the temptation to move out of her line of sight. He had rarely been the focus of her undivided attention.

"Poor Lynan, lastborn, you shall have the last Key." Lynan moved forward until he was touching the bed. Usharna's left hand crossed over to hold his in a firm, cold embrace. "I wish my hand was warmer," she said softly so that no one else could hear. "As warm as my heart whenever I think of you." With her right hand she passed him the remaining Key, a simple, golden circle.

Lynan nervously placed the chain over his head. The Key was surprisingly heavy against his chest. He thought he could feel everyone's gaze fixed on his face. He looked around and saw that it was so, except for Orkid who stared strangely at the Key itself. A shiver passed down his spine.

"The Key of Union," Usharna announced. "With this you represent the kingdom's commonwealth. You will be the king's representative to all our peoples."

The queen fell back against her pillows, her hands collapsing by her sides. Berayma and Olio were pushed away by Trion, her personal surgeon. He felt her pulse and temperature. "She has no other duties," he said somberly. "She needs to sleep now. Everyone must leave."

Berayma nodded and led everyone from the room. Besides his family, Orkid, Trion and Dejanus, there were nurses, attendants, and guards, including Kumul. They had all been standing quietly to attention against the walls, watching with fascination as power was passed from the dying queen to her four children.

The thought made Lynan frown. Power? What would he do with the Key of Union? He wasn't even sure he wanted it.

When they were all in the hall outside, Berayma ordered Kumul to set two guards at the door, and then advised everyone to return to their quarters.

"We all have much to consider," he said in his low monotone. "Grenda Lear has not seen such changes for a generation." He looked down uncertainly on Lynan as he said the last sentence. "But I'm sure our mother knows what she's doing. Age may have made her weary, but it will not have affected her mind, of that we can be sure."

"She won't live through the night, will she?" Olio asked, his voice tight.

"Enough of that," Areava said as kindly as possible, putting a comforting hand on Olio's shoulder. "It will do no good to think such thoughts."

Olio's eyes suddenly brightened. "Wait! I hold the Healing Key—"

"I can see where your thoughts are leading you, your Highness," Harnan interrupted, "but you must understand the nature of what the queen has done. She wielded the Key of the Heart herself, and it will have no effect on her now that she has surrendered it. Death is not a sickness for her, it is a relief and an ending." The old man blinked back tears as he spoke, and when he had finished, he hurried away.

Lynan felt a lump in his throat, so he quickly turned away from the others so they could not see his sorrow. They had shared little with him before, and he was damned if he was going to share his grief with them now. He was confused by the strange emotions he was feeling. He had loved his mother after a fashion, the way a servant might love a good mistress, but they had never been close.

The gift of the last Key, and her few kind words, had sharply reminded him of his loneliness and unhappiness as a child. *Why now, Mother, when it's all too late?*

"I will see you all tomorrow," he told the others. Berayma and Areava stared after him, the brother they had never before truly considered a brother at all.

Lynan fell asleep in his clothes, so when he was woken by Pirem for a second time that morning he felt uncomfortably cramped and pinched. Wan sunlight filtered through his room's only window high in the eastern wall.

"What news, Pirem?" he asked, shaking his head to clear away the cobwebs of interrupted sleep.

"I regret to have to be the one to tell you, your Highness, but your mother, Queen Usharna, is dead."

Lynan felt numb. "When?"

"Within the last few minutes. Word is being sent to your siblings right now. You must gather again at her bedside."

"Of course. Thank you, Pirem."

"Is there anything else I can do for you, your Highness?"

Lynan shook his head. *Why don't I feel anything? What is wrong with me?* "I will call you if I need anything."

Pirem bowed and made to leave but Lynan suddenly called him back. "Tell me, did you love the queen?"

"Why, yes, of course."

"Was she loved by the people?"

"Those I knew, your Highness." Pirem looked curiously at Lynan. "An' respected," he added. "She was loved an' respected. We've had a prosperous and largely peaceful quarter century. A people cannot ask for more. Is there anything else, your Highness?"

Lynan shook his head and Pirem left. *How much better simply to have been one of her subjects,* he thought.

8

IT was a golden morning. Sunlight poured through the windows in Berayma's chambers. Around him, servants and courtiers fussed over his robes and accouterments, making sure everything was in its right place and hung in the right way. His garments were resplendent, as befitted Grenda Lear's new king, even though he was being dressed to attend his own mother's funeral. Conversations were going on all around him, a constant background hum of human noise.

He stood ramrod stiff, arms out straight as a cloak was pulled behind him. He closed his eyes.

Not now, he told himself. *You cannot cry in front of all of these people. You would shame her memory.*

He swallowed hard. Everything he did, everything he thought, reminded him of his loss. Since the death of Usharna the morning before last, there had been no time to grieve alone. He understood that this was part of his duty now, to ensure a peaceful and rapid succession, but he longed desperately to have half an hour alone by his mother's white corpse, to let himself indulge in his own feelings one last time without concern for the kingdom's greater good, the kingdom's greater need.

I am being swallowed up, he thought unhappily, and squeezed his eyes tighter against the tears.

No more grieving. Not now. Not ever.

Areava breathed deeply as she strode determinedly down the hallway. She had been dressed for over an hour, but despite her heavy mourning clothes and the bright sun, she was cold. Her hands felt like lumps of ice. She fondled the Key of the Sword, found it ironic that she should be wearing it formally for the first time while garbed in clothes most unsuitable for war.

Oh, God, Mother, why did you leave us now? The kingdom still needs you.

She entered Olio's chambers without knocking. Servants, flocking around her brother like robins around a piece of bread, bowed to her and continued with their work.

Olio eyed her steadily. "You still m–m–mean to continue with your p–p–plan?"

The servants stopped what they were doing for an instant, their minds registering an opportunity for some palace gossip. Olio told them to leave. "I am almost ready. I can finish the rest myself."

When they were alone, Olio repeated his question. Areava strode to his dresser, picked up the Key of the Heart and with some stiffness placed it around his neck. "There, that's better."

"You are wrong in this, sister," Olio breathed, careful to keep his voice down.

Areava nodded. "Perhaps. But I know no other way to resolve the issue."

"It is only an issue for you," Olio responded, avoiding her gaze.

"No, brother, it is an issue for every citizen of the kingdom. The great families are great for a reason. They are destined to rule. We are all bred for it, trained from birth to take up the reins of running a kingdom."

"You forget—you *always* forget—that Lynan shares our m–m–mother's b–b–blood."

"I do not forget. You once accused me of hating him. You are wrong. I do not hate him. I don't even hold it against him that his father replaced our father as the queen's consort. But the kingdom must retain its strength and vitality, and it can only do that if those in power are true to their bloodline."

"You take a great risk. Lynan m–m–may p–p–prove to be worthy—"

"Olio, listen to me! This is not about Lynan!" Her words were sharp, and Olio stepped back. He looked down at the floor. She reached out to hold him by the shoulders, brought him close. "Poor, timid Olio, do not be afraid of me. Of all in this world I care for, I care for you the most."

Olio relaxed in her arms, returning her embrace. "I know, and will never forget it."

Areava sighed deeply and held her brother tightly for a moment more before releasing him. She lifted him with one hand and looked him directly in the eye. "Everything I do, I do for Grenda Lear. I am devoted to this kingdom and its peoples. I do not love them the way I love you or Berayma, but my life is theirs. I am born to serve, to serve by doing my duty as the daughter of Queen Usharna. This is not about Lynan, but about tradition, about the future, about what is right."

Olio had no more arguments. He nodded, surrendering to her. "Very well. Do as you m–m–must. B–b–but take care, sister. Usharna is dead, and a new order has arrived. For your sake, I hope your vision for Kendra is a p–p–part of it."

"It is up to us to make sure it is," she said evenly, and left him to finish his preparations for the funeral.

*   *   *

Lynan studied himself carefully in the full-length dress mirror. He wore gray woolen trousers, the ends tucked into his favorite boots—polished so brightly by Pirem that they were hardly recognizable—a white linen shirt with fashionably wide cuffs, and a short black jacket. His sword, sheathed in a metal dress scabbard, hung from gold rings attached to his finest leather belt. The Key of Union hung shining around his neck.

He noticed with some regret that although his clothes looked noble and dashing, his own physique still left a lot to be desired. He was shorter than average, and he suspected he was not going to grow much taller; by all repute, his father had been no taller than Lynan was now. At least his shoulders were straight and strong, and would become wider with age. But his torso appeared too long for his legs, and his neck too frail for the generous head perched upon it. His face was too round, too boyish still, to be considered handsome, and was topped with mousy brown hair.

"Well?" Pirem demanded impatiently.

"It's fine. Stop worrying."

Pirem snorted and told his charge to turn around. He attacked the youth with a clothes brush, using stiff, heavy strokes that stung Lynan's skin. When the old servant had finished, he stood back to admire his handiwork. "You'll do," he said in a resigned tone which suggested that no amount of extra work would improve things anyway.

Lynan nodded his thanks and left to join his siblings in the palace's great hall from where the royal mourning entourage would begin its march through Kendra to Usharna's funeral pyre near the harbor. He was the last to arrive, and Berayma stared reprovingly at him as he hurried to his position next to Areava and Olio and behind the new king. In front of Berayma stood Dejanus—now Berayma's Life Guard—and the court sergeant. Behind Lynan was the queen's bier, a simple wooden frame garlanded with hundreds of flowers. The bier was flanked on one side by priests led by Primate Giros Northam and on the other side by the five malefici, leaders of the theurgia, the magic circles of air, water, earth, fire, and stars, led by their superior, the Magicker Prelate Edaytor Fanhow. The bier was followed by a hundred-strong escort of the Royal Guard led by Kumul; the other nine hundred guards were already posted along the route to the harbor, under the command of Ager. Next came all the foreign ambassadors and provincial consuls, chief of whom was Prince Sendarus. None of the kingdom's minor rulers had been able to reach Kendra in time for the funeral. The rear of the entourage, led by Orkid looking even more severe and threatening than usual in his black mourning gown and hood, was brought up by various government officials and visiting dignitaries of lesser rank.

Berayma nodded to the leader of the court musicians waiting at the exit of the great hall. Trumpets blared, cymbals crashed, and the procession got under way.

It was a long march of nearly five leagues, planned to take the queen on a last inspection of her royal city. The court musicians kept a hundred paces in front, heralding the arrival of the entourage with a loud, military dirge. People thronged the streets, hung out of windows, and leaned over balconies, waving black handkerchiefs and wailing as they saw their queen for the last time, lying white and pale on her bier.

The first district they passed through, on the heights between the palace and the city proper, belonged to Kendra's wealthier and better-born citizens, in particular, members of the Twenty Houses. Tall stone-and-glass mansions glittered in the morning sun like giant jewels, surrounded by reserves of tall headseeds and stripe trees, resplendent in their summer dress. Farther down the slope the buildings became less grand and closer together, separated by formal gardens rather than glades. This was where the city's older families lived, those without claims to nobility but who strove to move upward socially and away from Kendra's growing middle class, whose quickly expanding district surrounded the city in a great semicircle, the ends anchored on the harbor shore. At last, the procession passed under the old city wall. The streets became narrower and darker, the tops of houses drooping toward each other and forming a sort of open archway. Most of these structures were centuries old and made of wood and mud and reed bricks. Fires in these quarters were common and difficult to control, but the people born here—merchants, craft workers and entertainers—would live nowhere else, for they believed they formed the heart of Kendra and therefore the heart of the kingdom itself.

The last district, which surrounded the great harbor like the dirt ring left in a washtub, was comprised of hovels crammed between warehouses. Many of its inhabitants slept in the open, scrounging what cover they could from the garbage left by those better-off Closer to the water the smell of the sea mixed with the not entirely unpleasant aroma of drying nets and tar, and the smells from the cooking pots of a hundred cultures that all great ports seemed to attract.

The procession reached the docks, continuing north until it again met the old city wall, where the funeral pyre was waiting for them. Usharna's bier was carried to the top of the pyre where Berayma set it alight. At first, the fire caught on only slowly, but a brief incantation from the Maleficum of Air brought in a fresh sea breeze and in no time at all flames were leaping high into the air. A thick column of brown smoke spread inland, hiding the morning sun and casting a gloomy shadow over the whole city, eerily mirroring the unhappiness of Kendra's citizens. There was a brief moment, as the cloud started to break up, in which it seemed to take on the shape of Usharna's face, and as it dispersed, it was as if her own soul was finally being released from its earthly prison. Lynan noticed that the subtle performance had strained most of the malefici and their faces were covered in fine films of sweat. He hoped the assembled citizens had appreciated the illusion.

The pyre burned fiercely for two hours. When the flames started to hiss and die and curl into gray tendrils of smoke, the entourage made its way back to the palace. This time there was no music to mark their procession, just the solemn tramping of the mourning march and the Royal Guards closing in behind it, their spears reversed.

The palace gates were thrown open for Usharna's wake, and everyone was welcome to come and celebrate the life of their late queen. There was plenty of food and drink, and soon people were laughing again, some nervously but most from relief. Usharna had been a popular ruler, but the dead could not be brought back to life and it was best to look forward to the future as hopefully as possible. There would a new monarch and a new beginning for Grenda Lear. The cloud from the funeral pyre had blown away, and the sun again shone down on the city. The only signs left of mourning were people's somber dress and the black flags and pennants that fluttered from the palace's tallest towers and from the masts of ships in the harbor far below.

Lynan found it difficult to join in the spirit of the wake. He was still confused about losing a mother he had hardly known, and yet who had, at the very end of her life, shown she had thought of him as a son. He managed to avoid the most patronizing and the most sycophantic of the wellwishers, people who, before his gaining one of the Keys of Power, would studiously have ignored him. As the celebrations became even more earnest and rowdy, he made his way alone—except for the company of a leather flask filled with red wine—to the palace's south gallery, a long, narrow room on the top floor decorated with fine paintings and tapestries.

The gallery's wide double doors were open to let in light and fresh air, and he stepped out on to the balcony. From here, he could see over all of Kendra and its three hundred thousand people, a large number of whom presently occupied the palace's courtyard and the grounds immediately beyond.

Lynan sipped his wine slowly, enjoying his privileged view. The sun was just beginning to touch the rising ground to the west, reflecting off windows, the color mixing with the red and green of the city's roofs to form a beautiful tapestry that merged with the lapping waters of Kestrel Bay, saffron in the afternoon light. In the distance he could just make out the rainforest-cloaked shores of Lurisia.

Lynan found himself absently fingering the Key of Union. *I am to be Berayma's representative in Lurisia and the other provinces,* he thought. *It's ridiculous. What do I know of such things? Who will teach me?*

He took a large swig from the flask and turned to leave, depressed by the weight of his new responsibilities. With a start, he saw Areava standing under one of the large double doorways, studying him closely.

"How long have you been there?" he asked, irritated that she had said nothing.

"Not long. We missed you downstairs at the wake."

"We?"

"Your siblings. There is a great deal we have to discuss."

Lynan snorted. "About the Keys of Power."

"Of course." She joined Lynan on the balcony. "You are very lucky, you know. Most of us believed our mother would leave you nothing." Lynan kept quiet. Areava shrugged, and continued. "You haven't been trained for such a duty, brother. What will you do?"

"I don't know yet. I'm still getting used to the idea of being accepted as a true prince of the blood."

Areava winced but recovered with a smile. "Possession of one of the Keys does not change the circumstances of your birth."

"You're right," he said dryly. "Usharna is still my mother."

"And your father was a commoner," she returned calmly. "Whereas Berayma's father, Milgrom, and my and Olio's father, Tafe, were noblemen, members of the Twenty Houses. There *is* a distinction between you and us, Lynan, and it will out eventually."

Lynan looked away so that Areava would not see his face burning. "I share with you the name of the Great House, Rosetheme," he said defensively. "The queen's blood flows in my veins as strongly as it flows in yours."

"Yes, but that's not all that flows in your blood, is it? Look, Lynan, I don't hold anything against you because your father didn't come from one of Kendra's original families, but let's face the truth. When our mother married your father, she thought she was well past the age for conceiving. If she had known she was still fertile, she would have married someone from one of the Twenty Houses."

"My father may not have come from the nobility, but he was the best general the kingdom ever had. Where the great families failed Usharna in her struggle against the Slavers and their mercenaries, my commoner father prevailed, leading his commoner troops in defense of the throne."

"I have never belittled your father for his deeds. He was a courageous and skillful soldier." She came closer and put a protective arm around his shoulders. His muscles tightened until they ached. No one had ever done that to him before, and he did not know how to react to it. "But it's you I'm thinking about. You don't really want the responsibility that goes with a Key of Power. You don't have the background, the training—the *inheritance*—to make it work for you."

"I haven't tried yet."

She let her arm drop, sighed sadly and deeply. "We don't want to see you get hurt, Lynan. You are our brother."

Lynan laughed bitterly. "Even though my father was a commoner?" He was suddenly curious. "What, exactly, is your offer?"

Areava smiled. "You hand the Key back to Berayma, and in return you'll receive a pension for the rest of your life. You and your descendants will be recognized as a branch of the royal family. Your children will become the first members of Kendra's newest noble family—the Twenty-first House."

"It's a very generous offer, but hollow for all of that. It does not give me anything the Key has not already supplied."

"But you will have none of the responsibilities, Lynan. The heavy burden of public office will be taken from your shoulders."

Lynan shrugged. "I might enjoy the burden."

Areava's voice tightened. "You are making this more difficult than it has to be. Everything would be so much simpler if you just agreed to face reality."

"Whose reality? Yours? The queen did not see things the way you do. The Key was entrusted to me by our mother. Indeed, it was her final official act. No, I don't think I can give it up."

He found the strength to meet her gaze. Her face had become hard. It was not hate he could see in her eyes, but something much less personal, much less familiar. *She thinks of me as nothing more than a peasant, as someone so far beneath her station it even pains her to talk to me.*

Areava said nothing more, but spun on her heel and left.

In the distance he could hear the wake continuing, but the sounds now seemed falsely optimistic.

And then Lynan heard someone else walking along the gallery. He was afraid it might be Berayma or Orkid come to throw the same argument at him—or worse, Olio, whom he liked—but the figure that appeared on the balcony was not much taller than he and walked with a peculiar, telltale stoop.

"I passed Princess Areava. She looked like a snow witch."

Lynan laughed bitterly. "She wanted me to surrender the Key of Unity."

Ager took a moment to appreciate the view before saying: "Surrender it now? She thinks of you as a defeated enemy already?"

Lynan shook his head. "I'm not sure how she regards me."

Ager nodded to the Key. "It still hangs around your neck. She was obviously wrong, however she thinks of you."

"I was tempted," Lynan admitted. "For a moment I was tempted. I have never held such responsibility before."

Ager sniffed the air. "You know the story about your father and the battle of Heron Beach?"

"Only that it was his first battle and that he won. Neither Kumul nor Pirem were there, and they have been my main source of information about my father."

"Well, I was there. Your father had a choice. He could pull back north of the Gelt River and await reinforcements, or he could launch an attack. He wasn't sure of the enemy's strength, but he did know that if he didn't pin them against the coast they would slip away, and it would be weeks or months before he could chase them down again. More importantly, he was unsure of his own ability to prosecute an attack."

"But he was a great soldier!" Lynan objected.

"No doubt about it, but before the battle of Heron Beach, no one, not even your father, knew what kind of a general he would be."

Lynan looked at Ager. "This is a fable?"

Ager shrugged. "If you like. But it is a true fable, and you *are* your father's son."

Ager patted Lynan affectionately on the shoulder and departed.

Lynan left the gallery himself soon after and stood at the top of the wide staircase that led down to the great hall. For a moment he watched the people below: women in long mourning dresses that swirled as they turned, and men in their finest clothes, all aglitter with jewelry and wine-induced smiles.

He wondered if it had really sunk in yet, that Usharna was dead and they had a new monarch. He thought they would miss her more than they knew.

Areava had intimated she was speaking on behalf of their siblings, but if Berayma was going to confront him on the same issue, Lynan reasoned, it might as well be somewhere very public where his actions would by necessity be tempered.

He saw a group of important-looking people enter the hall from the courtyard, Berayma in the middle of them and the center of their attention. Those gathered around him were civic officials from Kendra, chief among them the mayor, Shant Tenor, and the president of the merchants' collective, Xella Povis. The two made an odd couple: Tenor was an overweight, pasty-faced man in his late fifties who specialized in obsequies and bullying, while Povis was a tall, dark-skinned woman, originally from Lurisia, with a reputation for hard but fair dealing and a frankness that often offended the more polite mores of the court. Berayma stood a good head above them all, his expression patient but tired, trying to listen to the two of them talk at the same time.

Lynan descended the staircase and approached the circle, waiting until he caught Berayma's eye.

"Brother," Berayma said politely, interrupting the chatter. "Isn't it touching to see so many of Kendra's loyal citizens turn up to wish our mother a last farewell?" There was no irony in his voice.

"Touching indeed, *brother*," he answered, staring at the hangers-on until they had all bowed. *This is a new experience for us all, citizens,* he thought, smiling at them grimly, *so we'd better get used to it now.*

"It was the least we could do after nearly thirty years of her generous reign," Shant Tenor said loudly. He glanced up meaningfully at Berayma. "And to usher in what we're sure will be many decades of continued prosperity for Kendra."

Xella Povis smiled. "What he means," she explained to Lynan, "is that we hope your brother sees fit to continue the generous export subsidies and dockyard refits your mother instigated for the benefit of the city."

"What's good for Kendra is good for the kingdom," Shant Tenor declared pompously. "I hope you make the provinces understand that, young Ly . . . ah . . . your Highness."

"I look forward to carrying your message to them," Lynan replied dryly, and noticed Xella Povis regarding him with something akin to approval. He had the feeling that her opinion of the mayor was as low as his own. He faced his brother. "Speaking of my duties, could I have a word with you alone, please?"

"I don't see why not." He turned to his guests. "If you would excuse us for a moment?"

The others bowed and scraped and quickly moved away. Berayma nodded to his brother to speak.

Lynan took in a deep breath. "Areava has made an offer

for the Key of Union. I've decided to hold on to it. It was a gift from my mother, and I have no intention of surrendering it to her . . . or anyone else."

Berayma shook his head, his expression blank. "I haven't the faintest idea what it is you're talking about. Perhaps you had better start at the beginning."

As Lynan recounted his meeting with Areava, he saw Berayma's face go white with anger, but anger against whom he could not tell.

"I think I understand now," Berayma said. "It seems I need to speak with Areava. I knew nothing of this offer and do not condone it." He paused for a moment, avoided Lynan's gaze. "I admit I was surprised by our mother even recognizing you as an heir, let alone giving you one of the Keys of Power, but I would never go against her wishes. Our relationship must be renewed—or, rather, begun, since I admit I've made it a practice to ignore you since your birth. There is obviously a great deal I have to learn about my own family."

Lynan was stunned by Berayma's words. "I would like that," he replied lamely.

Berayma nodded stiffly. "It was what our mother would have wanted. There are still many official duties I must perform this afternoon and this evening, but I will discuss certain matters with you and our siblings over the next few days. You have courage and honesty, I see, and they are essential qualities. In time, I think you will make a good ambassador for the throne. The sooner we start you off, the better."

Lynan nodded, not sure what to say.

"This is a time of joy as well as sadness," Berayma said. "Our mother is free at last of all tribulations and pain. Drink to her memory, and to our future."

* * *

Lynan felt as if a great burden had been lifted from his shoulders. With Berayma's support, he was confident he would be able to handle his new responsibilities and, more importantly, he knew Areava and the Twenty Houses would not dare attempt to take away his newfound authority. For the first time in his life he thought of himself as a *real* prince, a scion of the House of Rosetheme. His chest swelled and he strode around the gathering with greater purpose and confidence, not shying away from those whom once he would have avoided because of his dubious birthright and their obvious arrogance. He was clever enough not to try and rub anyone's nose in his success, but could not help taking delight in the way everyone bowed and scraped to him. As the night progressed, and as he worked his way through his flask of red wine, he could not keep a swagger from entering his walk.

His progress was watched with amused interest by Kumul and Ager.

"Our young popinjay has discovered something about himself," Ager said.

"That he can preen with the best of them," Kumul noted sourly. "I hope he wears out of it. I am more fond of the old Lynan."

"The old Lynan may not have gone, Kumul, and the new confidence cannot hurt him."

"Unless someone tries to push him off his stool. Everyone's very sweet to him now, especially in the presence of Berayma, but they will find a way to harm and hinder him if they can."

Ager found it difficult to share the constable's pessimism. He had been truly sorry at the death of Usharna, but he could not help feel that with Lynan's new position, not to mention his own, things could only get better. For the first time in his life Lynan had a family, and for the first time in nearly twenty years Ager felt he had a home and companions with whom he could share it.

"Who's that he's with now?" Kumul asked.

Ager peered with his single eye at the woman Lynan was talking to and shrugged. "I do not recognize her. But I think she wears the tunic of one of the theurgia."

"There is a star on her shoulder, with a circle around it. She is a student."

"Probably here just for the wake. I can split them up if you like."

Kumul shook his head. "We cannot keep an eye on him all our lives, and I certainly don't intend to interfere with his love life."

"Oh, is that it?" Ager asked, more interested. "Is she pretty? I can't tell from here."

"Compared to what? You? Hell, my arse is pretty compared to your face."

"Well, compared to your arse, then."

"She is considerably prettier than my arse. In fact, she's pretty indeed."

"Good luck to him, then."

"Aye, although she seems ill pleased to be with him." Kumul looked around the courtyard and great hall, his expression bored. "I'd better start my rounds. You coming, or are you too busy squinting at the student magicker?"

"Oh, I've finished my squinting, Constable. Give me your orders."

Jenrosa Alucar had not intended to come to the queen's wake, but she had been bullied by her friends who were all excited by the prospect of seeing something of the royal home. In theory, all citizens were allowed to enter the palace's many public spaces, but in practice only those with business or who were associated in some way with the court ever saw within the palace walls. Even the Church of the

Righteous God, although they were based in the palace's west wing, held their celebrations in special churches and chapels located in the city itself.

In the end, it was her own curiosity that made her come—not about the palace, but about the royal family. She had never actually seen any of them except Usharna herself in a special celebration held years ago for the delivery of the fishing fleet after a severe storm. She had a vague idea of what Berayma looked like because his face had appeared on a special coin issue, and everyone thought they knew what Areava looked like because she was supposed to be a younger version of her mother, but no one she knew personally had ever seen Olio or the youngest one, Lynan. During the funeral procession she had seen glimpses of them all between crowds of official and soldiers, but always from behind.

When they reached the wake, Jenrosa and her friends played guessing games, placing wagers with each other about which two of the hundreds of well-dressed young men in the palace were Olio and Lynan. After losing half her weekly stipend, Jenrosa decided to drop out of the competition and instead found a drink and started wandering around the grounds marveling at the palace and all its decorations. She was admiring a particularly large tapestry hanging from the great hall's north wall when a voice behind her said: "*The Hunt for Erati*, by the Weavers Guild in Chandra. A special tribute to King Berayma III."

Jenrosa looked over her shoulder and saw a short youth with a round, pleasant face and thin brown hair that stuck up at odd angles. He was dressed in fine clothes and wore a sword that seemed strangely plain and dull in comparison. He smiled at her. The flask he held in one hand and the slight slackness of his jaw and glaze in his eyes told her he was someone to be avoided.

"It's quite spectacular, isn't it?" the youth continued. "It's one of the largest tapestries in the palace, and easily the most colorful. Do you like the way the line of the hunting pack follows through to the forest trail and finally to its prey? The eye just glides along."

"How do you know all this?"

"A man called Harnan told me."

"A friend of yours?"

The youth thought about the question. "I'm not sure how to describe him. Professional acquaintance, probably." He seemed pleased with himself.

"Well, thank you for the lecture notes." Jenrosa moved. "I am going to join my friends now."

"I could tell you about the other tapestries, if you like."

She shook her head, tried to smile kindly. "Thank you, no. My friends are waiting for me?"

"Banisters? Statues? Paintings?"

Jenrosa stopped and turned to face him. She decided to be stern and frowned at him. "What?"

Her frown did not work. He came up to her, still smiling far too easily for her liking.

"I can tell you all about this whole place. I could give you a tour." He was having trouble focusing on her.

"What makes you think I want a tour of this place?"

"Well, it's the palace, isn't it? Everyone wants to see inside the palace." He burped in her face. The smell of his breath almost made her faint.

"You know what I would like to see?"

The youth shook his head. "No. Tell me, please!"

"I would like to see you walk away from me and take your idiot grin with you."

Her words had the opposite effect than intended. He smiled even more widely. "Delightful!" he cried out loud enough to draw looks from those nearby.

"Why are you so *happy?*"

"Because today things are turning out so much better

than expected." He winked at her. "I've met you, for example."

Jenrosa shuddered. "Look, find a midden and bury your head in it."

Now the youth actually laughed. "You speak like Kumul," he said.

"And who is Kumul when he's not telling you where to go?" she asked, getting angry now.

The youth looked around, then pointed at a huge man about fifty paces away dressed in the livery of the Royal Guards. "That's Kumul."

Jenrosa checked herself. "He's a soldier," she said slowly.

"He's a constable!" the youth declared.

"But you're not a soldier, right?" She was playing it carefully now. She did not want to discover she had been insulting one of the more influential court members; inevitably, word would get back to her maleficum if she had.

He shook his head. "Oh, no. I'm too short to be a Royal Guard." He sighed deeply. "Alas."

"But you're a member of the court."

He had to think about that one. "Not really."

Jenrosa breathed a sigh of relief. "I *really* have to go now. My friends are waiting for me." She walked away. The youth kept up with her.

"Do you mind if I come?" There was a glint in his eyes Jenrosa did not like.

"You're too young," she said shortly.

"I can't be any younger than you."

"I'm eighteen."

"Well, a year younger."

"And all my friends are *much* older than me." She picked up her pace, but the youth matched it.

She stopped suddenly and he overshot her. He turned back and looked around. "Where are your friends?"

"What is your name?" she demanded.

"Pirem," he said quickly. "What's yours?"

"Leave me alone," she said.

He held out his flask. "Your cup is empty, Leave-Me-Alone. Would you like some more wine?"

"I've already told you what I'd like."

"Oh, yes. The midden." He giggled.

"You're drunk."

He considered the question then shook his head. "Not yet. Not truly, absolutely stonkered." He blinked. "Well, maybe a little."

Before she could say anything more, someone called out her name. Her friends appeared, including Amrin, who was as big as a bear. "*These* are my friends. The big one likes wrestling."

Amrin scowled at the youth. "Are you being bothered?" he asked.

"Not at all," the youth said quickly. "She's delightful."

"I wasn't talking to you," Amrin said forcefully.

"So, are you all magickers?"

"Students," Jenrosa said. "Now we have to go and study." Her friends looked at her strangely.

"Umm, yes," Amrin said doubtfully. "We have to go and . . . study . . ."

"Are you sure you all wouldn't like more to drink?"

Jenrosa turned on him suddenly. "I don't want to be in your company, Pirem. Nothing personal, but . . ." She shook her head. "Yes, it *is* personal. I'm sorry, but I find you annoying."

The youth appeared suddenly crestfallen. Jenrosa groaned inside.

"I see. Well, if that's the way of it . . ."

"That's the way of it," Amrin said, scowling again. He pointed to his theurgia's star symbol of on his tunic. "So if you don't want us to practice our magic on you, scuttle away!"

The effect on the youth was instant. His expression turned as cold as ice, and he met Amrin's gaze with suddenly clear brown eyes. "I carry a magic symbol, too," he said evenly.

Amrin guffawed. "Of course you do, little mouse."

The youth reached into his jerkin and pulled out an amulet on a silver chain. He held it up for them all to see. The students stared at it for a moment, then blinked. They all knew what it was. And Jenrosa knew what it meant. "Oh, God," she breathed weakly. "You're name's not Pirem."

"No."

There was a stunned silence among Jenrosa's friends. After a moment one drifted away, then a second and then a third. Jenrosa and Amrin were left to their own fate.

"I . . . your Highness . . ." Amrin was not sure what to say.

"You were only defending your friend. You have done no wrong. But you had best leave now."

Amrin nodded and melted into the crowd.

Jenrosa swallowed. "Your Highness, if I have given you offense—"

"I took no offense." He was starting to smile again. It had taken all his concentration to act sober.

"—then you got all you deserved."

Lynan's eyes widened in surprise, and then he laughed. "Other than my own siblings, you're the first person I've met today who hasn't tried to fawn their way into my favor."

"A bit late for that."

"To the contrary. What's your name?"

"Jenrosa Alucar, your Highness."

"Of course, your manners must not go completely unpunished."

Jenrosa said nothing.

"You must present yourself to the guard at the door to the inner palace when the wake is finished. That should be about sunset. He will instruct you where to go."

Lynan started to leave, but Jenrosa called after him. "What punishment?"

Without turning, he said, "You'll see."

9

JENROSA considered fleeing the palace, grabbing what she could from her dormitory at the theurgia, and trying to stow away on one of the merchant ships in the harbor. Or even better, stowing away on one of the ships of the foreign dignitaries who had arrived in time for the queen's funeral; then, at least, she could run away in relative comfort.

But then she used the same arguments against the plan that she had used to convince herself to stay with the theurgia: she had a home here in Kendra, she had a future as a magicker, and nowhere else could offer her that.

At sunset, accordingly, she presented herself to the guards at the entrance to the inner palace. One of them ordered her to follow him and led the way through a series of narrow corridors and flights of stone steps into one of the towers that ringed the monarch's own chambers and the throne room.

Well, at least I'm not being led to a dungeon, she told herself, but the thought did little to ease her apprehension. What sort of punishment had the prince in mind for her? Was he going to throw her off the tower? She knew in her mind that the idea was ridiculous; all the same, her anxiety was beginning to make her legs feel weak.

They eventually arrived at a narrow wooden door that looked as old as the roughly shaped stones that framed it. The guard knocked once with the butt of his spear, opened it and pushed Jenrosa through. The door closed behind her. She found herself at the foot of a set of stairs worn with ancient use.

The prince's voice said from somewhere above: "Come up, Jenrosa Alucar."

She hesitantly ascended into a circular chamber filled with the smell of dust and old books. The prince was standing in the middle of the room. He had changed into less formal clothes, and was without his sword and knife. His Key shone dully in the little light shining between the wooden shutters of the room's only window.

"You are still smiling at me, Your Highness," she said. "I hope that is a good sign."

"I'm glad you came," he said sincerely.

"It wasn't as if I had a choice," she pointed out, and looked around her.

The walls were lined with shelves inset into the stone, and each shelf was crammed with books that looked as old as the tower itself. "What is this room?"

"Kendra's first great king, Colanus, was part magicker. He made the Keys of Power. Some say that is how he gained the throne. This is his study. No one uses it anymore."

Jenrosa pulled one of the books from its shelf. She carefully opened the leather cover and looked in surprise at the writing on the first page. "What language is this?"

Lynan shrugged. "No one knows. Which explains why no one uses the study any more."

"The malefici would commit murder to get their hands on these volumes." She meant it jokingly, but the words seem to hang in the air between them.

"The malefici have already tried," the prince said lightly. "You know any history?"

"Very little, unless it is to do with the study of the stars." She was starting to get impatient. She wanted to be given her punishment so she could get back to her dormitory, away from the palace and away from this strange prince.

"Three hundred years ago a band of powerful magickers conspired to get their hands on the contents of this room. Their plot was discovered and they were thwarted by the king. He executed the ringleaders. Do you know what he did with the rest of the magickers?" Jenrosa shook his head. "Let them into the room to study the books on the condition they submitted to his will."

"But if he didn't object to the magickers seeing the books, why did he kill their leaders?"

"Because they conspired against him, of course. After several years of unsuccessfully attempting to read these volumes, the surviving magickers gave up."

"And what was the king's will?" Jenrosa asked, curious despite herself.

"That they form into the five theurgia with a ruling prelate elected from their own ranks who consults directly with the monarch."

"He got them under his thumb."

"In other words."

"Is that what you want to do to me?" she asked.

"I don't understand . . ."

"Put me under your thumb?" Her hazel eyes stared defiantly at him.

Not under my thumb, exactly, he thought, but feigned surprise. "Of course not."

"Then how are you going to punish me?"

"By offering you a glass of wine and a chance to see a sunset such as you have never seen before."

Jenrosa shook her head. "I'm not sure I heard you right."

The prince pointed to the window. On the stone sill were two glasses and a bottle. Her eyes widened in surprise. She had never drunk from glass before. In fact, she could not remember ever having drunk from a bottle. He waved her forward, then with some effort managed to open the shutters.

"See for yourself," he offered, and moved out of the way so she could see through the window.

She moved in his place and looked out, gasping at what she saw. The whole city was spread out before her like a glorious map. Kestrel Bay shone like liquid gold as the sun set far, far to the west, behind a range of mountains that were dim and dark in the distance. Seagulls played above the harbor, and farther out she could just discern the long, splayed wings of kestrels swooping low over the waves.

"It is . . . Oh, it is beautiful."

The prince joined her. He pointed south, to a green land mass that rose from the waters like a mirage. "Lurisia," he said. Then he pointed to the mountains in the west. "And that is the Long Spine, the farthest border of Aman." Finally, he pointed east. "That land mass is Chandra, and beyond that you can just make out the great Sea Between."

He pulled back again and carefully poured wine into the two glasses. "This is a bottle from the queen's own reserve." His eyes dulled for a moment, then he said, "Sorry. The king's reserve." He offered her one of the glasses, and she took it hesitantly.

"Some punishment," she said.

Kumul made sure the last of the guests at the wake had been ushered out of the palace before starting his inspection of the night watch. He began his round at the main gate and worked west from there, making sure the guards on roster were at their appointed places and that torches were lit along the palace walls and over each entrance way. He completed the circuit an hour after he started, and stood in the courtyard for a while watching busy palace servants sweeping and wiping and polishing the great hall to make it ready for business as usual the next day.

Business as usual, he thought grimly. *Constable under a king who doesn't like me, and who is friends with the Twenty Houses, none of whom like me.*

For a moment he wished he had given himself the night off to visit one of his many female friends in the city. Yet he knew that on this night of all nights he had cause to be on duty. It was his last act of service for Usharna, his dead queen, and once-wife to his beloved general.

Ager joined him, looking tired. "Where did you disappear to?" Kumul asked.

"Some of our guests had broken into the training arena. There were empty flasks and bottles everywhere, and some of them had used our equipment for practice."

Kumul grinned. "Did any impale themselves?"

Ager shook his head. "Regrettably, no. The arena's cleaned up now, and I've got a couple of the new recruits stowing away our gear."

"Well, check with them, then get some sleep. Tomorrow's going to be as busy as today. Berayma will want to talk to us about his plans for the coronation. I'm just going in now to see him before retiring myself."

"As you say." Ager left, and Kumul surveyed the courtyard and gate one more time. Everything seemed to be in its place. He resented it. He felt there should be some change, some sign, after the death of the woman who had ruled here for a quarter of a century.

But she was a ghost now, and ghosts had no need of palaces. He grunted to himself and went through the great hall to the Long Walk and made for Berayma's chambers. Before he got there, he heard running steps behind him and Dejanus called out his name. The Life Guard looked very worried.

"Kumul, I've found something."

"What?" Kumul asked sharply, suddenly alert.

"It's best you see for yourself. Follow me."

Without waiting for a reply, Dejanus led the way back to the great hall and then through a door leading to the servants' quarters. Kumul followed unquestioningly. Whatever had rattled Dejanus was something he wanted to see for himself. The Life Guard was setting a hard pace, stopping only to get a torch, but finally slowed when they reached one of the corridors leading to the cellars, part of the very first palace built hundreds of years ago, and dark and wet with mildew.

"It's around here somewhere . . . There! Do you see it?" Dejanus was pointing to a spot on the cobblestones.

"I can't see my own feet in this gloom. Lower the torch."

Dejanus did as asked. "It's fresh blood, and there's a knife . . ."

"I still can't see—"

Before he could finish, something slammed against the back of his skull. The dark air seemed to explode in his eyes. As he collapsed onto the cobblestones he heard Dejanus' feet running away, their sound echoing in his mind like the beat of his own heart. He tried to call out, but his senses fell away one by one and he knew no more.

Berayma rubbed his temples with the palms of his hands. Since late morning he had had a nagging headache, and the day's warmth and the afternoon's drinking had only made it worse.

"Could I get Dr. Trion for you?" Orkid asked solicitously.

Berayma shook his head. "It will go of its own accord. Let's get this business out of the way so I can get some rest. We have a busy day tomorrow."

"Indeed, your Majesty. You wished to see me about Prince Lynan. Is something the matter?"

Berayma did not want to discuss Areava's offer to Lynan

with the three other men gathered in his room. He did not yet trust the chancellor as his mother had done, and it was no business of Dejanus', who had appeared to let the king know that the constable had been unavoidably detained, and considering how Harnan Beresard collected gossip like gold coins, Berayma thought his private secretary probably knew already.

"Lynan has to consolidate his position as quickly as possible or, Usharna's will or not, he will find himself the object of continuous derision, court rumor and suspicion. He needs to be set on his path."

"Your Majesty?"

"I want him sent on a mission to Chandra as soon as possible, and I want you to accompany him."

"Your Majesty?"

"Must you always say that?"

Orkid looked ready to repeat his phrase, but closed his mouth in time. "I'm sorry. Why and when?"

"Why? Because I want him given the opportunity to prove himself as soon as possible. I also want him out of Kendra, so people, especially those in the Twenty Houses, have time to get used to the idea of his holding one of the Keys of Power. Chandra has been one of our most loyal subject kingdoms for hundreds of years, so the embassy will be relatively easy for Lynan to carry out. I need you to come up with some excuse, and to arrange for the Chandra Commission here to offer him an invitation."

"That should not be hard, your Majesty. I'm sure King Tomar would be glad to welcome the prince; he and Lynan's father were friends, I believe."

"Exactly. Can you arrange it for autumn?"

"I see no difficulty with that."

The king turned to the private secretary. "In the meantime, Harnan, send for Lynan. I want to discuss some issues with him tonight."

"Of course, your Majesty."

"And then get yourself to bed, old man. I will need you refreshed tomorrow, but don't come before mid-morning; I won't have got through all the papers you've already given me by then."

Harnan bowed and had started to leave when Orkid said, "Must you see Lynan tonight? You are already feeling over-tired . . ." Harnan hesitated at the doorway.

Berayma sighed heavily. "Yes, Chancellor. It must be tonight."

"But surely it could wait until—"

"Now!" Berayma shouted, and Harnan disappeared. Berayma groaned. "Orkid, I'm sorry. I should not have raised my voice like that."

"Do not trouble yourself about it, your Majesty," Orkid said stiffly. "I understand perfectly. It has been a long and trying day for you."

"Thank you for your patience," the king said sincerely. "I do not think there are any other matters to trouble you tonight. You may go."

"There is one small issue, your Majesty," Orkid said carefully. "Concerning your own recent embassy to Hume."

"Really?" Berayma was puzzled.

"I have received a message from one of my agents there. I think you should read it."

"Very well. We have some time before Lynan arrives."

"We should be alone," Orkid added.

Berayma nodded to Dejanus. "Leave us please. If you see the constable, tell him to wait until after I have spoken to Lynan."

Dejanus left, and Orkid placed a long sheet of paper in front of the king.

The recruits had finished putting away all the training weapons. Ager was checking the cabinets when he noticed

Lynan's knife was missing. He called one of the recruits over. "All the weapons have been found?"

"All that were on the grounds, Captain."

Ager pointed out the missing spot in the cabinet. "Do another search. I want the knife found."

The recruit gulped and called back his mates. For another half hour they scoured the training arena and fencing shed, but found no trace of the missing knife. They reported glum-faced to Ager.

"All right. Nothing more can be done here tonight. We'll do another search tomorrow in better light. In the meantime I'd better report this to the constable."

The recruits went pale, and Ager dismissed them before one of them passed out.

He went to the Long Walk and asked one of the two guards on duty if Kumul was still with the king.

"No, Captain. He did not see the king. He was on his way here when Dejanus called him away."

"Where did they go?"

"I did not hear, sir. But you can ask Dejanus yourself. He is in with the king now, and should be out soon."

Ager shook his head. "No. It's not important. I'll try the constable's rooms." He turned on his heel and left.

"If it's not so damned important, why did he bother me about it?" the guard asked his fellow when Ager was out of earshot. The two men laughed quietly. "Officers and whores," the guard went on, "always asking for something."

"Soldier!"

The guards snapped to attention. Dejanus appeared in front of them, his blue eyes wide with anger.

"What was that about officers?"

"Officers, sir?" The guard tried playing dumb; as often as not, it got you out of trouble.

"Come with me," Dejanus ordered, then turned to the other guard. "And I'll deal with you later."

Dejanus waved the first guard into what had been the queen's sitting room and closed the doors behind them. The guard had a sinking feeling that playing dumb was not going to get him out of trouble this time. He was afraid to turn and face the Life Guard.

"Look at me, soldier, and come to attention!" Dejanus ordered.

The guard snapped erect and wheeled about on his right foot. Before he finished his salute, Dejanus drove the knife he had been hiding up his sleeve deep into the guard's midriff, between the iron slats of his armor, forcing out of him a gush of air and his last breath. Dejanus caught him as he fell and eased him gently to the floor.

"And two to go," he said to himself.

Harnan Beresard had not found Lynan in his chamber, and so had gone to Pirem's room instead. He banged on the servant's door until Pirem appeared, rubbing his eyes and wearing nothing but a scowl.

"What the—!" Pirem blinked when he saw who it was. "Oh, forgive me, sir, I thought—"

"I am sorry to wake you, Pirem. But the king needs to see Lynan immediately. He is not in his room. Can you tell me where I might find him?"

Pirem shook his head. "He sometimes wanders around the palace if he can't sleep. But I'll find him. I know his favorite places."

Harnan nodded. "Very well, but see that his Highness sees the king tonight, or we'll both be in trouble."

Pirem disappeared back into his room and quickly dressed. He rushed to Lynan's room and, using the spare key he always carried, let himself in. He found Lynan's good coat and his father's sword and belt. He paused for a moment to consider what else the prince might need, then slapped his forehead. "Oh, hurry, you old fool," he told himself. "The king's not goin' to care what the lad looks like at this time of night."

He started his search in the gardens, then the south gallery, then along the palace walls, but without success. There was one place left, and that was a long walk followed by a long climb. But the king wanted to see him now! Berayma's chambers were on the way, and Pirem decided to let him know Lynan would be with him soon rather than letting His Royal Majesty sit alone, twiddling his thumbs and wondering where his brother had got to.

"Hurry, Pirem, hurry!" he urged himself, and set off at a trot.

"I see nothing so urgent about this report," Berayma said, handing the paper back to Orkid.

"Forgive me, your Majesty, but I thought the information about Queen Charion's plans to limit Chandra's trading rights were not only important but relevant, considering your intentions to send Lynan on an embassy to King Tomar."

Berayma carefully studied Orkid's face. The two had never get on, but Berayma had to admit he had made a very good chancellor under Queen Usharna, and had been absolutely loyal to her. He nodded slowly.

"And you were right to present it to me. The fact that I do not agree with your opinion should not deter you in future from presenting me any information you consider important."

Orkid bowed slightly, accepting the truce, and the implicit compliment. Dejanus returned then and nodded to Orkid.

"Your Majesty, the constable has not shown up?" the Life Guard asked.

Berayma shook his head. "I will give you his instructions. You can pass them on to Kumul when you see him."

Dejanus nodded and Berayma started to write instructions on a sheet of paper. The Life Guard looked over his shoulder as if to read the instructions as they were written. Then Orkid moved forward. Berayma looked up at the chancellor. "You can go, Orkid. Thank you for your advice tonight."

"Your Majesty." Orkid bowed deeply, and then before Berayma could react, the chancellor gripped Berayma's arms just below the elbows.

"What—!" cried the startled king, and pulled back, raising his head. Dejanus took out his hidden knife and drove it straight into the side of Berayma's neck.

Berayma lurched back, his arms breaking Orkid's grip and reaching behind him for his attacker, but at that instant Dejanus pulled out the blade. Blood spurted across Berayma's desk, spraying Dejanus and Orkid. The king tried to stand, but he started falling. He grabbed at his desk, scattering paper and ink, tried to reach for Orkid but could only grab his coat. As he lost consciousness and collapsed, he took Orkid down with him. He crashed into his chair, hit the floor, and was still.

As the jagged wound in Berayma's neck pumped blood, Orkid frantically jerked his coat loose from the dying king's hands and teetered to his feet. The flow of blood abated and finally stopped.

"Lord of the Mountain," muttered Orkid, his arms out wide, his hands and coat covered in blood. It had all happened quicker than he had thought possible, and was far bloodier and more terrible then he could have imagined.

Dejanus looked down grimly at his handiwork.

"No one saw you deal with the guards outside?"

Dejanus shook his head. "And I have ensured that the guards on duty at the gates are my men; all have some grumble against Kumul. They will be ready to believe whatever we say about him and Prince Lynan."

"We have to get things ready before Lynan appears."

"It would have been easier if Berayma had not called for him."

"Be that as it may, we are now committed."

Dejanus lifted his gaze to meet Orkid's. "I hope the rest of your plan goes more smoothly."

Before Orkid could answer, there was a cry from the door. Both men whipped around. They saw an old man standing there, his mouth agape, his eyes wide in horror.

"Pirem!" Dejanus shouted.

Pirem snapped out of the terrible shock that had frozen him in place. He backed away from the door.

"Kill him, Dejanus!" Orkid cried. "And then kill his master!"

Dejanus lunged forward, but his feet slipped on the pool of Berayma's blood and he fell heavily to his knees. He looked up in time to see the servant flee like an old rat with a cat after it. He jumped up, but before he could set off in pursuit, Orkid grabbed his arm.

"No, wait! There is a better way! All the pieces are in place, we only have to keep to our roles." He took Lynan's training knife from Dejanus' hand and dropped it on the floor near the body of the dead king. "Put the bodies of the sentries back in their place, then call out the Royal Guards." He could not help staring at Berayma's corpse. "The king has been murdered by Prince Lynan and his protectors, the constable and Pirem. What a pity they were slain trying to escape the palace."

10

THEY were sitting on the room's stone floor discussing magic.

"It isn't that I don't believe there is magic in the stars," Jenrosa was explaining to Lynan, "but that I think the theurgia is going about finding it in the wrong way."

Lynan nodded wisely, as he had learned to do while attending his mother's court, but mostly he was concentrating on Jenrosa herself and not her words. He decided she was more attractive than he first thought. He liked the snub nose with its spray of freckles. When she smiled, her face changed, became softer somehow, and when she frowned, he could not help the urge to stroke her cheek and console her. But, his alcoholic bravado gone, he kept his hands to himself.

"Why don't you present your argument to your maleficum?"

Jenrosa looked aghast. "Are you serious? Do you have any idea how much the hierarchy have invested in the old beliefs? How many decades—centuries!—of research and practice? They would throw me out! They would burn me at the stake!"

"We don't burn people anymore," Lynan pointed out.

"My grandfather Berayma VII banned that right at the start of his reign."

"Then they'll convince your brother to bring it back."

"Just for you?"

Jenrosa nodded. "God, yes. They hate heretics."

Lynan leaned forward and refilled her glass.

She took the bottle from him and shook it. "The wine is almost gone," she said sadly.

Lynan reached into a dark recess under one of the lower bookshelves and retrieved a second bottle.

"Magic!" she declared.

"So what would you like to see your theurgia study?"

"To begin with, the same things sailors and explorers have to study. They use the stars to get their directions."

"I know *that*," Lynan said. "Everyone knows that. Why should the theurgia study what everyone else already knows?"

"Because there is no formal system incorporating all the ways the stars are used for navigation. And more importantly, finding your direction implies having at least some idea of where you are at any given time. If we could refine the methods the sailors use, we may be able to devise a way of finding out exactly where we are, anywhere in the world."

Lynan considered her words, then smiled. "Ah, but what if it is a cloudy night!"

Jenrosa looked at him sourly. "You have to begin somewhere."

Lynan swallowed. "Speaking of beginning somewhere—"

"Oh, yes, of course! You now have one of the Keys!"

Lynan blinked. How did that happen? He was going to talk about *them*, not about him. "Yes, I have one of the Keys, but what I was trying to say—"

"What does it mean?"

"What does what mean?"

"Well, what responsibilities do you take on?" She waved her hands at him. "No, no, don't tell me! It's the Key of Union, right?" Lynan nodded, feeling a little adrift. "So that means you'll be responsible for administering the provinces?"

"No. That is the king's duty. I'll be a kind of ambassador. Berayma will use me to represent the throne outside of Kendra."

"A toast," Jenrosa said, raising her glass. "To the king's new representative to the provinces!"

Lynan raised his glass halfheartedly. "It means, of course, that I may not return to Kendra for many years. There are some things I would like to do before I—"

"You'll begin with a grand tour," Jenrosa interrupted. "Across Kestrel Bay to pay a visit to Goodman Barbell in Lurisia. Then west to Aman, and a word with King Marin; I hear he's a conniving old goat, so you'll have to be on your guard. And then farther west, into the Oceans of Grass, and you'll see all the tribes of the Chetts—"

"If I can find any of them," Lynan pointed out.

"—then east to Hume, and Queen Charion," Jenrosa continued, unabated. "I've heard she is the most cunning of all the king's subjects. Your will learn much from her, I think."

"She will undoubtedly learn a great deal from me," Lynan said dryly. "And where do I go after Hume?"

"South to Chandra, and King Tomar II."

"He was a friend of my father's," Lynan said quietly.

"Then it will be like visiting an uncle," Jenrosa said, moving closer to Lynan. "I spoke to him once. He was here on one of his state visits and came to the theurgia's school. He spoke to each of the instructors and students personally. He was round and jolly, with the saddest eyes I've ever seen."

"He lost his wife at sea about twenty years ago. Her ship was attacked by Slavers. They never found her body."

"That would explain the eyes," she said. "What part of the tour will you enjoy the most, I wonder? I think it will be the trek through the Oceans of Grass. You probably won't find many Chetts, but you'll see some amazing things." Her eyes took on a distant look. "Grass stretching from one horizon to the other, huge herds of strange animals with horns and long, flowing manes. Wild horses, thousands of them, not afraid of anything under the sky. Thunderstorms as big as continents sweeping overhead. Or maybe you'll like Lurisia the best. Everything's green in Lurisia, and it's always hot. Flowers the size of meat plates, insects with rainbows instead of wings . . ."

"Maybe you should make the grand tour," Lynan joked. "I'll stay behind to play at court."

Jenrosa shook her head. "Oh, no. Kendra is my home. I don't want to leave."

"The way you speak of all these distant lands it sounds as if leaving Kendra is something you want more than anything else."

"Believe me, your Highness—"

"Lynan, please."

"—I want to stay right here. But I can imagine you will enjoy yourself so much you'll never want to come back."

Lynan finished his wine and refilled the glass. "Well, Kendra has one thing in its favor. That's where you'll be."

She looked at him hard, then fidgeted uncomfortably and stood up. "I see." She looked like an animal that has suddenly realized it is in a cage.

Lynan stood up, too, drew in a deep breath to speak. Just as he opened his mouth, someone started banging on the door.

"Oh, damn!" he exclaimed, his breath coming out in a rush. "Go away!"

The banging only increased in ferocity.

"Who is it?"

"It's me, your Highness!" shouted Pirem. There was such urgency in his voice that Lynan almost went to the door immediately.

"Maybe the king needs to consult with his new roving ambassador," Jenrosa suggested.

"Pirem, couldn't it wait?"

"Now, Your Highness, please!" Pirem banged the door a few more times for effect.

Jenrosa laughed quietly. "You don't suppose he's been listening outside, do you, and wants to make sure you don't say anything too foolish?"

"Foolish?"

"Your Highness, please!"

Lynan could no longer ignore the pleading in his servant's voice. He stomped down the stairs to the door and opened it slightly. "This had better be important, Pirem—"

He managed to get no more out before Pirem, breathless and pale and carrying Lynan's coat and sword belt, forced his way in. He pushed his master away from the door, quickly glanced back at the corridor, then slammed it shut. He grabbed Lynan by the hand and dragged him up the stairs into the turret room. The servant's eyes looked as if they were about to pop out of his head. "Quickly, Lynan, you have to leave the pal—" His words died in his throat when he saw Jenrosa.

"How long has she been here?" he hissed.

"Pirem, you forget yourself! And what business is it of yours how long Magicker Alucar has been here?"

Pirem wrung his hands in distress. "Oh, I am sorry, your Highness, but not as sorry as you'll be if you don't leave the · palace right now! This very minute!"

Jenrosa stood up. "What's happening?"

Pirem thrust himself between her and Lynan. "How does His Highness know he can trust you?"

"What are you talking about?" Lynan demanded angrily.

"She may be one of *them!*" he hissed.

Lynan shook his head in frustration. "You have some explaining to do, Pirem. Be quick."

"Your brother's dead!"

"Dead? Which brother?"

"The king! He's been murdered!"

There was a stunned silence, then Lynan said sternly. "That isn't funny, Pirem. Your sense of humor is as sour as your tongue—"

"I don't think he's joking," Jenrosa said, carefully watching the servant. "Can't you see how terrified he is? Pirem, how can you know Berayma is dead? Who killed him?"

"I saw his body!"

Lynan grabbed his servant by the shoulders. "*Who* killed him, Pirem? *Who?*"

"Orkid! An' Dejanus!"

Lynan stared at Pirem, not knowing what to say, not wishing to believe his servant's words.

"Your Highness, please believe me. I haven't been drinkin'. I wasn't dreamin'. I know I'm an old fool sometimes, but I'm not an idiot!"

"Tell me what you saw," Lynan said, struggling to remain calm. "*Everything* you saw."

"There isn't time for that!" He took Lynan by one arm and tried dragging him down the steps. Lynan resisted with all his strength. "They want to kill you, Lynan!"

"Kill me?"

"I'll explain as we go," Pirem said and again pulled on Lynan's arm, at the same time handing Lynan his cloak and sword belt. "Follow me!"

There was enough of the boy in Lynan, and still enough authority in Pirem's voice, to make him obey the command. Pirem led the way out of the room and down into the main part of the palace, not far from Lynan's chambers. "You can't go back to your room, that's the first place they'll look for you. We have to get you a horse."

He led the way toward the royal stables, followed by Lynan and an uncertain Jenrosa. Lynan stopped and told Jenrosa to return to make her own way out of the palace. "I don't know what's going on, but there's no need for you to become involved."

Jenrosa agreed readily. "I want no part of a palace revolution." She turned to go, but froze at the sound of tramping feet and jangling armor coming from around the corner at the far end of the hallway. "Then again . . ." she said half-heartedly.

"Come now!" Pirem pleaded. "Quickly, before they see us!"

He ducked down a side corridor, followed by his two charges, and hurried through a maze of little used passages and servants' ways. They soon heard a commotion from the general direction of Lynan's quarters.

"They've just discovered you're missing," Pirem said grimly, then stopped suddenly.

"What's wrong?" Lynan demanded.

"I'm an idiot! They'll be waitin' for you at the stables!" His brow furrowed in concentration. "But you still need a horse." Then his eyes lit up. "The Royal Guards' stables! They won't think of that! Not yet, at least."

They started off again, and a few minutes later they came out into an area behind the palace, near the stables of the Royal Guards. Pirem turned to the other two. "Be quiet, for God's sake, or we're all dead!" he said between clenched teeth. "We'll have to work quickly and quietly to get you a mount, Your Highness."

"But where will I go?" Lynan asked, his voice rising.

"Away from here," Pirem answered, peering into the darkness as he spoke. "After that, I can't help you, an' I'll slow you down if I come with you." He peered into the darkness for a moment, then hissed, "The way is clear!"

At a half-crouch the three fugitives ran across the open ground to the first enclosure. Lynan's nose wrinkled.

"Don't they ever clean these stables?"

"Of course they do, your Highness, but only once a day. These aren't the Royal Stables. There, in the fourth booth, that looks like a good mount."

The horse was a fine-looking brown mare with a clean coat and a nose splashed with white. As Jenrosa led her from the booth, Lynan put on his coat and buckled on his sword belt. Pirem then helped him select a harness and saddle from those hanging from a wall opposite the entrance, and handed a bridle to Jenrosa.

"I was in my room, your Highness," Pirem started explaining suddenly, "when Harnan Beresard came asking me to find you an' tell you that the king wanted to see you right away." The two men lifted a saddle off its hooks and carried it to the waiting mare. As Lynan adjusted the saddle's straps, Pirem continued his story.

"I couldn't find you, o' course . . ." Pirem glanced at Jenrosa. ". . . so I went to tell the king there'd be a delay. When I got to his room, I heard voices, so I didn't go straight in, thinking it best to wait until whoever it was had finished their business with his Majesty. Then I recognized the voices as belonging to Orkid an' Dejanus. They were saying how some plan had to go right or somethin', an' I realized they could be talkin' for hours, so I crept up to the door quiet as a cat to catch someone's eye."

Lynan's fingers were fumbling at tasks that had been automatic for years. Jenrosa was having similar difficulties fitting the bridle.

"I was lookin' into the room . . ." Pirem grabbed Lynan's arm so tightly it hurt. His old, rheumy eyes looked up into Lynan's face, tears rolling down his cheeks. "The king was on the floor in a bloody heap! I think they stabbed him right in the . . ." Pirem gagged, but managed to finish the sentence in a burst, ". . . in the neck, your Highness, pierced like a sticker in a boar's belly, an' the blood was everywhere."

Jenrosa swayed and held onto the mare's head to stop herself from falling. Lynan was already crouching, but he too suddenly felt faint. He put a hand on the horse's flank to steady himself.

"They saw me! As I ran away, I heard Orkid tell Dejanus to kill me, an' then to come after you! But I know this place like the back of my hand, all the servants' ways, so I was able to get to you well before them. You know the rest."

Lynan slowly stood erect, taking the reins from Jenrosa. Pirem was resting against the wall, his hands shaking.

"Thank you, Pirem," Lynan said softly, trying to keep his voice even despite the fear threatening to overwhelm him. "You have risked your life to save mine. I will never forget it. Now you and Jenrosa must go. Find a place to hide, and I'll try and let you know what happens to me."

"What will you do?" Jenrosa asked.

Lynan shrugged. "I don't know. Maybe King Tomar will help. But the first thing I have to do is get out of Kendra."

Pirem moved to the stable door and waved to him. "There is still no one here. Go now, your Highness, while you can. Quickly!"

Lynan led the mare out to the open and mounted, then turned to say goodbye to his companions.

"You there! Get off that horse!"

Startled by the sound, the horse turned on its rear legs. Lynan saw five guards running toward him from the palace. Pirem jumped forward and slapped the horse on the rump. The animal bolted, almost unseating Lynan.

"Flee, Lynan!" Pirem shouted. "Flee for your life!"

Lynan did not know what to do. He wanted to ride away as fast as the mare could take him, but he could not just leave his friends like this. Pirem saw his indecision and drew his dagger.

"There is nothing you can do for us!" he cried. "Flee!"

Pirem turned and ran toward the guards, shouting an old war cry and waving his dagger above his head. The first guard tried to meet Pirem's assault head on, but Pirem had been a soldier longer than a servant. He dived under the sword and swept up with his dagger, lodging it into the guard's chest. As the man reeled back, Pirem wrested the sword from his hand and charged again.

After seeing the fate of their companion, the four surviving guards were more cautious. They kept their swords low and waited for the old man to come to them. Pirem swerved at the last moment to take the one on his far right, but his opponents were younger and more agile than he. There was a flurry of sword play, then Pirem cried out and dropped to the ground, his weapon clattering to the earth next to his bleeding body.

Jenrosa panicked and bolted, aiming for the servants' door Pirem had led them through. The guards set off in pursuit.

"Oh, God, no!" Lynan cried. He drew his sword, kicked his horse into action and galloped toward the guards. Two of them slowed down and spread out, trying to cut off his escape route. He charged the nearest.

The guard brought up his own weapon in a high block, but Lynan loosened his left foot from the stirrup and slumped low over the mare's right shoulder, swinging his sword up and out, striking the guard's jaw and slicing along his throat like a barber's razor. The guard grasped at the wound, dark blood spouting between his fingers, and collapsed without a sound.

Lynan wheeled the horse around to face the guard on his right, but it was already too late. Out of the corner of his eye he saw the silhouette of a man behind him. A hand grasped his left foot, still out of the stirrup, and pushed it up and over the mare's back. Lynan landed heavily on the ground, his breath whooshing out. A sharp pain in his side made him feel instantly nauseous. For a second he blacked out, and when he came to, he was on his back. Through a haze he could see a guard standing over him, his sword tickling Lynan's throat, and two others standing back a few paces, Jenrosa struggling futilely in their arms.

"Your Highness," the guard over him said in a bitter voice, "for what you did to King Berayma tonight, I'm going to skewer you like a bird on a spit."

Lynan saw him bunch his muscles for the killing stroke when suddenly a shadow loomed over both of them. The guard gasped as a spear sprouted from his chest. He was pulled back off his feet and sent spinning away. A second, misshapen shadow cut down one of the guards holding Jenrosa, and the last guard turned on his heel and ran.

A strong hand grabbed Lynan by the hair and pulled him to his feet. Lynan found himself staring at a salt-and-pepper beard and blue eyes.

"Are you all right, lad?"

"Kumul?"

"What a silly bloody question," the constable said. Still holding the prince by the hair, he spun him around so he could see the second rescuer.

"And Ager," Lynan said weakly. And then he remembered the magicker. "Jenrosa—"

"I'm all right," said her voice beside him. She was horribly pale and her whole body was shaking. She was staring at the body of the guard Kumul had killed.

"The last guard!" Lynan said, remembering now that he had seen him running away. "He will tell others where we are!"

"I'm too old to go chasing after him, and Ager here, for

all his agility, couldn't run after a lame infant." Kumul turned to Jenrosa and Ager. "We need another three horses."

Jenrosa looked up at the constable strangely, then hurried back to the stables, Ager hobbling behind.

"Do you think you can stand on your own, your Highness? I've got to help the others. We haven't much time."

Lynan nodded vaguely and immediately felt his support go. He spread his feet wide to steady himself and looked around for his mare. She was standing twenty paces away, not far from the guard Lynan had dropped.

I've killed my second man, he thought, and then felt wretched because the fellow had been one of the Royal Guards.

He tried to control the heaving, but without success. He emptied his stomach. Groaning, he wiped his mouth with the back of his hand, then tottered over to the horse. He returned to the stable, retrieving his sword on the way and cleaning the blade against his pants. Within two minutes he was joined by the others. All three mounted and the four headed down behind the stables and away from the palace. As they disappeared into the long shadows that covered the slope down to the city below, they heard behind them the first sounds of hue and cry.

"Ride hard!" Kumul roared. The four kicked their horses into a gallop, then hung on for dear life as they descended into the darkness.

11

ORKID stood in the doorway to Lynan's chambers while Dejanus searched the rooms for any hint of where the prince might be.

"He can't be far," Dejanus said. "My guards are at all the gates. He must still be in the palace."

"Unless Pirem found him," Orkid said.

Dejanus left the room. "His sword is gone, and the Key." He looked desperately at Orkid. "What now? We need his corpse to blame for Berayma's death—"

"There's no need to change the plan," Orkid said, thinking. "Not yet, anyway. Your guards may still find and kill him for us."

"I'll organize the hunt and make sure," he said.

"And I will wake Areava and tell her the tragic news about her brother." Dejanus started to leave, but Orkid held him back and whispered fiercely in his ear: "And never forget the plan! We can gather all the willing witnesses we need once we have Lynan's and Kumul's bodies. Areava will believe the worst of her brother. And remember when you see her that *she* is queen now. Make sure your guards treat her as such."

*   *   *

When Lynan and his companions reached the original city wall, they slowed their mounts to a steady walk. They needed to recover from their hair-raising descent, being almost as winded as their horses.

They passed as quietly as possible through the narrow streets and alleys of old Kendra. There were some people about, marking the passing of good Queen Usharna and the start of Berayma's reign, and the companions could hear snatches of song as they passed inns and taverns open late for the occasion.

Lynan had no idea where Kumul was leading them. He sat on his horse like someone with the weight of the world on his shoulders. He could not shake the feeling of nausea from his stomach, nor the images of Pirem's tragic death and the guard he had killed. He had to swallow continually to keep the bile down. Jenrosa rode beside him, dazed by events and her predicament. Behind them came Ager, grimly silent. Only Kumul seemed to show any purpose, his face a mixture of alertness and barely repressed anger.

They made their way southeast through the city. When Kumul pulled them up and ordered them off their horses, Lynan could smell the harbor not far away.

"We'll leave the horses here," Kumul told them. "It's best now if we go on foot."

"Where *are* we going?" Jenrosa asked.

"A friend's place," he answered. "Now, no more questions until we get there. The less attention we draw to ourselves with unnecessary chatter, the better our chances of surviving the night."

They slapped their horses to send them on their way; if unhindered, they would eventually return to their stable. In a few minutes the companions had reached the docks. Ropes and pulleys creaked and clanked in the onshore evening breeze, and rats scurried out of their way. The harbor smelled of sewage and bilge and rotting flesh. *Everything is death tonight,* Lynan thought bitterly.

Kumul, setting a rapid pace, led them east along the harbor for a league or so before heading north, back into the city proper. They passed warehouses smelling of exotic spices and busy taverns smelling of stale beer and urine. Skinny dogs sniffing for garbage scampered out of their way or growled at them defiantly. As the streets turned into alleys with houses dangerously leaning over them, the night air became strangled and still. The only sound was their own footsteps on the cobblestones and the occasional furtive scraping of a scavenging rodent or a hunting cat.

At last, Kumul slowed to an easy walk as he peered through the dark trying to recognize features and landmarks.

"It's around here somewhere," he whispered to himself.

For a few minutes more they kept on this way and then, with a satisfied grunt, he stopped and knocked impatiently on a door.

"Where are we?" Lynan asked.

Before Kumul could reply, the door opened and a man shorter than Kumul but just as wide came out on to the street. "Who the hell do you think you are, my friend, rousing me from my warm chair . . ." The man craned forward toward the constable. ". . . at this hour . . . Kumul?"

Kumul chuckled, a sound like a small avalanche of gravel. "Who else do you know who's as big as me, Grapnel?"

The one called Grapnel laughed in turn and put his hands on Kumul's shoulders, then noticed his companions. "You've brought friends, I see."

"Can we come in? It isn't safe out here."

"Not safe? Who in their right minds would be after you?" Grapnel asked, but he ushered them inside without waiting for an answer.

They were crowded into a narrow hallway. Grapnel

squeezed his way to the front and showed them into a living area. A bright fire was burning in a deep grate at one end of the room, and before it were mismatched chairs and a long table. The walls were made from whitewashed mud brick, and long beams supported a clinker-built roof.

Grapnel set chairs in a semicircle in front of the fire and bade them sit. He disappeared into an adjoining room, appearing a moment later with five mugs and a jug of home brew.

For the first time that night, Lynan saw that the close-cropped graying hairs at the back of Kumul's head were matted with dried blood, and a red smear covered the nape of his neck.

Lynan turned his attention to Grapnel. Their host had a wide, swarthy face with two raised white scars, one on either cheek, which joined the corners of his mouth, giving him a permanent and macabre grin. His brown hair was cut as close to the scalp as Kumul's, and each ear sported a large gold earring. Brown eyes were half hidden by drooping eyelids that made him look as if he would fall asleep at any moment. Although not as tall as Kumul, he still loomed over Lynan.

Their host poured beers for them, then sat back in his chair and waited for Kumul's explanation.

"This is Captain Ager Parmer, late of the Royal Guards," Kumul started, nodding in the crookback's direction. "He was once a captain in the Kendra Spears."

Grapnel leaned forward and peered at Ager's face. "By all the creatures in the sea, you *are* Captain Parmer. And you've had hard times, I see."

"And I remember you, Grapnel," Ager replied. "You were Kumul's lieutenant in the Red Shields."

Grapnel nodded, and then looked at Jenrosa. "And you are?"

"My name is Jenrosa Alucar. I am a student magicker with the Theurgia of Stars." She shook her head. "Or I was."

Grapnel looked questioningly at Kumul.

"She was Prince Lynan's companion tonight," the constable told him.

"Good grief, Kumul," Grapnel said, grinning slyly. "No wonder you're in trouble."

Kumul sighed. "And this is the prince in question," he continued, indicating Lynan.

Grapnel shot to his feet, his chair falling over behind him. His cheeks reddened, making the scars stand out like welts. "Grief, your Highness! My apologies!" He glanced at Jenrosa. "And to you, ma'am."

Lynan could not help a smile creasing his face, and he tried to hide it in his cup. Strong, bitter stout coursed down his gullet, almost choking him. Jenrosa blushed as deeply as Grapnel, but there was anger behind it.

"You misunderstand our relationship," she said quietly.

Grapnel started apologizing again, but Kumul interrupted him. "And this, Your Highness, is Grapnel Moorice, trader and ship owner. One of your father's most loyal and hard-fighting soldiers. And a friend." Kumul took Grapnel's arm. "Evil things have happened tonight. King Berayma has been murdered by conspirators, and now they're after Prince Lynan."

Grapnel's mouth dropped open. "On our friendship, Kumul, are you telling me the truth?" Kumul nodded. "How much do you know?"

Kumul shrugged helplessly. "For me, it started with Dejanus, Berayma's Life Guard." Kumul quickly explained how he had been fooled by Dejanus. "I think he thought I was dead; either that, or he had some other part for me to play before the night was over. When I woke, I was too groggy to think. I managed to reach the courtyard when Ager found me. We immediately went to Berayma's chambers in case Dejanus meant him harm as well, but we were too late."

"At first we didn't know what to do," Ager continued. "Kumul was still dazed. I left him there and went to give the alarm, but found out from a guard that it had already been raised and that the order was out for Kumul, Lynan, and Lynan's servant to be captured or killed because they had just slain the king."

"I knew Lynan could not have had anything to do with Berayma's slaying," Kumul said. "I also knew it was too late to make for his chambers—others would be well ahead of us—so I gambled that they would make for one of the stables."

"How did you guess we'd head for the Royal Guards' stables?" Lynan asked.

"They were closest," Ager said, and shrugged apologetically. "By that stage we figured we needed some luck."

Lynan then recounted what Pirem had said about the involvement of Orkid, then about their rush for the stables and Pirem's death.

"Pirem?" Grapnel asked. "The general's old servant?"

Lynan nodded.

"I am sorry to hear of his death. He was a good soldier. What happened next?"

"Then Kumul and Ager turned up."

"Thank God," Jenrosa said. "They saved our lives."

"That's half my job done," Kumul said grimly. "Now that you are both safe for the moment, I'll go back and kill Dejanus and Orkid." He stood up to leave.

"You can't!" Lynan exclaimed. Kumul had become his rock in the last two hours and he wanted to hang on to him for as long as possible. "They'll be looking out for you! That guard who got away couldn't have mistaken for you for someone else. As soon as you turn up, they'll kill you or take you prisoner."

"Not if I tell them what really happened," Kumul said. "Most of the guards are good and loyal lads. The ones at the stables tonight must have been Dejanus' favorites."

"Good lads or not," Jenrosa said evenly, "they'll still kill you."

"You don't know what you're talking about, girl—"

"Think for a moment, Kumul," she said sharply. "Who did Orkid and Dejanus blame for the king's death?"

"She's right, Kumul," Grapnel said. "They'll not ask questions. They'll kill you to make up for failing to protect Berayma."

"I can't let the king's death go unavenged," Kumul said bitterly.

"But what better way to revenge him than ensuring their plot fails?" Grapnel said urgently. "Keep Prince Lynan out of their hands!"

"And help me reclaim my rights," Lynan said.

Olio had been roused by a servant, and told that Areava wanted to see him urgently in Berayma's study. Olio dismissed the servant and dressed quickly, wondering what all the fuss was about. Probably something to do with Lynan again. He wished his sister would let the matter go; she was becoming obsessed with Lynan and his inheritance of the Key of Union.

The palace was awash with guards and officials, each hurrying on some task. Olio's curiosity gave way to a feeling of dread. Something was wrong for so many to be out and about at this time of night.

It must be Haxus, he thought. *Its ruler has decided to take advantage of Usharna's passing and invaded the north of the kingdom again.*

There were several people milling about the entrance to the king's rooms. Most stood as silent and white as marble statues. *God, it is war, then.*

He entered the dark chamber and saw his sister and Orkid deep in discussion in front of a large desk. Areava, noticing him, moved forward to greet him. Her golden hair was drawn back in a tight ponytail, and she was wearing linen breeches, leather jerkin, and riding boots; this was the way she dressed when she was at weapons training. Her brown eyes were deep and red rimmed.

Olio caught a glimpse of a body slumped behind the desk. At first nothing registered, and then he recognized the long, blue cloak that fell from the corpse's broad shoulders. He took a step forward and saw the floor was covered in blood.

"Olio—" Areava began, but he turned away from her, gagging. Areava waited for him to finish, came closer and put an arm around him.

"M–m–my God!" he wheezed. "It can't b–b–be . . ."

"I need you, Olio," she said calmly. "Stand straight."

He did as she ordered. He saw how pale her own face was. "When? Who?"

Areava turned to Orkid, who came to them. The chancellor's coat and hands were encrusted with blood. His fingernails were black. Olio could not help retreating a step.

"Who did this?" Olio asked.

Orkid cast down his gaze. "We have reason to believe it was Prince Lynan, your Highness."

"No!" Olio shouted automatically. "That's not p–p–possible. Lynan would not have done this." He faced his sister. "Areava, you know this isn't p–p–possible—"

"Olio, listen to me. I didn't want to believe it at first either, but the evidence is overwhelming. Listen to the chancellor." She nodded for Orkid to continue.

"We believe it was a conspiracy between Lynan and the Constable of the Royal Guard."

"Kumul, too!"

"And Lynan's servant, and that crookback captain our

mother healed," Areava said. "Others were undoubtedly involved, but we don't know who at this stage. What we do know is that Kumul, Lynan, and the crookback were seen escaping from the palace in the company of a young woman."

"A young woman?"

"We don't know her name yet, but her clothes identified her as a magicker," Orkid continued. "They killed four guards, Your Highness. I have a witness to the fact. Lynan's servant was also killed in the struggle."

"None of this m–m–makes sense," Olio said to himself.

Orkid placed a hand on his shoulder. "It is a terrible crime, and made worse by the station of its perpetrators. We are all in shock, but your sister is now Queen of Kendra. She will need your support, your steady hand. Let Dejanus and me take care of apprehending the murderers."

Areava took Olio's face in her hands, made him look at her. "Olio, the world has turned upside down for us. First our mother's death, and now this. But I will not shirk from my new responsibilities, and neither must you. You possess the Key of the Heart, and the kingdom will need healing."

He glanced again at his brother's corpse, still trying to comprehend what had happened, and nodded uncertainly. "What . . . what do you want m–m–me to do?"

"Stay by me, brother," Areava said. "Just stay by me." He felt her lean against him then, and understood what she herself must have been through. He put his arms around her.

"I am always at your side, sister," he said softly.

All eyes were on Lynan. He realized what he had just said, and although he knew it was his fear and anger and frustration speaking, he also realized it expressed his heart's desire. He was as surprised as his companions.

"I intend to claim what is mine by right," he said forcefully. He glanced at Kumul. "And when I do, I'll give you Dejanus to do with as you wish."

Kumul studied the prince's young face for a second, then nodded slowly. "And Orkid?"

"He's mine," Lynan replied.

Kumul smiled approvingly. Lynan felt his hopes flicker for the first time that night.

"Excuse me," Jenrosa said mildly, "but how do you intend to reclaim what is rightfully yours when the Royal Guard is probably scouring the city for your hide? And while you two are planning the downfall of the conspirators, what am I to do?"

"The first thing *all* of you will have to do is escape Kendra," Grapnel said.

Lynan saw the grief and horror in Jenrosa's expression. "I'm sorry," he said to her. "It's my fault this has happened—"

"Oh, enough," she snapped. "I know it isn't your fault, but I had a good life as a student and I don't fancy spending the rest of it on the run with three outlaws, one a prince of the blood possessing a head certain people want to cut off, and two others as inconspicuous as a pair of beached whales."

Grapnel laughed and slapped the table with a large hand, spilling beer from mugs. "What a jolly team we'll make!"

"*We?*" Kumul asked.

"Of course. You're going to need my help to get clear of Kendra. One of my ships is in port, so I can smuggle you out of the city."

"You've done enough for us already by giving us shelter tonight. I have no wish to place you in any danger, my friend," Kumul said.

"You've already done that by coming here. It's in my interest to make sure you get clear away."

"But get clear away to where?" Jenrosa demanded. "Where can Lynan—any of us—safely go?"

"Safely?" Grapnel said. "Probably nowhere for any length of time. But there must be some place you can stay until the immediate danger is over."

Lynan sighed, then pulled the Key of Union from out of his tunic. He looked at it sullenly, his earlier bravado gone now. *I wish now that I'd never seen this thing,* he thought glumly.

"What will Areava's position be?" Grapnel asked Lynan.

Lynan looked up in surprise, overwhelmed by sudden guilt. He had been so involved in his own plight he hadn't given a thought to Areava's situation, or Olio's. Had the assassins been after them as well? If so, surely they'd be dead by now. A groan escaped from his lips.

"I fear . . . I fear that they must be dead with Berayma. I only escaped through good fortune and the courage of my servant . . ." His voice faltered. He could still hear Pirem's cry as he fell beneath the swords of his attackers.

"You may be wrong about your siblings," Grapnel said. "The conspirators must know the kingdom, not to mention the Twenty Houses, would not tolerate one of them ascending the throne. They need a Rosetheme, one of the royal successors. There are no other claimants that I know of."

"You can't mean that Areava or Olio were involved in the assassination of Berayma?" Lynan declared. He glanced up at Kumul, seeking his support, but the constable's face was unreadable.

Grapnel shrugged. "I'm not a magicker, Prince Lynan. I can't see into the minds of others. All I know is that the conspiracy, to work effectively, must be wider than simply Orkid and this Dejanus, and the conspirators must place either Areava or Olio on the throne. A kingdom must have a ruler the people will accept, or there will soon be no kingdom."

"Areava. . . ?" Lynan said aloud, but more to himself than the others. "But she couldn't kill Berayma."

"There are some who love power more than anything else in the world, your Highness," Kumul said darkly.

For a while no one said anything. Finally, Grapnel sighed and stood up. "You must stay here tonight. Tomorrow morning I will go out and see what is happening. We will be in a better position then to determine what to do next."

Grapnel got some rags and vinegar to clean Kumul's wound, then gave his guests rugs and blankets to put on the floor before the fire. The four tried to rest during the night, but too much had happened, too much was at stake, for any of them to find sleep at first. They talked for a while, but the conversation soon died of its own accord.

Lynan, cocooned by the silence, tried to make sense of what had happened to him over the last few days. From being the invisible son of a distant mother and deceased soldier, he had suddenly become a recognized heir and prince of Kendra, the greatest kingdom known to history, then prey to the scheming of royal assassins, and finally—probably—made an outlaw in his own land.

It seemed so unfair that everything that happened to him occurred without his determination or agreement. He was a small, storm-tossed boat trying to keep afloat in political waters for which he had no map or compass. He was adrift, in danger of sinking, and without the means or wherewithal to do anything about it.

A new feeling sparked in him then, and he recognized it as anger. Not the flaring emotion that came with loss of temper, but a revolt against the huge injustices heaped upon him by a world that did not care if he lived or died. It was anger as foundation, the beginnings of something solid upon which he might start building his own life according to his own terms, and he held on to it as if it was a life raft.

Even as the thought occurred to him, he was struck by its

irony. Before he could do anything for himself, he had find a way out of his present predicament, and for that he was again relying upon the actions and motivations of other people.

How could he ever repay their loyalty? he asked himself, and the answer came almost immediately. By winning back his birthright.

12

"IT'S not your sympathy I want," Areava said evenly.

The man standing in front of her desk, bedecked in all the finery of his office as magicker prelate, the chief representative of all the theurgia, swallowed hard. Edaytor Fanhow's first audience with the new queen was not going at all well. Instead of being ushered into the throne room, as he had expected, he had instead been taken to her new private chamber, the very room in which Berayma had been murdered if the amount of dried blood on the floor was any indication. There were two guards standing on either side of the desk and another pair near the doorway. Fanhow had thought that offering condolences on the tragic and barbarous death of Berayma would soften the cold stare the queen had regarded him with since he had first entered the room. He glanced up to Olio for some sign of empathy, but the prince's face was set as hard as stone.

"What I want from you is help to find my brother, the outlaw Prince Lynan," Areava continued. "Can you provide that help?"

Edaytor spread his hands. His cloak billowed out behind him, and he now desperately wished he had dressed less formally when Areava's messenger had come for him in the hour before dawn. "It isn't that simple, your Majesty. Our arts are dependent on so many conditions, so many nuances—"

"Yes or no, Prelate," Areava interrupted. "I haven't the time for explanations. Is there a way that one of your magickers can track down Lynan's movements since last night, or find him for me now?"

Edaytor was about to spread his hands again but stopped himself just in time. "I cannot answer it so simply. I will have to consult my colleagues, the maleficum of each of the five theurgia. I know of no way this can be done without a good deal of preparation. However, new incantations and pathways are being discovered all the time."

Areava looked down at her hands, knotted together on the desk. She had never felt this tired before in her life. There was so much to be done in the next few hours, and so few people she felt she could rely upon to help. Orkid and Olio would offer whatever assistance they could, but she knew it would still not be enough. Who among the leading citizens, the chief bureaucrats, the merchants and traders, the generals and admirals, the Twenty Houses, and yes—the theurgia—could she trust?

"Consult with your colleagues, then, Prelate," she said at last. "But come back to me with an answer before noon today."

Olio nodded to Edaytor, and he got the hint. "Of course, Your Majesty. Right away. Before noon." He scurried off as fast as his legs could carry him.

Areava sighed deeply and rested back in her chair. "Useless. Absolutely useless. How did he make magicker prelate? I've met novices with greater wit than he has."

"That is exactly why he is p–p–prelate," Olio answered, without any trace of irony. "Why p–p–place someone with real authority over m–m–magic in a p–p–position where they will not be able to p–p–practice their arts? B–b–by all accounts Fanhow was a m–m–mediocre stargazer with a p–p–penchant for administration. No one ran against him for office, and he was voted in unanimously."

"Stargazer? He was a member of the Theurgia of Stars?" Areava asked. "So was this woman Lynan escaped with . . ." She scrabbled among the papers on her desk for Dejanus' note which held the woman's name.

"When Fanhow made p–p–prelate, Jenrosa Alucar was five years old. I doubt he holds any loyalty to her, or even to his old theurgia."

Areava nodded tiredly. "You are right, of course."

"You are exhausted," Olio observed. "You m–m–must rest at some point."

"Yes, but not this point. We must secure the throne." She glanced up at her brother. "And that means securing Lynan. While he is alive, the conspiracy still lives."

Olio's mouth tightened. He could find no reply to Orkid's accusations, but what he had come to accept in the middle of the night, however begrudgingly, seemed increasingly absurd to him in the light of a new day.

Before he could answer, the doors to the study opened to let in the chancellor. Areava looked up sharply. "What news?"

"None yet, your Majesty. Dejanus is supervising the Royal Guards as they scour the city, but there are so many places to hide. Who knows how long your brother and his fellow traitors have been planning this operation? They could have a dozen bolt-holes prepared." He set a thin, leather-bound book in front of her on the desk. "The list you asked for."

"What list?" Olio asked curiously.

"Of those who may have some reason to be involved in a plot to overthrow Berayma," Areava answered for the chancellor, and opened the book.

Olio looked over her shoulder and scanned the first page.

He stood back, shocked. "Orkid, you can't be serious! These are p–p–people who have been loyal to the throne and the kingdom all their lives!"

"Loyal to your mother, your Highness, which does not add up to the same thing," Orkid answered. "At any rate, the list does not contain those who are traitors, only those who are known to hold some grudge against the late king, your sister, or yourself."

For a moment, Olio was speechless. There was no way Orkid could have produced this list in the last few hours. The chancellor was staring at him fixedly with his dark eyes, and he had to avert his gaze.

"Xella Povis?" Areava asked, pointing to a name on the second page. "The head of the merchant guild? I know for a fact that she was a good friend of Berayma's. Why is her name here?"

"A good friend of your brother's, yes, but I know she has opposed you several times on issues concerning your late mother's policy of subsidizing ship building."

"Oh, this is ridiculous!" Olio said fiercely, still not daring to meet Orkid's gaze. "If you wrote down the name of every person in Kendra who ever had a bad thought about our mother or Berayma or Areava or me, the list would be ten leagues long!"

"It may well prove to be of no consequence," Orkid agreed patiently. "But if I err on the side of caution, I will not be ashamed of it. My duty is to your sister, and not to the niceties of polite society. I have included the names of all those of whom I have knowledge concerning some possible matter of dispute between them and a member of the House of Rosetheme."

Areava sighed. "Very well, Orkid. Thank you for your efforts. I will read the document and inform you of any action I consider necessary." She checked the shadow cast by the hour stick near the study window.

"I have an appointment with Primate Northam in a short while." Orkid's eyebrows lifted in inquiry. "To make arrangements for Berayma's funeral," she added testily.

Orkid cast his gaze down to the floor. "Of course, Your Majesty. I will inform you immediately of any developments regarding the search for Prince Lynan."

Areava stood up. "Do that." She turned to her brother. "Olio, you had better come with me. After all, this meeting with the primate is a family affair."

As Orkid turned to leave, Areava called him back. "By the way, I want the Key of the Scepter. It was still around Berayma's neck when he . . . when his body . . . was taken away."

"Then it must still be with him. I will give orders for it to be collected at once and brought to you."

As Orkid left, Areava whispered to Olio, "For without that Key, what authority have any of us?"

Lynan did not know how long it took him to fall asleep. He knew he had stayed awake longer than the others because he remembered hearing their snoring and snuffling and thinking how loud it was. He had never slept in a room with other people before, and found it most distracting. He also remembered the fire going out, leaving the room in unrelieved gloom. But one moment he seemed to be staring into the darkness, and the next he was blinking as bright sunlight poured into the room, trying to blind him. He sat up, rubbed his eyes, and moaned as the memory of the previous day's events flooded into his mind.

Jenrosa appeared, squatted by his side, and shoved a mug of hot cider into his hands. "Drink this, and when you're ready, pull on your boots; there's porridge waiting for you in the kitchen, but it won't stay warm forever."

Lynan thirstily quaffed the cider and followed Jenrosa into the kitchen. There was a large pot containing something gray and glutinous bubbling away on a stove. He scooped some into the bowl Jenrosa handed him and swallowed a mouthful. It tasted better than it looked.

"Good," he mumbled to Jenrosa as he wolfed down more.

"Kumul made it."

"Where is he? And where is Ager, and our host?"

Even as he asked the question, Kumul and Ager entered through the back door carrying armfuls of firewood. "Grapnel has gone to hear what is being said on the streets," the constable said. "He should be back soon."

Lynan returned to the main room with Kumul and helped him start a new fire in the hearth. Then, together, they looked out the window and onto the narrow street. Across the way was a baker's shop with a stall outside; business was already brisk—a queue extended some way down the street.

"I wonder what has happened to Areava and Olio," Lynan wondered aloud, his voice unhappy.

"There's nothing we could have done for them," Kumul said matter-of-factly. "Anyway, we'll know soon enough. Here comes Grapnel."

The front door opened and Grapnel entered. He quickly closed the door behind him and made sure it was locked, then waved Lynan and Kumul away from the window. Jenrosa and Ager heard Grapnel come in and joined them. Grapnel looked into their faces, and his own grim expression made their hearts sink.

"The news isn't good. Word's out that Prince Lynan murdered Berayma, then was forced to escape from the palace before he could kill Areava and Olio. Areava is now queen, and has ordered that you be found and brought to her for justice."

"My God! Areava is part of the plot!"

Grapnel shrugged. "Possibly, but remember, your Highness, that Orkid and Dejanus can argue their case with her, arrange the evidence any way they like. She may be innocent of any wrongdoing, yet still believe you guilty of the crime."

"Then I have to see her," Lynan said emphatically. "I will convince her of the truth." He gathered his coat from the floor and made for the door. "The sooner I go to the—"

Grapnel held him by the arm. "You wouldn't make it to see the queen," he said. "Dejanus would make sure you were brought to her with your head already removed from your shoulders. Even Kumul couldn't get you past the Royal Guards at the moment. They are devastated that they failed to protect Berayma, and are determined to prove themselves not only by killing you and Kumul, but by ensuring no one gets to see the queen without her explicit permission."

Grapnel turned to Ager and Jenrosa. "They know you two escaped with the prince. Warrants are out for all four of you. The Royal Guards have already started searching house to house. We don't have much time."

"Do you have any ideas?" Kumul asked.

Grapnel nodded. "Look down the street," he said, pointing to the window. Kumul did so and saw a long wagon covered in an oilskin parked outside an open warehouse. One of the sorriest looking nags in Kendra was hitched to the wagon.

"Yours, I assume," Kumul said.

"Aye, and full of bolts of cloth. I have a ship leaving for Chandra this morning, and this is the last part of its consignment. I'll get you down to the docks hidden under the oilskin."

Lynan looked up at Grapnel. "Then I am leaving the city?"

"You have no choice," Grapnel answered evenly. "You need to find a place where you will be safe for a short while, and where you will have enough time to plan your next move."

"Surely someone will be watching the docks," Kumul said.

Grapnel laughed. "Of course. An eel called Shehear, a snitch who does occasional jobs for the chancellor's intelligence network, is already down there waiting for something to happen. First sight of you lot and he'll be hurrying as fast as his legs can carry him to find the nearest detachment of Royal Guards."

"So what's the point?" Jenrosa demanded.

"As soon as you've boarded my ship, Shehear will be off. That's when we'll transfer you to the ship's shore boat. It has a sail, and is easy to row if the wind dies on you. You can follow the coast until you are well past the city. Meanwhile, the ship itself will head northeast, hopefully drawing all the attention."

"But I know nothing about boats!" Lynan declared.

"I know how to sail one," Ager said. "I've been second officer on too many merchanters to ever forget."

"And I can navigate," Jenrosa added confidently.

"Fine, but where will we go?"

Grapnel shrugged. "I have no answer to that, your Highness, but you haven't time to ponder it here in Kendra."

The Key of the Scepter shone dully in the sun of a new day. Orkid held it up by its chain, admiring its solid and functional beauty.

"The key to all power," he murmured softly. His free hand clasped it tightly. "The power to dissolve a kingdom, and to create it anew."

He closed his eyes, reminding himself to remain patient. So many decades of planning were now reaching their culmination, it was difficult for him to resist the temptation to force events to a faster pace.

But history will not be rushed. My people have waited this long, they can wait a few years more.

He unclasped his hand, noticing then the dried blood on his palm from the Key. He grunted, surprised he had not noticed it before. After all, he had himself removed it from Berayma's gory neck after the body had been removed. He wiped his hand on a cloth, and was about to clean the Key itself but changed his mind.

Areava wants it, and so she will have it, stain and all. This will be a sign for her, if she is clever enough to read it.

He put the Key back into the pocket behind his waistband. When he had first handled it, he had half expected to feel its power, its influence, but there had been nothing. He patted the waistband over the Key and wondered again about its significance. During the Slaver War he had witnessed Usharna using the combined keys to wield great magic—calling storms to protect Kendra's harbor, bringing confusion to the enemy's armies—but always at such great cost to herself that it had taken years, maybe decades, from her life. He had always assumed that the power stemmed from the chief Key, the one he now possessed, but in his hand it was nothing more than a pretty golden trinket. Alone, was it nothing more than a symbol, then? He wished he had been able to convince Usharna to forget tradition and leave all the Keys with Berayma instead of scattering them among her children. It would have made so many things easier.

He put it out of his mind. There was still much to be done, and little Lynan, poor orphan and dupe, was still free. Everything about the plan had worked until the prince had escaped in the company of Kumul. Orkid was much more afraid of Kumul than Lynan. The constable was respected by too many people in the kingdom, and his reputation as a soldier was second only to that of Elynd Chisal.

At least the Royal Guards would give him short shrift in

their present mood. They would do anything to revenge Berayma, and to prove their loyalty to Areava.

He smiled grimly to himself. It struck him as ironic how Areava had become, in one sense, a new Key of Power. Orkid allowed himself a small smile. She was one key he would never surrender.

Usharna had given Primate Giros Northam possession of the palace's west wing. Although not an enthusiastic adherent of any faith, Usharna appreciated the benign effect the priests had on much of the population of Kendra. The god they worshiped was a distant entity, long ago evolved from some primitive spirit of the sky, unlike many of those deities worshiped in some of the kingdom's outlying and less civilized provinces. The actual name of this god was known only to the primate and his chosen successor, and the religion it inspired had as its main objective the easing of poverty and the bringing of comfort, which had conveniently made it a valuable ally in Usharna's long struggle to destroy slavery in her realms, the same struggle that had cost the lives of her last two husbands. Besides, Usharna could not be sure the priests were wrong about the existence of their god, and if it indeed existed, it would do no harm to cooperate with its acolytes.

Northam had turned the square in the west wing into a cool garden, an oasis of peace apart from the normal bustle of the palace. The largest of the rooms had been turned into the royal chapel, and the others had been set aside for the library, the refectory, and priests' cells.

Areava and Olio met Primate Northam in his private office, but as soon as the main business of arranging Berayma's funeral was over, the three walked into the garden and sat under a large summer tree, its drooping branches protecting them from the climbing sun.

"It is a matter of whom to trust," Areava told Northam. "I

was not taken into my mother's confidence as much as Berayma. I don't know who her closest confidants were, nor whom she turned to besides Orkid for advice. There is so much to be done, and I'm not sure on whom to rely."

"You trust no one?" Northam asked, a little surprised.

Areava laughed lightly. "Olio and Orkid, I trust. And you, of course."

Northam nodded. "Perhaps I can offer some help, even though I was never a member of the court circle, as such." He glanced up at Olio. "You are right to place your faith in your brother. He is, I think, an upright man with a good heart."

Olio smiled and bowed mockingly to the primate. "You are generous."

"As for any others . . ." Northam paused to collect his thoughts. "I have had very little to do with the chancellor, but I know he was trusted implicitly by your mother. Xella Povis, from the city, I always found honorable—"

He stopped when he saw the look exchanged between Areava and Olio. "There is something wrong?"

Areava quickly shook her head. "No. I, too, have always felt the merchant could be trusted."

"And I," Olio agreed firmly, casting a glance at his sister that Northam could not interpret.

The primate mentally shrugged and went on. "I know one or two magickers from the theurgia that are worthy officials. Prelate Fanhow is honest enough but tends to the bureaucratic."

"And among the Twenty Houses?" Areava asked, swallowing her pride.

"Good and bad, as you'd expect. Many of the older members of the Houses became . . . accustomed . . . to your mother; I think you can expect their good will and devotion to carry on to her successors, for a while, at least. As for the younger members, much will depend on how you include them in your administration. I would expect some to be ambitious, which may be to your advantage, but keep a close eye on them."

Areava seemed to ready herself to ask another question, but said nothing.

"What ails you, your Majesty?" Northam asked gently.

"I need to know that I am secure," she said. "There is much to be done, but my actions will be circumscribed if I'm worrying about what is happening behind my back."

"The burden of every ruler, surely," Northam said.

"My mother had no internal enemies."

Northam laughed. "Not for the last years of her reign. But the first ten were fraught with danger for her. Intrigues within the Twenty Houses; enemies without plotting with enemies within; and the Slavers, of course. Usharna persevered, and was at times quite ruthless, until everyone grew to recognize her undeniable ability as queen. From this, and not from her inheritance of the throne, came her right to rule."

Areava nodded. With her whole heart and mind she wished nothing more than to serve the kingdom, but was depressed by the thought that she would have to prove her ability over a period of years or even decades.

Northam gently tapped her hand. "My chief advice is this. Reconvene the executive council. Your mother did something similar in her earliest years. Place in the council all those who wield some influence or power: representatives of the Twenty Houses, the merchants and army, the theurgia, your chief officials. Let them know they are there to provide advice, not share your rule. Make sure some of those on the council are those you believe may be against you, for then you can keep a closer eye on them. After a few years, when you are surer about your path and when you have bound to you those who are truly loyal to the kingdom, you consult the council on fewer and fewer occasions until membership is nothing more than honorary, an award you distribute to those closest to you."

"I like this advice," Areava said after a moment. "You, of course, must be one of its members."

Northam was taken aback. "It is not the place of the clergy to become so intimately concerned with politics."

"Nevertheless, you will make an exception in this case. I need my friends by my side."

Northam saw the determination in Areava's eyes. He spread his hands. "If that is your command, of course."

"It is my wish," Areava said gently.

Northam laughed at her choice of words, making his wattled throat jiggle. "In that case, how could I possibly refuse?"

The ride in Grapnel's wagon was stuffy, cramped, and bumpy. By the time Lynan and his companions got down to the docks, they were bruised and angry. They slipped onto the merchant ship as covertly as possible, protected from most prying eyes by bales of cotton and crates of squawking chickens. *Seaspray* was a small ship, perhaps fifty paces long and, at its widest, a dozen abeam. A single mast sprouted from the middle of the deck, its yard and sail strapped to its length to make it easier to work cargo on the ship. At the stern was a modest poop deck, and below and in front of it the wheel housing. There were two hatches: a large one forward of the mast and a smaller, man-sized one between the mast and the wheel housing.

A small, wiry sailor with forearms the size of hams shepherded the four refugees down the aft hatch to the main deck, where crew were busy shifting crates brought down through the cargo hatch.

"Wait here until Grapnel or the captain come to get you," the sailor said, grinning slyly, obviously enjoying being part of a ruse to fool the Royal Guards. He returned to the upper deck, leaving them to their own devices.

For several minutes they watched the sailors at work, admiring their strength and their skill with rope and tackle. Huge crates were moved with seemingly effortless ease, but the groaning of the deck planks attested to their great weight. Kumul shifted from foot to foot, uneasy to be idle when there was work to be done, and at one point actually moved forward to lend a hand but was quickly waved back by one of the sailors. "We know what we're doing," the sailor said curtly. Kumul returned to his position and resumed his dance.

A short while later they heard the sail drop and then crack as it caught the wind. The boat rolled for a moment, its ungainly width not made for tight maneuvering, until the prow steered clear of the dock and the city was astern. The rolling gave way to a steady pitch that was less nauseating.

Grapnel's head peered at them from the hatch, and he called them up to the deck. Lynan glanced aft and saw Kendra receding behind them. He wondered if he would ever be back.

Grapnel was standing beside a big woman with no hair and golden skin. "This is Captain Turalier," Grapnel told the companions, and they exchanged brief greetings.

"Shehear's taken the bait," Grapnel continued, "and is well on his way to the palace by now. We'll have passed the heads soon, and you can be off on your own journey. Hopefully, the attention of any pursuer will stay on *Seaspray*."

"You will be captured by the navy," Kumul said. "Their ships are faster than yours."

"But their crews are not as experienced or brave. We will head out into the Sea Between and far from the sight of any land. They will not pursue for long."

"And then what will you do?" Kumul asked him.

"I have friends in Chandra. I will hide away there for a

while." He shrugged. "Who knows what the future will bring for us all? Your path is more hazardous than mine, I think."

"When do we part?" Jenrosa asked.

"As soon as we're through the heads," Captain Turalier said, her voice surprisingly light for such a large woman. She checked the sail and the wind vane. "Probably before the next quarter of an hour. *Seaspray*'s boat is ready to be put in the water, and is well provisioned. We'll let it down and put you on board. Then you're on your own."

"I wonder how much of a head start we'll have," Ager said, also observing the wind.

"The navy always has some of its fastest cutters on standby," Kumul told him. "Mainly for courier work. If Shehear ran all the way to the palace, the alert has probably already been sounded. We should expect pursuit within the hour."

Turalier nodded. "Sounds about right. I'll lower the boat now and you can load her with whatever else you need."

She left to give the order and Grapnel was called away by the ship's quartermaster. The others stood together awkwardly. The four of them had been thrown together as a group through circumstances beyond their control. The realization was finally hitting them that for the foreseeable future they would be living in each others' pockets; more to the point, the life of each of them now depended on the fortitude and loyalty of the other three.

"We still have to settle on a destination," Kumul said after a while, looking out to sea as if the answer was to be found there.

Ager nodded to Lynan, his one eye regarding the prince keenly. "Your Highness?"

Lynan glanced up, surprised. Why was Ager asking him? He and Kumul were older, more experienced. . . .

"I'm . . . I'm not sure," he managed to say. He saw Jenrosa grimace, and suddenly felt he had let her down. Then he saw that Kumul also looked disappointed, as if Lynan had made a slip in basic weapons training.

Ager sighed. He opened his mouth to say something, then stopped. He was staring at the middle of Lynan's chest. Lynan looked down, noticed nothing out of the ordinary.

"What is it? What's wrong?"

"I'm an idiot," Ager told himself.

"What are you on about?" Kumul asked.

Ager reached out and pulled on the chain around Lynan's neck, pulling the Key of Unity out from underneath the prince's shirt. Ager stared at it shining in the sun for a moment before putting it back.

"Don't you see, you fool of a giant?" Ager demanded, grasping the constable's forearm. "That's it! The answer has been there the whole time."

"I wish you'd stop talking in riddles—" Kumul began, but Jenrosa cut him off.

"Of course! The Key of Union! The provinces!"

"What are you two talking about?" Lynan asked.

"Lynan, you're the throne's representative in the provinces," Jenrosa said. "The Key of Union was given to you by Usharna herself."

"I don't think we can count on Areava and Orkid allowing his Highness the opportunity to exercise his office," Kumul said sarcastically. "I can't imagine anyone taking his authority seriously, especially if they're under the thumb of the palace."

"Not everyone is under that thumb," Ager said evenly. "And there are parts of this kingdom where Usharna's authority never fully reached, but where the holder of the Key of Union will be obeyed implicitly if there in person."

"Not city or town in the kingdom fits that description," Kumul responded. "Maybe way out in the moors of Chandra, or the rain forests of Lurisia, or the grasslands of the

Chetts . . ." His voice trailed off as he realized what he was saying.

"Exactly," Ager said emphatically.

Understanding dawned in Lynan then. "You mean I should escape to one of the uncivilized lands of the kingdom, where Areava won't be able to find me."

"And where her agents and armies will tread only softly, if at all," Kumul added.

"And where you can form a rebellion," Jenrosa said.

The other three looked at her in surprise. For a moment, no one said anything, and then Kumul boomed angrily: "A rebellion against the throne?"

"Be quiet, Kumul!" hissed Ager. "Do you want the whole world to be party to our private conversations?"

"But—!"

"I meant a rebellion against the conspirators!" Jenrosa said fiercely. "A rebellion to see justice done, a rebellion to see Lynan reinstated as a loyal and trustworthy prince of the blood, to see Kumul reinstated as Constable of the Royal Guard and Ager as one of its officers, and to see *me* reinstated as a member of the Theurgia of the Star; a rebellion to let us all return home and get on with our proper lives."

Kumul and Jenrosa matched stares. Although he towered over her, she stood up close to him, her fists on her hips, her hazel eyes glaring into his blue ones.

Lynan cleared his throat. "I thought the idea was to lie low until things got a little quieter."

"Quieter?" Ager asked. "What do you mean, exactly?"

"You know. Not so dangerous."

"Things won't be so dangerous once Orkid and Dejanus have cut your throat," Kumul reflected, finally breaking eye contact with Jenrosa. "But I don't suppose that's what you mean by 'quieter,' either."

Lynan feel set upon. "What is going on here?" he demanded, crossing his arms.

"Grow up, Lynan," Jenrosa said impatiently. "Your life—all our lives—are in danger. We can't sit back and let events unfold as they will. If you ever want to return to Kendra, if you want to punish Berayma's murderers, you're going to have to face up to a few unpleasant truths."

Lynan looked sullenly at her.

"And it's not just what *you* have to do," Jenrosa continued. "For better or worse, you're not alone in this."

Lynan closed his eyes. He wanted to shut out Jenrosa's words, but each one struck home. He nodded slowly. "Well, for better, I think. For me."

Ager grunted. "So where is it to be? Chandra, Lurisia, or the Oceans of Grass?"

"I vote for Chandra," Jenrosa said. "I hear they appreciate magickers there, and King Tomar was a good friend of Lynan's father."

Kumul shook his head. "Chandra is too close to Kendra. And the province's wilder parts, the moors, will offer little support. They're thinly populated. A good place to hide, perhaps, but not for raising an army."

"The same can be said for the rain forests of Lurisia," Ager said. "With the added disadvantage that it has far too many merchants who know me."

"That leaves the Oceans of Grass," Jenrosa muttered dispiritedly.

"I thought you wanted to see the Oceans of Grass," Lynan observed. "What was it you said? 'Huge herds of strange animals, with horns and manes. Wild horses, thousands of them, not afraid of anything under the sky. Thunderstorms as big as continents . . .'"

"I was talking about *your* adventures," she said sourly. "I'm quite happy surrounded by civilization, thank you very much."

"The Oceans of Grass will be perfect for Lynan's purposes," Ager said. "Far from the capital, not locked in by mountain or sea, and traversed by a large number of tribes loyal to the throne in their own rough and ready way but not particularly attached to, or respectful of, the kingdom's officials."

"But loyal to whom?" Jenrosa mused.

"That's the beauty of it," Ager replied, pointing to the Key of Union. "Apparently they almost worship the two most responsible for destroying the Slavers, the scum who preyed so heavily on them."

"Of course," Kumul said under his breath. "Usharna and the *general*, who was himself half Chett."

"And Lynan is the son of both," Ager said smugly, folding his arms.

Captain Turalier rejoined them. "The boat is ready. You should board now. We'll be through the heads in a few minutes."

The four companions shook hands with the captain and Grapnel, he and Kumul embracing, then moved to the stern. Their swords were bundled together and placed in the boat, then Ager went down first and steadied the vessel as Kumul clambered on board. Kumul had obviously never been in a small boat before, and he found it difficult to keep his balance. The boat started rolling precariously.

"Sit down, you horse!" Ager barked. Embarrassed, Kumul plumped down on the mid thwart. Jenrosa went down next. Lynan watched her with envy as she lightly stepped into the boat, then stepped over Kumul to take the rear thwart and the rudder.

"All right, your Highness, your turn," Ager said. "Come down this side of Kumul and sit beside him."

Lynan swung over, but before descending, he turned to Grapnel. "Thank you for all you have done. I will never forget it."

Grapnel nodded. "Best get going, your Highness, or you won't live long enough to remember."

As soon as Lynan placed a foot in the boat, it started to move away from him.

"Shift your balance this way," Ager urged him.

Lynan edged toward him, but of its own volition one hand held on to a rope hanging from *Seaspray*'s gunwales.

"Your Highness, you'll have to let go sometime," Ager said, reaching out to grab him by a sleeve.

Lynan let go of the rope, overcompensated, and started waving his arms around in wide circles to maintain his balance. Ager lost his grip on the sleeve, and Lynan toppled backward into the sea with a huge splash. As he bobbed to the surface like a cork, he saw *Seaspray* pulling away from him, Captain Turalier and several of the sailors looking back with grins as wide as mainsails on their faces.

Kumul and Ager each grabbed a handful of the sorry prince and dragged him on board like a hooked tunny. He lay on the bottom of the boat, coughing and hacking, thoroughly wet and miserable.

"Have a nice swim, your Highness?" Ager inquired politely.

Lynan eased himself up to the mid thwart and wiped dripping hair away from his face. "Delightful, thank you."

Ager said nothing more, but with practiced ease erected a supple mast and unfurled a single, lateen sail. A moment later the wind caught the canvas and sent the companions away from Kendra and away from home.

13

ALTHOUGH Lynan had occasionally dreamed of visiting faraway lands one day, he had never actually been at sea. At first, wet and miserable, he sat shivering and feeling sorry for himself, his head down, but as the sun and the breeze dried his clothes and then warmed his skin, his temper improved.

He found himself taken over by the novelty of sailing over deep blue water, of having his hair whipped around his face like a loose sail, of the smell of brine untainted by the scent of human waste. He marveled at the seagulls wheeling overhead, at the cormorants that dived into the water so recklessly, and at the pattern of the waves running across the top of the sea.

After a while, though, doubts assailed him. He noticed how small the boat was, and wondered what fish might be lurking just under the hull for a chance at nibbling a dangling hand or foot. He could not help remembering how poor a swimmer he was—he had never taken to water. He drew away from the gunwales, trying to sit as closely as possible to the center of the thwart, and began to feel miserable again.

When at last they left behind any remaining signs of civilization, Ager told them they still had an important decision to make. "How are we to get to the Oceans of Grass?"

"The most direct way," Kumul said. "Surely the sooner we get there, the better."

"Perhaps," Ager mused. "But if Areava has guessed where we're heading, she'll try and cut us off."

"We have at least some head start," Jenrosa pointed out.

"For how long?" Lynan asked. "Areava has probably already sent messages to the provinces warning them to keep an eye out for us. If she sends those messages by postriders, they will not be far behind us. If she has sent them by carrier bird, which is more likely, the messages will already be arriving at Chandra and Lurisia."

"As much as possible we will have to travel under cover," Kumul said. "By night, by little used roads, by stealth. The four of us, no matter how determined, cannot hope to force our way through the whole kingdom."

"Then you think we should not take the most direct route," Jenrosa said dryly.

"No route will be entirely safe," Ager said. "We must weigh what we think the risks will be and choose the least dangerous."

"That *may* be the most direct route," Kumul said. "The least expected action is often the wisest, and time is important. If we take months to get to the Oceans of Grass, it will give our enemies the breathing space they need to secure their position, or to work on enough of the tribes of the Northern Chetts to stop any rebellion from ever getting off the ground."

"I can't dispute what you say, Constable," Ager said quietly. "In the end, of course, the decision isn't really ours to make."

"What do you mean?" Lynan asked, confused. "Why go through all this discussion otherwise?"

"What I mean, your Highness, is that Kumul, Jenrosa, and I cannot make the *final* decision. You must."

"Why me? We're all in this together—"

"Start thinking like a true prince, lad," Kumul said. "In the end, you have to make all the decisions . . . all the vital ones, anyway. This is *your* cause. Eventually, you will have to stand alone, especially if you're to lead a . . ." He glanced quickly at Jenrosa. ". . . rebellion. We can advise, even cajole, but we can't make policy, we can't decide what path the rebellion must take, we can't denounce your enemies for you. All of these things must be done by the leader— by you."

Lynan was silent. He did not want this responsibility. Not yet, anyway. Why were they forcing the decision on him now, when he knew no more than they about the situation?

For a while they sailed on, the water gently lapping against the side of the boat, the sun warming their faces.

"Lynan?" Jenrosa urged quietly.

"I'm thinking," he replied curtly, angry at his companions and conscious of them staring at him. At last he said, "I don't want to make this decision."

Ager sighed. "It's not a decision any of us want to make. Still, it has to be made."

Lynan muttered something.

"What was that?" Jenrosa politely enquired.

"I said we might as well go by the shortest possible route."

"Why?"

"What do you mean 'why'? Because you want me to make the decision, and that's the decision I've made, that's why."

"That's hardly an answer," Ager reproved. "As your followers—in fact, at this point, as your *only* followers—we deserve more respect and courtesy. Otherwise, your rebellion might be very short-lived."

"I don't understand any of this. You insisted I make the decision. I didn't want to—"

"Will you listen to yourself?" Jenrosa snapped. "You're starting to sound like a spoiled brat. We're not bees, Lynan, we're people. If we don't know on what grounds you've made the decision, how can we advise you and how can we respect your decision?"

"You mean every time I make a decision I have to explain it to everyone?"

"Not every time," Ager assured him good humoredly. "Just most of the time. Once you've shown you can make good and wise decisions on your own, no one will question you."

Lynan breathed out resignedly. "I think we should take the shortest possible route because, as Kumul pointed out, time is of the essence, and because we don't know yet whether or not Areava has blocked the way. If she hasn't, we'll get through to achieve our goals all the quicker. If she has, it won't be too late to choose another, longer, route."

"Well, that's pretty comprehensive," Jenrosa acknowledged.

"Yes, very sound," Ager agreed expansively.

"Excellent choice, your Highness," Kumul said. "That wasn't so hard, was it?"

"Thank you so much," Lynan said. "And I assume the most direct way is by boat?"

"Aye," Ager agreed. "We follow the coastline until we come to the mouth of the Gelt River, and then sail up the Gelt until we are within one or two days' march of its source in the Ufero Mountains, on the other side of which we will find the Oceans of Grass."

"How long do we stay with the boat?"

"About ten days, depending on the wind."

Wonderful, Lynan thought. *Another ten days over water. And it was my decision.*

As they sailed on, the coastline gradually changed in appearance. Close to Kendra, soft yellow beaches gave way to gently rolling farmland, but as they approached the Ebrius Ridge—the basalt uplifts that separated the Horn of Lear from Chandra to the north—the topography became increasingly steep until eventually high cliffs marked the boundary between sea and land. Lynan felt small and insignificant under the towering black wall, and vulnerable and frail against the white-capped waves that crashed into the cliffs, sending great sheets of spray into the air. Circling above them like thin strips of shadow was a cloud of kestrels, springing from their aeries in the face of the rock wall and searching for fish and other birds.

"They make me uneasy," Kumul muttered, staring at their flying escort with suspicion. "The kestrel is no longer a bird of good omen."

"I think they're beautiful," Jenrosa declared in their defense. "They mean us no harm." Her gaze lifted to a group of kestrels that broke away from their fellows and flew further out to sea.

"Let us talk about something else," Ager said. "Whether or not the birds bring us bad luck, there is nothing we can do about it."

"Let's talk about ships, then," Jenrosa said, still watching the kestrels.

"What type of ships?" Lynan asked.

"Whatever type is coming our way," she said calmly. The others looked up at her sharply, and then followed her gaze.

"I can't see anything," Ager said.

"Nor I," Kumul added.

"You won't for a while," Jenrosa said. "But I've been talking to sailors and navigators now for three years, and I know that kestrels have learned to follow our ships because of the refuse we throw overboard." She pointed to the birds that had left the cliffs. "And they are hovering above a ship."

"Damn," Ager swore under his breath. "She's right. I'm an idiot for forgetting. Lynan, help Jenrosa with the tiller. Kumul, help me pull down the sail. We must row."

"Row!" Kumul declared. "The waves will send us against those cliffs!"

"Lynan and Jenrosa will steer us very carefully, won't you? But with the sail up, we're too easy to spot."

Ager and Kumul quickly furled the sail and stowed the mast. They took the oars and sculled strongly and evenly toward the looming cliffs, Kumul pacing his stroke to match Ager's.

"When we're two hundred paces out, Jenrosa, steer us parallel to the shore," Ager said. "We daren't go any closer than that."

Jenrosa nodded. Lynan, constantly looking over his shoulder, was the first to see the approaching sail. "There she is!" he cried.

The other three peered toward the horizon. They caught a glimpse of a red sail, and soon after a long, sleek hull. The sail was emblazoned with a golden spear crossed by two swords. A warship.

"Do you think it's searching for us?" Lynan asked.

Ager shook his head. "Possibly, or it's carrying messages from Areava to King Marin of Aman. Either way, if it sees us, we could be in trouble."

They were very close to the cliffs now, and the waves were getting harder to resist, even with both Lynan and Jenrosa pushing against the tiller. They could see huge, jagged boulders at the base of the cliffs, and a curtain of spray hung permanently in the air, drifting over the sea and drenching them. The rudder seemed to have a mind of its own, twisting and flexing beneath the hull.

"We have to move away!" Jenrosa shouted, trying to be heard over the roar of crashing waves. Lynan glanced fearfully at the rocks, now less than two hundred paces from them.

"Keep your course!" Ager ordered. "The warship is closing. It must have seen us!"

"Its navigator was watching the kestrels, too," Jenrosa said, and ignored Kumul's sour expression.

The constable grunted. "If they've seen us, then at least we can use the sail again." He let go of his oar and started to stand.

"No!" Ager roared, but it was too late. As soon as Kumul moved, the boat's prow lurched violently toward the rocks. He sat down and reached for the oar, but it slipped out of his grasp as the blade bit into the sea. The boat spun ninety degrees, sending the oar into Kumul's side with terrific force and unseating him with a loud thwack.

Ager grabbed the oar and tried desperately to work it as well as his own, but his reach was not wide enough. Lynan and Jenrosa pushed on the tiller in a frantic attempt to keep the prow pointed away from the cliffs, but a wave picked them up and lifted the stern out of the water, rendering the rudder useless.

Ager pulled in the oars and moved astern to take the tiller, pushing the two young people forward and down to the bottom of the boat. The wave seemed to tire of them and dropped them behind its cap. Ager was ready, and he heaved on the tiller with all his strength. Kumul had recovered his breath by this time, and he lurched back to help. Together, the two men were able to move the prow to port, and the boat slid sideways for a second before compromising and moving forward at an angle, driven by current and momentum, still headed toward destruction on the rocks.

"Look out!" gasped Kumul, pointing to where the waves were breaking early directly in their path. But there was nothing either of the men could do. Almost as soon as Kumul cried out his warning, the boat was picked up by another wave. There was a tormented scraping sound as the hull was hauled over a barely submerged rock and the boat was shot forward again. It hit the sea with a crash and Lynan felt himself picked up and hurled through the air. When he hit the water, the shock of the cold made him open his mouth in a gagging scream, and the whole ocean seemed to rush in. He kicked frantically and broached the surface, only to slip under again right away. His clothes felt as if they were loaded down with lead weights, and he tore at them frantically.

Suddenly, a strong hand grabbed hold of his hair and jerked him to the surface. He heard Kumul mutter something about twice having to save him by his hair in two days, and then he was being dragged through the water like a river barge. Seawater still flowed into his mouth and up his nose with distressing ease, but he had the good sense not to struggle against Kumul's grip as he was pulled through the sea. He tried not to panic as the shadows of the cliffs fell across his face and made him almost rigid with fear. The pair suddenly rose in the air as a wave lifted them high. Lynan had a sensation of moving along very quickly and was aware of Kumul using his one free arm desperately in an attempt to at least steer some passage for them. They were surrounded by swirling white water. Lynan's thigh slammed hard against a rock. He heard Kumul gasp in pain. More white water, the sea surging over their heads.

I'm going to die, Lynan thought, and was surprised by the sense of calm that overtook him, like the moment just before sleep.

And then weight returned. It was as if having become part of the sea he was now being forcefully separated from it. His calves and ankles slapped against slippery rock. Kumul was lifting him out of the water, pulling him back with his last reserves of strength.

Even though Lynan had expended little effort in his own

rescue, he was exhausted. When Kumul finally released him, he could barely lift his head. He saw that he was lying on a long, flat basalt platform wet with spray, protected from the sea by a boulder balanced on the edge of the platform like a bird of prey on a perch. Ten paces away was Ager, bending over Jenrosa, trying to kiss her, and for the moment there seemed nothing odd about his behavior. Lynan tried to thank Kumul for saving his life a second time in as many days, but only managed a weak croak.

"Save your breath, your Highness," Kumul said gently. "You'll need it if we're to get out of this mess. We've lost our boat and with it our supplies and our swords—leaving us with nothing but knives to protect ourselves. We're at the bottom of a cliff. There is a warship looking for us on the other side of that boulder." He shook his head violently, as if to clear it. He faced the crookback. "Ager, how's the magicker?"

For the first time it occurred to Lynan that Jenrosa might be in danger, that indeed Ager had not been kissing her but trying to revive her. He tried to sit up, but it only started him retching. Brine burned up from his stomach and lungs, spilling out of his mouth as whispery spittle. The sound of him throwing up was matched by Jenrosa heaving and coughing.

"She'll be all right," Ager answered, and helped Jenrosa sit up. "What are our navy friends doing?"

Kumul half squatted behind the boulder and peeked over its edge. "They're about four hundred paces away. They're trying to retrieve the boat with hooks, but it's pretty smashed up. I can see archers behind the gunwales." He dropped down out of sight. "You're heavier than you look," he told Lynan wearily.

The young prince grinned stupidly and managed to join Kumul, his back against the boulder. He saw how the platform they were on jutted out of a crumbling cliff face that looked as if it was ready to finish slipping into the sea at any moment. It was a long way to the top, but the slope was nowhere near as sheer as Lynan had first thought.

Jenrosa moaned. Ager still held her, but after a moment she waved him away.

"I'm all right," she pronounced huskily, and slowly looked around. "We've got to climb that?" she asked, staring up at the cliff.

"Unless you feel like risking a five-league swim around the rocks," Ager said.

"Not today," she admitted.

"Well, we can't stay here either. Eventually a big wave will wash over us, and I don't give much for our chances of making it to safety a second time. Besides, the longer we wait, the stiffer our muscles will become."

Lynan carefully peeped over the boulder. "The warship is leaving," he told the others, and then saw the shattered remains of their boat swirling among the rocks below. "And they're leaving their prize behind," he added dully, and for an instant imagined that his own body was down there, broken and drowned. He recalled Kumul saying their swords had gone down with the boat. In his heart he felt a terrible pang—his sword had been the only thing left to him from his father. Suddenly he wanted to climb to the top of the cliff more than he had ever wanted to do anything in his life. He wanted to get away from the water, from the smell of the spray, from the call of the seabirds and the sound of waves smashing against the rocks.

"Let's go," he said, the plea almost sounding like an order, and stood uncertainly to his feet. Kumul's hand roughly pulled him down to the rock.

"Don't be an idiot, lad. Those on the warship would see us as easily as flies crawling up a white sheet."

They waited for nearly an hour, cold and regularly washed by spray coming over the platform. They huddled together for warmth and security, afraid that at any moment a big wave would throw them back into the crashing sea and finish them off. Eventually, Kumul could no longer see the warship's sail even when he stood up, and he led the way to the base of the cliff.

There were plenty of holds in the rock, but the basalt was sharp and cut into their palms. The first third of the slope was wet from the spray and they all slipped and gashed their faces and bodies. Their clothes tightened as they dried, stretching limbs like tight nooses. The worst part was the numbing exhaustion they all felt, exhaustion that turned muscles into string and bone into sapling, exhaustion so severe it became a physical pain starting in their joints and traveling throughout their arms and legs in excruciating spasms.

As they got higher, their rests became more frequent, and at times it seemed their ordeal would never end. Then, perhaps thirty paces from the summit, the wind hit them, a whistling, keening gale that whipped across the face of the cliff trying to hurl them back into the sea. Lynan knew he could go no farther. His mind started to wander and his senses were telling him that he was on level ground and that he could lie down now, that all he need do was release his grip and everything would be fine—he would wake in his bed in the palace in Kendra and the last two days would be revealed as nothing more than a nightmare.

Someone was talking to him. He tried to ignore the voice because it was spoiling the nice warm feeling that was creeping over him, but the voice would not go away and in the end he had to listen. *Lynan,* it was saying, *climb. One more step. Move up one more step.* So he moved one more step, and the pain was so bad it was like someone driving a nail into his knee. *One more step,* the voice repeated, and he recognized it as Jenrosa's. *Move, Lynan, you're so close to finishing. One more step, and then another, and another . . .*

And at last there came a time when he reached overhead with a hand and the slope was gone and there was soft vegetation underneath his fingers. For a moment his mind cleared enough for him to pull himself up the final two paces to the very top of the cliff. He collapsed into a bed of long, sweet-smelling grass, and darkness came and took him.

Speaking with Primate Northam had calmed Areava and helped focus her mind, which until then had been filled with a multitude of confusing facts and fears. The horror of her brother's murder, and the realization that Lynan must have been behind the crime, had almost overwhelmed her reason. The discussion with the priest had also made her realize that her first duty was to ensure a peaceful transition in rule from Berayma to herself. The kingdom must be her priority, not the pursuit of her brother's killers; Orkid and Dejanus between them were more than capable of hunting down Lynan and his co-conspirators.

However, when Dejanus intercepted Areava and Olio on the way back from the west wing to tell them that Lynan had been sighted boarding a merchant ship, her fury at her half-brother came on again like an irresistible tide and she had to struggle against it.

"Then see he is captured."

"I have already alerted the navy," Dejanus confirmed. "They will send out ships to intercept the merchant and bring your brother back for justice."

"And see to it he is b–b–brought b–b–back alive," Olio said firmly. "His dead b–b–body will leave too m–m–many questions unanswered."

Dejanus looked at Olio with an expression the prince couldn't read. "But if they offer resistance—"

"Alive, Dejanus," Areava insisted. "How else will we discover the extent of the conspiracy behind our brother's death?"

Dejanus nodded curtly. "I will see to it the ship captains understand your order." He left without further word.

For a moment Areava simply stood there, fighting the urge to close her eyes. "I am exhausted," she said weakly.

Olio put a hand on her shoulder. "Do you w—w—wish to see Trion? I can send for him and he will give you a draft to help you sleep."

Areava shook her head. "Not yet. Find Orkid for me and bring him to my study. We must form this council as soon as possible and plan the . . . the coronation. The administration of Kendra must continue uninterrupted."

Olio nodded and left her.

A moment later Areava looked around her. Except for a guard at either end there was no one else in the palace corridor, and there were no sounds other than the echo of Olio's receding footsteps. The palace's gray stone seemed to surround and cage her.

I am queen, she thought. *I am alone.*

When she entered her study, someone was waiting for her, a man in a long green cloak. His back was to her, and he seemed to be staring at the monarch's desk.

"Who—?" she began, and stopped when the man turned around. "Oh, Harnan!"

The private secretary bowed to her. He held his hands out, shaking.

"Your Highness. I came late this morning as your brother . . . the king . . . instructed me. I did not know . . . nobody told me . . ." His voice failed him, and tears welled in his gray, rheumy eyes and rolled down his old and whiskered cheeks. "I am sorry . . ." His voice faltered.

Areava came forward, overwhelmed with pity for her mother's oldest and dearest servant. She held his hands in hers. "Harnan, it is I who should apologize. I did not think. So much has happened. I should have thought to send someone to tell you."

"Oh, milady, no, do not blame yourself in your grief. But I am . . . confused. I don't know where to go. I don't know what to do." His lifted his chin and tried to stifle his tears. "Forgive me . . . but first your mother . . . now this!"

Without thinking, Areava used one hand to dab away the tears on his cheeks. "There is nothing to forgive, faithful Harnan." She stood back, looking him up and down. "As always, ready to do service. Berayma would be proud of you."

Harnan opened his mouth to respond, but no words would come.

Areava sniffed back her own tears, knowing that if she started crying now she would not be able to stop. She said in as businesslike a tone as she could muster: "I see you have your tablet and pens." She nodded to the wide purse hanging from Harnan's belt.

"Yes, your High . . . your Majesty. I was to write letters for your brother this morning."

"Well, since you are here, I need your assistance if you feel up to it. I need urgent messages to go out by courier to the provinces. As well, I'm reconvening my mother's executive council and I want it to meet before noon."

"Of course, your Majesty. It would be a relief to work."

Areava smiled then, suddenly proud of the old man. "Then, together, you and I will administer this kingdom with such energy that it will do full justice to the memories of Usharna and Berayma."

The pain in Harnan's face visibly eased. He sighed deeply and drew out the writing tablet and his favorite pen from the purse.

"At your service, Queen Areava, always," he said, his voice full of emotion.

She patted him on the shoulder and told him to take a seat. She went behind her desk and stopped suddenly. On the desk, on a square of white silk, lay the Key of the Scepter, its luster diminished by the blood of her brother. She touched it hesitantly. A spark jumped between the amulet and her finger. She drew back with a hiss.

"Your Majesty, are you all right?" Harnan asked, concerned.

Areava glanced up and nodded quickly. She cautiously touched the Key again. Nothing happened. She picked it up by its chain and put it over her head. Her dead brother's Key clinked against her own, the Key of the Sword. She stared at it for a long moment, lost in her own thoughts.

Magicker Prelate Edaytor Fanhow had changed into more sedate clothing. Gone was the heavy velvet robe with the gold twine, the baggy trousers and the broad silver belt he had worn in his first meeting with the new queen. In their place he wore a more practical set of linen pants and shirt with the magicker's traditional stiff collar, and his cap of office, a wide beret with the prelate's badge pinned to its front.

He returned to the palace just before noon, hurrying to meet Areava's deadline for new intelligence about Prince Lynan from the theurgia. When he arrived at the queen's offices, out of breath and sweating, the guards let him through automatically.

He entered, opened his mouth to formally greet Areava, and came to a stop, his mouth closing shut with an audible snap. The main room was filled with the best from Kendra society, the very cream of the most elite professions and trades, all dressed in their very finest clothing and ceremonial garb. Everyone in the room turned to look at him, and their expressions made him feel like a latrine washer who had accidentally barged in on a wedding ceremony.

The crowd parted to let someone through. Fanhow's head twisted from side to side, searching for someplace to hide, but there was nowhere. He found himself gazing into Queen Areava's hard brown eyes. She looked him over.

"Dressing down for the event, Magicker Prelate?" she asked innocently.

"Umm, the event, your Majesty?"

"Did not a message go to the magicker prelate?" Areava asked the tall, wizened man by her side. Edaytor recognized Harnan Beresard.

"Yes, your Majesty, but my courier could not locate him."

"Your Majesty, forgive me, but I have been urgently seeking answers to the problem you set me—"

"Not that it matters," Areava interrupted, looking at Edaytor but still talking to Harnan. "For the prelate has arrived anyway. Still, some hint of ceremony in his dress would have been appropriate."

"Your Majesty," Edaytor began again, his voice plaintive, "I was only returning to inform you of the result of the combined theurgias' search for your brother!"

"And?" Areava asked.

Edaytor looked downcast. "In so short a time, your Majesty, all they could discover was some relation between Prince Lynan and the element of—"

"Water," Areava finished for him.

Edaytor gaped. "How could your Majesty possibly have known—"

"He has escaped by sea," Areava said. "Though his freedom will be short lived." She eyed Dejanus, who stood behind her in the company of Orkid and Olio. "Or so I trust."

Dejanus nodded vigorously. "Your navy will capture him soon, your Majesty. Have no doubt."

"I have no doubt," Areava replied. And then: "Yet." She turned her attention back to Edaytor. "At least you returned on time, Prelate."

Fanhow bowed as deeply as his stout build allowed. "At your service, your Majesty."

"Indeed. And now that you are here, we can begin."

"Begin?"

"The first meeting of my executive council. You are, of course, as magicker prelate, one of its members."

Edaytor repeated his bow. "Your Majesty, I am honored."

Areava regarded him coolly for a moment. "Good," she said at last, and turned to the rest of her guests.

"We will begin as soon as you are all seated. The council room is ready."

The guests made way for Areava and her immediate entourage, only Olio hanging back. Everyone else fell in behind her, some using swift footwork to advance their position in line but all careful not to crowd the queen. Edaytor, still recovering from shock, was content to go last. He was surprised to find Olio walking by his side.

"You did well, M–m–magicker P–p–prelate," Olio confided in him.

"Too little and too late, I fear, your Highness," Edaytor admitted unhappily.

"And yet you still came to report. That took courage."

"I will always do my duty, your Highness," he said with such seriousness it seemed almost comical to Olio.

Olio let Edaytor walk on ahead and regarded the man with new consideration. *Yes, Prelate, more courage than I gave you credit for. Perhaps the theurgia, unknowingly, have done us all a favor by your promotion.*

Areava sat at the head of the table, with Olio to her left hand and Chancellor Orkid to her right. Members of the Twenty Houses and government officials occupied the long side of the table on Orkid's side, and those representatives of the various guilds, the city and the merchants sat opposite them, including Primate Northam. At the far end of the table sat Fleet Admiral Zoul Setchmar and Marshal Triam Lief, the heads of Her Majesty's armed forces. Missing was the third member of the military trio, Constable Kumul Alarn, recently declared murderer, outlaw, and fugitive. Members of the Royal Guards stood to attention at every window and the two entrances; Dejanus stood directly behind Areava.

"By now you are all acquainted with the tragic events of the last twelve hours," Areava began. "I have, as is my right through inheritance, assumed the throne. My first action as queen was to sign warrants for the capture of my brother, Prince Lynan, and his companions. My second action was to call together this executive council. I thank you all for attending on such short notice."

Areava paused until the round of murmured "Thank you, your Majesty" and "I was honored, your Majesty" died down.

"We have a great deal to do. Word of King Berayma's death will travel widely and quickly, not just throughout the kingdom but to our enemies as well. Some of them may wish to seek advantage from the succession, thinking that Kendra will be in some confusion. We must dissuade them.

"Four things must occur. First, I must be crowned as quickly as possible. Second, all official positions must be filled. I know that Berayma had plans to revise the bureaucracy after our mother's long reign. I do not feel this is the appropriate time to do so." There were some audible sighs of relief from the government side of the table. "Third, we must ensure the people know that the succession, though brought about by violence, was itself achieved smoothly and with the full support of the kingdom's leading citizens. Fourth, Lynan must be brought to justice, and the horrible conspiracy he led exposed completely so that it can be crushed once and for all; to do otherwise will eventually lead to doubts about the authority of the throne and the security of the realm." Areava paused long enough for her gaze to light on each of those present. "I will not allow this to happen.

"As far as the coronation goes, I propose the date planned

for Berayma's crowning. I have already made arrangements with Chancellor Orkid for this to occur.

"As to the second issue, I confirm Orkid as my chancellor and Harnan as my secretary. The rest of you are confirmed in your positions as well. The one change will be a replacement for the traitor Kumul, late Constable of the Royal Guard. His position will be filled by my mother's Life Guard, Dejanus."

Orkid threw a surprised glance at Areava, but she did not notice it, even if Dejanus did. The new constable allowed himself the faintest of smiles. No one present disagreed with his appointment, but not everyone looked pleased.

"Constable, you may take your place with the admiral and marshal."

Dejanus left his position behind the queen and walked with military precision to the vacant seat at the end of the table.

"Regarding the third issue, I expect all of you here to communicate to your colleagues and the members of your associations what you have witnessed here today: a ruler committed to their well-being and that of the kingdom. I expect to continue in my mother's footsteps. While I do not claim yet to possess her wisdom and experience, I do possess the same love for my people and the same desire to see them follow their own lives within a just and peaceful society. Furthermore, I will have the able support and advice of the same ministers and officers who assisted my mother in the last years of her reign."

Areava paused to take a deep breath. "Concerning Prince Lynan. You have already heard that he escaped the city. The navy is in pursuit, and we are confident that his capture is imminent. However, should the outlaw escape a second time, it is no excuse to panic. I have already sent messages to our provinces to warn them of his outlawry, and instructing them to ignore his authority as owner of the Key of

Union. My mother explicitly stated that ownership of the
Key meant swearing fealty to the crown. Lynan has betrayed
that pledge and so forfeits his Key to the crown. Many of the
provincial rulers will be coming here for the coronation. I
will talk with each of them before they return to their own
lands. Nowhere in Grenda Lear will be safe for Lynan and
his followers."

"Your Majesty, do we know where Lynan is heading?"
asked Elenta Satrur, the head of the Guild of Dyers, a small
man with a voice as wooden as an empty wine cask.

Areava nodded to Orkid, who cleared his throat and
adopted his most patriarchal expression. "The ship he is on,
called the *Seaspray* and owned by one Grapnel Moorice,
was carrying a consignment of goods bound for Chandra."

"Grapnel!" declared someone else at the table, obviously
shocked. "He is part of Lynan's party?"

Areava looked at the speaker, hiding her dismay when
she recognized Xella Povis. "Goodwoman Povis?"

Povis nodded. "Your Majesty, forgive my interruption.
But I have known Grapnel for many years. I would never
have imagined—"

"And did you think I could imagine my own brother capable of regicide?" Areava asked.

Povis lowered her gaze. "Of course not, your Majesty."

Areava indicated for Orkid to continue.

"The *Seaspray* was last seen sailing northeast. The navy
is already in pursuit."

"Why Chandra?" Shant Tenor, the city's mayor, demanded.

Orkid shrugged. "*Seaspray* was the only vessel belonging to Grapnel in the harbor at the time of the prince's escape, and the harbor master lists her consignment as going
there. But Chandra might not be his destination. We don't
know."

"Could King Tomar be involved in the plot against the throne?" Tenor persisted, his expression afraid.

"Enough!" cried Areava. "This is precisely the kind of talk I want to avoid. If we in the council will see conspirators in every shadow, every new turn, what can we expect to happen among the people? We must stay calm in this crisis. There is no evidence of any kind implicating King Tomar. Remember, he is my family's friend, not just Lynan's. He knew and loved Berayma."

"Your Majesty, there is one possibility we must consider this morning," Marshal Lief said quietly.

Areava frowned. "If this is more about Chandra, Marshal . . ."

"It is about the kingdom of Haxus, your Majesty. It will already have learned of Queen Usharna's death. Its ruler, King Salokan, has long hated and envied Grenda Lear, and he may be assessing his options to take advantage of the succession. When he hears of Berayma's death, it may embolden him further."

"I agree with the marshal, your Majesty," said Fleet Admiral Setchmar. "Salokan remembers with bitterness the defeat handed to his father by our forces during the Slaver War. He will harm or hinder the kingdom any way he can."

"You don't think he will invade, surely?" Areava asked. "Our armies would overwhelm him."

"Invade, no. But I believe he will test your resolve. Acts of piracy against our shipping, for example. Raids against farms and small settlements along our common border. He will test your reaction to such provocation."

"We will respond immediately to any incursion," Areava said firmly. "I have a realm to run, and no petty northern king will interfere with that."

Orkid cleared his throat. "Your Majesty, why not send a firm warning before there is any provocation? We already have a fleet and two brigades stationed in Hume to supplement Queen Charion's own forces. Send more cavalry; they will best respond to and repel enemy raids."

Areava looked at Lief and Setchmar. The admiral nodded. "Good advice," he said. "I can provide transport for a couple of regiments within two weeks."

"Our army is too dispersed, Your Majesty," the marshal said. "We can hire mercenaries for the duration of the emergency. It would be considerably cheaper in the long term than raising new troops for a short campaign."

"Very well," Areava conceded. "But arrange for the mercenaries to be embarked away from Kendra. I don't want rumors of a war to spread. That's all we need right now."

Lief and Setchmar seemed happy with her decision.

"We have dealt with the main matters," Areava told the assembly. "It is enough for the council's first meeting. My officials and I have had to work swiftly to contain the crisis, but in future I will rely heavily upon you all for advice and support."

Before any questions could be asked, Areava stood, forcing everyone else to follow.

"We will meet again very soon. Harnan will inform you of the day and time. Until then, remember that the people will look to you for example. I expect each of you to behave accordingly."

14

WHEN Lynan woke, the sun was almost down and there was a chill in the air. His whole body ached and he had difficulty moving at first, but eventually he was able to stand and inspect his new surroundings. Not far from him was Ager, still asleep, his breathing deep and even. There was no sign of Jenrosa or Kumul.

The cliff edge was ten paces away, and Lynan could hear the distant thunder of the waves crashing below. He dimly remembered making it to the top of the cliff and then collapsing. Someone must have dragged him the extra distance in case he rolled over while he was asleep and fell to his death.

He turned around. To the north and east the land gently climbed to the top of the Ebrius Ridge, falling away more sharply southeast toward Kendra and north where the province of Chandra lay. In the far distance he could just discern the outline of Kendra, and behind it the far end of Kestrel Bay, a smiling blue curve that emptied into the Sea Between. Looking southwest he could see the beginnings of Lurisia, and the edge of the rain forest that covered most of the province. A thin gray line cutting through the forest was the Gelt River, where Lynan and his companions had been heading before their encounter with the warship. Between the cliff and the sea he saw the wavering silhouettes of kestrels soaring with the day's last thermals.

The ground was covered in long grass which gradually surrendered to low shrubs as the land sloped up and away. On either side of the ridge denser vegetation took over: tall, broad fern trees and wideoaks, with a scattering of sharrok pines and sturdy golden fans among them. From among a clump of wideoaks on the ridge's southeast side appeared Jenrosa and Kumul, looking tired and bedraggled, but nonetheless smiling as they waved at Lynan. He waved back and went to meet them.

"How are you feeling?" Kumul asked.

"As though someone has pulled me apart and then clumsily put me back together again. What do we do now?"

"It's too late to descend Ebrius Ridge. We should move to the trees where there is some cover and we can use the leaves to keep us warm tonight. I don't think it would be a good idea to start a fire. From this height they will see the smoke as far away as the city."

Kumul walked over to where Ager was sleeping and roused him. The crookback got to his feet and stretched his arms. "I needed that nap," he said congenially to no one in particular.

The four of them made their way to the ridge line and moved down the northwest slope for a league or so until they came to a small dell that offered some protection from a freshening evening breeze whistling in from the bay. They gathered together four large mounds of leaves and settled down to sleep, hungry and still exhausted from the day's efforts.

It seemed to Lynan that no sooner had he closed his eyes than he was being shaken violently out of his slumber. It was Jenrosa. The sun had gone down, and the land was cloaked in the soft darkness of night. He opened his mouth to say something rude, but she clamped a hand over it and indicated for him to keep quiet. He nodded and she removed her hand, then motioned for him to follow her. She led the way to the lip of the dell, where Ager and Kumul were lying, staring out into the dark.

Lynan looked inquiringly at Ager, but the man shook his head and cupped a hand behind one ear. Lynan tried to listen for whatever it was that had disturbed the others. After a few seconds he heard a distant scrabbling sound, as if someone was pulling a rake across the forest floor. When he heard the sound again a moment later, it was definitely closer. He felt a tingle pass down his spine when he realized he was hearing a great bear snuffling among the autumn leaves, probably following their scent.

Lynan had only seen one once before, when Usharna had consented to his coming on a royal hunting party on Ebrius Ridge. He had vague memories of how big great bears were, twice as tall and twice as wide as a large man, with muscles like steel coils covered by bristly, brown fur. Their muzzles were filled with large pointed teeth; their claws longer and sharper than butchers' knives. He had been told that given enough warning a man could outpace one, but that the creature's turn of speed was remarkable for its size and over a short distances a great bear could easily catch the fastest human.

Again that shuffling sound, closer yet. Lynan could smell something heavy and musty in the air, something that caught at the back of this throat.

"It's definitely headed this way," Kumul whispered. "It has our scent, and is moving back and forth to pin it down."

"Nothing for it, then," Ager said. "Our only chance is to set an ambush. But to do that we have to get out of the dell."

As best they could in the dark, the two men scanned the immediate area for a likely site. Kumul pointed to a broad golden fan with low branches about forty paces away on the

other side of the dell. Ager nodded, and the four of them ran
to it. The branches were numerous and sturdy enough to
hold them all, and within a few seconds the entire party was
perched in the tree like a family of giant birds, armed only
with their knives. Lynan tried desperately to slow his yam-
mering heart, convinced it was loud enough for the bear to
hear whether or not it had their scent.

A short while later it came into view. It broached the lip
of the dell and jumped forward, landing on all fours. Its
snout weaved from side to side. It started keening, obviously
disappointed no prey was yet in sight. It reared up onto its
hind legs, made a sound that rose to a curiously high-pitched
scream, and sniffed the air around it. Curved, yellow teeth
glinted in the moonlight. The bear fell to all fours again, and
shambled forward, crisscrossing the dell until it regained the
scent. With a satisfied snort it headed for the golden fan.

Lynan's stomach knotted itself into a painful mass and
his mouth went dry. He tightened his grip on the knife and
found himself wishing fervently to be somewhere else—
back on the cliff face for example. The bear was soon directly under the tree, obviously confused that the scent was
once again lost. Before it could look up, Ager, screaming the
ear-piercing battle cry of the Kendra Spears, leaped from his
perch onto the beast's back and drove his dagger straight between its shoulder blades. At the same time Kumul dropped
in front of the creature and slashed at its head, cutting it
across the snout.

The bear reacted immediately and with astonishing
agility for something its size. It roared and swung round in
a wide arc. Kumul caught the full force of the bear's weight
and was flung away like a rag doll, his weapon spinning out
of his hand. Ager slid down the spine of the bear and landed
on his rump, his dagger still stuck between the creature's
shoulder blades. It turned again, looking for Ager, its jaws
opening in a wide gape, blood streaming from its wounds. In

doing so, it came directly under Lynan's branch and he dropped onto its back, using all his strength to drive his knife into the tough hide where neck met shoulders. The blade hit bone, skidded off. The bear shook its head, throwing off Lynan as easily as it had dislodged Ager.

Jenrosa had also left the tree by now and hurried to Kumul's side. The bear saw the movement and charged toward her. Seeing her danger, she swung up her weapon, catching the beast another blow across its snout. The bear screeched, lashed out with one foreleg, and connected with Jenrosa's skull, sweeping her aside.

Lynan shouted in rage when he saw the magicker struck down, and he lunged forward, thrusting his knife into the thigh of one of the bear's massive rear legs. This time the point found muscle rather than bone and it sank deep. Dark, warm blood spurted over his arms and face. The bear lifted its wounded leg and kicked. Lynan dodged the blow, darted in again to retrieve his weapon and struck again. By now Ager had caught his wind and he leaped again onto the bear's back, pulling out his blade and plunging it a second time between the shoulder blades. This time he found an artery. The bear reared up on its legs, tottered for a second, blood pouring from its mouth, then fell forward and was still.

For a moment there was silence. Lynan dared not move in case the bear suddenly came to life again. The aftershock came soon after; his hands and thighs began to shake uncontrollably. Ager came to his side and put a hand on his shoulder.

"Well done, Prince Lynan. Are you hurt?" Lynan shook his head. "Then see to Jenrosa, and I'll check Kumul."

Lynan went to Jenrosa and knelt down beside her. A wide, vicious-looking cut ran raggedly across her forehead. Blood streamed down her pale face and into her sandy hair, turning it dark. He tore off a piece of cloth from his own shirt and pressed it against the wound. After a while the flow of blood was staunched. He lifted the cloth carefully and inspected the wound. A large purple welt surrounded the cut. He put an ear to her mouth and listened to her breathing. It was slow but steady.

He was joined by Ager and a battered Kumul, carefully rubbing his left arm.

"How is she?" Kumul asked.

"Unconscious," Lynan answered. "The blow was a heavy one. At least the bleeding has stopped. I think she needs a surgeon. How are you?"

Kumul shrugged, winced in pain with the motion. "At worst a cracked rib or two, at best I'm badly bruised."

"I can make a sling for you," Ager told his friend. "As long as you don't use your left arm, you should heal quickly enough."

Kumul nodded at Jenrosa. "And her?"

"She needs a surgeon," Lynan repeated. "There are towns in Chandra not far from this ridge. We'll have to take her to one of them."

Kumul and Ager said nothing, but the expression on their faces said enough.

"She needs help!" Lynan argued. "You can see that for yourselves!"

"We can't risk it," Ager said grimly. "If we go into a town, someone is bound to report seeing us, and then we'll have a company of Royal Guards in pursuit, probably led by someone in Dejanus' pay, if not Dejanus himself. What do you think will happen to Jenrosa if we are apprehended?"

Lynan looked down, knowing the man was right, and hating himself for knowing it.

"Look, lad, we don't know the injury is that serious," Kumul said gently. "Jenrosa could be up and about in an hour. Her only chance—our only chance now that we're back on land and so close to Kendra—is to keep moving and to stay away from places where we're likely to be recognized. If her injury's serious, I think Jenrosa would rather be in our hands than the enemy's."

"We'll have to carry her," Ager said matter-of-factly. "She may not come around for a while." He used his knife to hack two long branches from the golden fan and tied his and Kumul's cloaks between them, then he and Lynan carefully lifted the magicker onto the crude stretcher and placed her own coat over her to keep her warm.

"Kumul can't help in his condition, and we'll soon tire out moving her by ourselves," Ager told Lynan. "So one of us will drag her along. We'll have to move slowly, though, especially going down the ridge."

"There are many streams at the bottom," Kumul said. "We can stop at one of them. We will need water and rest and should hide during the day."

"I'll go first," Lynan said, lifting up one end of the stretcher. Jenrosa's weight sank in the middle, keeping her in place. Her face was white and pinched, but the cut on her head was dry now and her breathing was still regular.

They started off slowly, Ager leading the way, Lynan in the middle pulling along the stretcher, and Kumul last. The dark made it impossible to always to pick the best course, and they frequently had to backtrack to find an easier route, especially for the first few hours when they were still climbing to the top of the ridge. Every hour Lynan and Ager took it in turns to pull the makeshift sled.

By dawn they had reached the northwest foot of Ebrius Ridge and saw spread out before them the farmlands of Chandra. Fields covered the land to the far horizon in a patchwork quilt of rich greens. Here and there, meandering streams, isolated woods, and small villages broke up the pattern, and over it all shone the light from a strong summer sun.

It was mid-morning before Jenrosa made any sound at

all, and then it was only a soft murmur. Her eyelids fluttered restlessly but remained closed.

"I think her color's returning," Lynan observed hopefully. "She's definitely looking better."

"I don't know how you can tell with all those freckles, but I'd look better, too, if someone had just carried me for ten leagues," Kumul said dryly.

They were following a narrow dirt track that led between fields of growing crops. Ager was scouting ahead, keeping his single eye out for any strangers or soldiers, as well as a safe site for their next break. Whoever had made the trail had thoughtfully planted tall wideoaks along it to provide shade, and the air was filled with the sound of singing birds and calling crickets.

"On a day like this, it's hard to believe that anyone would want to kill us," Lynan said sadly. "In fact, it's hard to believe that anyone in the world is in trouble."

"Don't let your imagination get carried away, your Highness. You'd bleed just as red and die just as easily on a day like this as you would on any other. If you need reminding, look behind you and think how Jenrosa's probably feeling."

"Do you think she can hear us?"

"I've no idea."

"She *is* looking better, you know."

Kumul only grunted. Ager appeared up ahead at the top of a small rise. He was running toward them in his rolling crookback stoop. When he reached them, he was out of breath and red from exertion. "There's a troop of mercenaries up ahead. They're still a league from here, but we haven't much time. There's a stream over this rise. We can hide among the vegetation along its banks."

Ager grabbed the other end of the stretcher and they moved as quickly as possible, Lynan telling his weary muscles to hold out for a while longer. By the time they reached the stream, a narrow ribbon of cool clear water, they were panting heavily and their hearts were beating like drums on a racing galley.

The trail crossed the stream at a narrow ford and continued on the other side of the bank, ascending gently to another rise. On either side of the stream there grew drooping spear trees and busy wideoaks. The companions made their way downstream into the thickest part of the gallery, carefully maneuvering their burden. They had barely enough time to hide themselves behind branches and two fallen rotting trunks before the troop arrived, ten riders, their fine gear jingling as the horses trotted down to the ford. Lynan cursed silently when they stopped at the stream to let their horses drink. The two nearest them were complaining about being taken from their billets at a local village.

"I was getting on fine with that widow who owns the farm by the dairy," one said. "She needs a good man to help her run the place. Another few weeks and I'd have been cashing in to take up life on the land."

"I didn't know you were so keen on dirt and weeds," said the other.

"Better than war and death."

"What war? Grenda Lear ain't been at war for fifteen years or more."

"I got ears. I heard the sergeant talking to the messenger who came yesterday and Haxus was mentioned often enough. Besides, we've got a new king, remember? There's bound to be trouble now that Usharna's dead. All the kingdom's enemies were terrified of her."

"Berayma will teach them to be terrified all over again, mark me."

"Aye, and that's my point—"

"All right, keep the chatter down," said an authoritative voice from the other side of the ford.

So rapt had he been in the troopers' conversation that Lynan had completely forgotten about his charge, and he started when Jenrosa let out a low moan of pain. He quickly clamped a hand over her mouth, making sure he left her nose free to breathe, but it was too late. The nearest trooper looked alertly in their direction, then turned to his friend.

"Did you hear something?" he asked.

"No," the other said, not really interested. He had pulled down his breeches to piss on the bank.

"I said to keep the chatter down!" complained their leader.

"But I heard something, Sergeant!"

"Probably a vixen with cubs," the sergeant replied gruffly. "And we haven't time to dawdle. We're expected in Kendra by nightfall."

The trooper's face drooped sourly, and he mounted his horse. "I'm sure it wasn't a fox."

His friend pulled up his breeches, mounted and drew along side him. "Perhaps two young lovers, eh? Not everyone's in a hurry. Just think about your widow and the trail ahead. No point in pissing off the sergeant."

By now their fellows had already left the stream and the two friends had to spur their horses to catch up.

Lynan was about to move when Ager grabbed him by the arm. "Wait," he whispered. "The talkative one may double back for another look-see." A few minutes later, when no one had reappeared, Ager released his grip and nodded. "All right, it looks like we're safe."

Lynan took his hand from Jenrosa's mouth; she mumbled some words, but he could not make them out.

"She's talking," he said excitedly.

"She nearly talked us into a grave," Kumul said tartly.

"If what those troopers was talking about is true and not rumor," Ager said, "we won't be able to take the most direct route to the Oceans of Grass. The highways and rivers will be busy with soldiers and supplies pouring into major cities."

"But there was no talk of war after my mother's death," Lynan said, puzzled.

"More likely Areava's just being cautious," Kumul said. "She should expect some trouble on her borders, especially with Haxus to the north. So she would call in the nearest soldiers and send them out by sea."

"Or, just as likely," Ager added, "start a war to divert attention from the goings-on in Kendra. Three rulers in as many weeks is bound to cause a stir with more than the kingdom's enemies."

"Then what route do we take?" Lynan asked.

"That's going to take some thought," Ager admitted. "For the moment, I suggest we find a place where Jenrosa and Kumul can recover. We can't keep on like this, two of us struggling with a stretcher. We'll finally get caught out in the open. We need a new plan and time to think it through."

"But where?"

Ager looked around him. "This is as good a place as any. We have fresh water and there's fish in the stream. The trees will provide cover and shade, and we can keep an eye on troop movements from here."

Lynan nodded. "All right. I can't think of anything better."

Kumul pointed upstream. "We'd better move first. We're too close to the ford, and we can keep an eye on it just as easily from another hundred paces farther upstream and be in less danger of discovery ourselves."

They fashioned rough tethers out of green twigs from a spear tree, and even rougher pegs out of wideoak, using them to construct a reasonably waterproof shelter by gathering together branches and pinning their ends to the ground. By using twine unthreaded from his cloak and a thorn from a nearby whip tree, Ager made a clumsy but nonetheless usable fishing line. They risked a fire that afternoon, cooking Ager's whole catch of small fish in one go. The next day,

Lynan and Ager took turns to reconnoiter the area while the other attended Jenrosa. Lynan had dressed the wound on her scalp as best he could and kept it clean, and was relieved when no infection set in. At first, she would eat nothing, drink only what was dribbled between her lips, and made hardly a sound. On three occasions she mumbled more words, but still they made no sense. Around noon, she regained consciousness, to everyone else's great relief. They made a fuss over her, offering her water and a little fish and some berries Ager had found on one of his explorations; she gratefully ate what she could but fell asleep soon after. Her color was almost normal, however, and Lynan was sure she would be up and ready to move within a few days.

By now Kumul felt well enough to take his turn to look around the local area. His ribs were obviously not cracked after all. His side was still bruised, but he could move his arm freely, though with some pain. On the second night of their stay, the three men gathered to discuss their next move.

"Between us, Kumul and I think we have devised the best way to get you to the Oceans of Grass and the Northern Chetts," Ager told the prince. Lynan nodded for him to continue. "Twenty leagues to the north lies the Forest of Silona, a thinly populated and well covered area that will protect us from prying eyes for the next stage of our journey. The forest is nearly sixty leagues long, south to north, and will take us several days to get through."

Lynan could not help notice Kumul's grim expression. "Is there something you're not telling me?"

Kumul sighed. "I have heard stories about this place."

"A soldier's tale," Ager said dismissively.

"Maybe, but most soldiers' tales have a kernel of truth."

"What stories?" Lynan asked.

"The forest is left alone by people who live nearby," Kumul said. "It is a dark place, an old place, inhabited by foresters who have little liking for company. I have only seen it myself from a distance, and it still made my blood run cold."

"We've discussed this," Ager said angrily. "We both know the *real* risks. The forest is our best chance to make up distance and time and still go undetected."

Kumul nodded resignedly. "I know. I have no other plan."

Lynan was distinctly unsettled by the conversation, but he told Ager to continue.

"Once on the other side of the forest, we are fifty leagues from Sparro, Chandra's capital. From there we can find passage on a boat going up the Barda River to the Ufero Mountains. After crossing the mountains we can reach the Strangers' Sooq—the main trading town between the Chetts and merchants from the east."

"How many days will it take us to get to the Oceans of Grass if we go this way?" Lynan asked.

Ager glanced at Kumul, the scars on the skin over his dead eye looking like crevasses in the wan moonlight. "We think it will take as long as four weeks. If everything goes well, we may cut that down to three. If things go badly, it could take as long as five or six weeks."

"Is time no longer of the essence, then?" Lynan asked, raising an eyebrow.

"Of course it is," Kumul answered shortly. "But Ager and I agree it is the quickest way for us to get to the Oceans of Grass without being captured. There are safer routes, perhaps, but they would take several months."

"And, again, it is to be my decision?"

"Yes."

"So if I insist we continue with the original plan, you will not argue with me?"

"No, but we may not follow you. We can't speak for Jenrosa, but at the moment neither can she."

"This leadership is a hollow thing, I think," Lynan murmured bitterly.

Ager pulled gently on one ear lobe. "Your Highness, leadership is not hollow, it is two-edged; too many regard it as a privilege and not a responsibility. I've suffered too much at the hands of those who misuse it." He looked up and saw Lynan's expression. "No, lad, not your father, but I've served under other generals, not to mention a bounty of ship's captains."

"I will follow your advice."

The two older men nodded solemnly.

Jenrosa woke again that night. She was confused and did not have the strength to sit up without assistance. She ate willingly, listened patiently to Lynan as he described what had happened since the bear had struck her down, but fell asleep again before he could tell her about the change in their plans.

"It's all right," Ager assured him. "There'll be time to tell her everything when she's fully recovered. When she wakes tomorrow, she'll probably remember nothing of what you've told her tonight."

"But she'll be all right, now, won't she?"

"Now that she's climbed out of her deep sleep, I think so. I admit, I was afraid she would die on us without ever coming to. I've seen it happen before."

Ager lay back and closed his eyes. Lynan sat in the darkness of their makeshift shelter, Jenrosa's head in his lap, listening to a chorus of frogs from the stream's banks. He could also hear the soft footsteps of Kumul outside, restless as a tiger. Absently, he stroked Jenrosa's hair and wondered what her life had been like before he and his problems had set it astray. Were her parents still alive? Did she have any brothers or sisters? Suddenly it was important for him to know.

He was aware his feelings for Jenrosa had become stronger since their escape from the palace, but what those feeling were, exactly, left him confused. He had never before felt so protective about someone. He was attracted to her, but the emotion churning inside of him involved more than his desire to bed her.

And what of her feelings for him? Her attitude had been standoffish, even resentful, and this hurt him. She said she did not blame him for her predicament, but there was no doubt it was his fault she was now on the run, her life in constant danger. However, he could not help being glad she was in exile with him, nor help feeling guilty that he should be the cause of her unhappiness.

And her injury, he reminded himself. What if she dies? It would be his fault.

He had no answers to his questions, and they filled his heart like a great leaden weight.

The next day Jenrosa tried standing. She managed to walk a few paces before falling back into Lynan's arms. Ager had been right about her memory, but Lynan patiently recounted everything a second time, adding the change in plan.

"I wonder if I'll ever get back to Kendra," she mused aloud, and Lynan felt a pang of homesickness also. "I don't have any choice but to go along, do I?"

"The kingdom's soldiers can't look for us forever. When things quiet down, perhaps you can go back to a life in one of the cities or towns."

"But not Kendra."

Lynan shrugged. He did not know what to say.

"I don't know how fit I am to travel," Jenrosa said, "but I'll try not to slow you down too much."

"We can wait here for a day or two more," Ager said, "but not much longer. We're pushing our luck by staying in one place for so long. Eventually, some local will notice our smoke or stumble across our shelter."

"The most dangerous part of the journey will be from here to the Forest of Silona," Kumul said. "It's all open farming country, and we'll stick out like trees in a desert. So rest well now, for when we start, we must move quickly."

They never got their extra day. The next morning, soon after the four had eaten a light breakfast, Lynan accompanied Jenrosa as she tried to exercise, intending to walk her to the ford and back. At first her feet were unsteady, but by the time they had reached the ford she was walking normally if more slowly than usual.

"How do you feel?" Lynan asked her.

"Like someone's inside my skull trying to break out with a hammer. If I move too quickly, I think my head will explode, and all my joints turn to jelly. But I'll survive." She turned and smiled at him, touched by the look of concern on his face. "I hear you saved my life."

Lynan blushed. "It's my fault you're involved in any of this at all. The least I could do was stop you from being killed."

Jenrosa laughed at his words, then groaned and held her head between her hands. "Laughing hurts, too. It's ridiculous, isn't it . . ."

There was a sound of approaching feet from the other side of the stream. Lynan glanced up, expecting to see Ager or Kumul. Instead, he saw an armed man dressed in stained brown leather and carrying a long sword. Lank, shiny black hair fell down to his shoulders, and wide brown eyes stared at them eagerly from out of a round, pockmarked face. The warrior gave a triumphant yell and charged the two friends, swinging his sword over his head.

Both Jenrosa and Lynan reached for their daggers, but it was too late to do anything effective against their attacker.

The warrior was only two paces from them when Kumul charged into him, hurling him violently into the stream. Kumul's momentum carried him forward and he tripped over the stranger, but he quickly scrabbled to his feet. He turned to face the warrior, but he was lying down in the water, unconscious.

"Get back to the shelter!" Kumul roared at his two friends. "Tell Ager to hurry!" He bent down and retrieved the stranger's sword.

"Kumul—" Lynan began, but Jenrosa yanked hard on his arm.

"For God's sake, do as he says! Come on!"

Even as Jenrosa spoke, four other men, dressed and armed similarly to the first, came running over the rise. They skidded to a halt when they saw Kumul standing astride the ford, their fallen companion at his feet.

Lynan pushed Jenrosa away from him. "Go on!" he shouted. "Get Ager!" Without waiting to see if she left or not, he ran back to Kumul, stopping behind him because the ford was not wide enough for them to stand side by side.

"What the hell are you doing here?" Kumul hissed at him.

"I'm not running away," Lynan replied, sounding more determined than he felt.

"And what do you think you'll do with me between you and the enemy? Stab at them with your knife between my legs?"

"If I have to."

"You'd better be bloody sure of your aim, lad," Kumul said grimly.

Having decided that four against two was reasonable odds, even if one of them was halfway to being a giant, the soldiers on the rise started moving forward.

"Don't be fools," Kumul warned them, his voice almost paternal. "Do you really think any of you can take me on?"

The four hesitated, glancing uncertainly at each other, but then continued their advance.

"I wish I could brag with Ager's conviction," Kumul whispered out of the side of his mouth.

"*I* was convinced," Lynan confided.

Kumul laughed, and this made their opponents even more uncertain.

"Hang this. We can't afford to let any of them get away. Do you think you can take out one of them if I provide you with a sword?"

"Sure." Lynan's voice sounded a little too high for his liking. "Maybe two."

"Just worry about one to start with."

The strangers arranged themselves into a line and were about to start across the ford when Kumul sounded his battle cry and charged forward, scattering them back, two of them tripping over. Kumul jumped over them to reach the bank, sidestepped to the right and swung his sword at the startled soldier in front of him, the blade cutting into the man's head just above his left ear. There was a sickening crunch, a fountain of blood, and the man collapsed. Kumul picked up the man's sword and threw it grip-first to Lynan.

Lynan caught the gift and enthusiastically engaged the other soldier left standing, only to find his task harder than Kumul's. His opponent was a better than average swordsman, and although Lynan's training gave him the edge, he was used to the weight and feel of his father's sword. His blade flickered and slid against his enemy's in a search for an opening. He heard combat resume behind him as Kumul defended himself against the two remaining soldiers who had now regained their feet.

Desperation fueled Lynan's attack, and he found the extra speed he needed to parry a thrust from his opponent and send the point of his own sword into the soldier's throat. The man gurgled and fell backward, his hands clasping hopelessly over his fatal wound.

Lynan spun on his feet and charged into the melee around Kumul, screaming something he hoped sounded bloodcurdling.

One of the enemy turned to face him but had to retreat under the barrage of blows Lynan directed against him. The soldier lost his balance and slipped forward, straight onto Lynan's sword. Lynan twisted his weapon out from between the man's ribs. By then Kumul had dispatched the last of the enemy, and stood panting over him, his arm covered in blood.

"That was a good fight," he said admiringly. "They were better than I thought they would be."

"Who were they?" Lynan asked.

"More mercenaries. When they saw you and Jenrosa alone out here, they probably thought they'd have themselves a little easy money, and perhaps some fun with the woman."

"Will there be more?"

"Almost certainly. They were probably a scouting party out to find a place to camp for their company, probably half a day behind. We'll have to hide these corpses and get moving."

There was a sound behind them and both men turned quickly, swords raised.

"You could have kept one for me," Ager said. He was accompanied by an exhausted looking Jenrosa.

"They were too eager," Kumul said matter-of-factly.

"You're wounded," Ager observed, pointing to the big man's bloody arm.

"Kumul!" Lynan exclaimed in concern. He assumed the blood had belonged to one of the dead mercenaries. "Why didn't you say something?"

"I did," Kumul replied. "I said 'That was a good fight,' and then I said . . ."

"That isn't what I meant." Lynan could not hide the exasperation in his voice.

"It isn't serious, your Highness, or I would have mentioned it." He looked up at Ager. "I was a mite slow. My side's still a little stiff."

"You may not think it's serious, but you won't be lifting a sword for a few days," Ager said, carefully examining Kumul's wounded arm. "Lynan, go to a sword bush by our camp and take Kumul with you. Pick some of the leaves and bruise them between your hands, then rub them vigorously into Kumul's wound."

Kumul turned white. "Oh, no. I've had that done this to me before, when I received a cut to my left leg, and I still remember the pain!"

"And you still have your left leg. Now go with Lynan." Ager turned to Jenrosa. "And you need to rest. We'll have to move on as soon as it's dark, and you'll need all your strength." He surveyed the four corpses. "At least now we'll all have swords."

"They'll have had horses," Kumul said. "We can't use them ourselves if we want to remain unnoticed, but we can't leave them wandering around here."

"I'll lead them a couple of leagues farther up the trail," Ager said. "Now go."

The three moved off as ordered. Lynan remembered the first mercenary, still alive but unconscious. He turned to warn Ager, in time to see him lift the head of the mercenary in question, stick the point of his dagger in the man's throat and pull it with a savage stroke. There was a tearing sound, a great gush of blood, and that was it. Ager looked up and for a moment locked eyes with Lynan, and for the first time the prince saw loathing and pain in them.

Shivering, Lynan turned around again.

15

AREAVA was woken early by a messenger from Dejanus. He had someone in the Royal Guard's office
with information concerning Prince Lynan. In no mood to
suffer the new constable alone, she had Olio roused as well.
Dejanus' guest, sitting on a stool and looking exhausted and
sorry for himself, was a man dressed in the livery of a naval
officer; the long red stripe on his jerkin's sleeves indicated
the rank of captain.

When the queen and her brother arrived, the captain
stood up so quickly the stool toppled over. He managed a
salute. Areava could see that he was terrified. What had Dejanus been saying to him?

"Your Majesty, this is Captain Rykor of the *Revenant*,
one of the ships sent after Grapnel Moorice's *Seaspray*,"
Dejanus told her. He looked at the captain with barely dis-
guised contempt. "He has a tale for you."

Areava nodded for Rykor to tell his story. In a nervous
voice he told Areava and Olio about a small boat that had
fled from his ship the previous day, and which had been
wrecked against the rocky cliffs north of Kendra. His description of the events was sparse but left out nothing.

"How many did you say were in the boat?" Areava asked

the captain when he was finished. She glanced at Dejanus standing behind the captain like a nemesis, brooding and threatening. For a moment Areava herself felt threatened by his presence, but then she heard Olio's steady breathing behind her and she felt safer.

Captain Rykor swallowed, cast his gaze down to his feet. "Four, Your Majesty. Three men and a woman."

"Did you recognize any of them?"

"Not as such, Your Majesty. But the largest one had the build and look of the const . . . I mean . . . of Kumul Alarn." He cast a frightened glance toward the new constable. "We were never close enough to see their faces."

"And there were no survivors," Dejanus said, a statement and not a question.

"No," Rykor confirmed. "We waited for several minutes. No one survived. There were no bodies. The undertow there is horrific. If they are not . . . well, eaten . . . one or two of the bodies might wash up on the shores of Aman or Lurisia in the next few days."

Areava sighed deeply.

"How did you find the b–b–boat?" Olio asked. "I thought you were sent after the *Seaspray?*"

"Three warships were sent out, Your Highness," Rykor answered. "Besides my own *Revenant*, there were *Moonlighter* and *Windsnapper*. My ship was out last, and my lookout saw kestrels above a boat northwest of our position, though he saw no actual boat at that time. I knew that both *Moonlighter* and *Windsnapper* each had the necessary speed to catch *Seaspray*, so I decided to follow the new sighting, just in case."

"As well you did," Olio said gently.

Areava nodded to Dejanus, who tapped Rykor on the shoulder. The captain saluted the queen and left.

"I want patrols increased along that coast, both by sea and by land. If any bodies resurface or are washed up on the shore, I want them returned immediately to Kendra for identification."

Dejanus nodded. "It may be hard to recognize any remains, Your Majesty. Thrown against those rocks, and what with the sharks and other creatures . . . well . . ."

"Nonetheless," Areava insisted, "I want it done. Is there any word from the captains of the other two ships?"

Dejanus looked dejected. "They lost the *Seaspray*, Your Majesty. She went too far out to sea. There was a fog, some shoals . . ." His voice trailed off.

Areava nodded stiffly, turned on her heel and left, not waiting to see Dejanus salute her. Olio followed her.

"I had hoped it would all be over by this morning," Areava said dully.

"It m–m–may b–b–be all over. I don't think anyone could survive b–b–being thrown into the sea so close to the rocks near those cliffs."

"And what of the conspiracy?" the queen wondered aloud. "Without Lynan or one of the others, we may never know who else was involved."

"And it may never m–m–matter. If Lynan and Kumul were both involved in B–B–Berayma's death, then they were almost certainly the ringleaders. Who else could have been? And without them, any other conspirators aren't likely to b–b–be a threat."

"*If* Lynan and Kumul were involved? You still doubt it?"

Olio shrugged. "The evidence against them is overwhelming, I admit, but it is entirely circumstantial. Think, sister: if the conspiracy was set against you or m–m–me as well as B–B–Berayma, do you think either of us would be here now to talk about it? Poor B–B–Berayma was the target, not the whole royal family. And if that is the case, what profit did Lynan gain from the king's m–m–murder?"

Areava nodded. "Perhaps he argued with Berayma on the night."

She stopped suddenly and looked up, wide-eyed.

"What's wrong?" Olio asked.

Areava had just remembered her conversation with Lynan on the south gallery only a few hours before Berayma's murder. She had consciously tried to suggest to Lynan that Berayma supported her approach. What if Lynan had confronted Berayma about it that night? What if in anger and frustration and confusion Lynan had lashed out, killing Berayma?

It was my fault, she told herself, then shook her head fiercely. *No. If Lynan went that far, it was his own base nature, not my words, that drove him.*

Olio looked on, bemused, wondering why her expression was so bleak one second and then so angry the next. "Sister?"

"Perhaps he argued with Berayma on the night," Areava repeated.

They resumed walking. After a moment Areava continued, "We may never know. Of most concern to me is the loss of the Key of Union." She looked down at the two keys that now hung around her own neck. "I do not know what power the Keys hold, but I fear that the loss of even one Key will weaken them."

There was the sound of footsteps running behind them. Areava looked over her shoulder to see Harman scurrying after them, his writing implements and pads tucked under one arm.

"So soon, old friend?" Areava called out to him.

"The business of the kingdom waits for no man or woman, your Majesty," Harman replied, catching up with them. "Not even the queen herself."

"Tell me, was it always like this for my mother?"

"Always, Your Majesty."

"How did she live so long?"

Harman smiled slightly. "I think she actually grew to enjoy it."

"That is something I will never do, I think," Areava said wistfully.

"Give it time," Olio said in her ear. "You are more like our m–m–mother than you think."

Dejanus left his office in high spirits. When he passed a patrol of the Royal Guards that forgot to salute him as constable, he merely reminded them of their duty. *They will learn,* he told himself.

Captain Rykor, whether he knew it or not, had lifted from Dejanus' mind his greatest fear: that Lynan would be captured alive. Exactly how much the young prince knew of Dejanus and Orkid's part in Berayma's murder he did not know, but his predecessor Kumul was certainly clever enough to have figured out most of it, and was sure to have told Lynan. Now that both Lynan and Kumul were dead, however, Dejanus was secure in his new position.

At last I am safe, he thought.

Ever since Orkid had discovered his betrayal of Grenda Lear during the Slaver War, Dejanus had lived in fear of being exposed to Usharna, but from the moment he had pierced Berayma's throat with Lynan's dagger he had as much against Orkid as the chancellor had against him.

He stopped for a moment, frowning. And what of the deal with Orkid? For helping with the assassination of Berayma, the chancellor had promised to ensure he was made constable . . . and yet . . . and yet Orkid's expression had seemed particularly displeased when Areava had announced Dejanus's elevation at the first meeting of the executive council.

The constable shook his head. There was nothing the chancellor could do. If Dejanus was brought down, then Orkid would come down with him. And now that Lynan and

Kumul were dead, no one except the pair of them knew the whole truth about Berayma's death.

He breathed a sigh of relief, and for the first time in his life knew he no longer had to look over his shoulder to the past. Only the future mattered now.

Amemun held up his glass to the light, admiring the color of the fine red Storian wine. He sipped it carefully, enjoying its full body and woody aroma.

"We have nothing like this back home," he said.

Orkid offered his friend a smile and drank from his own glass. "Trade is one of the things we will improve. Usharna was loath to surrender the crown's monopoly on luxury goods such as wine; it added so much to her revenue. I could never make her understand how reducing restrictions would increase the flow of commerce and so increase her revenue in the long term."

"She was shortsighted, then."

Orkid shook his head. "In some ways perhaps. She could be hidebound, with monopolies for example, but in other things she was remarkably progressive. After all, she made me chancellor, the first citizen of the kingdom not from Kendra itself to hold such high office."

"To our benefit," Amemun said without irony.

"To the benefit of Grenda Lear as a whole," Orkid pointed out without pride.

"As your brother, the noble Marin, foresaw all those decades ago when you were first sent to Usharna's court."

Orkid nodded. "Aye. Farseeing, indeed."

"What of our co-conspirator? Do you think he will cause you trouble?"

Orkid shrugged. "I had hoped to tie Dejanus to me even more closely, but Areava announced his promotion without consulting me. From her point of view it was the right thing to do, but regrettably it happened before I could suggest it to her myself. Dejanus is not the most brilliant man I've ever met, but he's not stupid. Knowing that I was working on his behalf would have confirmed our relationship."

"But you have a hold on him anyway. His secret past is enough to ensure his obedience, surely?"

"Perhaps. But don't forget Dejanus now has a hold on me as well. We are like two great bears with their mouths around each other's throat."

"So how do you intend to proceed to the second part of the plan?" Amemun asked.

"Sendarus has been doing most of the work unwittingly for us, but it may require a little prompting on our part. The people will soon be demanding Areava provide an heir, especially after the events of the last few days. And fortunately for Aman, King Marin's son is available."

"And if the queen marries him, a day will come when the kingdom will be ruled by someone with the blood of both Kendra and Aman." Amemun grinned into his glass. "A pity your brother had no daughter. Then Berayma could have lived."

Orkid shook his head. "No. His closeness to the Twenty Houses meant he would never have married outside of them. Areava was our only chance."

"And what of Olio, and that Harnan fellow?"

"I thought I knew Olio. He was always such an inoffensive boy, lurking timidly in the background, but I did not give enough credit to the relationship between him and his sister. She has needed his strength since Berayma's death, and he has provided it without hesitation. I must work on him, bring him around, make him trust me as much as his sister does.

"And Harnan is so devoted to his duties he does not always see what is going on around him. He and I have always worked well together. I see no reason for that to change."

Amemun pursed his lips. "There is one other matter

Marin has asked me to report on. The Keys of Power. I do not think he was aware they were to be divided between the heirs. You should have warned him."

Orkid grunted. "I had hoped to convince Usharna not to proceed with her plan, and for a long time thought I was succeeding. Given another day or two, I might have won her around, but . . ."

"But now they are apart. They have lost their power. If Areava and Sendarus have issue, we will want the Keys brought together again."

"You forget, Amemun, that Lynan was wearing one of the Keys. They can never be together again. Their power is broken."

Amemun's face clouded. "This is dark news."

"The individual Keys hold some energy, I'm sure. They may work still, though not as effectively as in the past. Other rulers have survived without such tokens. So will Areava's heirs."

"Other rulers haven't had such a large kingdom to administer," Amemun pointed out. "And power or no, they still have an influence over the people. We must work to unite the surviving Keys."

Orkid held up his hand. "Patience! There is more than enough for us to deal with at the moment. The Keys can wait."

Amemun nodded reluctantly. "I hope Marin sees it the same way."

"He will forget all about the Keys when Sendarus and Areava are engaged," Orkid said.

"Oh, aye, there's no doubt about that." Amemun raised his glass. "For Aman!"

"For Grenda Lear," Orkid replied.

Olio left the palace as surreptitiously as possible, not wishing to be seen by his sister or any member of the Royal

Guards. Under present circumstances they would have insisted on providing him with an escort, but Olio needed time alone, time to think, time away from the palace itself and everything it represented.

He wandered for a while along the wide avenues of the higher, richer districts, but gravity and inclination slowly drew him down into the old city, the heart of Kendra. He was dressed plainly, and the Key of Healing was hidden beneath his jerkin. In the crowded streets no one looked closely enough to identify him.

Olio reveled in the anonymity. No one fawned over him, no one expected him to respond to a salute or greeting. He was no more than a citizen of the city, and this meant more to him than his official rank. Like Areava, he believed heart and soul in the kingdom, in the good it had achieved, in its civilizing influence and the peace it had brought its many millions of inhabitants. But he was also aware of how much more it could achieve, given the will and determination. Around him were signs of poverty: people living in the streets, poor sanitation, children laboring away at a hundred different crafts from cobbling to sail making. He walked carefully along rises and curbs to avoid stepping in human and animal excrement.

In time, he found himself in a short alley darkened by the leaning roofs of the old timber houses that lined it. Garbage and filth clogged the worn, shallow drains on either side of the cobbled paving. Two children dressed in little more than rags ran past him, squealing with laughter as they went. An old man sat in a doorway, trying to mend a tattered shirt with a bone needle and coarse twine.

Olio paused. He looked up and around, counting the houses. Twelve along one side, eleven on the other. He wondered how many families lived in each. One or two, maybe more? Say three to six members for each family. In a space no longer than fifty paces or wider than thirty, there probably lived between a hundred and two hundred people, many of them children, and many of them would not live long enough to reach adulthood.

This is also Kendra, Olio thought. *This is also the kingdom.*

He started to walk on when he caught sight of a familiar cloak. Its round owner was just stepping out of one of the old houses the prince had been considering.

"Well, well," Olio said loudly, "M–M–Magicker P–P–Prelate Edaytor Fanhow."

The prelate turned, obviously not expecting to meet anyone who knew him. His expression showed twice as much surprise when he recognized the prince. He bowed uncertainly, still not quite believing his eyes.

"Your Highness! What are *you* doing down here?" He looked around curiously. "And where is your escort?"

"I am walking, sir, taking in the sights. And as for escort, why, I have n–n–none."

"No escort?" Edaytor scurried to the prince's side, and took his arm. "Then, your Highness, stay close by me. I will see that you come to no harm."

Olio laughed lightly. "Why should any harm come to m–m–me?" He looked up and down the alley. "I see no thieves or scoundrels. We are quite safe, I think. At any rate, you yourself have no escort."

"They know me around here, Prince. They know I carry nothing on my person worth stealing except my cloak, and no one would buy that from a thief, for it is generally believed to protected by magic."

"And how comes it that the m–m–magicker p–p–prelate is so well known in this desperate slum?"

Edaytor's expression became guarded. "My duties carry me to every part of the city, your Highness."

"There is no theurgia hall here."

Edaytor said nothing, but tried to guide Olio out of the

alley. The prince pretended to go along, but stopped suddenly when they came to the house Edaytor had appeared from.

"Definitely no theurgia hall."

Even as he spoke, the door to the house opened and an old woman came out carrying an empty basket. She saw the prelate, came over quickly and kissed his hand, then scurried off in the opposite direction.

"Who was that?" Olio asked mildly.

"I . . . I don't know her name," Edaytor admitted.

"She certainly seemed to know you."

"Only in the last hour. Her son was a student magicker in the Theurgia of Fire. He died last week in an accident at the armory foundry. She had no money coming in at all, so I gave her some coins."

Olio absorbed this information, but said nothing. Edaytor misinterpreted the silence, and blurted, "But I used my own money, your Highness, no theurgia funds."

"Oh, I wasn't thinking that." Olio patted Edaytor's hand still resting protectively on his arm. "One day, P–P–Prelate, I think you and I should sit down and have a long talk."

"About what?"

"Why, sir, about the kingdom."

Left alone in her bedroom, her ladies-in-waiting gone at last, Areava slumped in a chair. She was exhausted and wide awake all at the same time. The sheer emotional and physical load of the last few days pressed down on her like a heavy weight, but a thousand thoughts were racing through her brain, all competing for her attention. Details about the Twenty Houses and their allies, Orkid's list of possible traitors, the missing corpses of her youngest brother and his co-conspirators, the hiring and billeting of mercenaries, the impatient demands of the trade guilds for their protective tariffs to be kept in place, the impatient demands of merchants for the tariffs to be lifted, the invitation list for the coronation . . . The urgent, the sublime, the foolish, and the unnecessary all combined, and it was all new to her.

She had no way of knowing how to cope with the sudden flood of details and facts overwhelming her, and which was added to every morning by Orkid with his heavy solemnity and bearded, brooding face. Olio and Harnan helped where they could, but Olio was as new to administration as she was and Harnan had his duties as private secretary to keep him busy without having to answer all her foolish questions. She found herself constantly being given information she did not want to know about, applications she did not want to read, appeals she did not want to judge, and blandishments she did not want to hear.

She stood up angrily. The night was still warm—the last hurrah of summer before autumn's cold sou'westerlies began and brought with them the icy winds up from the lands of snow far south of Theare—but she still felt the need to stoke up the fire; anything to help fill up the vacant space in her room. And the vacant spaces in her life left by the deaths of her mother and brother.

She lay on her bed and closed her eyes in an attempt to find sleep, but it was futile. Restless, she left her room, startling the two guards on post at her door. Ignoring their concerned expressions as they trailed behind her, she soon reached the south gallery. She headed over to the balcony and stopped short. There was a figure on the balcony, looking out over the city and the waters beyond. For a terrible moment she thought it was the ghost of Lynan come back to haunt her at the very place they had last spoken. The figure turned, and Areava recognized the tall and slender profile of Prince Sendarus. Her breath gushed out in relief.

"Your Majesty!" Sendarus exclaimed, and bowed deeply. "I did not know you were there!"

"I have just arrived. I am sorry to have disturbed you. I came to get away from my rooms."

"I understand. You wish to be alone. I will leave now."

"What were you looking for?" she asked.

"Your Majesty?"

"Can you see Aman from there? Are you homesick?"

Sendarus laughed lightly. "No, it is too dark for that, and I am not homesick."

"I thought you might miss your father."

"I did at first. But I have found my attention quite diverted."

"The city has that effect on people seeing it for the first time."

"That is not what I meant," he said seriously.

Areava joined him at the balcony and felt a breeze on her face. She closed her eyes and pretended she was not queen and that her mother still reigned, and that all was right with the world.

Sendarus watched her carefully, watched her hair blown by the breeze, watched a small pulse in the curve of her throat, but said nothing.

16

IT took Lynan and his companions six days to reach the outskirts of the Forest of Silona. The encounter with the mercenaries had made them all jumpy, and they could ill afford further trouble now that Kumul was temporarily incapable of wielding a sword; though much better, Jenrosa still lacked stamina. Besides, the open farm land they were passing through encouraged caution.

They walked from dusk to dawn, keeping to side trails where possible, and rested during the day, taking turns to keep watch. They ate whatever food they could scrounge on their journey—berries, nuts, once a runaway chicken—and used ground leaves from whip trees and sword bushes to harden the skin on their heels and toes and reduce the risk of infection from the blisters that blossomed on their feet.

They had one more close encounter with mercenaries before reaching the forest, another troop of cavalry, but they had heard the horses from a distance and were able to hide in time.

The Forest of Silona was made up of towering wideoaks, summer trees, and headseeds, packed more closely together than any such trees had any right to be. Their branches blocked most of the sunlight from reaching the forest floor, and a sad wind passed between them, making a sound like wooden pipes playing a dirge. The air smelled rich and loamy and left a musty taste on the back of their tongues. There was something forbidding about the place, about the wood green darkness, which made all four travelers hesitate before entering its cover.

"It'll be safer for us in the forest than out here in the open," Ager said reassuringly, his voice hiding a quaver. He grunted, squared his shoulders as best he could, and strode, lopsided, in among the trees.

"There. It's done, and I haven't dropped dead. Come on, the sun's already up. The sooner we start, the sooner we'll be out the other side."

"Is nowhere safe anymore?" Lynan asked forlornly, of no one in particular. He followed Ager. Once under the heavy shade of the trees his feeling of dread eased somewhat. It was like jumping into a cold river—after a few seconds it did not seem nearly so cold.

"It's all right," he said encouragingly to Jenrosa and Kumul. "It's . . . safe."

Jenrosa stood with her fists on her hips for a moment as if she was about to dispute the fact with Lynan, then sighed and crossed the boundary into the forest.

Kumul still hesitated. "I cannot forget the stories I have heard about this place."

"We've all heard stories," Ager muttered. "Soldiers make them up about every forest or river or city. You haven't paid them any heed before."

"I haven't been *here* before," Kumul countered.

The muscles in Lynan's back started to tighten. Kumul's words were frightening him. Instinctively, he drew closer to the other two, fighting the urge to leave the forest and let pure sunlight bathe his skin again.

Kumul looked back the way they had come and watched as a breeze calmly ruffled the stalks of ripening wheat and barley which filled the fields stretching north to the horizon. Then he looked at the trees, scowled into his beard, and followed the others in. Immediately, some of the tension left his body, but his expression remained grim. "Let's get on with it, then," he grumbled, and led the way deeper into the gloom.

"That's curious," Lynan thought aloud.

"What's that?" Ager asked.

"I don't hear any birds."

It was true. There was not the slightest sound made by a bird, not even a raven's desolate cawing. Except for the companions, everything was still and silent. The trees closed about them like a silent escort, shepherding them north and into the forest's heart.

They used trails when they found them and stayed with them as long as they led north. Most of the tracks had not been in use for many years and were difficult to follow, but some had been abandoned only recently and undergrowth had not yet made the way difficult. Occasionally they come across small, abandoned huts, their open doorways and windows making them leer like skulls, their wooden floors covered in cobwebs and dust. At night the huts provided welcome refuge from the damp leafy ground outside and some protection from the creatures they assumed roamed the forest as soon as evening settled on the trees, although the only spore they saw belonged to rabbits or hares and the occasional badger. When forced to sleep outdoors, the companions would take turns on watch, guarding a tiny, precious fire and listening anxiously for any sound. Even the snuffling and pawing of a wandering bear in the blackness just beyond the circle of flickering light would have provided some measure of comfort and reassurance, for, in fact, there were few signs of any life apart from the creaking of timber, the sighing of the canopy far above, scattered spoor in the morning, and the half-ruins of deserted human habitation.

On their third night, however, when Lynan was taking his turn on watch, he did hear a sound from somewhere in the night. At first he thought it was nothing more than a settling branch, the sound of wood moving, but the second time he was sure it was closer, and its quality was different somehow from a tree's random swaying, as if caused by a definite movement.

He held his breath and peered out into the darkness, but could see nothing. He stood up and drew his sword silently from its sheath. He wondered if he should wake the others, but told himself it was his own fears and wild imaginings that were disturbing him.

And then the sound came again, from a different angle but closer still. He twisted around, staring into the dark forest, trying to make out some hint of movement, some sign of life. But, again, there was nothing to be seen.

He finally convinced himself he was overreacting, sheathed his sword, and was squatting to sit down by the fire when he saw two eyes—green slits that burned unnaturally—staring back into his own. He cried out involuntarily and leaped to his feet. The vision disappeared.

Kumul jumped up and grabbed his sword. He scanned the area slowly, then settled his gaze on the prince. "What the hell are you bellowing for?"

"I . . . I thought I saw something."

"What?"

"Eyes. A pair of eyes. Green eyes. Before that, I heard movement."

"Movement," Kumul said dully. Ager was now sitting up as well. Both men stared out around them. "I hear no movement and I see no eyes."

Lynan blushed. "Sorry to wake you," he said stiffly.

Kumul and Ager exchanged weary glances. "You're

doing fine, lad," Kumul muttered halfheartedly. "Such alertness commends you." The soldier dropped back to the ground, and both he and Ager returned to sleep almost immediately.

Lynan angrily poked the fire until the flames were much higher. He walked to the limits of the light it cast and studied the ground as best he could. There were no tracks, nothing unusual.

Oh, you are a mighty warrior, he told himself. *Shadows and creaks and fear make enemies for you, as if you didn't have enough real ones already.*

He sat down by the fire and tried to relax, but when he was relieved from the watch by Jenrosa not long afterward, he was still so tense it took him another hour to find sleep. When he woke the next morning, he was tired and irritable and could not shake from his mind the memory of those two green eyes.

The companions carefully rationed the dried fish and berries they had brought with them, but their food was gone entirely by the end of their fourth day in the forest. They managed to find a few handfuls of wild blackberries and nuts, but it wasn't enough to keep away the increasingly urgent hunger pangs that disturbed their sleep. At least, they came across enough streams to quench their thirst.

On the morning of the fifth day they discovered a wide and apparently recently used trail. Fresh human footprints patterned the dirt, and they found a dropped nail and close to it a brooch, still shiny with recent use. After a few hours they heard sounds up ahead: human voices and the grunting of a pig or two. The travelers' spirits lightened, but they proceeded cautiously, not sure of what they might find.

Soon after they came upon a hamlet comprising a dozen or so huts gathered around a level area, at the center of which was a well. The place was teeming with small children, all dressed similarly in plain smocks gathered at the waist by rough cords. Moving to and fro between huts and the well were women, wearing long woolen dresses and wide leather belts, and carrying heavy baskets of washing or wooden buckets of water. They carefully lifted their loads above the heads of the children who swerved and careened around them with carefree abandon.

As soon as they saw the companions, everyone in the hamlet stopped what they were doing. The happy faces of the children changed to expressions of uncertainty and fear, and the women dropped their baskets and buckets and retrieved long curved knives from the back of their belts. The blades shimmered in the soft light filtering through the canopy.

"Friendly lot," Jenrosa murmured.

"Have you noticed how many there are?" Kumul asked Ager.

The crookback nodded absently, and Lynan realized that indeed there seemed to be a large number of people for the small number of huts. Then he noticed the frames of several new huts lining the trail as it left the hamlet on the other side.

Kumul motioned his companions to stay where they were, and cautiously moved forward ten paces, his arms spread out and his palms held upward.

"We mean you no harm," he said.

"We'll determine that," a woman near the well said. She was shorter than most of the other women, but something about her voice bespoke authority. She came forward to within a few paces of Kumul. "Who are you and why are you here?"

"They're hounds, Belara!" another woman said, her voice full of alarm. "They're Silona's hounds!"

There was a ripple of fearful moans from the people, but none of the women lowered knife or retreated.

"Don't be foolish, Enasna," said the one called Belara. "It is just past midday. No hound walks at this hour."

Kumul shrugged, looked at the woman called Enasna. "As you can see, madam, I have two legs, not four. I am no hound, but a traveler." He faced the first woman. "You are Belara, I assume. My friends and I are an embassy from our village to King Tomar in Sparro. We have been sent to ask for lower taxes; the past season has been cruel to us and our crops were poor."

"There are easier routes to Sparro than through the Forest of Silona," Belara said, her voice taking on a menacing edge. "And you don't dress like any villagers I've ever seen. You're soldiers, and the woman carries magical designs on her tunic."

"Our village sits on the northern foothills of the Ebrius Ridge. This is the most *direct* route, and the sooner we reach Tomar's court the sooner my village will have relief. As for our clothing, we live in a hard land and must defend ourselves. And it is true that the woman knows some magic, but she is only young and still learning."

While Kumul spoke, Belara had been studying his companions. "What's wrong with your bent friend?" she asked, pointing at Ager with the knife.

"My friend's injury is an old one, inflicted when he fought for Queen Usharna during the Slaver War."

"And why is your arm in a sling?"

"We were beset by bandits. I was stabbed in the arm, and the woman is recovering from a blow to the head."

"Did the bandits get much?" she asked, her curiosity getting the better of her.

"A shallow grave each," Kumul said gruffly.

The woman laughed suddenly and lowered the point of her knife. At that, all the other women lowered their blades as well. The children came forward then, milling around the companions, but especially Ager, pointing at and touching his crookback. Many, too, were fascinated with Kumul; they had probably never seen anyone so large. Kumul introduced himself and his friends, using only first names.

"You look like you could do with some food and rest," Belara said. "Take what water you need from the well, and then come to my home," she pointed to a hut not twenty paces away, "and I'll see what food I can scrounge up for you. We may even be able to do something for your arm."

"We do not need much," Kumul lied. "We have no wish to be a burden."

"We never refuse hospitality to travelers." She paused, losing her smile, then said, "We get so few. At least stay the night."

Belara's home was larger inside than any of the abandoned huts the companions had rested in so far on their journey through the forest. A bleached woolen rug separated sleeping quarters from space set aside for housework and cooking. Planks made from summer trees and sanded back to a fine finish made the floor, and rougher planks were used for the walls and caulked with dried mud. Two small children, neither older than three, were sleeping in a large wooden cradle near a slow-burning fire in the middle of the living area, the smoke rising to a hole in the branch and twining roof. Furniture was sparse but comfortable and practical, comprising a long table and an assortment of hand-made chairs and stools, all beautifully carved.

While Belara tended Kumul's wound, she asked many questions about the outside world. Ager now did most of the talking, careful not to admit to any knowledge someone from a small village would not have.

"These are your children?" Lynan asked Belara during a lull in the conversation, pointing to the two in the cradle.

"The oldest, Mira, is mine. The other belongs to Seabe. She's out gathering food with some of the other women."

"Where are your men?" he asked. "Out farming?"

Belara looked at Lynan strangely. "You would have little success farming in this forest. The men are out cutting timber. Every half year we hire oxen from those farmsteads surrounding the forest and use them to haul the timber to the Orym River, where merchants buy it and float it down to Sparro. We use the money to buy what we can't supply ourselves. We get fish from the streams, and trap rabbits when we can, and the forest supplies all the berries and roots we need."

"I'm surprised no one's cleared parts of the forest for cultivation."

"Some have tried," Belara said fatalistically. "But clearings don't stay cleared for long. The forest always grows back before any crop can be harvested."

"I don't know that I like the sound of trees growing faster than wheat," Jenrosa said.

"This is an old part of the world," Belara told her. "The forest was here long before the kingdom, or even Chandra, existed. It never seems to change. It doesn't grow, it doesn't shrink. But it provides well enough for those who take out of it only what they need. Most of the time, anyway." She was now applying some lotion to Kumul's wound, making him wince.

"Most of the time?" Kumul asked.

Belara stared at her guests, then shook her head. "There's no need for you to know. It's our problem."

"Why is this the only inhabited hamlet we've come across so far?" Kumul persisted.

Belara was wrapping a clean bandage around Kumul's wound. "There used to be a dozen or more. There are only three or four left now, though I would have to ask my husband, Roheth, to tell you for sure. He travels through the forest all the time, finding the right trees for us to take."

"Is this problem you mentioned behind people leaving their hamlets?" Ager asked.

Belara's hands stopped their work. "Perhaps," she said in a subdued voice. "But that, too, is something better asked of Roheth." She finished dressing the wound and moved over to the fire to place a gridiron over it, then packed the gridiron with round lumps of seed dough she quickly kneaded between her hands.

"There are many people in your hamlet," Grapnel said innocently. "Far more than I would have guessed from the number of huts."

"We are two hamlets," Belara said in a small voice.

"Seabe and her child come from the other hamlet," Ager guessed aloud.

"Yes. She is staying with us until a new hut can be built for her." She turned to face them, her face suddenly light and smiling. "Do you think King Tomar will listen to your appeal for reducing your taxes?"

Caught off guard, Ager parried the question valiantly. Lynan could only admire his skill, and was relieved the question had not been directed toward him.

Having successfully deflected any more questions about the forest, Belara made sure the topic was not raised again. When Seabe, a large, quiet woman with sad eyes, came home carrying a wooden basket filled with hard nuts, Belara set her guests the task of breaking open their shells and cleaning the fruit.

An hour before nightfall, Roheth and Seabe's husband, Wente, returned. Children in the village had told them of the arrival of the four strangers, so they were not surprised to see them when they entered the hut. They were tall, gangly men with long, wiry arms, and their hair and full beards were black and shaggy. Soft brown eyes stared out of long, angular faces, the contrast startling. After introductions, Roheth studied his guests carefully before saying: "You say you're from Ebrius Ridge?" He didn't sound convinced.

"A small village just north of the Ridge," Ager replied. "Novalo, it's called. About ten days from here."

"How small a village?"

Ager shrugged, wishing Roheth would change the subject. Eventually, he knew, he would be caught out by such persistent questioning. "Around eighty or so."

"You don't know exactly?"

"There were three women pregnant and near their time when we left," Jenrosa said quickly. "The village could have eighty-three souls by now."

Roheth faced Lynan. "Where did you say you bumped into these bandits?"

"We didn't," Kumul replied for the prince. "But it was two days out from the edge of this forest."

Roheth nodded knowingly. "Aye, well, you don't get bandits *inside* of the forest. Except for us woodcutters and our families, you don't get much of anyone here. You lot are a bit of a surprise. Haven't had any strangers come this way for . . . now what would it be, Belara? . . . Three years, maybe four? . . . A long time, anyway. Certainly no one just passing through." The companions said nothing, content to let Roheth enjoy his fishing. "Did you see anyone else in the forest on your way here?"

"Anyone else?" Jenrosa asked.

"A woman," he said, and his throat tightened. Lynan immediately recalled the pair of green eyes he had seen staring at him from the darkness, but he said nothing. He was still ashamed of the reaction from Kumul and Ager when his cry of surprise had woken them.

"No, we saw no one else," Jenrosa said.

Roheth shook his head, as if he was chasing away a persistent fly. "So, you're off to see the king in his court about taxes? I wish you luck, then."

"Are you taxed heavily here?" Kumul asked.

"Us? Taxed?" Roheth actually laughed. "No tax collector's been here for nearly a century. They don't like the forest. Lucky, that."

Roheth and Wente had each returned with a brace of rabbits, and these were wrapped in leaves and baked for dinner, served with roasted nuts and a dark gravy made from some mushrooms Seabe had collected that afternoon. The gravy was mopped up with the fresh bread Belara had baked, and it was all washed down with a few flagons of forest mead.

Lynan enjoyed himself more than at any time since fleeing Kendra. His hosts were considerate and, after a few mugs of the mead, joyfully boisterous. There were odd moments throughout the meal, though, when the forest dwellers would inexplicably slip into a kind of deep melancholy, as if a great tragedy had touched all their lives and memory of it refused to leave them. As the night wore on, the bouts of melancholy became deeper and more frequent, and their laughter sounded forced. The companions began to feel uncomfortable, and started making excuses to leave.

"We can't let you sleep outside," Roheth protested. "There's more than enough room in here for all of us." His arm moved in a wide arc, encompassing the hut crowded with people. "Plenty of room," he insisted somewhat groggily.

"It's all right, Roheth," Jenrosa said. "We're used to sleeping on the ground."

"It won't do. Tell them, Belara."

His wife stirred uneasily. When she talked, her eyes were downcast. "Roheth is right. We cannot let guests sleep outside when there is more than enough room in our home."

"Your generosity is overwhelming," Ager said to the hosts.

It was another hour before the forest dwellers had drunk themselves into a near stupor. With great effort, they gathered together their sleeping children and withdrew behind the woolen rug into their sleeping quarters, leaving their guests to stretch out how they liked in front of the fire.

Lynan woke just before dawn, not sure what had roused him. The fire had burned down to a few glowing embers, and the air was chill. He pulled his cloak tighter around his body and tried to get back to sleep. His mind was just beginning to drift when he heard a scraping sound. He sat up, peering into the eerie gloom. The others were all asleep. He heard the sound again and realized it was coming from outside. Something was scratching on the door, trying to get in.

A part of his mind was surprised he was curious instead of frightened. What if it was a bear or wolf? *No,* he told himself, *that sound is not being made by claws.* What if it was one of the children, gone outside for a piss and not able to get back in? He threw off the cloak and stood up, being careful not to step on anyone. The scratching became more insistent, almost frantic, as if whatever was doing it knew someone was coming to open the door. Lynan stretched out his hand, touched the wooden handle and began to turn it.

"No!" hissed a voice behind him.

Lynan nearly jumped out of his skin. He spun around and saw Jenrosa sitting up, holding her cloak protectively around herself.

"Don't open the door, Lynan, whatever you do!" she pleaded.

"What's wrong? It could be one of the children trying to get back in . . ." Even as he said the words, he knew with utter certainty it was no child outside. He whipped his hand away from the handle and stepped back, his skin crawling with instinctive revulsion.

The scratching stopped. For a moment there was no sound at all, then something with an inhuman throat started wailing. It was almost inaudible at first, but it grew louder and more keening until it had become a scream of anger and hatred that made every nerve in Lynan's body vibrate in pain. The cry then pulled up and away from the hut, as if its source had taken wing and was flying above the hamlet and heading into the forest. In a few seconds there was silence again, and Lynan found he could move once more. His body started shaking uncontrollably, and Jenrosa had to help him into a chair. By now everyone in the hut was awake. The sound of two mewling children came from the sleeping area.

Roheth and Wente stumbled into the living area, sharp axes in their hands, followed by Belara and Seabe holding their babes. Terror was on all their faces. At first, no one said anything. Belara placated Mira and put her in the cradle, then heated up a mug of spiced mead and gave it to Lynan. There was a heavy knock on the door, and before Lynan or Jenrosa could say anything, Ager had opened it. A wide-shouldered woodsman entered, and like Roheth and Wente he carried an ax.

"We heard her," the stranger said to Roheth.

Roheth nodded. "Everyone is safe. Thank you for coming, Tion."

"She'll be back now," Tion muttered, glancing disapprovingly at the guests. "Unless something is done."

Roheth ushered Tion outside and followed him. When he came back a few minutes later, his face was gray and worried.

"What is going on?" Kumul asked levelly.

"What was it?" Lynan added.

"*She* was Silona," Roheth said heavily.

Kumul did not look surprised. "So the stories are true."

"Oh, yes. She exists, all right."

"Excuse me," Lynan interjected, feeling annoyed. "But who is Silona?"

"She is part of the forest," Belara said quietly. "She's been here since time began, guarding the trees."

"Is she dangerous?"

"Mortally dangerous," Roheth answered. "You are a very lucky young man. By rights, you should have died tonight."

"If she's so dangerous, why don't you hunt her down and kill her?"

"Oh, men have tried before. Over the centuries, every generation throws up its heroes and its fools. Those who go after her are never seen again; at least, not as man or woman."

"How often . . ." Lynan swallowed hard and started again. "How often does she kill?"

"Most of the time she's asleep. Every few years she wakes to take the blood of three or four humans, then goes back to sleep."

"Blood?" Lynan's hands started shaking, and had difficulty putting the mug of mead to his lips. He drank deeply.

"She is a wood vampire," Roheth explained. "Perhaps the last of her kind. The fact that the borders of this forest have stood for so long shows how strong her will is."

"How does she take the blood?"

Roheth shrugged. "No one has ever seen her, let alone watched her feed, and lived to tell about it. One day you wake up and someone in the hamlet has died. There are no marks, but the body is drained of blood. We burn the corpse. Sometimes she takes travelers, and if their bodies are not found by the next night, they will walk the forest seeking out new victims for her."

"The hounds of Silona," Jenrosa said, glancing at Belara.

Roheth nodded. "When we find them, we cut off their heads and burn them. We give them rest."

Lynan was feeling sick. *I almost let her in.* "Why . . . why did she not just break down the door if she wanted someone inside this hut?"

"Legend says her victims must come to her willingly," Roheth replied, looking sideways at Lynan.

"I'm sorry, Roheth, I didn't know what I was doing . . ."

"I'm not blaming you. It's impossible to resist her, which is why our families crowd together when she is awake and haunting the forest."

"That explains all the abandoned huts we found on the way here," Ager said. "They belong to woods people who leave to join other hamlets."

Roheth nodded.

"How do you know when it's time to gather together?" Kumul asked.

"When we find the first victim," Roheth replied bluntly.

"I think we are lucky not to have met this Silona before," Kumul said. "To think of all the nights we were sleeping in the open."

"She stalks the hamlets and the forest surrounding them, mostly." Roheth caught Lynan's attention. "But now that's changed. If she's felt your mind, she will pursue you."

"But I am safe here?"

"Not anymore. You've frustrated her once. She will keep on returning to our hamlet until she takes you, or some other unfortunate falls in her way."

"We can keep watch," Kumul suggested, his voice becoming strident. "We will set a trap for her—"

"Do you think we haven't tried this before?" Roheth demanded. "Our traps never work. Watchers fall asleep where they stand, or become victims themselves. She is used to the ways of people: she knows us the way we know the boar we hunt or the fish we spear."

"You mean that our presence is placing all your lives in danger?" Ager said.

Roheth nodded reluctantly. "That's what Tion wanted to talk about. He believes I should ask you to leave, for the sake of the hamlet."

"Will you force us to go?" Jenrosa asked, appalled.

"No. I cannot do that. You are my guests. If you wish to

stay, I will do what I can to protect you." Roheth's face was bleak as he said the words.

"We'll go of our own volition," Lynan said, startled by his own decision. Ager and Kumul stared at him in surprise. Jenrosa looked aghast. "From what you say, Roheth, we're no safer here than in the forest, but while we're here, we increase the danger to you and your family." He turned to his companions. "A prince's decision. Isn't that what I'm supposed to be making these days?" The woods people looked at their guests with puzzled expressions.

Ager nodded resignedly. "What a time for you to practice your leadership skills."

"Any of you who want to stay are welcome to," Roheth said. "Not all of you have to go."

"Just the one Silona touched?" Lynan asked.

"Yes. The others are safer here if *you* leave the hamlet. It is you Silona will be after."

"We'll all go," Kumul said definitely, and Ager nodded his agreement. Only Jenrosa gave no indication of what she was thinking.

17

THE light of the morning sun struggling through the tree canopy found the four companions saying their farewells to the people of the hamlet.

"Keep your campfires burning high and bright," Roheth advised them. "Legends say she finds strong light uncomfortable. Other than that, there is not much else that will help. Except maybe this." He offered Lynan his own coat, a finely made woolen garment dyed the dark green of the forest.

"Does it carry a magic charm?" Lynan asked, wide-eyed.

Roheth laughed. "No, but you'll need it to keep you warm if I take yours."

"Mine? I don't understand."

"If we keep something of yours with us, it may fool Silona into thinking you're still here, for a night or two at least."

Lynan gratefully exchanged coats and shook Roheth's hand. Berala handed them seed bread and strips of dried rabbit which they crammed in their pockets.

"Good luck, Lynan," the forester said somberly.

Lynan smiled weakly, already frightened of what might lay ahead.

The companions kept to the main trail heading north out of the hamlet. They talked sparingly, each feeling the tension build in them as the day wore on. They stopped briefly for a meal around noon, then continued on their way until they came across a narrower, less-used trail that headed northeast. Ager suggested they take the less-used trail, reasoning that if Silona came hunting for Lynan she would follow the main trail first.

The way was gloomy and overgrown, and they often had to struggle through brambles and tall bushes. Tempers frayed. As evening approached, Lynan's stomach started to compress into the now familiar knot of apprehension. His knees no longer seemed strong enough to support his whole weight.

"We should stop soon and make camp," he suggested.

"I thought you'd want to be as far away as possible from the hamlet," Jenrosa said.

"What I want is enough time to gather so much firewood that our campfire will shine all night like the sun."

"One thing about a campfire is that it'll draw attention to us," Jenrosa said helpfully.

"Then what would you suggest we do?" Lynan snapped.

She shrugged, looking miserable. "I'm sorry. I don't know what to do. It seems to me if we're not being chased by guardsmen or warships or mercenaries, then it is bears and vampires. What's next, do you think? When do we stop running?"

"We stop when we reach the Oceans of Grass."

"What makes you think Areava won't stop hunting for you, even as far as the Oceans of Grass?"

"It's easy to hide in the grasslands," he said with more confidence than he felt. "They go on forever. Areava can't spare the troops or the money to search for me forever."

"Face it, Lynan, you're not simply *fleeing* Kendra, you're going into exile. All your life you're going to be a wanted man. I don't want to be a part of that, but I don't know how I can get out of it. As long as your life is in danger, so is mine."

"Then why didn't you stay behind in the hamlet? You could have stayed there until the danger with Silona was passed and then made your own way elsewhere."

"Elsewhere? I only have one home, and that's Kendra. And eventually even the foresters will hear of Berayma's murder and the four outlaws accused of it. Besides, I'm not interested in wielding an ax and hunting rabbits and being surrounded by nothing but trees, vampires, and screaming children. With you, at least, I have the protection of Kumul and Ager."

"And me," Lynan added quietly.

Jenrosa glanced at his sideways. "I need to be by myself for a while," she said, and increased her pace to pull ahead of him. Her place was taken by Ager.

"Adventures aren't all they're cracked up to be, are they?" the crookback said.

"Adventures?"

"What we're all going through now, your Highness. It's an adventure, really, when you look at it properly. Think of all the things we've done in the last few days. I'd call it an adventure."

"I don't think I'd call it that. More like finding increasingly unpleasant ways to die."

"But that's what adventures are when you're actually experiencing them. They don't become adventures until afterward, when you're sixty-three years old and sitting in front of a huge fire with your grandchildren all around you."

"It's not the adventuring that worries me, Ager. It's the fear. I always seem to be frightened, sometimes so frightened I want to throw up. I want to rest. I want to be able to go to sleep on a soft warm bed and know that not only will

I wake up the next morning, but that I won't have to get up just to do more running."

"I don't know when you'll be able to do that again," Ager said.

"Jenrosa doesn't think I'll ever be able to. She said I'll be an outlaw for the rest of my life."

"She's scared too, Lynan. I don't think she really believes that. Things will seem better when we leave the forest. This is a dark place, and makes for dark thoughts."

"And hides dark things, Ager," Lynan reminded him.

They found a space among the trees which, if not large enough to be called a clearing, at least allowed in some light and made them feel less closed in by the forest. They gathered as much wood and tinder as possible and started a large fire.

Kumul arranged the watch. "From what Roheth told me, this demon usually comes in the hours before dawn, so I'd rather Ager or myself faced it. You take the first watch Jenrosa, followed by Lynan, then Ager, and lastly myself."

"What will you do if it comes?" Jenrosa asked him.

"Cut its bloody head off," he said grimly.

The forest was completely still. No animal came snuffling at the perimeter of their camp, no wind moved among the trees, no insects called out in the night. Lynan sat as closely as possible to the fire without risking his forester's coat catching alight. He turned constantly, peering into the dark. Whenever a log cracked in the fire, he jumped and then cursed his own cowardice.

Time stretched until seconds seemed like minutes and minutes seemed like hours. Lynan wondered if he would ever be relieved from the watch. Perhaps Silona was sorceress as well as vampire and had frozen time until she could find the mind she had touched so softly the night before.

Twice before, he told himself, remembering those green eyes in the forest.

When at last Ager did rouse himself from sleep, stretching like a misshapen bear and grinning like a child waking on its birthday, Lynan felt so much relief he wanted to laugh.

"How did it go?" Ager asked him.

"No problems at all," Lynan lied.

Ager nodded and made himself comfortable on an upturned log.

For a while Lynan watched the confident crookback with envy, then closed his eyes and fell into a deep sleep as if he had nothing in the world to worry about.

The sixth day after the companions left the hamlet the trees started to thin out and they could track the sun against the sky. The air was cooler, drier, and they could smell a river and ripening fields as well as bark and moss and humus. The old trail they had been following for so long now turned east, so they headed north among the trees, confident they would soon come to the borders of the forest.

Early in the afternoon Lynan stopped suddenly and looked up. The others halted, hands going to weapons.

"It's all right," Lynan told them. "Listen."

They all cocked their heads and listened. They kept still for over a minute. Jenrosa opened her mouth to make some comment about her feet turning into roots when the clear, beautiful fluting of a bird reached all their ears. Jenrosa smiled with pleasure and Kumul and Ager laughed.

"I never thought I'd be so pleased to hear birdsong again," Kumul admitted.

"Not long now," Ager said. "Maybe only one more night in this forest and then we're out."

They set off with renewed energy and a longer stride, even Ager stretching his strange lope without complaint. None of them cared what dangers faced them out in the open because nothing could be worse than the constant fear they had endured over the last six days.

That evening they had no trouble finding a suitable place to make camp. They celebrated their last night in the forest by eating the last of the dried meat the foresters had given them.

"We'll have to find another stream tomorrow or we'll have nothing to eat," Ager said.

"Unfortunately, I haven't a bow, but I could try and trap some game," Kumul offered.

"As long as we're out of this forest, I don't care if I don't eat for a month," Lynan said.

When Lynan took his watch, he was alert but more relaxed than he had been for many nights. He was reassured when he heard the sounds of crickets among the undergrowth, and even the occasional soft padding in the dark of something considerably larger than an insect. Nevertheless, he kept the fire high and bright, and was glad of the warmth it gave.

Toward the end of his watch he heard someone stir, and he turned expecting to see Ager rising early, but it was Jenrosa. She had turned in her sleep, throwing open her coat. Lynan walked quietly to her and closed the coat around her and then, on impulse, softly touched her hair. The skin on his fingers tingling, he retreated, feeling that perhaps not all was wrong with the world after all.

He turned and saw, at the edge of darkness and light, a girl. She was small, dressed in green cloth, with long blonde hair that reached down to her waist. Her face was hidden in the night.

Lynan studied her, unafraid. She took a gliding step forward, as if her feet were not actually touching the ground. He could see her face now. It was round and beautiful. Deep, dark eyes returned his stare. She looked younger than Lynan. She took another step forward and held out her hand.

Lynan started walking toward her. A part of his mind was telling him to stay where he was, but he ignored it and kept on walking until he was only a few paces from the girl. He noticed absently that it was not green cloth that dressed her but parts of tree and bush and moss, and somehow it all seemed a part of her, not something she wore at all.

"I have been searching for you for many nights," she said, her hand still held out to him. Her voice was as deep and dark as the night surrounding them, and it drew him forward. He reached out with his own hand and took hers. Her skin was as smooth and cold as glass. Her nails dug into his palm and he felt warm, sticky blood trickle between his fingers.

She leaned forward and whispered into his ear. "I want you. I need you." Her breath was like the sighing of the wind. He could see now that her eyes were the green of the forest itself. She raised his wounded hand and softly licked the palm. He reached out with his other hand. The green surrounding her fell away, and he saw two small white breasts with dark brown nipples.

He put his bloody hand over one of her breasts. He felt no warmth, but still desire flamed within him. She took his hand and moved it to the other breast, and then the flat of her stomach, smearing blood over her ivory skin.

"Kiss me," she said, and pulled him toward her.

He wrapped his arms around her waist and brought his lips against hers. He kissed her gently, ignoring the smell of decay on her breath and the sharp teeth that filled her mouth and the rough, rasping tongue that touched his. She drew him away and smiled, her mouth wet with saliva. He saw her eyes brighten, and her pupils distend into slits like those of a cat. Her nails stroked the back of his head and neck.

"Kiss me again," she said.

Lynan submitted, lost in her, and shivered when her teeth bit into his lower lip. The metallic taste of his own blood flooded his mouth and a small germ of panic wormed its way into his mind. He tried to draw back but found that he was held fast. He grabbed her arms and immediately let them go—they felt like the strong, young branches of a wideoak, the skin rough as bark. A cry started somewhere deep in his throat and escaped as a pitiful moan. His lover threw her head back and laughed, an eager and malevolent sound that finally brought him to his senses and he saw her for what she was.

The face was still that of a girl, still beautifully alluring, but it rested on a body that was half-human and half-tree. The limbs were covered in gray skin, and her body was as hard as wood. Her hair was made from green wisps that smelled of moss and twigs and made a clacking sound when she moved her head. A long, green tongue with three hollow tendrils flickered between her lips.

"Do you desire me?" the creature asked, and laughed again.

He felt her grip tighten around him, and his breathing became labored as he felt his rib cage bending under the pressure. He put his hand under her chin to keep her mouth away from his face, but she was far too strong and slowly she forced her head closer to his.

Suddenly the night was filled with flaring brightness. Lynan was flung away from the vampire like a child's toy, and he landed heavily on his side. He heard a scream of such pain and torment that his mind reeled in shock. He shook his head and looked up to see Jenrosa, a flaming brand in one hand and a sword in the other, confronting Silona. She was thrusting the brand at the creature's face, forcing it farther and farther away from Lynan. He saw that Jenrosa was also drawing herself farther into the forest. He cried out to her and tried to stand, but was still so dazed he could only manage to get to his knees.

He heard more cries behind him as Kumul and Ager

leaped to their feet and scrabble for their weapons. With a greater effort Lynan stood up and tried to run to Jenrosa's assistance, drawing his sword as he did so. By now Silona was fighting back, hissing fiercely at the magicker and trying to knock the brand from her grasp. The vampire moved to Jenrosa's left, forcing her to follow, then quickly leaped back to her right, her arm whipping up and connecting with the magicker's right shoulder. Jenrosa cried out in pain but managed to hold on to the brand. Silona now struck with her other arm, and her nails raked across Jenrosa's right shoulder. This time the impact sent the brand flying out of her grasp to land fizzing on the ground twenty paces away. Silona cried in triumph and moved in for the kill, but the cry turned into a scream of rage as Lynan's sword sliced into her arm. Lynan felt the blade bite into the vampire's limb, making a whacking sound as if it had embedded itself in a block of wood. Silona pulled back, the blade popping out of her arm. Pale blood seeped from the deep cut, pink in color and almost transparent.

Lynan swung the sword over his head for another blow, but Silona had seen Kumul and Ager running toward her, each bearing a brand as well as their own weapons. Her body writhed and her back split open like a seed case. Two huge black wings sprouted, dark flowers against the light of the campfire. The wings came together with a crack and the vampire lifted into the air. The wings flapped a second time and she disappeared into the night.

The four companions stood together, peering into the darkness, but could see nothing of her. A second later they heard a wail of frustration and pain echo through the forest. Lynan's whole body shuddered, and he collapsed to the ground.

When Lynan came to, it was morning. The fire was still burning brightly, keeping him warm in the chill air. He propped himself onto his elbows and tried looking around, but he felt dizzy and his head fell back with a clunk.

"I don't know what your skull's made from," said an interested female voice behind him, "but it's tougher than iron."

His eyes rolled back in their sockets and he saw Jenrosa sitting on the ground.

"I feel terrible," he managed to say.

"It's amazing, isn't it, the collections of cuts, bruises, and bumps our little party has managed to collect since fleeing Kendra. Can you imagine what we'll be like in a year's time? Or a decade?"

"Are we still in the forest?"

"Yes, but Ager thinks the border is only one or two hours' steady walk from here."

"Where is he?"

"With Kumul, trying their hand at trapping. As soon as they're back, we'll move, if you think you're up to it. I don't fancy spending another night in Silona's Forest."

Lynan shuddered with the memory of last night's events. He remembered how easily he had been beguiled by the vampire and felt ashamed. "I almost got you killed last night."

"But you saved my life from the bear, so don't lose any sleep over it."

Lynan laughed grimly. "You're determined to keep behind your fortress walls, aren't you?"

Jenrosa stood up and brushed off her pants. "I don't know what you're talking about."

"Help me up, will you?"

Jenrosa hooked her a hand under one of Lynan's arms and lifted. He was unsteady on his feet for a few seconds, but soon he could walk around without falling over. He managed to complete a circuit of their camp and was beginning a second when he saw something at his feet. Jenrosa joined him and looked down where he was gazing at a patch of blackened leaf litter and scorched ground.

"That's just where my brand hit the ground," she said.

"That's your brand over there," he said and pointed to it. He knelt down and stretched out his hand. "See, there's some—"

"That's her blood!" Jenrosa cried.

Lynan jerked back as if he had been about to pat a snake. He stared at it, fascinated. "You're right, it *is* her blood."

"Leave it alone, for God's sake. Haven't you had enough to do with her?"

Her words made him feel suddenly stubborn. He pulled out his knife.

"What are you doing?"

He ignored her and cut off a triangular section of Roheth's coat, then used the cloth to scrape up the blood.

"What are you doing?" she insisted.

"A souvenir," he said, waving the cloth at her. "Besides, I'm sure you've heard stories about vampire blood: it's supposed to have magical properties."

"What if it helps Silona track you down again?" Jenrosa spat at him.

Lynan hesitated, his face pale. "Do you think. . . ?" He shook his head. "No. Once we're out of the forest, we're free from her."

"How can you be so sure?"

"Silona is a wood vampire. If she leaves her forest, she dies."

"You don't know that."

Lynan put the sample in his coat pocket and stood up. "I'm prepared to risk it."

Jenrosa spun away from him. "You're a fool, Lynan. You'll get us all killed yet."

$$\langle\ 18\ \rangle$$

AFTER a week of searching for reasonable billets for his men in Kendra, Captain Rendle found a message from the quartermaster's office of the Grenda Lear army waiting for him at his inn. All mercenary companies had less than ten days to gather at the port town of Alemura if they expected employment in the coming demonstration against Haxus. Rendle was too experienced a soldier to be disappointed with the vagaries of the military bureaucracy, but he was angry he would lose the deposit he had just laid down for the billets.

He rode out of the city to where his company of mercenary cavalry had camped. He was greeted enthusiastically, his troopers expecting him to bring news that from now on nights would be spent with a proper roof over their heads, plenty of food and wine in their bellies, plenty of women in their beds, and an easy few months of employment at the expense of the new king. What they got were new marching orders and the news that they were to be employed by Grenda Lear's new queen.

Rendle's second-in-command, a whip of a man named Eder, asked him what was going on. In a few terse sentences

Rendle told him of Berayma's murder, Areava's ascension, and Lynan's outlawry and subsequent drowning.

"I'm not keen on serving under a Kendran queen," Eder said.

"Nor am I," Rendle replied brusquely, "not after fighting against the last one in the Slaver War; but for the moment we'll take her money and salute her pennant. At least until she moves us up north."

"So we are going to fight Haxus?"

"Not if I have anything to do with it. Haxus always paid better than Grenda Lear."

Eder smiled thinly. "I think I like the idea of taking coin with both hands; it seems a fairer way of doing things."

"What about our missing patrol? Any sign of them?"

Eder took him to a tent on the edge of their camp. He opened the flap and Rendle saw jerkins, belts, and knives laid out, all of them covered in damp soil. "One of the scouts I sent back found their graves near a stream about two days' ride from here. Their horses were nowhere to be seen. They all died from sword wounds."

Rendle's jaw clenched in anger. "Where are their swords?"

"None in the graves."

"And no sign of their attackers?"

"The scout said too many companies like our own had passed that way since. The tracks are all mixed up. He did find two of their mounts wandering alone on Ebrius Ridge."

"Do the others know about this?"

"Hard to disguise a scout carrying so much extra equipment and leading two riderless horses back to camp. They know."

Rendle led the way back to his tent where he rummaged in one of his chests and retrieved a large hand-drawn map. He laid it out on the ground outside.

"I don't like losing my men," Rendle said tightly. "And I don't understand this. None of my people are so stupid as to bother a village or hamlet by themselves. They might have tried to steal a chicken or pig, or annoy a farmer's daughter, but a farmer hasn't a chance in hell of doing anything about it."

He studied the map carefully. He had been roving over this part of the world for nearly thirty years now and knew most of it like the back of his hand. He pointed to a series of trails and streams at the north base of Ebrius Ridge which intersected the road the company had taken to reach the Horn of Lear. "They were sent ahead of us to here. When we passed by, there was no sign of them, so chances are whatever happened to them occurred in the six hours after they left the company and we reached this point."

There were a few villagers within a half-day's ride of the road, but little else. Ebrius Ridge itself had mediocre soil and the constant threat of great bears to worry any settlers, so people tended not to farm in the immediate area.

Rendle tapped the map angrily with one finger, then started circling out in a spiral. He traced over the main road, the ridge itself, the edge of Kestrel Bay, back to Chandra . . . His finger stopped, then retraced to the coast.

"I was told Prince Lynan had been drowned off these cliffs here, but his body was never recovered."

Eder looked over his shoulder. "Was he by himself?"

"No. He had at least three companions. A cripple, a girl, and Kumul Alarn. None of their bodies was found."

Eder's eyes widened. "The Constable of the Royal Guards was in on the king-killing plot?"

Rendle nodded. "According to official proclamations."

"I saw him once, during the Slaver War. The biggest, ugliest bastard I've ever laid eyes on. I'm not sorry he's left this world."

"But what if he and his friends didn't drown and instead made their way up the ridge? Where would they go? They couldn't return to Kendra, and they couldn't stay on the ridge. And it all happened at the same time we were making our way here from the other direction."

"You don't think our patrol met them?"

Rendle shrugged. "Impossible to know." He bent over the map again, his gaze moving north along Chandra's length and into Hume, then west to the Oceans of Grass. "So where could they be heading?" he asked himself.

"You going to report this to the queen?"

"Report what? That we've lost a patrol to unknown attackers? We have no evidence one way or the other about how they met their fate."

"Except that it was violent and their swords were taken."

"Another mercenary patrol could have done that. Old Malorca was moving through that area with his archers the day before us; he's always willing to take a snipe at a competitor."

"We'll have to fix him one day," Eder said gruffly.

"But not this day. The new queen is offering enough contracts for all of us right now." Rendle was still studying the map. He jabbed at a place marked as Arran Valley. "I don't suppose Jes Prado is still settled there?"

"Last I heard, and with a good portion of his men settled nearby. They moved there to take care of some minor trouble in the region and stayed. But you never liked the man. What's on your mind?"

"I think Prado's a whining excuse for a soldier, but we've never had any problems with him and he's a straight dealer. Send a message to him."

"I'll organize a rider—"

"No. I need something faster. Go to Kendra and buy a pigeon carrier."

"What's the message?"

"I don't know exactly. I'll think on it over the next hour, but it will have to mention money, and a lot of it."

*   *   *

Olio reached the rendezvous at Kendra's harbor ten minutes before the agreed time. Prelate Edaytor Fanhow had agreed to guide the prince through the city's worst slum, a tangle of streets behind the docks where sailors' widows and orphaned children, whores and smugglers, fugitives and the unemployable all congregated like ants around a honey pot. Olio was determined to do something for the poor in the city and Edaytor had reluctantly agreed to show him the worst poverty Kendra had to offer.

The prince found a place to sit in the sun and watched a merchant ship from Lurisia being unloaded. Stevedores manhandled a winch over the ship while the crew set about tying thick rope around the biggest logs Olio had ever seen. It was rain forest wood, as red as flame and as hard as iron, and Lurisia's main export to the rest of Theare. Three logs were bound together, the winch hook was slipped under the top knot, and the stevedores heaved back on their ballast until the load was raised above the ship's gunwales. The final maneuver had the stevedores swinging the load across to the dock and slowly releasing the ballast so the logs could be placed gently in a waiting cart. When the first load was dropped, the ballast was released too quickly and the cart lurched, scaring the four oxen tied to it. Only the quick wits of the driver, who pulled back sharply on the horns of the lead ox, stopped the cart from being pulled away before its load could be secured.

There were sharp words between the ship's captain and the stevedore boss, and then the second load was made ready and attached to the winch. As the winch was swung over the dock, the top knot holding the hook slipped and the load lurched heavily. Stevedores scattered from the winch, but the hook held and two of them hurried forward to release the ballast. As they set hands to the winch, the knot unraveled completely. The logs fell with an awful crash and the winch careened sideways, the ballast slamming heavily into the two stevedores who had tried to rescue the load. Olio heard the dull thump of the collision and then terrible shouts and cries as people ran to help the injured.

Without hesitation, Olio rushed to the scene. He elbowed his way past a gawping bystander and stopped suddenly when he saw the broken and twisted remains of one of the fallen stevedores. Blood pooled around his feet and he stepped back.

"This one's alive!" a voice said, and Olio looked up to where the second victim was lying, his head supported by the crew boss. The prince stepped over the corpse and knelt down next to the injured stevedore. The man's breathing was labored and blood flecked his lips.

"He's dying," the boss said grimly. "His chest is crushed."

Olio grasped the stevedore's hand and squeezed gently. The man's skin was cool and clammy. His eyelids fluttered and opened, showing dilated pupils.

"Is there n–n–nothing you can do?" Olio asked the boss.

"He's dying," the boss repeated dully.

Olio reached inside his coat with his free hand and grasped the Key of the Heart. It felt cold to his touch. He waited for something to happen, not knowing what to expect. He felt nothing, nor sensed any change in the man whose hand he held. He closed his eyes and concentrated, searching for some sign in his mind about how to use the Key. He remembered the sheer power he had felt after Usharna had healed the crookback. His hand around the Key started to tingle, but still he felt nothing passing from him to the injured stevedore, felt no surge of whatever it was that the queen had used. The stevedore moaned, then coughed. Blood spattered Olio's face, but he ignored it.

"He m–m–must n–n–not die," he stuttered under his breath. He bowed his head and tried praying to God, but the vague faith he held to gave him no sign. And then a hand lay softly on his shoulder and he heard words in a strange tongue spoken above his head. The Key in his hand seemed to come alive with sudden heat so fierce he wanted to let go of it, but he held on as the heat spread from the Key to his hand and then his arm, flowed into his chest, making his heart beat twice as fast, and then on through his other arm and the hand that held the stevedore. He could sense rather than see the aura of light and power that took shape around him and the injured man, and he could physically feel the stevedore's ribs and lungs bend and warp and reshape into their normal form. The stevedore let out a great cry of pain, but no blood came from his mouth and his eyes were keen and alive.

As quickly as it had started, the surge of power ebbed away until at last Olio let go of the Key and stood up. He immediately swooned and started falling back. His vision was blurred and he could not make out the face of the man who caught him and pulled him away from the wondering crowd, but then he heard a familiar voice say: "I did not think we could do that."

"Edaytor?" Olio asked weakly. "What *did* you do?"

"Added my knowledge of magic to the power lent you by the Key of the Heart. Can you walk, your Highness? I am not strong enough to carry you any farther. I want you away from this dock before someone recognizes you."

Already some of the stevedores were pointing at the pair and using the word "miracle." Olio nodded and staggered a few feet before Edaytor put his shoulder under one of the prince's arms and helped him away from the harbor. They continued like that until they had reached one of the dark, narrow back streets behind the warehouses that lined the docks. They collapsed together against an old brick wall.

"I really wish you would bring an entourage with you when you leave the palace, your Highness," Edaytor gasped, trying to catch his breath.

"What good would that do? Everyone would know who I am, and curtsy and p–p–prithee and p–p–petition. How could I explore the city then?"

"Better curtsied and pritheed and petitioned than stabbed by some malcontent. Especially down here on the docks where many are not from Kendra but the provinces and so less respectful of rich young noblemen and their purses."

"Oh, God, a shame to die because someone thought I was a m–m–member of the Twenty Houses," Olio joked, but his laughter sounded forced.

"I thought your family was one of the Twenty Houses."

"Don't tell my sister that." Olio stood upright and immediately felt dizzy again. Edaytor was by his side instantly with a steadying arm. "What happened b–b–back there?"

"You healed a dying man."

"B–b–but not by m–m–myself. It was your m–m–magic that m–m–made the Key work."

Edaytor shook his bald head. "I don't think so, your Highness. I've never been able to do anything like that before, and I've handled many magical artifacts. The Key worked because you were the channel."

"Then why didn't it work b–b–before you helped?"

"I don't know. Maybe it is an ability you must develop. Were you ever tested for magic when you were young?"

"N–n–no."

"Yet I suspect it runs in your family. That is not unusual. Certainly, your mother had the power. It also may be that the Keys only work effectively when they are all together, and singly need an outside source of magic. There is much to ponder on this."

Olio smiled shyly. "B–b–but together, Edaytor, we *can* work it."

"At a price. We are both exhausted."

Olio nodded wearily. "I'm afraid I am going to have to

call off our tour. I cannot remember ever feeling so tired b—b—before."

"Nor I. Come, your Highness, I will walk with you back to the palace."

"B—b—but your own offices are near here. I am fine."

Edaytor insisted, and together they made their way back up the avenue that wound its way through the city, ending in the climb to the palace's main gate and two of the Royal Guards. Edaytor left the prince in safety. Olio watched the round prelate start his journey back to his own offices, wondering what he had done to deserve such devotion.

"Your Highness, we didn't know you were out," said one of the guards as he saluted him in.

"That was the whole p—p—point," Olio said under his breath.

He paused in the courtyard, befuddled by exhaustion and all the questions in his head about what had happened on the docks. He badly wanted both to talk to someone about it before going to sleep. He decided to see Areava first; he thought she might have some knowledge from all her reading that might explain how he and Edaytor had performed their magic. He glanced up to her chambers and saw her figure silhouetted in the window. She was not alone. Olio did not have to guess who her companion was.

Well, sleep first, after all, he told himself, smiling. *I will not disturb the love birds.*

"I have your final spearman," Sendarus said, holding up the piece in victory.

Areava ignored him and carefully studied the polygonal board in front of her. True, all her spearmen had been discovered and destroyed, but her city was still protected by two lancers and a duke, and she was sure her defenses would not easily be overcome.

Who knows, she mused to herself, *he might even be foolish enough to send his sappers under my walls.*

"Now the game is reduced to its essential," Sendarus continued. "One player striving to breach the last barrier between him and his heart's desire."

"Your metaphor strains like a constipated old man," she told him without looking up. "I forgo a move."

"That is your last pass, your Majesty." Sendarus rolled the numbered knuckle bones. "I count five."

"That is a four. That bone is on its side."

"Four, then." He reached for one of his sappers and placed it under Areava's parapets. Areava removed an ivory shield to reveal her neat row of waiting swordsmen. "Your piece is taken." Sendarus blinked in surprise. "Swallowed whole like so much bait."

"You played the whole time for defense!" Sendarus protested. "You never had any intention of attacking my city!"

"And now that your last offensive piece is devoured, I am left with all the high points. My game."

Sendarus rested back in his chair and laughed. "You played me for a fool."

"Not at all. I played you like a fish."

Sendarus laughed even harder. Areava beamed.

"You fought hard, though," she conceded. "I was not sure if you had started the game with the sapper or the battering ram. I could not have stopped the latter."

"You can always stop me, your Majesty." He caught her gaze. "And I will always surrender."

She blushed, and stood quickly to hide it. "This has been a pleasant diversion, my lord, but I have business to attend to." She pulled a bell cord near her desk.

"A diversion? Is that all I am?" He asked the question lightly enough, but his expression was tense.

Areava gently placed a hand against one of his cheeks.

"There is no other diversion like you in my kingdom," she said.

He reached for her hand, but at that moment the door opened and Harnan bustled in, his arms filled with papers and scrolls.

Areava withdrew from Sendarus; he took the hint and stood, placing his hands behind his back. "I will see you later?" he whispered.

"Perhaps," she said, but not unkindly.

He bowed to her and left, nodding to Harnan, who tried to bow and hold onto his papers at the same time.

"We have much to get through, your Majesty," Harnan told Areava, and dumped his load on her desk.

"There is never a day when we don't," she said dryly.

"The life of a monarch has little pleasure, I know, your Majesty."

The corners of her mouth curved into the slightest of smiles. "Oh, I don't know about that."

"You will not say your farewells to Sendarus?" Orkid asked.

Amemun shook his head and mounted the horse Orkid was holding for him. "We talked last night. There is no need for further words between us. Nothing I could say would make him fall more in love with your queen."

"Our queen," Orkid said.

"Yes, of course," he said absently.

"That is the whole point of this exercise," Orkid persisted. "If she had no legitimacy in our eyes, then there would be no value in bringing her and Sendarus together, and any progeny from them would have no more right to claim our fealty than a child from a whore."

"It is not her legitimacy that concerns me, my friend. It is you."

Orkid's eyes opened wide in surprise. "What do you mean?"

"Marin had no choice but to send you here. He knew you agreed with his plan wholeheartedly and would never waver from our country's cause. And though your years here have not blunted your love for Aman, they have given you time to learn to love this city and its rulers."

"And why not, Amemun? It will soon be as much Aman's kingdom as it is Kendra's. But we must never forget the kingdom was built by those who came from here, not by our own people."

Amemun nodded. "I don't dispute any of this. But if things go wrong and do not turn out the way we have planned, then a time may come when you have to choose between your loyalties."

"Aman need never doubt me," Orkid said passionately. "I long for the day when I may return to my home."

Amemun patted the chancellor's hand, something no one had done since Orkid was a child. "I know. Keep your patience and your own counsel. The time will come, I am sure of it."

"Praise God," Orkid said.

"Praise the Lord of the Mountain," Amemun replied, not entirely in jest. "Good-bye, Orkid. Keep our prince safe!" He spurred his horse into a canter and left the palace for the docks where a ship waited to return him to Aman.

"Journey well," Orkid said quietly after him, and wondered when he would see his old friend again.

19

THEY were tired and hungry, but Lynan and his companions walked without stopping across yellow meadows and slowly undulating hills under a bright clear sky until the Forest of Silona was nothing but a green border on the southern horizon. For the first time in over a week they felt free, more at ease than at any time since their flight from Kendra. They all wore smiles like badges of distinction.

The sun was low in the west before Kumul called a halt. They were on a low hill that gave them a good view over a wide, shallow valley stretching some ten leagues north to south and half that east to west. Along its middle ribboned a blue stream, partnered by a wide dirt road. From their vantage point it looked as if most of the valley was under cultivation, divided into small squares of various shades, the pattern broken occasionally by small hamlets of twenty or so houses and one large town not far from their position.

"Mostly orchards," Ager observed. "This must be the Arran Valley. That means we're seventy leagues from Sparro, about a week's journey."

"I remember this place from one of my geography lessons," Lynan said. "This valley is famous for its peaches."

"And its wine," Ager added, licking his lips.

"And its archers," Kumul warned them. "They can put an arrow through the eye of a raven at a hundred paces, so let's stay alert. If anybody asks any questions, we spin the same yarn we gave the foresters."

"You don't think they believed us, do you?" Jenrosa asked.

"The point is, it's a story we know, and if we continue to use it, we'll get better at telling it. Just don't get imaginative. Keep it plain, and if you have to invent anything, let the rest of us know so we can speak the same lie."

"We'll need new names," Jenrosa said. "We can't go around declaring ourselves to be Lynan, Kumul, Ager, and Jenrosa, poor peasants whose names and looks happen to exactly match those of four outlaws from Kendra." The others agreed. "Then I'll be Analis," she said. "It was my grandmother's name, so it will be easy to remember."

"Then I will take my father's name," Ager said. "Nimen."

"Well, I had no mother or father to speak of," Kumul said, "so I'll be Exener, the name of the village I came from." He turned to Lynan. "You could you could take your father's name. Elynd is common enough, and many boys born around the same time as you were named after the General."

Lynan shook his head. "I wouldn't feel right about it."

"What about Pirem?" Ager said.

"No," Lynan said quickly. "Never again."

"Migam," Jenrosa suggested.

"What?"

"Migam. It's a nice name and it's easy to remember."

Kumul and Ager were looking at Lynan impatiently. "Yes, all right," he conceded. "Who was Migam, anyway?"

"My mother's pig," she replied, smiling.

Kumul and Ager burst out laughing, and in the end even Lynan joined in. "I hope he was a noble animal."

"He was small and hairy and he farted a lot, but he had his winning ways."

Against the continued guffaws of the two men, Lynan decided to change the subject. "Shall we camp here tonight?"

"I don't know about you, but I'm starving," Ager said. "Let's make for the town and see if we can't get some food and shelter. There's bound to be an inn or hostel there."

"What do you suggest we use for payment?" Jenrosa asked.

"We can work for it. Places like this always need seasonal labor, especially in autumn. Besides, it might also be a good way for us to get information about recent developments."

The others agreed, and less than an hour later they were walking down the town's main street where they found they had three inns to choose from. "This is a market town," Ager told them. "Some weeks the population here must treble."

They went to the largest inn and were immediately met by a burly man no taller than Lynan, with a red face impaled by a generous nose. Watery blue eyes stared out beneath a well-furrowed brow, and thin lips barely protruded from a forest of whiskers.

"Lady an' gents, welcome to the Good Harvest. You'll be wantin' board? We have a wide selection of rooms for you to choose from—"

"We have no money to speak of, landlord," Lynan said quickly. "But we would appreciate shelter and food for a night in exchange for any work you have."

"Food and shelter for work, eh?"

"Only for one night. We are on a mission for our village to the capital and must depart tomorrow morning."

"And what makes you think I have any work for you?"

"If you don't, we'll try one of the other inns," Kumul said bluntly.

The man regarded the giant for a second, then Ager and his crookback. Eventually he put his hands up. "Not so quickly now! Yran did not *say* he had nothin' for you to do!" He rubbed his chin with one hand. "In fact, I've got wood that needs cuttin', an' a beast in the outshed ready for dressin'." He pointed a finger at Lynan. "You ever dressed a beast before?"

Lynan blinked. Was the man serious? And what kind of beast? Before he could open his mouth, Ager stepped forward. "I've carved up sheep and goats," the crookback said.

Yran nodded. "Well, then, close enough to a steer, I expect. If you an' the big fellow do the dressin', an' the boy an' girl reckon they can cut all the wood into cords before it gets too busy tonight, you'll have a good meal, a comfortable bed, an' I'll even throw in a few ales in front of the big fire. If I'm in a good mood tomorrow mornin', you might even get breakfast out of it."

The companions accepted the offer, and Yran took them out back. There was a large pile of uncut wood against the rear wall, and nearby was the outshed. "You'll find the tools you need in the shed, includin' an ax an' a whetstone. Call me when you've finished."

The ax was made for someone with bigger muscles than Lynan or Jenrosa, so Kumul agreed to do the wood cutting in exchange for Lynan helping Ager with the carcass. At first, Lynan thought he had the better of the deal, but when he walked into the outshed he started having doubts. The steer had been slaughtered recently, and its hide still smelled of blood and shit. Its cut throat grinned obscenely at him, and dried gore matted the animal's fur. Seeing the massive weight hanging from a huge iron hook on the traverse beam, he realized how big a job lay ahead of them.

"I don't think we'll get this done in time," he muttered.

Ager ignored him. He opened the back of the shed and

half-pulled, half-dragged the carcass along the traverse beam until it was outside.

"Bring me the slop buckets and butchering knives," he told Lynan, and pointed to two wooden buckets in one corner with three different-sized knives in them—a heavy-bladed straight edged chopper and more finely bladed but wickedly sharp carvers. The buckets were black with grime and gore. Lynan felt like gagging, but brought the equipment with him, together with dirty white aprons he found hanging from the shed wall. The aprons covered them from neck to knee.

Ager, with a carver in one hand, walked around the beast a couple of times then nodded to himself. "Not too different," he said and stabbed the knife into the steer's groin. Lynan could not help flinching. With all his strength Ager pulled the blade down toward the neck until it met with the gash, then made quick cuts at the base of each of the limbs.

"Right, now comes the hard part," he told Lynan, and indicated he should take hold of the hide on one side of the long cut. Lynan did so, and on Ager's word they both pulled away from each other. The hide slowly, tortuously, separated from the flesh for about a hand's span. Ager then punched at the tegument connecting hide to muscle until it loosened and started peeling again; Lynan copied him on his side of the beast. Eventually the hide was taken off completely, revealing white tendon over pink muscle and ribbons of veins and arteries.

"This is what we all look like inside," Ager told Lynan merrily. "During the war I came across the remains of our scouts the Slavers had captured and skinned. They looked something like this." He patted the prince on the back. "And now comes the fun part." He used the knife again, carefully cutting around the intestines and other internal organs. The stench was overbearingly warm, as if the steer was still alive and breathing. The organs fell out together in one great glistening movement and slopped to the ground.

With great effort they unhooked the beast from the beam, and then with something like relish Ager cut off its head and quartered the body using the chopper. Then they worked at the internal organs, putting the ones that could be used for food into one bucket and discarding the others.

When day's last light evaporated, Yran came out with torches so they could continue their work. He quickly checked on their progress, seemed happy enough with it, then disappeared back into his inn, taking with him some of the offal and one of the quarters slung over his back.

An hour later, Ager, covered in sweat and flecks of fat and dried blood, finally stood up and stretched his arms. "Well, that's as good a job as Yran would manage, I dare say," he told Lynan. "We'll put this lot in the safe box and then help the others stack the cords." Lynan found the safe box tethered high in a nearby headseed tree and let it down. They loaded in the remaining quarters and offal, closed the mesh, and hauled it back up again.

"Just in time," Ager said, pointing to a mangy looking dog and one very fat porker that had come around to investigate the discarded organs.

By the time both tasks were finished, Yran had filled an old iron basin in one of the bedrooms he assigned them with hot water and next to it placed scented fatblocks and clean washers. Ager and Lynan let Kumul and Jenrosa clean first, then deliriously enjoyed wiping the gore off their own faces and hands. All the time they could smell the night's meals being prepared, and their stomachs rumbled in hunger.

They left their coats, cloaks, and swords in the bedroom and found Yran, who then led them into the main room and showed them to their table, already laden with large tankards of warm peach wine and wooden platters burdened with grain bread steaming from the oven. The room was still

largely empty, only a few travelers present and none yet of
the locals, but the main fire burned fiercely, filling the inn
with the scent of sweet-smelling resin.

The companions were thirsty and tired from hard work.
They swigged down their drinks and stuffed their mouths
with the bread.

"Swinging that ax for three hours was harder than fighting," Kumul said, pulling at his shoulder. "It's the same action again and again, and wears your bones away."

"You'll live," Ager said without sympathy, and turned to
Lynan. "I'll bet our young friend has never gotten his hands
so dirty."

Lynan felt his ears burn. "I've done hard work before."

"In the training arena, I'm sure. But this was different,
wasn't it? It's the work your servants have always done."

"Hush," Kumul warned them. "We know nothing of such
things, remember?"

But Lynan was not quite so ready to let the matter drop.
"I'm willing to learn, Ager. You should know that by now."

Ager regarded him with sudden affection, his one eye
bright. "Aye, that's true. You've never shirked from hard lessons."

Any further discussion was forestalled by Yran joining
their table with a tankard of his own and a huge jug. "The
kitchen hands can finish off the stews an' porridges, an' the
meat's crispin' nicely," he told them, refilling their drinks.
"How long have you been on the road, did you say?"

"We didn't," Kumul said carefully. "But close to three
weeks."

"You ever been to the Arran Valley before?"

"Once, a long time ago," Kumul replied. "I was a soldier
many years back, and came through here on the way north."

"Oh, aye. You had that look and walk about you, I must
say. Many soldiers have settled here over the years."

"It's a beautiful valley," Jenrosa said matter-of-factly.

Yran visibly swelled with pride, and started talking animatedly about the valley. He knew all the best streams for fishing, where the choicest fruit was grown, which farms had the best soil, and where the best rabbits could be caught. When he finished with the geography, he moved on to the valley's history. Tired from their exertions, the four visitors listened as politely as possible to family trees and accounts of great storms, but the going was heavy until Yran mentioned the valley's annexation by a king of Chandra some five centuries before.

"An' more recently, of course, Chandra's marriage to Grenda Lear."

"Recently?" Lynan objected. "It was over a hundred and fifty years ago."

Yran scratched the side of his large nose with a chipped fingernail. "Recent to some, as might be," he said reasonably. "An' the way things are goin', it might not be too far in the future before Chandra's a spinster again."

"What do you mean?" Lynan asked tightly, and Ager gently placed a hand on the youth's arm.

"Well, I've heard Tomar's naught happy with the new queen. Fact is, some in the valley are sayin' our peaches and plums would make better rulers than any of Usharna's mixed brood." Yran did not notice Lynan and Kumul stiffen, nor Ager firm his grip on the youth. "Maybe they're right, with one murdered, one drowned, one an idiot by all accounts, an' the girl on the throne untimely."

"Why is Tomar unhappy with the queen?" Ager asked.

"There's rumors of war. She's callin' in mercenaries to boost her armies, and a lot of them are marchin' through Chandra to get to the capital, which makes Tomar feel about as comfortable as a slug on a salt lick. An' then there's the accusations against General Chisal's son. The court's sayin' he did in his own brother! Poor little bastard drowned tryin' to escape, they reckon. Chisal and Tomar were friends a long time ago, an' the news hit him hard, folks say."

Lynan resisted the temptation to ask what the accusations said about him in detail, and instead said: "War with whom?"

"Why, Haxus, of course. Trust those bastards to make trouble as soon as Usharna passed on. An' if they weren't thinkin' of it then, Berayma's murder must have convinced Salokan to try his luck by now. At least, that's what everyone's mutterin'."

"But surely the queen is organizing to defend all of Grenda Lear, including Chandra," Ager argued.

"Maybe, maybe not. An' then there's that bastard from Aman makin' everyone in Chandra unsettled."

"The bastard from Aman?" Lynan asked. "You mean King Marin?"

"Lord, no, he's too far away to trouble anyone. It's his brother, the chancellor."

"The man's enough to make the dead unsettled," Kumul agreed. "But he's been chancellor for years now."

"An' never had so much influence, folks say. Look at that mountain prince he's fittin' up with the queen."

The four companions looked blankly at one another.

"You have been out of touch!" Yran declared. "King Marin's son—Sendarus!".

"What's this about Sendarus and Areava?" Lynan had met the man briefly before Usharna died, and he had seemed halfway decent back then.

"They're playin' all sweet together, and Orkid's budgin' them on for all he's worth. Accordin' to talk, the way they're goin' at it, Areava will have an heir by the end of next year."

By now the inn was filling up with customers. Yran stood to leave. Lynan wanted to hear more about the goings-on in

Kendra, but Yran waved him down. "I have work to do, lad. Maybe we can talk again later."

Soon afterward bowls of thin beef soup arrived, and before they had finished those, plates with steak rounds and baked parsnips. The four wolfed down the food, more hungry than they could have believed possible.

When he was finished, Lynan rubbed his stomach. "It is a long time since we have had such a meal," he said.

"Even longer since I enjoyed one so much," Jenrosa added, looking reasonably content for the first time since their escape from Kendra.

Lynan took the time to look around at the crowd. Some were travelers, garbed in riding leathers and dirt-stained coats and cloaks, but most of Yran's guests were locals in for a drink rather than a meal, farmers dressed in the same garb he himself had once worn to fool Ager on the night when they first met. *That was less than four months ago,* he reminded himself, *but it feels as if years have passed since then.*

Exhaustion crept over him, and he tried to shake it off. He wanted to speak to Yran again. His needed to know what was going on back in Kendra. He glanced up at his companions and saw they were equally tired. A full night's sleep would do them all good, and who could say how long it would be before they would get another one.

"Why don't you all go to bed," he suggested. "I'll stay up a while." Jenrosa nodded, but Kumul and Ager looked unsure.

"One of us should stay up with you," Kumul said. "Someone might recognize you and try something."

"I've drowned, remember? No one is looking for me anymore. And if anybody had recognized me, don't you think they would have given the alarm by now?"

Kumul could find no counter to the argument, and his body cried out for rest. "Well, don't stray outside of the inn," he warned, and then he and Ager left with Jenrosa to go to their rooms.

Lynan finished the dregs in his tankard and refilled it with the last of the peach wine. He noticed a collection of more comfortable chairs arranged in a semicircle around the main fire, all unoccupied, and left the table to claim one. Lynan found himself watching the dancing flames like a mouse hypnotized by the movements of a snake. His exhaustion returned and he tried to shrug it off, but the warmth and smell of the fire, and the peach wine, were making it impossible to keep his eyes open. He caught himself nodding off and tried sitting up, but after a moment his eyelids drooped again and his shoulders slumped forward. In the background he could hear the voices of Yran's guests merge into a single low drone, and sleep stole over him like night over day.

Lynan woke with a jerk, shaking his head to clear it. Pins and needles sparkled under his thighs and he changed position. The fire was burning low and he felt colder. His empty tankard hung from his right hand. He looked over his shoulder and saw that the inn was almost empty now. A couple of travelers were sitting together, hunched over their drinks in serious conversation, and a group of farmers were telling each other stories at another table. With relief, he noted that Yran was still working, clearing tables and sweeping the floor. He caught the innkeeper's eye, and Yran nodded back. Lynan took that as an encouraging sign and decided to wait a while longer. There was a sound on the stairs and he looked up to see Jenrosa. She came and took the chair next to his by the fire.

"Couldn't sleep?"

She shook her head. Lynan liked the way the fire reflected in her sandy hair. "It's like that sometimes, when you're so tired you can't even close your eyes."

"Especially if something is on your mind, and you've had your fair share of troubles since we met."

Jenrosa shrugged. "The truth is, things weren't going that well for me back in Kendra. I was proving to be a disappointment to my instructors."

"You couldn't do the magic?" Lynan had heard that it could take years for magickers to develop their skills and, conversely, years to discover that their latent potential was not magical at all but some other gift or ability.

Instead of answering, Jenrosa put her hands out in front of her, palm outwards, and muttered three words. The flames in the fireplace brightened noticeably, and golden sparks shot up the flue.

"I'm impressed," Lynan admitted. "I didn't know a student could do that, especially a student in the Theurgia of Stars."

The look she gave him was almost pugnacious. "You don't really think Silona was scared off by nothing more than a burning branch, do you?"

Lynan could not help shuddering at the memory of that night, but he remembered how brightly Jenrosa's brand had burned.

Jenrosa shrugged. "Party tricks, of course. I can't start a fire, for example, only increase the brightness and heat of one that already exists, and then only for a short while." Even as she said the words, the fire in front of them descended into old age again. "But my ability, for what it's worth, does stretch across several disciplines. I think that's why my maleficum and the theurgia's instructors let me stay on for as long as I did."

"You were in trouble with them?"

"I was bored with them," she said. "The pointlessness of so much of the instruction, repeated from generation to generation for no other purpose than maintaining a tradition. They are never sure which bits of their rituals and incantations actually perform the magic, so they keep it all. Can you imagine how horrifying it will be for students a thousand years from now? They'll be ninety before they graduate."

"Still, at least you had a home with them."

"Not for much longer." She turned her head to meet his gaze. "But I would rather be here right now than back in Kendra. I know it's easier to say this sitting in a dry and comfortable inn than it is in a forest inhabited by a vampire, but there you are."

Lynan nodded, not sure what to say in response, so he offered a thank you. It seemed to have the right effect. Jenrosa smiled and got up. "I think I'll be able to sleep now," she said, and left.

Lynan watched her climb up the stairs, a part of him wishing he was climbing up with her, and all the way back to her bed. However, another part told him it would be exactly the wrong thing to do just then, and he took the advice.

He was not aware at first of the figures moving behind him, but when he looked over his shoulder to see where Yran was he found himself gazing into the steady brown eyes of one of the farmers. He was a light-skinned man, past middle age, with thick gray hair twisted into tight braids. He carried a paunch still kept in some control by broad muscles. His face was a macabre collection of scars and a crooked nose. Behind him were two taller men, their faces as disfigured, their hair almost as gray; they were so similar they could have been twins.

"We told the innkeeper you were asleep, and so he's turned in himself," the first man said, and casually sat in the chair just vacated by Jenrosa. The other two stayed behind Lynan.

Lynan looked at the man blankly. "What?"

"A wonderful purifying thing, fire," the seated man said. "Did you know that in some cultures only males are allowed to start a fire, and in others women are considered the guardians of the flame?"

Lynan shook his head. He wanted to leave, but found himself cornered by his own uncertainty. *These were farmers,* that was all, he assured himself. *No reason to go screaming for Kumul. I cannot spend all my life jumping at shadows and doubts.*

"Wonderful and purifying," repeated the farmer. He cocked his head and glanced at Lynan out of the corner of his eye. "I know you, young sir, I am sure of it."

"We've never met," Lynan replied, trying to keep out of his voice the frog that had suddenly appeared in the bottom of his throat.

The man extended a hand and Lynan felt compelled to take it. "Jes Prado." He pointed to the two men behind him. "And these are Bazik and Aesor."

"Migam," Lynan returned shortly. "Are you a farmer hereabouts?"

Prado nodded. "I know your face. Do you have a brother?"

"No."

"A cousin, then?" Jes stretched out his hands to warm them by the fire.

"Possibly. I don't know all my uncles."

"Then maybe it was your father."

Lynan swallowed. "I don't think so." Shame burned his face.

Prado wagged a finger. "Now, I know there's some connection." He held a hand up. "No! No, don't tell me. I'll remember. Where are you from, Migam?"

"A village, just north of Ebrius Ridge."

"I haven't spent much time in that region, I'm afraid. No clue there. Is your father a merchant? Someone who travels?"

"No. He was a farmer. He grew wheat."

"*Was* a farmer? He's dead? I'm sorry to hear it. Did he ever buy slaves for his land?"

Lynan looked up, horrified, before he could stop himself. "No!"

"Ah, then maybe we haven't met," Prado said evenly.

Lynan stood up, but two heavy hands rested on his shoulders and gently forced him back into his seat.

"There was a man called Elynd," Jes continued. "He was much like you, Migam, if older and broader, but I can see you will fill out with time. He was husband to a great woman, but he met with a terrible accident."

"He was murdered," Lynan said sullenly, no longer seeing any point in continuing the pretense of not knowing whom Jes was talking about.

Prado shrugged. "He was a victim, Migam, a victim of a political decision." He cupped his chin in his hands and stared into the fire. "If I have it right, Elynd had a son with this woman, a son now wanted for regicide, a crime generally regarded as being even more terrible than slavery." The man laughed softly, sending a shiver down Lynan's spine. "And here you are."

Lynan tried again to stand up, but the grip on his shoulders became painful. Fingers dug under his collarbone.

"And the big one in your company must be Kumul Alarn. There are few others who would fit that description. I can't remember the names of the other two, but they're unimportant. I think the largest reward will be for you. Large enough, in fact, for me to re-form my company. What do you think of that?"

Lynan glared at the man, saying nothing.

Prado sighed, extracted a small knife from behind his belt buckle and leaned across. Lynan tried to pull away. "Bazik," Prado said, and the man holding him placed one strong hand behind his neck and used the other to cover his mouth. Lynan struggled even harder, but the second man now came and stood in front of him and punched him once under the diaphragm. All the wind in his lungs exploded from him, and his eyes watered in shock and pain.

Prado smiled disarmingly as he placed the point of his knife against Lynan's jaw, just in front of his right ear. "Rendle did not say in what condition you were to be given him, only that you were to be alive. This will teach you to answer questions from your betters."

Lynan's head exploded with excruciating agony as the small knife bit deep and dug across his jaw in a line to his chin. His cry was stifled by the hand across his mouth.

"In the old days, when I was a slaver and not a captain, I would not have marked my merchandise in so visible a place. But I have to admit it was satisfying doing that to the son of Elynd Chisal." Prado wiped the knife on his boot and tucked it back behind his belt. "Think of this as your initiation into adulthood. Welcome to a life of pain, although in your case it sadly looks like being a short life." He pulled out a kerchief and wiped at the blood streaming down Lynan's throat and neck, then forced it into Lynan's hand. "Keep it against the cut. It will serve until we have more time to do a better job."

Lynan closed his eyes and desperately tried to overcome the pain threatening to make him pass out.

Prado nodded curtly to the man holding Lynan, and he yanked his prisoner to his feet.

"Keep quiet," Bazik whispered in his ear, "or Jes will cut you again."

Prado led the way out of the inn, the other two taking Lynan. It was raining outside, and the shock of the cold made Lynan gasp. Blood and water ran down his shirt. He was pushed and dragged around the side of the inn where three horses were tied to wall stakes; full saddlebags and swords hung from their saddles.

Prado held Lynan by his hair. "You can make this ride

easy on yourself. You do what you're told and you'll be reasonably comfortable, but cross me and I'll match your new scar on the other side of your face and you'll be dragged behind like a legless dog on a lead." He patted Lynan's head and laughed. "Don't look so bloody miserable, boy, things will get a lot worse than this for you before your life is over."

"What about his friends?" Aesor asked.

"Too many for us to take on by ourselves. This is our prize." Prado mounted one of the horses and put an arm out for Lynan. Lynan hesitated and he was punched in the kidneys for his trouble. Strong hands hooked under his armpits and lifted him behind Prado. "Hold on, Your Highness; you don't want to fall off."

The other two mounted their horses. Prado gave a hand signal and the party moved silently out to the main street and then north headlong into the rain, the sound of their passing lost in the night.

20

IT had been as unexpected as it had been desired. Areava and Sendarus had been in her bedchamber discussing a future that might include the two of them together. Neither had mentioned the marrying of royal houses, or the combined destiny of two great peoples; it had been about making one life out of two, about having children, about growing old together. And then, as if predestined by God, the talk had turned to holding and passionate kissing, and finally to making love.

Afterward, when Sendarus lay sleeping with his head across her belly, she had felt the Keys of Power glowing with a bright warmth between her breasts. She traced a finger along his spine, his neck and cheek, and kissed him lightly on his forehead, then gently moved his head aside and left their bed.

She wrapped herself in a cloak and went to the window to look out over her city and her kingdom. She was not sure what it was she was searching for—a sign perhaps—but she was content to see that everything lay still under the moon and stars. It made her feel as if the universe had expected what had happened between her and Sendarus, and accepted it as part of some destiny. She turned back to her bed and silently watched her lover sleeping on, his mouth curved in the slightest of smiles, and then she saw her blood on the sheets. She was surprised there was so much, and then felt the stickiness between her own thighs.

Perhaps all great things begin with blood, she thought. *Love and birth and death. And new reigns.*

A breeze stroked the nape of her neck and she shivered. It felt like the caress of a cold hand.

Olio knew as soon as he saw his sister the next morning. He did not say anything to her but watched her and Sendarus closely during their breakfast together. The habits they had fallen into as a courting couple were still there, but changed with a new knowledge of each other. Olio wondered who else would know. Areava's ladies-in-waiting, of course, which meant the whole court would hear the news before the end of the day. That made up his mind for him. When the plates had been cleared, Olio leaned over and kissed her lightly on the cheek.

"What was that for?" she asked, clearly pleased.

Olio did not answer but smiled knowingly at the couple. Sendarus blushed.

"Is it that obvious?" Areava asked. Olio nodded. "Then it is just as well it happened with a prince," she said dryly.

"Indeed," Olio said. He licked his lips, and asked carefully: "Are you intending to go further?"

Areava and Sendarus said "Yes" at the same time.

"And when will you m–m–make a formal announcement?"

"We had not discussed that," Sendarus said.

"It is something we cannot decide by ourselves," Areava said, and sighed. "We are of royal blood. Our engagement and wedding will be state occasions. Our love is ours alone, but our marriage will be a public affair. As well, the coronation is next week. One thing at a time."

"The Twenty Houses will not like the news," Olio pointed out.

"Good," Areava said simply.

"They will accommodate themselves, surely?" Sendarus asked, still surprised the royal family had not the unstinting support of the nobility. His father, with less power and authority among his own people than Areava among hers, would nonetheless never tolerate open dissent; he would force the issue and decide it in his favor, as always.

Areava exchanged glances with Olio. "Since I have no intention of accommodating them, they will have to."

"Softly, sweet sister," Olio advised. "They are still recovering from your ascension."

"As am I," she said stiffly, her brown eyes hardening. "But they must learn the kingdom's welfare comes before their own."

"And again I say, softly. You have p–p–problems in the north, and can do without new p–p–problems here in Kendra as well."

"Haxus?" Sendarus asked. "I have not heard of this."

"Nothing has happened yet," Areava told him. "But reports from our posts in Hume indicate Haxus is moving troops to our common border. King Salokan has tried nothing yet, but may before the coronation."

"The coronation would be a good time to announce the engagement," Olio suggested. "Tomar and Charion will b–b–be here. And your father, Sendarus. It would m–m–make it a double celebration."

Areava nodded. "That makes sense. If it is to be a political event, then we must use it to best political advantage. The Twenty Houses may not like the news, but the provinces will be pleased."

"It would have been simpler had I been a scion of one of your Twenty Houses," Sendarus said lightly.

"Then you would not be with me now," Areava said

tartly. Sendarus was taken aback by the change in her voice.
She reached out and took his hand. "Forgive me. But I find
little in my uncles and cousins that amuses me."

Duke Holo Amptra found little about his niece, the
queen, that amused him. He sat on a stone seat in his garden
watching the birds in the trees bicker and fight, swoop and
peck. It reminded him of the Twenty Houses and their relationship with the Rosethemes.

*If only Usharna had had a brother, none of the Houses'
present troubles would exist. She would never have ascended to the throne, and the Keys of Power would not have
been held all together in the hands of a woman. It was not
right that so much power be concentrated in a single person.*

For a brief moment he had believed everything had been
put right with Berayma's ascension to the throne. But then
that hybrid spawn of Usharna, the despised Lynan, like his
father before him, had struck at the core of the Twenty
Houses. The fact that Lynan had drowned while trying to escape made up little for the crime he had committed. But at
least Lynan had been a true son of Kendra, unlike this foreign prince who had so easily—so casually—plucked the
new queen as if she was nothing more than ripe fruit. It
seemed to Holo that things were going from bad to worse,
and he prayed with heart and soul that on his death his son
would come into his inheritance in a world put right again.

He saw Galen enter their grand house and a moment later
appear in the garden.

"You were not at the palace for long," Holo said.

"No need to. Everyone is talking about it. The rumors are
true. Areava and Sendarus are to marry."

"When will they announce it?"

"Probably at the coronation. That is what I would do."

"It must be stopped."

Galen shook his head. "It cannot be stopped. We can do

nothing against Areava. Grenda Lear has suffered enough shocks the last few weeks, and Salokan will need little excuse to try his hand against the kingdom."

"Then *those* rumors about Haxus are true as well?"

Galen sat down next to his father. "I think we will soon be at war."

"You realize what will happen if the marriage does go ahead and there is issue."

"Yes. The royal line will be separated from the Twenty Houses, perhaps forever. Once Areava marries someone not of us, a precedent has been set."

"It is disastrous."

"Perhaps not, father."

Holo looked up at his son in surprise.

"Perhaps, father, what the royal line needs is new blood. Perhaps including the kingdom's other royal houses in our own royal line is best for Grenda Lear."

"We *made* the kingdom," Holo argued, his voice almost pleading. "It is the Twenty Houses who have always provided the kingdom's rulers, who have united almost all of Theare under one crown. We have not failed yet."

"Our family failed in one thing; our loyalty to the crown."

Holo turned his face away. "That was a long time ago. My brother was punished for his crime."

"But not the Twenty Houses. We all let him thrive, Father. He was our responsibility."

"This is not something I wish to discuss. It has been kept a secret for many years now."

"But *we* cannot afford to forget."

Holo sighed deeply. "You think Areava should marry this Amanite?"

"No. But I do not think I have the right to stop it. None of us do. And more pressure from us would only further determine Areava along her course."

"Then we are lost."

Galen shook his head. "Nothing is ever completely lost."

"The Rosethemes would put a rabbit warren to shame, and Marin's family is little better."

"I have no doubt of the couple's ability to have children. But royalty is vulnerable and always seeking support. We must bide our time and, when our support is called for, step back into our rightful place in the shield wall. We must win back our influence, not force it on Areava. You know how she will react."

"So again we must wait."

"Yes, but perhaps not for long. War has a habit of uniting the great families behind their rulers, and of binding rulers to their great families."

Somewhat reluctantly, Primate Northam had heeded the urgent message from one of his priests in the city. It was a wet, blustery day, and his cloak did little to protect him from the weather as he made his way cautiously down cobblestone alleyways made treacherous with rain. He found it ironic that on those days when weather made poor lives even more miserable, the old quarters of the city where most of the poor lived looked at its best. Under a bright sun the leaning, two-story oak-and-clinker-board houses appeared faded and dark, but rain made the wood and peeling whitewash glisten, temporarily giving them the illusion of newness and even a kind of gaiety.

There were three chapels in this quarter, and Northam prayed he was heading for the right one. It had been some time since he had last personally inspected them. The rain forced him to keep his gaze downcast and he almost passed by the chapel sign. He knocked on the door and hurried in as soon as it was open. He threw back the cowl of his cloak and immediately smelled the stained wood of the pews, a bitter smell that always reminded him of his childhood. In the background he could also smell porridge cooking, and he heard the voices of people chatting in the kitchen. Certainly nothing seemed awry.

The priest who let him in took his cloak. He was smiling.

"Your message said it was a matter of utmost urgency," Northam said. He pretended to look around. "I see no emergency." The voices from the kitchen broke into laughter. "I certainly hear no emergency."

The priest did not look remotely apologetic. "Believe me, your Grace, it is an emergency. Please come into the kitchen."

Trying to look patient rather than cross, Northam followed the priest down the hallway, through the chapel proper and into a brightly lit room. He smelled more than porridge now. Cider and bacon, as well, and fresh bread. The priest had two guests. The primate cursorily inspected their faces and then froze.

"P–p–primate Northam!" Prince Olio stood to greet him. "How wonderful you could join us."

"We will make a merry company," Prelate Edaytor Fanhow said, rising as well and shuffling sideways along his bench seat to make way for the newcomer, something made difficult by the prelate's girth.

"Your Highness! I had no idea! And Prelate Fanhow!" He looked at the priest, who was grinning from ear to ear. "This is a surprise . . ."

"God's teeth, Father, sit down," Olio ordered, and waved at the space Edaytor had made for him. The primate did as he was instructed. "We have a wonderful p–p–plan to help those in Kendra, but it needs your cooperation and . . . well, silence."

"My cooperation *and* silence, your Highness?" he asked. The priest placed a spoon and an iron bowl filled with porridge still bubbling with heat in front of him. Northam tried to hide his discomfort. He felt like a rabbit who had been invited to tea with a wolf. He looked up at Olio's smiling face. Well, a genial wolf, perhaps, but were they not the worst kind?

"Eat your p–p–porridge, man," Olio commanded. "Edaytor and I want to set up a hospice."

Northam gingerly tasted the porridge. It had been laced with honey and made him feel warm inside. He swallowed a whole spoonful. He had forgotten how good porridge could taste, especially on a cold, wet day. "A hospice? Where?"

"Right here," Edaytor said. "This is the largest of your chapels in the old quarter."

"But who would run it?"

"Ah, that's where you come in," Olio said. "We need an extra cleric. Or a lay servant if you can spare one."

"Your Highness, forgive me. As much as I admire your wish to help the poor of Kendra, one priest cannot do much by himself, especially for the seriously ill. You need surgeons for that, and in the whole of Kendra there is only one with any skill and that is Trion, and he already does what he can at his own hospice."

"That's true," Olio admitted. "But the p–p–priest would have assistance."

"Assistance? From where?"

"From the theurgia," Edaytor said. "I will supply magickers to deal with the healing."

Northam dropped his spoon in the bowl. "Magickers? Since when do magickers heal the sick?"

Edaytor and Olio looked at one another as if they were sharing a private joke. "The magickers would not be healing the sick," Edaytor continued. "At least, not by themselves."

Northam sighed. "You are playing games with me, Your Highness."

Olio laughed lightly, and his soft brown eyes seemed to shine. "Not at all. I will p–p–provide funds for the hospice to operate, and pay for any herbs and m–m–medicines it will need. And for the seriously ill, well . . ." He slowly pulled out from underneath his shirt the Key of the Heart. ". . . I will deal with them."

The primate stared at the prince for a long moment. "Your Highness, you can't be serious."

"I have never b–b–been m–m–more serious in m–m–my life."

"The Healing Key is for only the most sacred duties, your Highness."

"And what is m–m–more sacred than saving life?"

"But how do you know it will work? You've never used it . . ." His voice trailed off as he saw the expressions on the faces of Olio and Edaytor. "You have used it, haven't you?"

"A few days ago, down at the docks," Edaytor said. "The Key worked when both the prince and I used it together. We saved a man's life. Well, the Key saved his life."

"I am a p–p–prince of Grenda Lear with p–p–position and great wealth," Olio said. "And yet I have no p–p–power to assist the people of that kingdom. At least, I thought that was the case."

"You cannot spend your life down here, your Highness. You have duties in the palace—"

"I have no intention of spending all m–m–my time in the hospice. I would only visit when the m–m–most serious cases needed the power of the Key."

"You cannot heal all the sick and dying," Northam said sternly. "How will you choose who to save and who to let die?"

Olio's face darkened. "I will depend on your p–p–priest for advice on this. I know I cannot help all. The old m–m–must be allowed to die in peace, but even there the hospice can help. It will give them a place where their p–p–pain can be eased. But many die unnecessarily, from disease or accident, or worse. These I can help. These I will help. I will be a p–p–prince to them."

Northam regarded Olio with new respect and something like awe. He sighed deeply and said, "It is one of the great burdens of our calling that we cannot do more for the poor and the ailing. Since the end of the Slave War, it has some-times seemed to me that the church has been seeking a new cause to further its mission. Perhaps you have given it to us. You will have your priest."

There were no shouts of joy from the others, but Northam sensed a feeling of quiet relief. "There were two things you needed from me. The first was my cooperation. You have that, and gladly. The second was my silence. Silence from whom?"

"M–m–my sister," Olio said, as if the answer should have been obvious. "And anyone involved with the court. Can you imagine what would happen if Areava found out what I was doing?"

"She would commend you heartily!" Northam declared. "Do you doubt the queen's mercy?"

"Of course not. But she would insist on giving m–m–me an escort. People would come from everywhere to see Olio do his m–m–magic. The hospice would become a circus, not a p–p–place of healing. My p–p–part in this m–m–must be kept secret."

"But you will need some protection," Northam insisted.

"Why? Why would anyone suspect I was involved with the hospice? And if I was in any danger, there will be Eday-tor's m–m–magickers around to p–p–protect m–m–me from any harm."

"You must be discovered eventually," Northam argued.

"I m–m–must insist on this, Father," Olio said firmly. "I will do this m–m–my way."

Northam nodded, but his face showed how unhappy he was with the situation. "If you insist, Your Highness, I will keep your secret, though in the end I think it will do you little good."

Olio reached across to take the primate's much larger hand and patted it like a child comforting his father. "We will worry about discovery if and when it happens."

21

IT was a woman's scream that woke Kumul. He leaped out of bed, dressed only in his linen undergarment, and rushed into the inn's main room with his sword drawn and ready. The room was empty. He heard sobbing from the kitchen.

Ager joined him, more completely dressed and similarly armed. "Lynan's not in his room," the crookback said tersely.

Kumul cursed loudly, and together they went to the kitchen, fearing the worst. They found the body of Yran slumped on the floor, a thick pool of blood surrounding him like a halo, his throat cut from his left ear to the middle of his larynx. Ager knelt beside the body and touched the man's neck and hands. One of Yran's kitchen helpers had collapsed into a chair and was crying uncontrollably.

Kumul rushed out the kitchen door, but Ager called out: "No point, Kumul! The man's been dead for hours. His neck and fingers are stiff as bone."

Kumul ignored him.

Ager grabbed the kitchen hand by the arm. "When did you get here?"

"Not five minutes ago, sir! I started the scrubbing outside, and came in to get the saucepans and found Master

Yran lying there! Oh, God, it's horrible . . ." Her voice started rising in a scream again, but Ager shook her hard.

"Listen to me! Do you have a grieve?"

"Yes, sir."

"Then get him, and quickly. And get whoever was working here last night!"

"Yes, sir," she repeated, and scrambled out of the kitchen, her tears stopping now she had something to do.

Kumul returned, his face filled with fury. "There were three horses tied around the side of the inn, and four sets of footprints in the mud, about five hours old."

"Was Lynan's among them?"

Kumul shrugged. "I can't be sure. We should never have left him alone last night!"

"There's nothing we can do about that now."

"Jenrosa and I can carry out a wider search."

"Better get dressed first; you don't want to frighten the townspeople. By the way, I've asked the women to get the grieve."

"What if he recognizes us?"

"For God's sake, man, what if he suspects us of killing Yran? At least by helping find out what happened, we may avoid that."

Kumul looked as if he was about to argue the point, but then nodded and left to get Jenrosa. A little while later, a short, round man wearing the orange sash of a grieve entered, out of breath and flustered. He carried an old dress sword as if he did not know what to do with it. He ignored Ager and stooped over the dead innkeeper, sucking his teeth and shaking his head.

"Oh, dear. We've had nothing like this for years. And Yran of all people! Oh, dear me." He breathed through his nose like an angry bull.

"I've asked the woman who found him to bring back all

the people who were working here last night," Ager said. "They might be able to tell you something."

The grieve looked at him in surprise, as if Ager had just appeared from thin air. He quickly studied Ager's face, then his crookback, and then his face again. "Did you, my friend? Well, that was uncommonly straight thinking. And who are you?"

"A traveler. I was staying here last night with three companions."

The grieve immediately looked suspicious. "Strangers, then?"

"Strangers who want to help," Ager said quickly. "It's possible that whoever did this also harmed one of our party. He is missing from his room."

"Or did the deed and ran in fear for his life," the grieve said.

"He had no reason to do this."

"Yran was not a poor man. For some, a handful of gold coins is more than enough reason to kill an innocent."

"Then maybe you should see if any gold coins are missing," Ager countered.

The grieve shot up as if he had been kicked. "Dear me, more uncommonly straight thinking. I wonder where Yran kept his takings?"

Just then the kitchen hand reappeared, followed by some of the cooks and servers Ager had seen last night. They gathered around Yran like pups around a dead bitch, whining and lost. The grieve tried comforting them all, but his words only seemed to make things worse, and the whining turned into bawling.

"The money," Ager reminded the grieve.

The man nodded. "Lewith," he said, grabbing one young man by the shoulders. "Listen to me, Lewith. Where did your master keep his takings?"

"He's dead, Goodman Ethin," Lewith cried at the grieve. "God's pain, he's dead!"

Ethin gave the man a firm shake. "Now, Lewith, you must tell me. Where did Yran keep his takings? We have to know if his killers were thieves."

Lewith pointed under the carving table, a huge wooden block on cast iron rollers. "Under there. There's a loose floorboard."

Ager did not wait for the grieve, but pushed aside the table and squatted down. He used the point of his sword to test the boards. He found one that lifted, prized it up and put his hand down the hole. He scrabbled around for a moment then stood up, his hand holding a rusted metal box. He shook it, and all could hear could the jangling of several coins.

"It needs a key," Ager told the grieve.

"On a cord around his . . . his neck," Lewith whispered, pointing now at Yran's corpse.

Ethin hesitated, and Ager impatiently bent down by the body. He slipped a leather cord from around Yran's bloody neck and used the key on it to open the metal box. He showed everyone that it was half full of coins, some gold, most copper.

"Is this about right for a night's takings?" Ager demanded of Lewith.

"More, sir. That's easily the money from two nights' trade. He would have been taking that to Master Shellwith for safekeeping this morning."

"Master Shellwith?"

"Our magistrate," Ethin told Ager. "He has a strongbox in his office." He met Ager's stare and nodded. "So if it was not for theft, why was Yran killed?"

"To keep him out of the way while my friend was taken," Ager said. "Another of our party has searched outside the inn. There are signs there of three horses but four sets of footprints, about five hours old. Yran has been dead for about that time. You can feel his fingers if you doubt me."

The grieve shuddered. "I believe you, sir." He said to Lewith: "I want you and the others to go into the dining room. Get a good fire started. I will come and talk with you soon."

As soon as they had shuffled out, Ethin turned his attention back to Ager. "Now, my friend, why would anyone want to take your companion away from you? Is he worth a ransom? Did he owe money?"

"We come from a farming village, and we are not worth much more than the clothes we wear."

"You don't talk and act like a farmer."

"I was a soldier once, as was another of our company; but the one missing is not much more than a boy, callow and unused to the ways of the world."

"Then we come back to my question. Why was he taken?"

Ager could only shrug. He could think of no story that would convince the grieve; better to shut up and see how things played out. For a man who on first sight seemed particularly unsuitable to be a town's keeper of the peace, the man had a habit of asking the most awkward questions.

Kumul—now fully dressed—and Jenrosa came into the kitchen, their boots caked with mud past the ankle. Jenrosa's face was pale with shock. Kumul looked at Ager and shook his head. "The main road is mucked up badly after the rain, but there are three clear sets of horse prints heading north from the town." Kumul nodded at Ethin. "You're the grieve?"

Ethin nodded, obviously in awe of the man's size.

"He was about to questions the cooks and workers about last night's guests," Ager said for him.

Ethin nodded and made a move toward the main room. "That's exactly right."

Kumul grabbed the grieve by the arm. The man jumped as if he had been struck by a snake.

"God's sake," Kumul said gruffly. "I only want to ask you a question. Is there a place we can get horses around here?"

"We have two stable yards. I know Gereson has horses for sale at the present."

"What do we pay him with?" Jenrosa asked.

"Can you deputize us?" Kumul asked Ethin.

"Deputize you? Why would I want to do that?"

"To catch the bastards who took our friend and killed Yran," Kumul replied sharply.

Ethin was taken aback by the suggestion. "I've never deputized strangers before . . ."

"Who else in this town will pursue the murderers as ardently as we?" Ager asked.

"Well, no one, to be straight," the Grieve admitted. "Pursuit of dangerous criminals is not the main objective in life for farmers and shopkeepers."

"Then deputize us," Kumul insisted.

"What for, sir? You intend to go after your friend at any rate. What difference would it make to you?"

Kumul licked his lips. "Because then you can advance us the scrip for our services."

"Advance you a scrip?" Ethin looked shocked. "I have no resources for hiring deputies!"

Ager shook Yran's money box. "You have this. Advance us enough coin against Yran's estate to purchase horses for ourselves. We have none ourselves, and without them, we will never catch Yran's killers."

Ethin frowned in thought.

"Yran's death cries out for revenge," Ager added.

Ethin breathed through his nose and took the money box from Ager. He selected a handful of quarters and half-royals and gave them to Kumul.

"With that, you can buy four good horses, three for yourselves and another for your friend should you save him, but bugger the scrip. Yran had no family I know of, and I don't think he would begrudge the amount if you revenge his death. You'll find Gereson at the other end of town. While you arrange for your horses, I'll question Lewith and company and see if I can get you more information."

"I'll stay with Goodman Ethin," Ager told the others. "I'll meet you at Gereson's when I finish here."

Kumul nodded and left with Jenrosa. They found the stable yard and presented their coins to Gereson, who, for that amount, said they could choose any four horses they liked and he would throw in saddles, bridles, and packs as well. By the time they had selected four mounts, fit mares with even temperaments, Ager had joined them.

"The only visitors at the inn who were still drinking last night after Yran let his workers go included Lynan, a pair of travelers, and three farmers. The grieve found the travelers still in their rooms, and they told him that when they went to their beds, only the farmers and Lynan were left in the main room and Yran was in the kitchen. Then one of the cooks said she knew the names of one of the farmers, and that he owns land in the east of the valley, on the slopes."

"So we go there first?" Jenrosa asked.

"We follow the tracks you and Kumul found. I don't think they're heading back to the farm."

"Why not?" Kumul asked.

"Because he must have known he was recognized last night, and that the grieve would come and at least ask questions, if not actually make an arrest. Besides, the farmer's name was Jes Prado. Sound familiar?"

Kumul thought for a moment, then nodded slowly. "Never met the man, but he was a mercenary captain who fought for the Slavers during the war. Most captains on the other side took the queen's amnesty and disbanded their companies after the war and settled down somewhere. I assume Prado chose this valley."

"Well, I'll wager he's leaving the valley now. Most importantly, he's not heading south."

"So?" Jenrosa asked.

"Prado would not have taken Lynan unless he knew who he was and that he was outlaw, but he's not heading straight for Kendra to deliver his prize to Areava. That means there's more to it than we presently understand."

"Maybe Areava doesn't want Lynan to be seen in the capital," Kumul suggested. "She may think he has support there, among the commoners at least."

"Then why not kill him outright?" Ager countered. "I think there others involved, and Prado is on his way to meet them. More than that, Prado knows we'll follow him, so he won't stay on the road for long."

"Then we're running out of time," Kumul said brusquely, and mounted the horse he had chosen for himself, a large roan with a black streak on her forehead.

Before the other two had mounted, the grieve appeared. "I don't know what it is about you, Crookback, but I trust your face."

"Thanks for that," Ager said dryly.

"I won't come with you. I'm no horseman and could never hope to keep up. Find Yran's killers and, if you're able to, bring them back here for justice."

Kumul looked darkly at the grieve. "We make no promise on that, but we will do what we can."

Ager and Jenrosa mounted, and Kumul took the reins of the fourth horse. They rode north out of town, each desperately hoping that Lynan was still alive to be rescued.

Lynan slipped sideways off Prado's horse and fell to the ground. He was barely conscious, and the shock of hitting the hard earth barely registered in his fogged brain. He heard curses and then commands. Rough hands half-carried him to softer ground. He was dimly aware of an argument going on in the background. Something grabbed his jaw and pain lanced through him. His vision cleared and he found himself looking into the face of Jes Prado, his head haloed by the soft light of a damp, cloudy dawn. He moaned. He had hoped in his delirium that all that had happened to him was nothing more than a nightmare.

"I'm going to stitch you up, boy," Prado breathed into his face. "But first we have to clean your wound."

Lynan started slipping back into the fog when a thick unguent was rubbed into his cut. Again, terrible pain tore through him. There was a brief moment when he thought it was over and he could retreat back into his troubled sleep, nightmare and all, but it was only the lull before the storm. His whole body spasmed when Prado used a heavy needle and sinew to close his wound. Prado was sitting on his chest to stop him moving, and his thugs held onto his head and legs. Lynan screamed, then slipped back into unconsciousness.

He did not know how long he remained unconscious, but when he came to, he found his hands were tied to a pommel and Prado's arms were coiled around his waist. Ahead, he saw Bazik, and he could hear Aesor clopping along behind. His jaw throbbed with a terrible ache, and it felt as if it was twice its normal size. His tongue filled his mouth, and he tried to ask for water but could only manage a wheeze.

"Our friend is awake," Bazik said, looking over his shoulder. Prado only grunted.

Lynan tried turning his head to look around, but the pain in his jaw only got worse, so he twisted from the waist instead. They were following a narrow but well-worn trail that wound its way up a gentle tree-covered slope. Leaves dripped water on him. A weak sun shone from a pale blue sky through the canopy, but the light made him feel colder. He again tried asking for a drink, but was ignored.

After a while the trail leveled off and the trees started thinning out. Lynan glanced quickly at the sun and saw they were heading north. He could see the Arran Valley to his right, its broad descent ending in a patchwork of fields and orchards. To his left, the ground was largely flat and covered in long grass with occasional clumps of wideoaks and heart-seed breaking the skyline. Farther east, the horizon was lost in a green haze which he thought might be a river valley.

The Barda River, he told himself hazily. *Why are they taking me this way? We are heading toward Hume and not Kendra.*

As the day drew on, it got warmer, and Lynan's drying clothes started to tighten around him. They left the shelter of the woods and headed into the plain, making their way from copse to copse, Prado obviously seeking cover wherever he could. As the sun neared its zenith, they stopped under the shade of a group of wideoaks. Lynan's bindings were cut and he was pushed from the saddle to the ground. Prado knelt next to him and inspected his handiwork.

"You'll live. There's no infection and the stitching is holding. You won't chew for a while, though." He forced Lynan's head back and held up a flask. Water splashed over the prince's mouth, some of it spilling down his throat. He coughed and spluttered and his jaw felt as if it was splitting open, but Prado grabbed a handful of his hair and yanked his head back again, forcing him to drink more.

Bazik came over and tapped Prado on the shoulder. "Captain, you should see this."

Prado followed Bazik to the edge of the copse. They peered westward, back the way they had come. They talked urgently among themselves. Prado gave a command and returned to Lynan, forcing him to his feet with a kick to his back. Bazik and Aesor lifted him to Prado's horse and tied his hands to the pommel again. The horses were tired and needed a rest, but Prado started off at a hard canter, heading straight east.

Lynan tried desperately to match the horse's rhythm, but found he was bound so tightly to the pommel he could not lift above the saddle. He was being jolted with every fall of a hoof and the agony was too much for him to bear. He cried out, but was ignored. He tried to focus on the horizon. The valley seemed as far away as ever. He cried out again, and Prado cursed. Lynan heard a sword being lifted from its scabbard. Before he could react, Prado brought down the hilt of the sword against the back of Lynan's head, and he fell into a black pit.

Kumul kept the lead, able to maintain his mount at a brisk trot and at the same time keep his eye on the road. The others followed behind, Ager deep in thought and Jenrosa doing her best to stay in the saddle. She knew how to ride but had not had much experience of it since living in Kendra.

They rode for three hours before Kumul called a halt. "I've lost the trail," he told them. "The ground is drying and I can no longer tell the old tracks from the new." He slapped his thigh angrily.

"We should keep on, anyway," Ager said stoically.

"What if you're wrong?" Kumul asked. "What if Prado doubled back and is now heading south for Kendra?"

Ager shrugged. "There is nothing we can do about that. We must continue and hope to pick up some sign."

Kumul looked up and saw Jenrosa dismounting. "What are you doing? We can't rest yet—"

"Have you anything of Lynan's?"

"What the hell has that to do—" Kumul started angrily, but Ager waved him quiet.

"I have his sword and the coat the forester gave him," Ager said.

"Cut me a piece from the coat."

Ager unwrapped Lynan's coat from his roll and did as instructed. He handed Jenrosa a strip of cloth. Kumul opened his mouth to demand what they thought they were doing, but again Ager waved him still.

"If she is doing what I think she is doing, my friend, we will soon know in which direction Lynan is being taken."

Kumul closed his mouth and watched on impatiently.

Jenrosa squatted near the road's edge and gathered a handful of damp grass which she rubbed vigorously between her hands to dry. She then made a small mound from the grass and the cloth and withdrew a small glass from her pocket, using it to focus the sun's light onto the mound. For a long time nothing happened, and Kumul became increasingly fidgety. His horse felt his frustration and started pulling on the reins.

"The grass is still too damp," Ager said, but even as he uttered the words a thin stream of smoke started from the mound. Jenrosa chanted something under her breath and suddenly the mound was afire and blazing merrily.

"Bloody wonderful," Kumul fumed. "Now we can all roast chestnuts."

Jenrosa and Ager ignored him. When the fire burned out, she gathered the ashes in her hand and stood up. She chanted something once more and threw the ashes into the wind, carefully watching which way they scattered before settling to the ground. Jenrosa pointed east. "That way," she said.

"This is mumbo-jumbo," Kumul declared to Ager. "She is only a student magicker—"

"Kumul, which way is the wind blowing?" Ager asked him.

"From the north. What has that to do . . ." His question died in his mouth.

"And the ashes blew east," Ager finished. "There was a trail about two leagues back."

"I remember it," Kumul said, "but there were no recent tracks on it."

"Prado would have cut across from the road to the trail," Ager said. "I think that is the way we must go."

"North and then east?" Kumul asked. "Where *is* Prado going?"

Ager shrugged. "We must follow, whichever way he goes."

Kumul nodded stiffly. Jenrosa remounted and they rode back until they reached the trail. They had only followed it for a short while before it started to climb out of the valley, and they entered the beginnings of a wood.

Kumul pointed to the ground. "It is still wet here, and there are tracks of three horses, one set deeper than the others." He looked up at Jenrosa and offered a smile. "You were right."

"I'm glad I'm useful for something," she said without humor, but was surprised to find Kumul's words made her feel better.

"You forget you saved Lynan from Silona," Ager told her. "You may have saved him again."

"Not yet," she replied grimly.

The slope forced them to a slow walk, and Kumul ordered them to dismount and lead the horses to give them at least some respite from carrying their weight. Less than an hour later he stopped suddenly and studied the ground beside the trail. "They stopped here. Someone was lying on the grass. There is some blood."

"God," Ager muttered weakly. "They have wounded him."

"We must go faster," Kumul said, and mounted. He patted his horse's neck. "I am sorry, but we need your strength," he said to the mare.

The trail was still slippery from the night's rain and the going was hard, but the thought of Lynan being wounded spurred them on, and their mounts seemed to sense their eagerness. They reached the eastern lip of the valley an hour before noon and risked a ten-minute rest to give the horses a break, then went on, their pace picking up as the slope became easier and finally leveled out. By the time the sun was at its highest point they had broken through the woods and looked out over a great plain.

"That is the Barda River in the distance," Ager said. "I have sailed along it many times when working for merchants. They use barges to carry goods from Sparro to Daavis."

"Well, that answers Kumul's question," Jenrosa said.

The two men looked at her. "What question?" Kumul asked.

"Prado is heading for the river," Jenrosa said. "Ager said he must be meeting someone. What if the rendezvous is far from here, like in Hume? He can't ride the whole distance and hope to stay ahead of pursuit—he's carrying royal baggage, remember?"

Ager's eyes widened. "Of course! Why didn't I think of that? Prado is going to use the river. He'll make much greater time! If Jenrosa hadn't set us on the right trail, we would never have found out. Lynan could have been lost to us forever."

"But what rendezvous?" Kumul asked. "This is making less and less sense to me. Why risk taking Lynan if not to return him to Kendra? Who could Prado possibly be meeting? Lynan's not worth anything as hostage. Areava would pay to have him killed, not rescued."

"He might not be worth anything as a hostage," Ager said lowly, "but he's worth something as a symbol."

"What are you getting at?"

Ager shook his head. "I'm not sure yet—"

"Look!" Jenrosa cried, pointing. Kumul and Ager peered out across the plain but saw nothing. "Under those trees," she said, almost shouting.

"Which trees?"

Jenrosa moved her horse so it was standing next to Kumul's roan, and physically moved his head with her hands. "Are you blind! Those trees!"

At first Kumul noticed nothing, but after a moment he could see shapes moving in the shade of the small copse Jenrosa had found for him. He straightened in the saddle.

"That's them," he said with certainty.

By now, Ager had seen the distant figures also. "That was well seen, Jenrosa. It's hard to be sure with only one eye, but I reckon they're at least four hours' ride ahead of us."

Kumul lined up a finger with the copse, looking along the line with his right eye and then his left. He muttered a quick calculation and said: "Closer to three hours."

"They're moving," Jenrosa said. "They're riding out, heading straight for the river."

"If we get to the Barda before they find a barge, we have them," Ager said.

"The sooner we're there, the better, then," Kumul answered, and the companions kicked their horses into a ground-loping canter, trying to conserve the mares' strength for a last dash. They left the wood behind and rode out onto the plain into the light, their hopes high for the first time since they had discovered Lynan missing.

The horses beneath Prado and his men could not continue their canter for long, and Prado slowed them down to a steady walk before they were blown.

"They will catch up!" Aesor shouted.

"We will get to the river first," Prado told them. "That's all that matters. Their horses cannot continue that pace for any longer than ours."

"They could have fresher mounts," Bazik said.

"And at least ten leagues to make up," Prado angrily returned.

"But what if there are no barges at the river?" Aesor asked.

"The Barda bends sharply here, forming a steep bank. Pilots anchor there for the night. We'll find something."

"I bloody hope so," Bazik said to Aesor in a voice low enough for Prado not to hear. "I'm not keen on tangling with Kumul Alarn."

Aesor looked sourly at Bazik but did not reply. He fought the temptation to spur his horse into a gallop, but knew that if they exhausted their mounts too soon they were lost. He threw a glance at the prince, still slumped in Prado's arms like a sack of wheat, and wished he was as blissfully ignorant of events. He told himself to concentrate on staying on his horse, but could not resist looking furtively over his shoulder every few minutes; each time he looked, he was sure the enemy was closer. He saw that they alternated riding between a quick walk and a canter. Bazik was right, they had fresher mounts and were pushing them to the limit.

They were over a league from the river when two things happened. The prince jerked into consciousness and groggily sat up; the sudden shift in weight upset Prado's horse, and Prado had to pull back on the reins to stop the beast pulling to one side. Aesor cursed and for the hundredth time looked behind him.

"Prado!" he cried. "They've gone to the gallop!"

Prado savagely kicked his horse and it bucked, tossing its head high before breaking into a gallop and heading straight for the river, with Bazik and Aesor close behind.

Lynan had no idea what was happening, and all he could make out was the green blur of the plain and the smell of fresh water somewhere up ahead. His captors were in full flight, and he could tell from the rigid expressions on their faces that they were afraid. A deep recess in his mind figured out his friends might be the threat, but he had not the strength or the will to do anything about it. He tried closing his eyes to regain some kind of clarity, but the effect made him feel so unbalanced he had to open them again.

They were riding between trees now and their pace slowed. Lynan heard shouts behind him, distant and carried on a breeze. He recognized Kumul's rumble and tried to shout back but could manage only a croak. The horse swerved to avoid a thorn tree, galloped forward again, then came to a halt when Prado pulled back on the reins. It stamped its feet and shook its head, foam whipping from its mouth.

Lynan could see a river about fifty paces ahead, and what looked like two broad-beamed boats at anchor near the bank. Bazik and Aesor appeared next to them, and Prado shouted, "Now! Our last chance!"

They spurred their horses forward again. Just before they reached the bank, Bazik and Aesor dismounted. Aesor ran to the barge on the right, the smaller of the two, and Bazik to the one on the left. Prado dismounted and took the reins of all three horses. Again, Lynan heard Kumul's battle cry.

"Kumul!" he shouted, but it was a weak call, and only Prado heard. The mercenary lifted a foot and kicked the prince in the knee. Lynan cried out in pain and twisted sideways, only his binding keeping him in the saddle. He heard shouts in front of him and then screams. Prado used his sword to cut the rope and free Lynan's hands, then hauled him off the horse. Aesor reappeared and pulled on Lynan's hair until he stood up.

"Move!" Aesor ordered, and shoved him from behind.

Lynan tottered forward, carefully moving one foot in front of the other to keep himself from falling over. He reached the bank, and rough hands directed him to a plank, then guided him across. He felt the world shift under his feet and he remembered the last time he had tried to board a boat. "Oh, no . . ." he groaned, but before anything could happen he was manhandled aboard and pushed to the bottom. He tried to raise his head and received a punch in the face for his efforts. His jaw seemed to explode and he screamed. He heard the neighing and stamping of the horses as they were led on board. Twice, hooves missed his head by no more than the width of a finger. Prado was shouting orders and he felt the boat move out onto the water. Kumul's cries were now closer than ever.

"Kumul . . ." Lynan tried again to lift his head, but it felt as if it weighed more than all the stone in Kendra's palace.

Then he heard a loud crack, and he rolled on his back. A white sail flurried, fluttered, and then filled above him, and Kumul's voice trailed behind and was eventually lost.

Kumul waited until he was sure the horses could make the distance, then lifted his head and shouted the war cry of the Red Shields, kicking his mount to the gallop. Ager and Jenrosa matched him. Kumul drew his sword and leaned over the saddle to hold it forward, parallel with the horse's head; he had seen enough enemies peel away from him in a charge to know how formidable a sight he made in full flight, and he hoped it was enough to make Prado and his men panic and do something stupid.

They had obviously seen him, for they whipped their own horses to a gallop. It was now a race to the river, and Kumul realized with horrible certainty that unless something happened to stop them, the mercenaries with their prize would win the race easily. His heels dug into the roan's flanks, trying to urge more speed from her tired muscles, but her head was beginning to sag and he knew she could give no more. Ager and Jenrosa had started to fall behind.

In fury and anger he shouted his war cry again and again. He saw the enemy disappear behind the trees of the river when he was still five hundred paces from them. The next minute was one of the longest in his life. He started pulling on the reins when the first trees whisked by him, and he looked for a clear passage to the river. He heard the sounds of fighting ahead and to his left, and he jerked the mare toward them. The vegetation grew more dense and at last he had to dismount. He started to run, tripped over a root, picked himself up, and rushed forward again. He burst through the last ring of trees and bushes and saw a barge starting to pull away from the bank, Prado with his men and horses aboard. He could not see Lynan, and a cold fear clogged his throat. He sprang forward, but by the time he reached the bank the barge was in mid-stream and the sail was unfurling.

He noticed the second, smaller barge and ran toward it, then stopped in his tracks. A man lay dead on the bank, his head split open from forehead to chin, and beside him were a snapped rudder oar and the torn remains of the barge's sail.

"God's death, no!" he cried. "Lynan!" But as he got closer he realized the dead man was too big for his prince.

Ager ran by him and knelt down next to the corpse. "A pilot," he said grimly. He stood up and pointed at the retreating barge. "They still have him," he added.

Joined by Jenrosa, they looked out over the river and watched the receding barge until all they could glimpse was the top of the sail, and soon that, too, disappeared from sight.

22

COLD water splashed over Lynan's face, and he woke with a start. The first thing he noticed was that the pain in his jaw was reduced to a dull and constant background ache; the terrible throbbing had eased, and when he realized it was night and the sky really *was* dark, he knew his sight had finally returned to normal. Prado stood over him like the remains of his last nightmare, a bronze ewer in one hand.

"Well, at least you're still alive," Prado said levelly, and then ignored him.

Lynan moved experimentally and found his arms and legs reluctantly but surely obeyed his orders. He stood up slowly, letting himself get used to the gentle swaying of the boat. It was not as bad as he remembered, but last time he had been at sea and this time the vessel was sailing over nothing more dangerous than the quiet waters of the Barda River. The boat was loaded with bales of what looked like flax and hay, and his captors' horses were tethered to the single mast. Aesor was sitting in the bow and Bazik amidships with the horses. He himself was at the stern with Prado, and next to him was a man by the rudder. The stranger sported a nasty gash on the forehead. Lynan saw the blue stripe on one of the man's sleeves, and realized this was the barge's pilot.

He was a short, thin man with golden skin and hair as dark as the night; a Chett, Lynan dimly realized.

"Welcome, sleepy one," the Chett said in a deep singsong voice, and offered a faint smile. His right foot rested on a pedal leading to the rudder oar, and his hands held sheets that led through a complex of pulleys to the sail.

"My name is Gudon," he said. "What is yours? Ouch!"

"If you don't want to be kicked again, cut the questions," Prado ordered.

"A timely reminder to keep my mouth shut. Thank you, beneficent master."

Lynan did not know if Gudon was being sarcastic or not; nor, by his expression, did Prado. Gudon stared out over the river, looking blameless.

"Where are we going?" Lynan asked Prado.

Prado ignored him, but asked Gudon: "How far from Daavis?"

"Two days to Daavis, master, with a good wind. With no wind, it will be four days or more. With a bad wind, at least seven. With a really bad wind—"

Prado cut him off. "Fine, whatever. Just make sure we're there in two days, or I'll finish splitting open your head and then I'll throw you into the river." He tapped the hilt of his sword for emphasis.

Gudon nodded eagerly. "Oh, yes. Do what I am told, make the wind obey me, and get you to Daavis in two days. Otherwise I get the point."

"Watch them both carefully," Prado ordered Bazik, and moved forward to talk with Aesor.

Gudon glanced down at Lynan. "You are not a villain, then?" Lynan shook his head. "And are you getting off at Daavis?"

"Enough talking," Bazik snapped from amidships. He jabbed a finger at the pilot. "You tend to the steering, and you," he said, jabbing the same finger at Lynan, "you just keep quiet."

Lynan rested against the stern rail. He gingerly touched the side of his face and was surprised how thick the stitching and weal running from his right ear to his jaw felt. He wondered what he had done to deserve it, having only vague memories of his first conversation with Prado. Had it only been the night before? It seemed so distant in his memory now. He saw Prado cut into one of the bales of hay and spread it around for the horses to eat. Watching him, Lynan realized that for the first time in his life that he hated someone so much he would gladly kill him and not regret it afterward.

The wind changed direction from northerly to nor'easterly. Gudon expertly jiggled the sheets so the barge's sail would stay full, but the hull slipped sideways for a moment before righting itself. The horses neighed and stamped, and Bazik and Aesor rushed to help Prado calm then.

Lynan saw Gudon smile at him and he wondered if the barge's slide had been entirely accidental. "Is your wound all right?" he whispered while his captors were distracted.

"Oh, yes, master. I've applied my haethu potion to it, and all will be well."

"Haethu potion?"

"A wonderful thing. It heals small wounds, adds spice to sauces, flavor to water, and if you slip it in a girl's drink, she will fall in love with you and become more fertile than all the seas in the world."

"Where are you from, Gudon?"

"From the river, little master. Always."

"But you are a Chett."

"Truth. But I was a traveler in my youth, and journeyed far from the Oceans of Grass. When I first saw this noble water you call the Barda, I was born again. So I say to you, I come from the river."

"What tribe are you from?"

"The tribe of the pike and the trout, the silver belly and the fly-catcher, the yellowtail and the carp."

Lynan pursed his lips. "You come from the river."

"Truth," Gudon said, still smiling. "And where do you come from?"

Lynan sighed. "It might as well be the river," he said despondently.

"Then we are brothers, you and I," Gudon said. "And to prove it, we will both wear scars on the face."

"Thanks to Jes Prado."

"Thanks to destiny."

"How far, really, to Daavis?"

"Are you so eager to get there?"

"No."

"Then maybe forever," Gudon said mysteriously. Before Lynan could ask what he meant, the pilot nodded toward Bazik, coming to the stern now that the horses were settled. "Watch the river, little master, and watch the banks that glide by like dreams. There are worse ways to spend your time."

His heart eased somehow by his strange conversation, Lynan was able to ignore Bazik's glowering presence. He took the pilot's advice and stared out over the river, its wide curves a glistening road under the moonlight. Lynan wondered if it was a road with an end, or if was just one more way to the next disaster in his life. He remembered Kumul's voice a few hours before, calling after him as the barge pulled away from its anchorage, and he hoped his friends were all safe. He had not known before the strength of his feelings for them. A part of him wished they would stop following him, afraid for their safety, but another part—the stronger part, he realized guiltily—desperately wanted them to find him and free him from Prado's grasp.

As the night wore on, Prado ordered Bazik to get some

rest and kept watch at the stern himself. Lynan squatted down against the hull and tried to sleep, but without success. His jaw still troubled him enough to keep him awake, and his apprehension grew as the hours passed and the barge made its slow but steady progress upriver toward Daavis. His only consolation was that he was being taken farther from Kendra, and closer to the Oceans of Grass. If he could manage to escape, he might yet find sanctuary of a kind among the free Chett tribes that wandered the plains astride their tough ponies, moving their great herds of cattle from one feeding ground to the next.

Soon after midnight, Bazik relieved Aesor on the bow, and an hour before dawn Aesor relieved Prado at the stern. Aesor was still tired, and as Gudon started singing in a low voice, he angrily told the pilot to shut up.

"But your master has instructed me to reach Daavis in two days. I must sing to the wind to keep it true and steady."

Aesor grumbled something, but said nothing more as Gudon resumed his singing. It was more like a lullaby than anything else, and Lynan found himself finally drifting off to sleep. Then Gudon's foot tapped him softly in the ribs.

"What is it?"

"Our guardian has joined his dreams again," Gudon said, nodding at Aesor slumped against the bales. "The other one will not hear us talk if we speak as quietly as the river."

"You weren't singing to the wind, were you?"

"Oh, yes. But some songs are meant to slow down the wind. I need to warn you, little master."

"Warn me?"

"Do you wish to leave the company of these villains?"

"Very much."

"I have a plan, but it will be dangerous for both of us."

"Dangerous? How dangerous?"

Gudon shrugged. "Can you swim?"

"Yes, but not quickly."

Gudon frowned. "Do you think, if you had reason to swim quickly, you could learn?"

"What reason?"

"I am thinking it is best you do not know yet."

"When must I learn?"

"Soon. Before the sun is fully up. Before the beneficent master is awake to stop us."

"Us?"

"Truth. It is time for me to leave the river. I have a need to travel again."

"You would do this for me? Why?"

"There are signs, little master. We are both wounded in the head. We are both prisoner. We both wish to avoid the fate the beneficent master has in mind for us, for I do not believe he will let me live after you reach Daavis. And the river is telling me it is time to go. I listen to its waters very carefully. I told you before, it is destiny."

"Destiny hasn't served me too well up to now."

"Ah, but destiny serves no one. She has her own secrets, her own plans, and although we may sometimes read them, we may not change them."

Lynan noticed the barge was edging closer to the shore.

"You are going to beach the barge?"

"I could, but then the others would just pursue us, and on horses they would catch us."

Lynan remembered Gudon's questions about his ability to swim. "We are going to dive overboard and swim to the shore?"

"Yes, but not yet. It is not dangerous enough. Otherwise, the others would then beach the barge and still be able to pursue us."

"I'm not sure I like the sound of your plan."

"It is a good plan, little master, with only small problems."

"What small problems?"

Gudon pointed to the left bank about sixty paces away. "Those small problems."

Lynan stood, and in the soft pink light glowing in the eastern sky he could make out drooping spear trees and tangle weeds.

"I see nothing dangerous."

Aesor snorted and his eyes fluttered open.

"That is because you do not see properly," Gudon answered quickly, pushing the rudder away from him and drawing back on the left sheet at the same time. The barge swung noticeably toward the spear trees.

Aesor snorted again and stumbled to his feet, blinking. His action woke Prado in turn, who stood up and stretched his arms above his head. He looked out over the river, turning in a circle. He saw how close the left bank was and gave an order for Gudon to veer away. Gudon ignored him.

"You heard the captain!" Aesor roared. "Bring us back to the middle of the river!"

Again Gudon ignored the command.

Aesor started drawing his sword. Gudon kicked hard at the rudder pedal and yanked back on the sheets. The boat lurched as its stern swung out and Aesor lost his footing. Lynan did not hesitate. He lashed out with his right foot, connecting with Aesor's head. The man grunted and collapsed. Lynan reached for the sword and stood up in front of Gudon.

"I pray to God you know what you are doing, Pilot."

"Just one god?" Gudon asked, keeping his eye on the spear trees on the bank. "You should be more generous, little master."

By now Bazik had joined Prado, and together they advanced toward Lynan, their swords drawn.

"Come on, boy, don't be a fool. You can't take on both of us."

"I can," Lynan said with more confidence than he felt. In

an open arena, with his own weapon and without a jaw that
throbbed in pain, he was sure he could have taken on the two
thugs. Right now, however, he was not sure he could take on
an angry rat and win. He was relying on Gudon's plan coming up with a real surprise in the next few seconds.

The barge drove into the overhanging branches of the
spear tree. The ends of several of the branches disappeared
beneath the surface of the river and offered more resistance
before finally giving way to the barge's momentum. They
whipped up and over the gunwales, and Lynan saw large
boles attached to each of them, with white stolons growing
from them that seemed to wave like tendrils. Many of the
boles flew up so rapidly they tore from the branches and
arced over the barge. Prado and Bazik watched them pass
and then splash into the water on the other side. Lynan saw
several of them split open, releasing seething black masses
that quickly disappeared beneath the surface.

Lynan quickly looked over his shoulder at Gudon.
"They're not—"

"Yes! Jaizru!" Gudon shouted before he could finish the
question.

Lynan felt his blood run cold. He knew he had to find
cover, but was paralysed by fear. Gudon pushed him hard in
the back and he fell to the deck, the pilot on top of him. He
heard sounds like whole sheets of linen being ripped apart,
then the soft thwacks of things landing on the deck, and on
the bales and on the horses. And then the screams started,
coming from the horses and, he thought, Bazik.

"Now!" Gudon shouted in his ear, and stood up, dragging
Lynan with him. Gudon pulled him to the port side. Lynan
caught a glimpse of thin black strips of wriggling eels with
wide, dark red fins. Most were gaping on the deck, but many
had landed on warm flesh and were using their small mouths
filled with needle-sharp teeth to rip and tear. Prado was
dancing a macabre jig, trying to shake off one that had

latched onto his sword arm. Bazik was writhing in his own blood on the deck, covered in four or five of the eels, one of them gorging in his eye socket. The horses were bucking and kicking, trying to break loose from their tethers around the mast.

"Jump!" Gudon ordered, and half-lifted him over the gunwale. The prince fell over and down. The cold, dark water punched him in the chest and face. He kicked furiously, broke the surface and sucked in lungs full of air. He saw Gudon's face looking down at him.

"Swim for the bank!" Gudon shouted. "As fast as you can! Get out of the water!" Then Gudon disappeared.

Something bit at his hair. He screamed and splashed, swallowed water, spun in a circle. He caught a sight of the bank and swam toward it. Teeth punctured his boot and scratched his skin. He furiously shook his foot and lost his rhythm. Teeth bit into his knee—it felt as if he had been stabbed with a fork. He wanted to scream a second time, but managed to keep his mouth closed and start swimming for the bank again. He was bitten on the hand, under the armpit, on the groin. A low keening forced its way out between his teeth. He knew he could not take much more of this. His hand touched something beneath him and he jerked it away, but then his other hand touched something as well. It was soft, yielding, and he realized it was mud. He brought his feet down, took three strides and heaved out of the river.

A jaizru flapped by his face, its fin touching his cheek, and it landed on the grass about three paces in front of him, writhing as it asphyxiated. Another one smacked into his back. He ran, waving his hands about his head in panic. He slipped, got up and slipped again, and could do no more. He curled up into a ball and waited for the next attack, but after several seconds none came and he slowly looked up. He was at least twenty paces from the river, and the eels could not glide that far. A dozen of them were wriggling uselessly on the ground halfway between him and the bank, their white teeth glistening moistly in the dawn light.

Lynan started shaking uncontrollably. He tried standing, but his legs would not support him. He ended up sitting on the grass, and then he remembered Gudon. He could see the barge, rocking from side to side as the horses, which had now torn loose from their tethers, skittered and slid across the deck. They seemed to be covered in hundred of black streaks. Blood streamed down their flanks and heads. One went down, and then a second. He heard the pitiful whinnying of the dying beasts. He saw no sign of Gudon, or Prado and his men. After a while the barge settled and a dreadful silence settled over the river.

Two horses? he thought suddenly. *But there were three . . .*

He managed to get to his feet. He wiped his face with a hand and noticed it was bleeding. A savage, serrated cut jigsawed across his palm. He felt no pain, only a strange numbness. He checked his feet and legs, and saw that he was bleeding in at least four other places.

He walked to the bank, making sure to stay out of range of the flying eels, although the water was perfectly still now. He called out Gudon's name, but there was no answer. He edged toward the clump of spear trees, crouching down to peer among the branches that hung above the river. There was no sign of his savior. He called out his name again, and this time heard a weak reply. He glanced around but saw no one.

"Gudon?" he cried out, louder this time.

Once more, a weak reply. He was sure it had come from his left. He hurriedly made his way along the bank. There was a small copse of thorn trees in the way, and as he circled around it, he heard a man's voice coming from amid the thickets.

"Gudon?"

"Truth, little master, that was worse than I thought it would be."

Lynan pulled away some of the branches, ignoring the cuts they made on his skin. The pilot was lying, bleeding from several bites. His eyes were fluttering. In one hand he held a leather bag which he was trying to draw to himself.

"I had no idea the spear tree held so many nests."

Lynan knelt down beside him. Many of Gudon's wounds were as slight as his own, but the damage around his right knee was horrific; he could see the white of bone.

Gudon tapped the bag. "Inside. My potion."

Lynan lifted the bag and opened it. Inside was a small wooden bottle with a cork stop wired into place.

"My haethu," Gudon said weakly. "Pour a little on my knee."

Lynan untwisted the wire, pulled out the cork with his teeth, and carefully spilled a few drops on the wound.

Gudon flinched and shouted between clenched teeth. "All the gods! I have never felt so much pain!"

Lynan replaced the cork and resecured the wire. "What are you doing in here?"

"It was the only place I could drag myself to that would protect me from the eels." He pointed and Lynan saw several of the fish impaled on the branches.

"Things have quieted down," Lynan said. "I will pull you out of here."

Gudon laid a hand on his arm. "Not yet. Let the haethu do its work. You must find the horse."

"Horse? You managed to get one off the barge?"

"Oh, yes. I mounted one and it was in such a panic it was easy to make it jump over the side. I had to keep tight control of it or it would have bit and kicked furiously at the jaizru and drowned. Unfortunately, it meant I could not move my legs from around its girth. I am paying for that now."

"Where is it?"

"As soon as we reached the bank, it threw me and ran off. You must find it, otherwise we will have to walk, and truth, little master, all the haethu I own will not help me do that for a long, long while."

"I will build us a shelter and you can rest—"

"No, no. We must leave here as quickly as possible. When the villains do not arrive in Daavis, someone may come looking for them."

Lynan had not thought of that. "Wait, then. Which way did the horse run?"

Gudon smiled thinly. "I was in no condition to see. Away from the river."

Lynan nodded, gingerly withdrew from the thicket, and searched the ground near the bank. He found the horse's hoofprints easily and started to follow them. Ahead the land began to rise, gradually at first, but more steeply in the distance until it reached a crest covered in thick woods about five league away. He was praying that the horse had not run that far when he heard a soft whinny. He stopped, looked around, and saw the horse to his right, no more than a league from him. As he got closer, it looked up at him nervously but stayed where it was, occasionally lowering its head to crop at the grass. Lynan took his time and made his final approach a step at a time, making soft, reassuring sounds, his hands held out palm upward. The horse must have decided it wanted human company again, for it closed the last twenty paces between them and snuffled his hands for a reward.

"Nothing this time, I'm afraid, but if you carry me and my friend to safety, I promise you all the sweet hay I can buy."

The animal was covered in dozens of small bites, but a cursory inspection showed nothing too serious. He wondered if Gudon's haethu worked on horses. He took the reins and started to lead it back toward the river. At first the horse walked behind him without trouble, but as it smelled the river getting closer, it started pulling back and eventually refused to go any further. Lynan tugged experimentally, but only succeeded in losing the reins. The horse retreated a few steps and stopped.

Lynan glanced toward the rising sun. He would have to carry Gudon here to the horse. He cursed softly under his breath.

Orkid found it both amusing and satisfying to see Areava and Sendarus together in public. Amusing because no matter how hard they tried to keep their attention on whatever matter was at hand, in this case a public reception for the capital's leading commercial lights, they could not keep their eyes off each other for longer than a minute, and satisfying because their love for each other represented the culmination of all his work since arriving in Kendra as a young man. The lovebirds' plan to announce their intention to marry at Areava's coronation was the worst kept secret in the kingdom, and while the reaction from most of the members of the Twenty Houses could best be described as thinly veiled hostility toward Sendarus, the rest of the court seemed pleased by it, and as far as the rest of the citizenry was concerned, it was the only bright news after the black weeks just passed.

Sendarus' own generous nature and good looks helped the cause a great deal, of course. It was hard not to like him, and those who might otherwise have been opposed to their queen marrying outside of the Twenty Houses found themselves won over to the extent they became enthusiastic supporters of the union. People such as Shant Tenor, for example, whose prejudice was renowned, could not help clinging to the Amanite prince like a limpet to a rock. Tenor kept on talking about the commercial advantages of closer ties between Kendra and the provinces, something that would have been anathema to him only weeks before.

Others, such as Xella Povis, were more circumspect about the idea of the marriage, but were canny enough to keep their opinions to themselves and make the best of it.

Then there were those like Primate Giros Northam, even now talking with the queen and Sendarus, who would support Areava in all things. That Northam was a good man, Orkid did not doubt, but he was also wise enough to see that the queen was his church's most valuable supporter. Although the poor would always pray, in a kingdom where simple faith struggled against the more obvious and demonstrative powers of magic, royal approval gave it greater currency and respect among the nobility, especially among those eager to display their loyalty to the throne by paying some kind of obeisance to Northam's god. Orkid was less sure of Father Powl, Northam's right hand man. He was a small, thin man with a ready smile but eyes as hard and gray as steel. As Areava's confessor, his standing had improved recently, but Orkid had been told by Usharna that Northam had not nominated Powl as his successor. Orkid suspected this was because of Usharna's express wish, and Northam had complied. According to the church's dictates, only Northam and his nominated successor could know the true name of their god; did Father Powl expect to hear it still, or did he know he was not destined for the primacy? There might be another lever there for Orkid to pull.

The royal group was joined by Magicker Prelate Edaytor Fanhow. He and Northam exchanged a courteous greeting. Orkid had always thought Usharna's greatest achievement as queen was to ensure the church and the malefici were allies and not rivals. By giving the church her protection and by maintaining her authority over the prelate's office, she made sure both powerful factions were supporters behind her throne instead of enemies bickering in front of it. A split between them would give the enemies of Rosetheme a dangerous lever, and Orkid would do everything in his power to make sure that would never happen.

The chancellor wandered around the reception, fending off a flock of flatterers and pleaders with well-practiced blandishments, studying the reactions of those near Areava and Sendarus. Hovering over the royal couple was the ever present shadow of Dejanus, his face fixed with his usual quizzical half-smile, his eyes alert for any threat to the queen. For one moment the gaze of Orkid met that of Dejanus, and the chancellor felt the wary coolness there. Well enough, he told himself. We know too much about each other to be enemies, but we will never be friends. It was better that way, Orkid knew; it was so much harder to eliminate a friend.

The thought had come unbidden to his mind and he faltered for a second. His hangers-on stumbled around him. He smiled at them easily, apologized, and pretended to give them half an ear, but his mind was backtracking to find out from where the thought had arisen.

His gaze fell to his hands, the same hands that had held down Berayma's arms as Dejanus had stabbed the king in the neck. Orkid had been overwhelmed by the amount of blood. The room had filled with a stinking lake of it. And yet he had felt no remorse. He had never liked Berayma, and the greater cause had fortified Orkid for over twenty years, so the act itself—with all its gore—was more like an ablution than a murder. He could as easily have done the same to that whelp Lynan. But what of the other two surviving children of Usharna?

He gaze lifted again to Areava, and for a moment he thought he was seeing the old queen as she had been two decades before. His heart jumped a beat. Yes, he liked Areava a great deal, could even learn to adore her as he had her mother, but there was something more about her that stirred something deep inside of him. With some guilt he realized it was a pang of jealousy, jealousy toward his own nephew. The understanding shocked him, and he turned his thoughts to Olio.

The shy prince had changed over the last few weeks, become stronger and more confident. He was still cursed by his awful stammer, but his manner had more authority in it now. Was it the Key of the Heart that was transforming him, or his sister's need for support? Orkid liked Olio, always had, but wondered if the time was coming to be afraid of him. Olio had always been a fervent believer in Grenda Lear being more than Kendra and its self-interested Twenty Houses and merchants, and Orkid had long looked on him as an ally, but a more assertive prince working in the same court as Areava and Sendarus could prove harmful to Aman's long term interests. Yes, Orkid told himself, he would have to keep a careful eye on the young man.

Speaking of which, where was he today? Orkid looked around the hall, finally discovering him by the knot of minor officials clustering around him to get his attention. Not long before, Olio would have been flustered by all the attention, but now handled such situations with calmness and almost infinite patience. Even as Orkid watched, he extricated himself from the group and made his way to his sister. Olio and Areava exchanged a few words, then he bowed and left, taking Edaytor Fanhow with him.

Those two have been spending an unusual amount of time together, Orkid thought. *Whatever do they find to talk about?*

As soon as Olio was out of hearing of his sister, he asked the magicker what news he had of the hospice.

"It is ready, Your Highness," Edaytor said, smiling broadly. "Primate Northam has been as good as his word. There are ten beds for the sick, and he has assigned another priest to the chapel to care for them full-time. I have already recruited several magickers to play their parts."

"Now all we need are the sick themselves."

"The priests will take care of that for us. They visit the poor regularly, and will bring those most in need to the hospice for treatment. It will not be long before the sick come of their own accord."

"Will ten b–b–beds be enough?"

"For the worst affected. But the primate is now thinking of building a dispensary that can deal with less serious cases."

Olio nodded. "This is much better than I expected. At last I can do something for my own people."

Edaytor put a finger to his lips in thought, but hesitated to speak.

Olio sighed. "Out with it, sir."

"I am still concerned about how the healing will affect you. You know how tired you were after the first time."

"Surely, as we gain more experience in this, the healing will become easier."

Edaytor shrugged. "This is new to me as well, Your Highness. Truly, the more one practices magic the easier it becomes, but the Key is no ordinary talisman. I remember how weak your mother was after she healed the crookback."

"But she was old and ill herself."

"Undeniably, but nonetheless neither of us is sure that continued use of the Healing Key will not have some deleterious effect."

"I will be careful," Olio assured him.

Edaytor heard the excitement and eagerness in the prince's voice, and wondered if being careful would be enough. He would have to instruct his magickers to make sure Olio did not overextend himself.

* * *

There were plenty of barges heading down river, but it was not until well after dawn that Jenrosa sighted the first sail heading in the opposite direction. She called the others, and as the barge came into view they waved their arms and shouted. The pilot waved back and continued on his way. They were still cursing him when a second barge appeared sailing upriver, and they repeated the demonstration. This time the pilot, a short, thickset woman, steered closer to the bank. She looked warily at the giant Kumul and the crookback Ager.

"What is it you want?"

"Passage!" Kumul cried out. "And some food!"

The pilot surveyed them and their four horses for a moment and replied: "How much do you offer?"

"We have no money, but can give you one of our horses for payment," Kumul shouted.

The pilot considered for a moment, then brought the barge close enough to drop her anchor and push out two planks to touch the shore. As they started leading their horses aboard, she told Kumul she was going no farther than Daavis.

"That will suit us," he said grimly. He had no idea how far upriver Prado was intending to take Lynan, but getting to Daavis would at least give them a chance to catch up some of their lost ground.

They tethered the horses to the central mast and then helped bring in the planks and anchor.

"You're carrying a light load," Ager observed.

"I make my profits the other way, carrying ore to Sparro. This consignment will cover my costs." She nodded at the horses. "And on this trip one of those will bring me a profit."

The pilot seemed disinclined to talk, so the three companions found spaces for themselves among the bales and boxes up forward.

"How will we find Lynan again?" Jenrosa asked.

Kumul shrugged. "We reach Daavis and make inquiries there about the barge he was taken on. If it did not stop there, then we follow the Barda upriver until we discover some clue to his whereabouts."

"What if they backtrack?"

"There is nothing we can do about it," Kumul said gruffly. "We do what we can."

"I think Prado was in too much of a hurry to get to his destination to try anything so clever," Ager said. "My bet is he's heading for Daavis, either to meet someone or as a staging post for a ride north into Hume."

"This just gets stranger and stranger," Jenrosa said. "They are taking Lynan farther away from anyone who cares if he is alive or dead."

"Queen Charion would probably appreciate having him," Ager said, thinking aloud. "If she turned him over to Areava, she could not help but gain leverage in the court in her trade disputes with Chandra."

"Then all is lost," Jenrosa said gloomily. "They will get to Daavis before us, and that is Charion's capital."

Kumul looked up suddenly, and said carefully: "Or Prado is taking him to Haxus."

"To King Salokan?" Ager looked dumbfounded. "What would Salokan do with the son of his worst enemy?"

"Slay him!" Jenrosa said, horrified.

Kumul shook his head. "No. Ager said it before, and I should have seen it then. Lynan may not be simply a hostage, but a symbol."

"What are you talking about?" Jenrosa asked.

"King Salokan's no fool, and he has his spies in Kendra, as we do in his court at Kolbee, so will know what has happened over the last few weeks. He will use Lynan as a weapon against Grenda Lear, set him up as a pretender and invade the kingdom. Many will flock to Salokan's banner then, or at least offer only halfhearted resistance."

"That is not so different from what we intended," Ager said.

"Of course it is different!" Kumul said vehemently. "Our intentions were to bring the kingdom to its senses, to see Lynan reinstated and Berayma's real murderers caught and punished. Salokan wishes the kingdom harm, and would not hesitate to use Lynan to bring it about. He cares nothing for what is right, or for the justice in this matter. We do!"

Jenrosa was taken aback by Kumul's fierceness, and could not help wondering if he had been speaking as much in his own defense as that of Lynan's cause, and in turn it made her think about the conflict going on inside his heart. Kumul was—still was, in his mind, she was sure—Constable of Grenda Lear, and it was his duty to put things right in the kingdom. She wished she could have some of his nobility of purpose, but for her the goals were more immediate: to rescue Lynan. It occurred to her then that she and Kumul had more in common than she would have thought possible. She studied the giant more carefully, and for a moment thought she could see the man beneath the constable's livery and responsibilities. His regard for Lynan was due more than his loyalty to the youth or to the memory of the general. He was more like a father to Lynan than a guardian, and he was fighting for his son's life

That insight made her understand at last how she regarded Lynan. He seemed like a brother to her, and not a lover. Did that make Kumul her father, then? The thought made her smile. No, not a father. Something more perhaps, something she could not yet describe nor properly give voice to. She blushed involuntarily and turned her gaze out over the river. These were the stirring of feelings she did not ever properly understand herself.

Ager lay down on the deck and shaded his eyes from the sun. "Well, there's no point in worrying about what to do next until we reach Daavis. I'm going to get some sleep."

Kumul grunted, and looked in no mood to sleep. Jenrosa left them to stand at the stern and looked down into the river's brown water. For a moment she wished she was a fish down there, gliding along in life without a care in the world.

No you don't, she told herself. *For the first time ever you're actually starting to enjoy your life.*

The thought made her smile for the second time.

⟨ 23 ⟩

UNTIL they reached the base of the wooded crest, both Lynan and Gudon rode on the horse, but Lynan dismounted as the slope increased to reduce the animal's load and to guide it over jutting roots. Gudon hung on as best he could, not once complaining about his badly wounded leg. About midday, they came across a small stream, and Lynan called a halt. He eased Gudon off the saddle and made him comfortable before applying more of the Chett's haethu.

"I should bandage it," Lynan told him.

Gudon shook his head. "It has stopped bleeding. Truth, air is the best thing for it."

"It will go bad."

Gudon held up the bottle of haethu. "Not with this on it, little master." He offered the bottle to Lynan. "Put some on your wound. It will heal more quickly."

Lynan dabbed some on experimentally. The wound and the tips of his fingers became numb almost instantly. He handed the bottle back with thanks.

"Will you be all right by yourself? I have to find us something to eat."

"We should have taken some of the dead jaizru with us. They make a good stew."

Lynan's face wrinkled in disgust. "After what happened this morning, I could never eat one."

"But they were prepared to eat you; it is only just to eat them in turn."

Lynan did not have to search far for food. He found berries and nuts and a colony of mushrooms, and on his way back discovered the white flowers of honey tubes. The pair ate quickly, then drank their fill from the stream.

"This crest is near the middle of the Ufero Mountains," Gudon told Lynan. "I came east this way many, many years ago. If we continue northwest, we will stay under cover and find plenty of streams and food until we get to the other side of the range."

"And then what?"

"From there, you must decide what to do next. I must go to the Oceans of Grass. It is time for me to go back to my people. But you can head north to Haxus or back south, if you wish."

"I was taken from friends. They will be looking for me."

"Where were you headed?"

"The Oceans of Grass."

Gudon looked surprised. "It is rare for people from the south to go there."

"We had our reasons," Lynan said darkly.

"I do not doubt it." Gudon slapped Lynan's shoulder. "Then we must go on together. Your friends will come and look for you there."

"Not if they think I'm dead."

"If they truly are your friends, they will know you are still alive, little master."

"Please, Gudon, stop calling me that. I am not your master."

Before Lynan could react, Gudon reached out and put his

hand under Lynan's shirt and brought out the Key of Union. "Forgive me, but you are wrong."

Lynan grabbed it back and hid it again. "How did you know. . . ?"

"When the beneficent master brought you aboard my barge, the Key was hanging loose from your neck. I recognized it, of course. What Chett wouldn't? It is the symbol of your family's rule over us. I must have looked too hard, for Prado struck me down."

Lynan retreated from Gudon. "What will you do about it?" he asked suspiciously.

"What I am doing now. Helping you get to safety."

Lynan swallowed. "I'm sorry. I have learned to trust very few."

"Then if you learn to trust me, I will count it as an honor . . . your Majesty."

Lynan shook his head. "No. I am not king. My sister, Areava, rules in Kendra."

"So we on the river had heard," Gudon said carefully. "I will not apologize for calling you what I did, but best I take you to my people. There are those there who will grant you refuge, and perhaps more."

"More?" Lynan asked, his heart skipping a beat.

"I cannot say. You must go and see for yourself."

They set off again as soon as the horse had rested. The ground became rockier and their going slower. The trees closed in around them and the air became heavy and moist.

After a while, Lynan said: "How long did you pilot a barge?"

"Oh, many years. My youth was spent on the river."

"But you did not set out to be a pilot?"

"No. I did not know how my journey from the Oceans of Grass would end. Destiny made my feet follow the path to the Barda."

"Destiny and instruction," Lynan said quietly.

"Now what can the little master mean by that?"

"As a pilot, you have reason to travel between the capitals of Hume and Chandra, you listen to gossip and tales from your passengers, you see what cargo is being carried, including the movement of armies, and you have an excuse to talk to travelers."

Gudon smiled easily. "Destiny takes many shapes and forms. In my case, it was not a king but a princess, although she is a queen now. And it is my turn to ask you your question: what will you do about it?"

"What I am doing now," Lynan replied without trying to hide the irony. "Helping you get to safety."

The pilot saw the deserted barge and swore loudly. Kumul stood up to see what the problem was.

"Poor Gudon!" the pilot wailed. "He did not deserve such a fate!"

By now Ager and Jenrosa were standing as well. It did not take them long to see what the pilot was keening about.

"Is that. . . ?" Jenrosa started, but could not finish the question. She did not want to know the answer.

"Take us closer!" Kumul told the pilot.

"I do not dare! See the spear trees, and how some of their branches end below the water? They are holding jaizru nests! If we get too close, they may attack us as well!"

"Take us closer, damn you!" Kumul ordered, and went astern to make sure she obeyed his order.

The pilot started her wailing again but gently eased her vessel closer to the bank. Ager climbed the bow gunwale and peered into the abandoned barge. "It's a fucking mess," he said. "I see at least two dead horses."

"Any bodies?" Jenrosa asked.

"It's hard to tell. The deck is covered in blood and dead eels. Maybe one . . . no, two! Get us closer!"

The pilot shook, but under Kumul's glowering stare

pushed harder on the rudder. Ager asked Jenrosa to hold on to his coat as he leaned even farther over the water. "One is too tall to be Lynan. The other . . . I just can't tell. There is not enough left of the face and too much blood to tell by the clothing." Jenrosa pulled him back in and the two of them joined Kumul astern.

"We must get off," Kumul said.

Just then the water boiled to the starboard and several shapes, black and red with teeth like shears, flew out of the river. The landed just inside the barge and flopped uselessly on the deck, all the while trying to bite whatever was in reach. The three companions jumped back. The pilot kicked the rudder and pulled on the sheets. The barge lurched and then slid into the middle of the river.

"I am not stopping here, even if you cut me with your sword," she told Kumul, her eyes wide in fear.

"She is right," Ager said, his voice taut. "The river is too shallow here for the barge to get close enough to the bank. We would have to wade through the water, and probably all be dead before our feet touched dry land."

"But what of Lynan?" Kumul cried. "What if he is still alive? He could be on the bank somewhere, needing our help . . ."

"If Lynan survived the river, he is either dead from loss of blood or long gone from here, in which case we will have to find his trail and follow it."

"Where is the closest point we can disembark?" Jenrosa asked the pilot.

"About three leagues from here if you want to take your horses with you."

"But which side of the river?" Kumul asked.

"I do not think he would have survived if he tried to swim for the eastern bank," Ager answered. "The eels would have had more than enough time to finish him off. If he is alive, he is somewhere to the west of the Barda."

"Then that is where we go," Kumul said.

The barge seemed to take hours to reach the disembarkation point, but the sun had still not reached midday when the pilot pulled over and dropped anchor. The planks were not quite long enough to reach land, and the horses had to be pulled and pushed up the slippery bank. They left one of the horses with the pilot as payment.

"I did not take you to Daavis as agreed," the pilot said, and gave them two days' worth of food to make up the difference. "Journey well. I hope you find your friend."

Less than an hour later they reached the clump of spear trees and the deserted barge with its cargo, already starting to stink under the hot sun. They quickly found the prints of two humans and a horse.

"I think these are Lynan's," Ager said. "They are too small for Prado or one of his men."

"These ones are long, but the stride is short and there is much blood," Kumul said.

"It could be the pilot," Jenrosa suggested.

"Or not," Ager answered grimly.

Kumul followed the second set of prints to a thicket of thorn bushes. "The tracks meet here, then Lynan's set off west . . ." He stopped and stooped to the ground ". . . and come back again . . . and then set off once more, but the impression is much deeper. He is carrying something heavy."

"The other survivor," Ager said, joining Kumul. "Then Jenrosa is probably right. It must be the pilot. He would not bother to carry Prado or one of his men."

"But Prado had two men with him," Jenrosa pointed out. "Where is the last of them?"

Ager shrugged. "Dead in the river, most likely; probably nothing more than a skeleton now."

With hope rekindled in their hearts, they followed the tracks west for half a league on foot before rediscovering the horse's trail.

"They are riding west," Ager said, and pointed to the crest in the distance. "They are heading for the woods."

"Smart boy, that Lynan," Kumul said under his breath. "They can't be more than four hours ahead of us."

"They will pull ahead, even though their horse is carrying both of them," Ager said. "We have to ride slowly to keep to their trail."

It was mid-afternoon before Lynan reached the top of the crest. It had been hard work, climbing and leading the horse. Gudon had slipped into a kind of sleep, stirring only occasionally to pat the horse and smile at Lynan before nodding off again. Now that they were clear of most of the trees the sun woke him fully, and he tried to slip off the horse.

"What are you doing?" Lynan cried, and tried to stop him.

"No, no, young master! I need to stand. I haven't been on a horse for many years, and my thighs and back feel like they have been stretched forever out of shape." He balanced himself on his good leg and held onto the saddle, then slowly stretched his muscles.

A cool wind blew around them. From their vantage point Lynan could see that the crest fell more sharply on its western side—leveling out in a broad dry plain with no trees and no sign of life—but extended north until it joined the saddle of a much larger rise. Beyond that he could see the peaks of several mountains, some of them high enough to shine with snow. He looked behind him and saw more mountains, though none as high as those in the north.

"That is the Lesser Desert," Gudon told him, pointing to the plain. "It follows the Ufero Mountains along almost its entire length. South of here is the source of the Gelt River, which flows into Kestrel Bay."

Lynan dimly remembered that the Gelt River had been the original destination for him and his companions on leaving Kendra. How much easier their journey would have been if they had not been forced onto the rocks by that warship, he thought. They could have sailed halfway up the Gelt, then strolled the rest of its length to these mountains. No great bears or vampires or Jes Prados or jaizru.

"North of here there is a pass through the mountains, called the Algonka," continued Gudon. "It is part of a well-used caravan route, and will take us to the start of the Oceans of Grass. There is a water hole at the end of the caravan route called by us the Strangers' Sooq."

"We will find refuge at this sooq?"

Gudon shrugged.

"How far away is this pass?"

"Two days' journey at least. We must stay this side of the mountains to find water, and the way is not always this easy."

Lynan wiped the sweat from his brow. "Wonderful," he muttered.

Gudon used his arms to mount by himself and grimaced when his injured knee bumped into the saddle. "Truth, it could be worse," Gudon said between his teeth.

"How worse?"

The Chett grinned at Lynan. "It could be me walking instead of you."

It was late at night, and Rendle, tired and fed up from hours arguing with Charion's quartermaster about supplies for his company, was not in a good mood when Eder opened the flap to his tent and just walked in.

"This had better be good."

"You have a visitor," Eder said shortly and moved aside. At first Rendle did not recognize the lumpen shape that entered, even when Eder lit another candle.

"Who . . ." But then something about the mouth and crooked nose sparked a memory. "Prado?"

"The same," Jes Prado answered, and without invitation sat himself down on Rendle's bunk. He was cradling his arm, and his clothes were bloody and torn.

Rendle poured wine into a mug and passed it to Prado. "What happened to you? I wasn't expecting you for another day, at least. Did you find the prize?"

Prado swallowed the wine in two gulps and held out the mug for more. Rendle obliged.

"We found the prince, all right," Prado said, his voice rough with exhaustion, "and got him as far as the Barda River. Then we lost him."

Rendle's face went as hard as stone, but his voice remained level. "Lost him?"

Prado drunk some more wine, then started retching. Rendle took the mug away from him until he had finished, then handed it back. Prado met his gaze, but turned away when he saw the look in Rendle's eyes.

"But I know where he's going," he said quickly. "We were chased by Kumul and two companions—"

"The crookback and the girl?"

"Aye. We made it to the river just in time and took a barge. The pilot played along for a while, then drove the barge into a clump of jaizru nests."

Eder blanched; Rendle did not even blink. "And then?"

"The eels killed my two best men and two of my horses. I saw Lynan pushed over the side by the pilot, then the pilot mounted one of the horses and forced it into the river. I saw them being attacked as they made for the bank. More jaizru were flying at the barge. I jumped over the other side, thinking the eels would be too busy with the pilot and the horse. I was mostly right." He held up his arm to show the wounds he had received. "I have more on my back and neck."

"And then?" Rendle prodded without a trace of sympathy.

"I reached the bank and collapsed. I don't know how long

I was out for. When I came to, I saw Lynan carrying the pilot away from the river, heading west."

"What about the horse?"

"I didn't see its carcass in the river. I think it must have gotten away."

"And where do you think Lynan is going?"

"The pilot was a Chett," Prado said. "I think they'll head for the Oceans of Grass. Where else can the prince go?"

"How did you reach Daavis?"

"I caught another barge upriver. I had to give the pilot the last of my coins." He finished the wine, but did not dare hold out the mug again.

Rendle and Eder exchanged glances. Eder nodded and left the tent. "Do you think you can ride?" Rendle asked.

"Give me a night's rest and I'll—"

"Now," Rendle said. "We must ride tonight if we're to make the Algonka Pass in time to intercept the prince. If you are right about Lynan heading for the Oceans of Grass, that is the only way through."

"How many men will you take?"

"I will take my company, Prado. I'm not going anywhere near the Chetts without plenty of swords to back me up."

Eder returned. "I've sent out the marshals. The company will leave Daavis in small groups and meet four leagues north of the city."

"Get our tents down," Rendle ordered. "We won't be coming back here." He turned to Prado. "And you come with us. If we capture Lynan, I may forgive you for what you have done. If not . . ." He poured more wine into Prado's mug. ". . . I may sell you to the Chetts."

24

THE next morning Gudon's knee seemed no better to Lynan, but the pilot insisted the pain was less. Lynan applied more haethu to both their wounds. They ate a handful of berries they had found nearby and then they set off once more, traversing steep slopes made slippery with loose stones. Lynan discovered the hardest part was not climbing but descending; he had to use all his strength to keep his footing and at the same time concentrate on leading the horse along the firmest ground. The muscles and joints in his legs felt as if they had been so overused he would never walk normally again; and as far as he could see, for all his efforts they were making barely any progress at all. The terrain seemed the same no matter which way he looked. But Gudon, with gentle humor and confidence, continued to give directions and encouragement.

The sky was covered in high clouds which made Lynan feel dreary, and though it made the air cooler, it also made it more humid. They stopped regularly to let both Lynan and the horse rest, and near midday they were lucky to find a gully with trees for extra shade and a brook with water so cold and fresh it helped invigorate them. Gudon actually tried standing without support and managed to walk three paces before Lynan had to help him sit down. "You see, little master, I told you it was healing."

"I wish it had healed enough for you to lead the horse for a while. It does not like these slopes."

"Any more than you," Gudon pointed out.

"How far to the Algonka Pass?"

"We will reach it tomorrow, probably in the morning. The descent to the road will be hard, but once there it is easy going all the way to the Strangers' Sooq."

"And how far from the pass to the sooq?"

"Another day."

Gudon started suddenly and began digging at the base of a tree Lynan had not seen before. "It is rare to find these on this side of the Ufero Mountains," the Chett said excitedly. He dug until he had exposed enough of the tree's roots to get a hand around one of them. He pulled twice and the root lifted into the air, then used a small knife he retrieved from a sheath at the back of his shirt to sever it from the main stock. The outer layer peeled off easily, revealing a milky-white core. Gudon cut it in two and passed one half to Lynan.

"We call these gods' roots," Gudon said, and bit off a mouthful. "We use it to spice our food."

Lynan copied him. The flesh was softer than he thought it would be, but very fibrous. At first, he thought its taste seemed sweet, but then he felt the mild tingling along his tongue and down his throat that told him worse was to come. A moment later, he was spitting it out and gulping water from the brook.

"What do you use it to spice? Leather?" Lynan's tongue and throat felt as if someone had stuck a burning branch down his gullet.

"The Chett use it widely in cooking. If you leave it in the sun for several days, then pound it into a dust and add water to it, you get haethu. If you add a handful of the dust to a pond or river, the fish come belly-up to the surface and are easy to catch. If you rub the juice into your skin, flies and mosquitoes stay away."

"I'm not surprised."

"It is the most wondrous of all plants."

Lynan felt his stomach rumble. He hoped they would soon have more to eat than the occasional handful of nuts and berries.

The clouds disappeared during the afternoon and the heat became another burden for Lynan to bear. Although the slope became less treacherous, the ground was now made up of large rocks rounded by weathering. The horse became increasingly skittish and difficult to handle. Gudon sang to it, which calmed it for a while but also brought a warm wind blowing up and over the mountains from the Lesser Desert.

"One must be careful with the songs," Gudon said. "There is always a price to pay for using any magic."

"Apparently," Lynan said wryly, blinking furiously to keep the sweat out of his eyes. He could feel the skin on his ears and nose starting to burn. "So why did your princess send you to the Barda?"

Gudon did not seem surprised by the question, and he answered without hesitation. "Because it was the mercenaries working out of Hume and Haxus who were the center of the cursed slave trade, and my people were its main victims. They used the Barda River to take us down to Daavis for selling."

"But that was many years ago."

"We have a long memory. We keep watch, we listen, we smell the air. We will not let the Slavers arise again and take us as they did before."

"But the Chetts are famous warriors. Why didn't you stop them back then?"

"For many centuries the Chetts lived in small tribes of a hundred or so. It doesn't matter how brave you are if your enemy is three or four times your strength and you have children and cattle to protect. We finally started coming together to make larger tribes, but there were many arguments among the chiefs about who should be in charge. We fought each other as much as we fought the Slavers. In the end the father of my princess won a great battle against other Chetts near a waterhole called the High Sooq, and we started planning to hit back against the enemy."

"Your army was big enough to take them on?"

"Not in one battle, little master. The Oceans of Grass are very wide and hold more people than any in the east suspect, but not so many to take on the rich lands of Hume or Haxus. But we could raid and harry. In the end, it never came to be."

"Why?"

Gudon leaned over and tapped Lynan on the shoulder. "Because of your mother and because of your father. She ordered the destruction of the Slavers, and he carried out her command in a great war."

Lynan blushed. For as long as he could remember, he had been proud of his father's record as a general, but it had always been a private thing, without real understanding of what Elynd Chisal's efforts had meant for other people. Lynan blinked with a sudden thought.

"Prado was one of the mercenary captains who worked for the Slavers?"

"Oh, yes. I have never seen him before, but all Chetts know what he looks like, and know his name. I hope the jaizru fed off him."

"So do I," Lynan said, touching the wound on his jaw. "So do I."

"Here!" Ager cried. "Over here!"

Kumul and Jenrosa stopped their search of the ground and joined Ager at the edge of a gully. Ager held up a white misshapen lump.

"Congratulations," Kumul said. "What is it and what are you going to do with it?"

Ager threw it to Kumul, who caught it and looked at it. "See the tooth marks?"

"They could be from anything—"

"And how the root is cut neatly at one end?"

Kumul looked more closely. "Yes, you're right."

"And here," Ager said pointing to the ground. "They're hard to see because the ground is so hard, but hoofprints, for sure."

Jenrosa breathed a sigh of relief. "So Lynan did come this way."

"Afraid your magic had failed you?" Kumul teased.

"I told you which direction they were traveling," she said reproachfully.

"Well, now we can be sure where they're heading," Ager said quickly, throwing warning glances at them both. The two of them had become short-tempered since losing the tracks they had been following the previous night.

Kumul nodded. "The Algonka Pass."

"It makes sense. We had always planned to make for the Oceans of Grass, and from here that's the only route."

"At least he's not trying to cross the Lesser Desert."

"He might have if the pilot he rescued did not know the way," Ager said.

"Common sense would tell him not to go through the desert," Kumul scoffed.

"But not how to move along the Ufero Mountains, and not which direction to travel."

"How long ago were they here?" Jenrosa asked.

"Five hours ago, maybe more."

"They are pulling ahead of us, despite the injured pilot."

"That's because we had to rediscover their trail. Now we know for sure that they are heading for the Algonka Pass, we can make for it directly. We should get there soon after they do."

"Why not try and get there before them?" Kumul asked. "We could walk through the night."

"Along this route? I don't think so, at least not if you want to keep the horses. It's bad enough in daylight."

Kumul did not argue the point. "All right, but let's get moving. The more ground we make up before the sun goes down, the less anxious I'll be."

Prado was beginning to wish the jaizru had eaten him. It took the last vestiges of his strength to remain seated on the horse Rendle had given him. The company rode for four hours until the first signs of dawn lit the sky, then rested for half an hour. Rendle sent a surgeon to look at Prado's wounds and the man applied some foul-smelling ointment that took away some of the pain but none of his exhaustion. They rode all that morning, always keeping the Barda in sight, heading northwest toward the Ufero Mountains and the Algonka Pass. Farmers threatened them when they rode over their fields, and Eder would disdainfully throw each of them a handful of coins. Merchants leading long lines of pack horses and mules would swear at them as the passing column upset their animals and sent huge clouds of dust sweeping into their faces; these Eder ignored.

Rendle ordered a halt again before midday. They ate cold rations of dried-beef-and-yogurt strips. Rendle sent his fastest outriders ahead with orders to locate Lynan and if possible detain him until the main force caught up, or, if they encountered Chetts in any numbers, to ride back with a warning.

The company rode during the worst heat of the day. Eder asked him to ease up, but Rendle ignored him. When horses fell away—blown, lame, dropping from thirst—their riders were left behind to fend as best they could. When the road bent west and came right alongside the Barda, Rendle let the company rest for another half hour while the horses were watered. And then they were off again, the mountains slowly growing in size, their shadows stretching far across the land.

Prado twisted the reins around his hands and somehow hung on. There seemed to be dust everywhere and he wished he could breathe clear air. The reins started to cut into the skin around his fingers, but the pain was nothing to that he was already suffering.

Rendle kept them going until it was too dark to ride. When he called a halt, men fell off their saddles and horses stood shaking and sweating. Rendle went around, not resting himself until he had spoken at least a single word to all his men, encouraging them, bribing them, warning them. When he had finished, campfires were already alight and the horses watered and brushed down. He then stood alone at the end of the camp, staring out toward the mountains as if by sheer will he could make them come to him. Eder joined him after a while with a mug of hot stew. Rendle gulped it down and handed back the mug.

"One more day," he told Eder.

"They cannot ride like that again. The horses will drop dead."

"We'll take it easier tomorrow." He turned when Eder sighed in relief. "But not too much easier. We must get there in time to find Prince Lynan."

"Prado may be wrong. Lynan may be heading somewhere else."

"Where else can he go? He is outlaw everywhere in the kingdom. Only in the Oceans of Grass can he hope to hide."

"He could be going straight north, to Haxus," Eder suggested.

"No. Not Elynd Chisal's son. Haxus was the main base for the Slavers' armies during the war."

Eder spat on the ground. "You're right. How sweet it will

be to turn him over to King Salokan." The thought made him smile.

Lynan stared at the night sky. The only star he knew was Leurtas, and he could see it just above the southern horizon. *That way lies Kendra,* he thought. He expected to experience a bout of homesickness, but instead all he felt was detachment. Maybe Kendra was no longer his home. He searched his feelings for anything about his previous life he did miss. Security came into his mind immediately, and the certainty of day-to-day life. He thought some more. What about relations and friends? He would have liked to see Olio again, and Pirem. But Olio was closest to his enemy, his sister Areava, and Pirem was dead. And all his other friends in the whole wide world were somewhere out there, either searching for him or trying to find a place to hide, or even dead. He would have given anything then to hear Kumul bark at him, or Ager suggest a bout with short swords, or be the victim of one of Jenrosa's cutting remarks.

He shut his eyes to think about Jenrosa. He had fancied her once upon a time; now he did not know how he felt toward her; she was his friend, his companion, but nothing else stirred in him. That disappointed him. Maybe he should have followed her to her room that night in the inn; at least then Prado and his thugs would not have been able to steal him away.

Gudon stirred in his sleep and muttered something in a language Lynan could not understand. *Here I am, in the middle of a mountain range, with a lame Chett and a tired horse for company. I should be hiding under a rock in despair.* But instead he was feeling . . . he could not quite find the word, but was surprised to find that "content" came closest. It was not what he had expected. But even as he questioned it, he realized the reasons for it. He was still alive, he was within two days journey of at least some kind of refuge, and when his powerful enemies thought of him at all, they thought of him as a threat.

He found Leurtas again and glowered at it, as if it represented everything in the south that wanted him dead and gone and forgotten. Anger sparked a cold fire inside of him, and the contentment was sharpened by a new determination.

I will survive, he promised the star. *And I will return to claim what is mine, no matter who tries to stop me. I am Prince Lynan Rosetheme, son of Queen Usharna and Elynd Chisal, and I hold a Key of Power.*

25

ONE moment Lynan and Gudon were surrounded by stunted trees and harsh saltbush, their feet and the hoofs of their horse slipping on the scree, and the next they half fell, half stumbled onto level ground. The flanks of the Ufero Mountains towered above them like stone giants, gray and grim. For the first time in two days Lynan saw flowering plants: mountain daisies and summer trees, shinbark and sharrok pines. And there were birds. He could not see them, but he could hear them. He could also hear water.

"Is this the Algonka Pass?"

"The south side. You can hear the Algonka River a few hundred paces from here, marked by that line of trees. Beyond that is the road."

They did not set off immediately but rested briefly from their descent, and Lynan applied more haethu to Gudon's knee and his jaw. Lynan had to admit the haethu was working; he could no longer see bone in Gudon's wound, and the flesh and skin were starting to knit into an ugly scar. His own scar was smoother now, and there was no longer any pain.

"I think I will have a limp," Gudon said almost cheerfully, patting his leg.

"No need to sound so happy about it."

"Considering I almost lost the whole leg, it is a pleasant alternative. Besides, we Chett live in the saddle." He rubbed his backside gingerly. "Well, most of us. My life on the river has spoiled me."

The Algonka was indeed shallow, and although the water was incredibly cold, they had no trouble crossing. They passed through the opposite river gallery and stopped. There was a huge caravan making its way on the road, its start lost in the haze to the west, and its end lost somewhere in the east. Great wagons drawn by teams of ten or more horses trundled by, their huge wheels sounding like milling stones on the dirt road. Dust hung over the caravan like a brown shroud. Lynan saw men riding shaggy looking ponies and mules, keeping an eye on their property and occasionally lashing the labouring horses to keep them moving. Lynan had never seen anything like it. Almost all goods coming into Kendra made it by boat.

"The Failing Sun Caravan," Gudon said. "I was hoping we would run into it."

"The Failing Sun?"

"The last great caravan before winter sets in and makes this road impassable. All the merchants from Hume and even Chandra who can contribute to it do so. They bring metals and wine, weapons and tools, and take back thousands of cattle and horses. It is easier going west than going east, believe me. You don't want to journey accompanied by so many beasts. I have tried it."

"What do we do? Just join it?"

"Truth. There are so many in the caravan, two more will make no difference. The merchants and their guards will ignore us as long as we ignore them."

Lynan tugged on the horse's reins, and they moved forward and merged with the great stream of traffic. Around them milled merchants on horseback or on foot, their servants scurrying behind or riding on the wagons; some children ran past playing a game of catch-me; one old man on a donkey was selling honey wine from a huge flask strapped to his back. They ended up following a wagon loaded with painted pottery, all packed in straw boats. Lynan spent most of the next hour avoiding horse droppings, but in the end gave up and just trudged on, oblivious of what he stepped in. After a while the dust thrown up by the caravan had coated his face and gotten in his mouth and ears. He suggested to Gudon they move away from the center of the caravan and closer to the river.

"I do not think that is a good idea, little master. Here we are lost among so many. No reason to make ourselves stand out."

"I am dying of thirst, Gudon."

"Well, then, I will see to that." He hailed the vendor of honey wine and offered some of his haethu in exchange for two glasses; the vendor agreed willingly. Lynan hesitantly accepted the dirty glass, but the wine that poured down his throat was the sweetest thing he had ever tasted, and seemed to take all the dust on its way down to his gullet. They carried on, moving in the middle of the great beast. He noticed people munching on biscuits as they walked or rode. "Does no one stop for a meal?" he asked Gudon.

"The caravan only stops at night. It is too much effort otherwise, and there is protection in numbers."

"Protection from whom?"

"There are bandits hereabouts who prey on merchants foolish enough to get separated from the caravan. Some from Hume, some Chett, some from distant lands who cannot make a living doing anything else except preying on the weak and vulnerable."

After climbing along the slopes of the mountains for two days, Lynan found it easy to keep pace with the large wagons. He watched all about him with great curiosity, and now and then Gudon offered a commentary. "That one has come all the way from Lurisia—see the timber in his wagon? The tribes will use that to make their bows and shelters. Over there, I do believe, are priests of the Lord of the Mountain from Aman, coming to make converts among my people; they have wasted their journey, I fear. The merchant with the tall hat is from Sharrock; it will take him nearly half a year to return home . . ."

And these are all from Theare, Lynan thought to himself. Indeed, most of them were from some part of Grenda Lear. For the first time in his life he had a notion of just how diverse was the kingdom's makeup. The maps he had seen did not do it justice. He felt a surge of pride that he was a scion of the family that had united all of these peoples under one crown.

Gudon tapped him on the shoulder. "Do not turn around, but wait for him to pass. A tall man on a big horse."

A moment later Lynan saw the man come into view. He was dressed in leather armor and was inspecting every one he passed. He threw Lynan and Gudon a lingering glance, but moved on.

"Mercenary," Lynan said.

"Truth. Searching for us. Prado or one of his men must have survived, and their friends have come looking for us."

"How do you know that? They could be looking for someone else. . . ." The argument sounded hollow even to him. "Why didn't he look us over more closely?"

"Think, little master. If you were searching for a prince and a pilot, who would you assume was on the horse?"

Lynan laughed. "Your injury may yet do us good."

"This time, but perhaps not next time," Gudon cautioned. "We must become even less conspicuous. Early in the morning, before the dust rises, we will be more obvious."

The wagon in front of them hit a hole in the road. The load of fragile pottery shifted, and the straw boats at the back started to slip through a loosened knot. Lynan threw Gudon the reins and rushed forward. He tightened the rope across the back of the wagon and retied the knot. A short, bearded man appeared on a donkey. He raised a cane to strike at Lynan's hands.

"Good sir!" Gudon cried out. "He has saved your goods from destruction!"

The merchant hesitated, holding his cane high in the air.

"Sir," Lynan said in as meek a voice as possible, "the rope was loose. See the knot I have tied? Is this yours?"

The merchant lowered his arm and leaned over the donkey to see the knot. He had a small, sharp face, and his eyes gleamed like a rat's. "My father's soul," he sighed, shaking his head, "that is not my knot. Forgive me, sir. You have done me a great favor and I would have caned you for it." The merchant sucked through his teeth. "But there is an obligation. You will eat in my tent tonight."

"That is too much generosity," Gudon argued. "It was only a knot!"

Lynan scowled at Gudon. They had no food, and the crazy pilot was throwing away a free meal!

"Too much generosity!" cried the merchant. "I will show you too much generosity! Not only will you eat with me tonight, you will sleep with me and my servants so you will be safe from brigands!"

Gudon bowed his head. "You are munificent."

The merchant puffed himself up. "Yes. *And* I am generous."

"Indeed," Gudon agreed, smiling faintly. "My name is Gudon. My friend's name is—"

"Migam!" Lynan said quickly.

"Migam," Gudon confirmed.

"Good to meet you, I am sure. I am Goodman Gatheras, merchant from Sparro, dealer in the world's finest pottery. Have you seen my wares?"

"Indeed," Gudon said. "We have been following your wagon for several hours and admiring the pottery."

"The Chetts will buy all of this?" Lynan asked.

"Most of it," Gatheras replied. "Much of which they will then sell on to merchants from Haxus in the spring. I also sell some of my wares to other merchants like me. The Failing Sun Caravan is a great opportunity to meet those from far-away lands." He looked downcast then. "Alas, it is also a great opportunity for thieves." He blinked at Lynan. "For which I mistook you."

"An innocent mistake," Lynan told him.

Gatheras sat erect on his donkey, a proud king dressed in a merchant's finery. "Not only am I munificent and generous," he declared, "I am also plenteous. Not only will you share our food and our tent, but I offer you the protection of my company all the way to the Strangers' Sooq."

"Ah, benevolence!" Gudon cried, raising his arms in supplication. "What fortune to have tied your knot!"

The merchant nodded stiffly, accepting the compliment. "I must see to the knots on my other wagons. Excuse me." He tapped the donkey with his cane and trotted off into the dust, muttering to himself: "Munificent . . . generous . . . plenteous . . . benevolent . . ."

"Your good deed has served us well," Gudon said to Lynan.

"The mercenary returns," Lynan said under his breath.

The rider in leather was in more of a hurry going back down the line. He barely glanced at the pair.

"The real danger will be at the sooq," Gudon said. "It will be easier for them to discern between merchants and freeloaders like us."

"How are we going to find Lynan amid all this?" Jenrosa asked. She coughed as even more dust found its way down her throat. All around her trundled wagons, herds of people and stamping horses. She desperately wanted to ride, to try and get above at least some of the dust and confusion, but Kumul had insisted they stay on foot. It was the only chance they had of making himself and Ager even remotely inconspicuous.

They had reached the pass an hour before. Ager had known of the Failing Sun Caravan from his work with merchants, but Kumul and Jenrosa were overwhelmed first by the spectacle and then by the confusion. They felt like grains of wheat floating helplessly with the current of a great river. The sun, low in the western horizon, was shining full on their faces; it looked obscenely distended and red in the haze, but its light was still strong enough to make them squint.

"We have no chance of finding him in this crowd without bringing attention to ourselves," Ager said. "We will have to wait until we reach the Strangers' Sooq at the end of the pass."

"How long?" Jenrosa asked.

"I have never traveled this road, but I have been told the journey from Daavis is four days with a wagon: two days to reach the Algonka Pass and two days to cross and reach the sooq. We came onto the road about halfway along the pass. So a day, maybe two, at the most."

"And if we do find Lynan there, what next?"

"Into the Oceans of Grass," Kumul said, not sounding too happy about their prospects. "If we have figured all of this out, then so have the mercenaries."

They had noticed the scouts moving up and down the line and had dismounted before being seen, taking cover behind a large wagon carrying sheep hides built up into fleecy hills.

"We might have seemed nothing more than guards for some of the merchants," Ager suggested weakly.

"We have no reason to expect fortune to favor us so suddenly," Jenrosa said.

"She is right," Kumul said. "They will recognize us if they see us."

"Then, when the caravan halts for the night, we must find our way to its center," Ager said. "There is some obscurity in numbers."

Kumul agreed. "If Lynan is among this lot, then we may find him there, too."

"We might do better to search for his wounded companion," Jenrosa suggested.

"Good idea," Ager said. "But our main objective at this point should be to remain unnoticed until we reach the sooq."

They trudged on, keeping an eye out for any sign of more mercenaries. Jenrosa tried to take in what was going on around her, the merchants and their colorful clothes, the different goods being carried by the wagons, but she had to concentrate on moving one foot in front of the other. She was more tired than she could have imagined possible back in her slow and comfortable life as a student magicker. She wondered if she would ever have that again, that feeling of not being hunted, of not desperately seeking some kind of sanctuary. That, in turn, made her think of the Oceans of Grass; the very name suggested vast distances where an army could lose itself, and a germ of hope kindled in her heart. Perhaps there, an insignificant speck, she would find peace again. Even as she had the thought, something inside of her rebelled against it. Life in Kendra may have been comfortable, but it had also been numbingly boring. Would the Chetts allow her to practice her magic? What magic did they use? Could they teach her?

These were questions she would have to find answers to. She found her steps becoming lighter.

Eder gave Rendle the latest report from the scouts as they rode along Algonka Pass, the company following behind four abreast. They were still three hours' ride behind the caravan and would not reach it before nightfall. His captain heard him out without speaking a word. "At least there are no signs of Chetts in any number," Eder offered halfheartedly when he had finished.

"There will be at the sooq," Rendle spat. "And if we don't find the prince soon, that's where we'll end up."

"Do you want to wait in the pass, then?"

Rendle shook his head. "Even if we don't find him, I still intend to head north to Haxus. This new queen in Kendra is sitting loose on her throne. Why else hire mercenary companies and send them north? Destiny blows behind Salokan now. He will need trained bands like ours. Prince Lynan was just an extra bargaining chip. Even if we turn up without him, we can let Salokan know he is still alive and still an outlaw."

Eder nodded at Prado, riding a few paces behind and hanging half off his horse. "He will not last to Haxus."

"He only has to last to Strangers' Sooq. He can identify the prince and the pilot for sure." He slapped his thigh with frustration. "Are you sure the scouts saw no pair fitting Prado's descriptions?"

"They saw several traveling in pairs, some with one horse, some with two, some just walking. All different sizes. Some were Chetts. Unless they actually stop and interrogate them all, how can they be sure? And that will only antagonize the merchants and their guards."

"Send out more scouts," Rendle ordered. "Even if we just identify them, we can wait until we reach the sooq to take the prince."

"The Chetts and merchants won't like that," Eder complained. "The drawing of weapons is forbidden there."

"What can they do about it? We have over two hundred armed riders. No one can stop us, and before the Chetts can organize a war party, we'll be long gone, riding hard for Haxus."

Eder left to give the order. Alone, Rendle felt his anger and frustration rising. He wanted to lash out at someone. Anyone. He slowed until Prado had caught up and punched the man in the back. Prado shot up like a branded colt.

"Keep in your saddle, Prado," Rendle said fiercely. "You haven't finished yet."

Prado glared at him. "You would not treat me like this if my veterans were here. I always led a better company than your ragtag collection."

"But you don't have your veterans with you, and you never will again if we don't recover the prince and turn him over to Salokan. No money, no company. Right now you're nothing more than a poor old soldier who's fallen on evil times." Prado turned his face away from him. Rendle angrily grabbed a handful of his hair and jerked his head back. Their horses skittered to a stop and Rendle's men rode around them like water flowing around a rock. "How sure are you the prince escaped the river? You're not lying to me, are you?"

Prado pulled his head away, leaving a handful of hair in Rendle's fist, and gave the captain a jagged grin. "If I am, you won't know until it's too late. What do you think the Chett will do when they see Captain Rendle appear at the Strangers' Sooq with his company of hated riders? They haven't forgotten you, old slaver, mark my words."

"Then they won't have forgotten you either," Rendle returned and spurred on his horse, Prado sneering after him.

Lynan could not sleep. Gatheras had overwhelmed them with his benevolent, munificent and plenteous generosity. He could not remember ever having eaten so much. The merchant must have had a whole wagon devoted to supplies, most of it food and wine. There had been roast pig and fowl, potato and pea soup, hard wheat bread with dried fish and spiced yogurt spread, sesame balls made with honey, and white wine and red wine, and a sickly mead at the end of the meal that made him feel dizzy and slightly nauseous. All of it now roiled in his stomach, unused to such splendor.

If I sleep, I will have nightmares, he told himself. *From now on I eat nothing but berries and nuts.*

He groaned and tried turning in the bedding Gatheras had loaned him. He wanted to see the stars, but he and Gudon were now sharing ground with Gatheras and seven of his eight servants under a huge tent. Snores and snuffles mumbled in the background, and the smell of silent burps and not-so-silent farts filled the air. Giving in to his insomnia, he got up and carefully made his way to the flap. Outside stood the eighth servant, standing guard with a huge club. Lynan rubbed his belly and made a sour face. The guard smiled knowingly, patted his own belly and belched loudly.

Although he could now see the sky, it was made faint by the forty or more campfires that burned brightly in the caravan camp. He was still surrounded by sleeping bodies. Hundreds of them. Dozens of tents, some of them even bigger than Gatheras', swelled in the darkness like beached whales, and circling the camp were the wagons forming a wooden wall. He made his way to the piss trench, gingerly stepping over heads and arms. He could hear the Algonka River gurgling nearby, and something else. He quickly relieved himself and listened more carefully. Sounds of horses, many of them. The occasional clink of steel slapping on steel or leather. He edged around the side of one of the wagons and peered into the darkness. The ground sloped gently down to the river and a small glen, and between the trees of the glen he could make out the dark shapes of horses. Now and then he saw men dressed in leather gear, just like the mercenaries he and Gudon had observed riding up and down the caravan during the day.

God's death! he thought. *It's Prado and his men!*

His first reaction was to run back to Gatheras' tent and raise the alarm, but he stopped himself. What good would raising the alarm do? Why would anyone care? It was no concern of Gatheras or his fellow merchants. Lynan forced himself to think calmly. If the mercenaries *were* after him, either they did not know he was in the camp or had decided they could not move against him yet; otherwise he would already be their prisoner. He had to warn Gudon, but knew that until they reached Strangers' Sooq there was nothing either of them could do.

His stomach forgotten, he returned to Gatheras' tent and gently shook Gudon awake.

Gudon listened wearily and said, "Since there is nothing to be done, I suggest you try and sleep." He closed his eyes again.

"Sleep? How can I sleep now?"

Gudon sighed, sat up and gently pushed Lynan down. He started to sing. Lynan blushed. "I'm no babe to be sung a lulla . . . lull . . ."

His eye lids fluttered and closed, and he sensed a dark sheet falling over his mind.

26

SOMEONE was kissing his cheek. He tried to open his eyes, but it was much harder than it should have been. The kissing was getting harder. Odd, he thought, dimly remembering where he was. A horrific image of Gatheras taking advantage of him gave Lynan the extra encouragement he needed to prize open his eyelids. He looked up into the face not of Gatheras but of Gudon, and Gudon was not kissing him, he was slapping him.

"What are you doing?" he mumbled.

"Waking you up, little master."

"It's dawn already?"

"Not yet."

"What's wrong?"

"I have to go."

Lynan shook his head to clear it. "What did you say?"

"I have to go. I must leave before it is light."

Lynan sat up straight. "What are you talking about?" He could not hide the catch in his voice. He was being set adrift again.

"I want to get to the Strangers' Sooq before the caravan. I must find my friends to arrange things."

"Can't I come with you?"

"The mercenaries have set guards. They will not worry too much about a single Chett—many of us travel along the pass—but they will decidedly pay attention if they see you."

"But what will I do?" He tried not to sound desperate. He searched for courage, but it seemed far, far away.

"I have asked Gatheras to let you stay with him. I told him I would make sure he gets favorable treatment from the Chetts. He agreed, and will take you with him to the sooq."

"But what will I do when I get there?"

"If I am not there to greet you, you must find a Chett dealer named Kayakun. You can trust this man. He will know what to do. You must follow his instructions precisely. Do you understand?"

Lynan nodded, not really understanding but at least willing to trust Gudon. "What about your knee?"

"Gatheras will help me to the horse. I will have no trouble riding to the sooq. It is not that far for a single rider." Gudon patted Lynan's shoulder. "You will be all right. Keep your eyes open. Talk only to Gatheras. If I am not at the sooq, find Kayakun."

"Are you ready?" Gatheras said behind Lynan, making him start in surprise.

Gudon nodded and Gatheras approached and offered the Chett a hand up. Gudon left the tent without another word. Lynan hugged his knees. He wanted to curl up into a ball and let the world pass him by. He did not want to stand, or leave the tent, or go to the Strangers' Sooq, or find a man called Kayakun. He wanted the past weeks to evaporate into a nightmare and leave him warm and safe in his bed back in Kendra's palace.

He stayed like that for several minutes. Gatheras returned and squatted down beside him. "It is the small things in life that make it worthwhile," the merchant said in a businesslike tone. "Take, for example, the knot you tied on the rope around my wagon. It was a little thing, but it meant a great deal to me. I will take you to the Strangers' Sooq. It is a little thing, but I think it will mean a great deal to you. Am I right?"

Lynan nodded.

"Good. Now you must do a little thing. You must stand."

Lynan met Gatheras's gaze. "I am—"

"Do not say afraid. No one is afraid to stand up." Gatheras stood up, his arms out wide as if to embrace the idea. "A little thing."

Lynan swallowed and stood up. "A little thing," he said, his voice wavering.

Gatheras held out a tunic. "This carries the sign of my house. You will wear it until we reach the Sooq. This is a particular request from Gudon."

Lynan took off his coat and exchanged it for the tunic.

"Now everyone will think you work for me and not spare you a second glance."

Lynan frowned. "How much did Gudon tell you about me?"

Gatheras smiled mysteriously. "Are you hungry?"

Remembering the huge meal he had last night he started to say no, but when he thought about it he realized he was hungry. "Yes," he said.

"Then the next little thing we will do is eat. I cannot have my servants passing out from lack of food. Come with me."

Gudon kicked the horse into an easy trot. As he rode from the camp, the ground started sloping gently toward the west. It would level out a few leagues on, and an hour's hard ride after that he would reach the first Chett outposts, single warriors hidden in grass hides who watched the comings and goings of everyone leaving the Algonka Pass.

A mercenary guard rode toward him, keeping parallel until Gudon waved at him and held up two string baskets, each holding one of Gatheras' beautiful pots. The mercenary shook his head, Gudon shrugged and continued on. After a while, the mercenary dropped back to resume his station.

Gudon thought he had made it through when a second mercenary appeared suddenly from a copse near the river. Gudon did not want to appear like a fugitive, so he slowed and waited for the mercenary to catch up. The rider wheeled his horse in front of Gudon, barring his escape. He was a thickset bruiser with hairy arms and ragged black hair tied back in an ivory pinch. He smiled genially enough and rubbed his chin with a callused finger.

"Early start?" he asked.

"Indeed, master." He held up his baskets. "I intend to be the first to tempt the markets with my employer's wares."

"Who is that?"

"His name is Gatheras; he comes from Sparro."

The mercenary nodded, then pointed to Gudon's leg. "Nasty wound. How did you get it?"

"I was bitten by a horse, master."

The mercenary laughed. "This one?"

"Oh, no. I ate the one that bit me."

"I heard the Chetts eat those who attack them, even humans."

"Forgive me, master, but that is a myth. We never eat anything that walks on two legs. So no humans, and no birds."

"That sounds reasonable." The mercenary edged his horse closer. "I think I would like you to come with me. My captain would like to talk with you."

Gudon expressed surprise. "Your captain is interested in pottery?"

"Among other things." He leaned over to take the reins of Gudon's horse and never saw the thin bone knife Gudon drove into the nape of his neck. The mercenary gasped once and fell from his saddle. He was dead before he hit the ground.

Gudon quickly reached to grab the stirrup of the mercenary's horse. The animal whinnied and stamped but did not try to pull away. Gudon tied the reins to his own saddle before carefully dismounting, putting his weight on his left leg. He bent over the mercenary and used his knife to cut out a small square of his cheek muscle, then swallowed it whole.

"In your case, master, I will make an exception about eating my enemy."

He slipped the knife back into its sleeve behind his neck before quickly tying a rope around the mercenary's hands and looping it over the saddle of the dead man's horse. He then hobbled to the other side and used all his strength to pull the mercenary over the saddle. He got back on his own horse, took the reins of the second mount and set off again, singing softly to the paling sky overhead.

"I am starving," Kumul groaned. He got up from the ground, dusted off the coat he had been lying on and scratched his graying hair.

"Think of all the beef that awaits you at the Oceans of Grass," Ager said. "Thousands—millions!—of cattle, all waiting to be devoured by a carnivore like you."

Kumul's stomach growled so loudly people nearby turned to see what the disturbance was.

"Then again, do not think of it," Ager suggested. "Think instead of being small, of being invisible. Particularly think of making no sound that will attract attention to you."

Kumul scowled at the crookback. "I cannot help it. We haven't eaten properly in days."

Jenrosa joined them, leading their horses. "The first wagons have set off."

"Did you see any sign of—?" Kumul began, but Jenrosa shook her head. "Lynan is here. I know it. I can *feel* it."

"You are not a magicker, Kumul," Ager said. "Don't raise

our hopes too high. He may already be ahead of us." He
looked across to the river where the mercenaries were wa-
tering their horses. "At least they haven't got him."

"I think Kumul is right," Jenrosa said. "And I *am* a magicker. I can feel something as well, and I trust my senses in
this."

"Be that as it may, we can't be obvious about it and go
searching for Lynan. We will go with the caravan to the
sooq. When the caravan breaks up, we may spot him."

"The mercenaries are leaving," Kumul said. The others
looked up and saw the company moving out, riding at a trot
to get ahead of the caravan and its dust. He wished they
could do the same. He noticed that some of them stayed behind. Kumul pointed to them. "They will keep back to keep
a lookout from the caravan's rear."

"I'll return soon," Jenrosa said and left for the river, taking the horses with her.

"What is she doing?" Ager asked Kumul, alarmed when
he saw her walking toward the mercenaries waiting for the
caravan to pull ahead.

Kumul grunted his approval. "What we cannot do ourselves. With my size and your crookback we would be recognized right away."

They spent a nervous few minutes watching her water the
horses and refill their leather bottles. Two mercenaries were
standing not ten paces from her, talking between themselves.

When she returned, they started off, keeping as close as
possible to a large wagon that hid them from any casual
search.

"Did you overhear them?" Ager asked impatiently.

"They know their captain is searching for someone, but
not who he is. They are worried that he is taking them so
close to Chett territory. They are scared of them."

"Did they say who is their captain?"

"No, but it isn't Prado. They talked about him being with their chief, but they did not seem fond of him."

"Not surprising," Kumul noted. "Not after he lost their prize catch."

"There was something else," Jenrosa said. "They kept on talking about not going back to Hume. They were upset about it."

Kumul and Ager exchanged glances. "You were right," Kumul said. "They are going north."

"With or without Lynan," Ager said. "That could mean that if we find Lynan and hide him from them, they will eventually give up their search and leave."

"I think, as we get closer to the sooq, the mercenaries will become more desperate," Jenrosa said. "It's important we find Lynan first."

"We talked about that and agreed—" Ager started, but Jenrosa cut him off with a sharp wave of her hand.

"No, *you* talked about it. I agreed to nothing. I am going to find Lynan. You two stay here. And don't worry, no one will be bothered about me."

She gave Kumul the reins to her horse, and before either man could stop her, she ducked around the rear of the wagon and disappeared.

"She will get us all killed," Ager complained.

Kumul shook his head. "No. No, I don't think so. She will be fine."

Ager thought he heard something more than respect in his friend's voice. He looked keenly at Kumul but could read nothing in his expression.

A wind blew up and sent dust into their eyes. They bowed their heads and ploughed on.

Lynan was riding on one of Gatheras' wagons when he saw the lush green circle of growth that surrounded the Strangers' Sooq. He stood up on the board to get a better view. South of the sooq began the Lesser Desert, its gray rocky ground dull under the bright autumn sun, but to the west and north of the sooq started the Oceans of Grass. It was not the brilliant green he had imagined, but a washed-out green, like thin agate. And it moved. He held his breath in wonder. Breezes played across the grass like invisible hands. It seemed to him that the whole plain was alive.

"It is beautiful," he said aloud.

The driver beside him snorted. "I have been here during drought. It is dead then, as dead as the desert."

Lynan did not believe this place could ever be truly dead. *This is the greatest life I have ever seen,* he thought.

"Sit down, boy," Gatheras hissed, pulling along side on his donkey. Lynan sat down in something of a daze. The merchant saw Lynan's expression and chuckled. "Quite a sight the first time, isn't it?" he said.

"It is beautiful."

Gatheras looked thoughtfully at him. "The only people I have heard call it that before were Chetts."

"My grandmother was a Chett," Lynan said absently, his attention still focused on the plain.

"Indeed? She must have been very short for a Chett."

Jenrosa had walked as casually as possible from wagon to wagon, trying to see the face of every person she passed without being obvious about it. There were no mercenaries riding with the caravan anymore, but that was not to say they did not have their spies here looking out for anyone behaving oddly. She passed wagons carrying dried fruits, spices, pottery, iron and copper ingots, ropes and cloth; she walked by merchants and servants, fellow travelers and priests. And no sign of Lynan.

Her attention was distracted when the sooq came into view. The sight of the verdant water hole and the vast distances beyond made her gasp. The plains drew out to meet the sky at some distant horizon. The grass seemed to move in time with the scattered clouds that scudded overhead. She breathed in deeply, and smelled grass and air and . . . and freedom. It was like nothing she could have imagined, but now that she had seen it she knew that somehow it was what she had been looking for her whole life. *A new world,* she thought. *A home.*

Angry words roused her from her reverie, and she dodged aside as a wagon loaded with lumber trundled past, its driver still swearing at her. She swore back and was stomping off, pretending high dudgeon, when she saw a youth had also been captivated by the sight of the sooq. He was standing on a wagon hauling pottery. Someone came up on a donkey and said something to him and he sat down, still staring ahead. She noted the livery he wore, and because she became conscious of it was able to imagine the youth's build without it.

She stopped in her tracks. *Oh God oh God oh God . . .* She started running to catch up with the wagon, but then changed her mind and stopped again. A man walking with a long stick swerved to avoid her and muttered something indecent. She ignored him. She could not just go up and grab Lynan and hug him and cry in relief. That would draw more attention than either of them wanted. She thought quickly. *She knows where he was now.* She had to get the others. They would trail behind and make their move when the caravan reached the sooq. She could barely contain her excitement.

She turned back to find Kumul and Ager, and soon discovered them trudging beside the same wagon she had left them with. She tapped both on the shoulder as she came abreast. She made sure her face was downcast, but it was a struggle.

Kumul glanced at her. "At least you tried," he said encouragingly.

"True," she said, sighing.

"I still think it was a dangerous thing to do," Ager commented, but his voice was concerned, not angry.

"True."

"I wonder where is right now, and what he's doing," Kumul said.

"Sitting on a wagon tending a load-full of pottery," Jenrosa suggested casually.

Kumul snorted. "Probably."

They walked on for a while in silence until the sooq came into view and Kumul and Ager saw it for the first time.

"Quite a sight," Ager said. "I think Lynan would be impressed."

"He was," Jenrosa said.

They fell quiet again. A minute later Ager looked sideways at Jenrosa. "What did you say?" Jenrosa feigned puzzlement. "You said something about Lynan."

"I did?"

Silence again. And then, despite all her efforts, the laughter came. First, just the pressure of air against her throat, then a sort of explosion through her nose, and finally a great guffaw that startled her companions. She could not speak. Eventually, the guffawing weakened to a persistent giggling that hurt her ribs. Ager's eyes lit up with sudden understanding and he joined in. Kumul looked at both of them as if they were mad. His expression made Jenrosa and Ager laugh more violently. They finally got it under control, reducing their mirth to a hoary wheeze.

"People are looking," Kumul hissed at them.

"Right," Ager said tightly, and that set him and Jenrosa off again.

"God's death!" Kumul snapped. "What's so bloody funny?"

"Don't you see?" Ager said, forcing the words between fits of laughter. "Jenrosa *found* him!"

Revelation made Kumul's face go pale under his close-cropped beard, and then the broadest smile Jenrosa had ever seen lit up his face, and seeing it, her own heart lifted even higher.

Lynan could now make out among the trees buildings made of white stone. They were all two stories with flat roofs and curved corners. The road ribboned around the sooq and ended in a cleared area to the west. And there, in their brown leather armor and with their glinting weapons, were the mercenaries. Most were dismounted, but there was no pretense of making a camp. They were waiting. Lynan could see some of the locals watching them from between the trees. He hoped Gudon had made it through.

Lynan asked Gatheras if he knew where he could find Kayakun.

The merchant shook his head. "Apparently, Gudon was going to arrange for him to meet us."

"If Gudon reached the sooq," Lynan said.

"I do not know this Gudon as well as you," Gatheras said, "but if he is only half as competent as every other Chett I've met, he not only reached the sooq but has probably arranged rooms for us at the only inn and prepared a five-course meal for us as well."

By the time they reached the cleared area it was already filling up with wagons and merchants putting up covered stalls and tents. Many locals, most of them Chetts, were wandering around to get an idea of the goods being put up for sale and trade. Lynan tried not to look at every Chett that wandered by as he helped unload Gatheras' wagons. They built small pyramids with the pots so every shape and size could be displayed. Gatheras made sure to ask after the health of every visitor, and Lynan could not help admiring his ability at always turning the conversation toward the necessity of owning pots to carry food and wine and grain and spices—indeed, to carry anything of value.

The work was hard and seemed to go on for hours. When he and Gatheras' servants had finally finished unloading the wagons, the sun was only a hands span from the horizon, and despite a warm breeze starting to blow from the plains toward the mountains, the temperature had dropping noticeably. Some of the servants got a fire going and started cooking the evening meal. Even more locals were visiting the stalls now, taking advantage of the cooler air and drawn by the distractions offered by the visiting caravan.

Lynan noticed that the Chetts, unlike their brethren in the east, all wore traditional Chett clothing: tight-fitting linen trousers and loose shirts with a v-shaped opening for the head; some wore wide heavy ponchos decorated with bright symbols denoting tribe, clan, and family. It was livery of sorts, but much more colorful than the designs worn by soldiers and servants in any of the provinces on the eastern side of the mountains.

By now Lynan could not help wondering what had happened to Gudon. He had seen no sight of him, and no one had approached him on Gudon's behalf.

As the other servants were about to start their evening meal he was called over by Gatheras. The merchant was standing next to a Chett tall even for his own people, his dark hair streaked with gray and his golden skin as rough as a lizard's. The Chett looked down his nose at Lynan. "This servant?" he asked.

Lynan studied the Chett closely. Was this Kayakun? He was about to ask when Gatheras grasped his arm tightly in warning.

"I know he is small, sir, but Migam is stronger than he looks. He will carry the three pots without falling behind." He turned to Lynan. "This noble gentleman is purchasing several of our wares, but he needs three samples to show

other Chett buyers who are staying with him while the caravan is here. You will carry them to his home for him."

Lynan nodded curtly. His stomach was doing somer-
saults. "Which pots, sir?" he asked the Chett, trying to keep
his voice even.

The Chett did not bother speaking to Lynan but merely
pointed to the three he wanted. Lynan groaned inside. They
were big. He put them one in the other and lifted the lot up
to his left shoulder like he had seen the other servants do.
The Chett walked off and Lynan followed. They crossed the
camp and were soon among tall spray trees, their trunks sec-
tioned in rings; beautiful lion flowers grew from them, nodding in the evening breeze. They reached a dirt track and
started passing homes and shops still open for business. The
smell of food was everywhere, reminding Lynan that he was
hungry again.

"Do not turn around, but we are being followed," the
Chett said casually. "Five men wearing cloaks, but I can see
leather armor underneath."

Lynan's heart started racing. "Sir, I think they mean me
harm."

"Probably," the Chett said, but seemed unconcerned by
the prospect. "I would prefer any confrontation not to occur
in such a public space." They passed an outdoor tavern and
turned left down a narrow alley crowded on both sides by
buildings.

"But this is a dead end!" Lynan cried.

"Walk ahead of me and put down your pots," the Chett
said calmly. As Lynan passed him, he turned on his heel and
drew a long knife that had been hidden beneath his poncho.
None too gently, Lynan rested the pots against a wall and
stood behind the Chett. Five men turned into the alley, shadows against the setting sun. They stopped when they saw the
armed man facing them. One of them, the biggest, stepped
forward.

"We are not after you," he said to the Chett. "We want the lad."

"You can take the pottery, but I am responsible for the boy until I return him to his master."

The mercenary spread his arms in a wide shrug, simultaneously showing the long cavalry sword hanging from his belt. "We wish him no harm. My captain has business with him." He reached for a pouch on his belt and shook it. Coins jingled. "We will pay you to leave him in our care. You could tell his master he ran away. No one will be the wiser."

The Chett considered the offer for a moment. Lynan readied himself to pounce. If he could take the Chett's knife, he might be able to force a way through the soldiers before they had time to react. Then, to his surprise, the Chett shook his head.

"No, I think not."

The mercenary sighed and waved for his fellows to join him. The narrow alley forced them into pairs. As one they threw their cloaks over their shoulders and drew their swords. "I am sorry to hear you say that," the big one said, and he advanced with his weapon held out in front of him. The Chett suddenly leaped forward in a move that surprised Lynan as much as the mercenaries. His knife flicked once, twice, and he sprang back again. The leader fell, hitting the ground face down with a satisfying whack. Blood seeped from underneath his body. The other mercenaries hesitated and threw each other nervous glances.

"I can dispose of four of you in this confined space without much difficulty," the Chett said, his tone almost bored.

"He's right," one of the mercenaries said. "Three of us can wait outside the alley while the other gets help."

There were mumbles of agreement and they started to retreat. Because they kept their gaze on the Chett and Lynan, they never saw the two figures appear in the mouth of the alley behind them, one huge and the other somehow malformed. They heard the snick of steel sliding against scabbard, but before they could turn, three of them were savagely cut down. The fourth yelped, twisted to face the Chett, then desperately twisted again to meet the threat behind him. A giant shadow loomed over him. For a split second, light sparked off a sword swung high in the air before it was brought down so hard it split the mercenary's head in two. Blood fountained into the air and what had been a face slapped into the dirt. Amazingly, what was left of the mercenary remained standing, his body teetering, the blade that had drunk his life lodged in bone and tendon. The giant twisted the sword and pulled it away. The dead man fell back against a wall and crumpled to the ground. His legs and arms twitched obscenely and then were still.

Another, slighter figure appeared at the end of the alley. "Lynan?"

Lynan took a hesitant step forward. He recognized the voice, and the shapes of the two swordsmen, but dared not believe it.

"Grief, your Highness, you've led us on a long run," the giant said.

"Do you know these people?" the Chett asked.

In answer, Lynan ran forward. He jumped onto the giant, his arms wrapping around the broad shoulders, his hands slapping the back. "Oh, God, Kumul! Kumul!" Tears stung his eyes but he did not care.

The giant hugged Lynan in turn and lifted him off the ground. "I thought we had lost you forever, lad," he croaked.

Ager and Jenrosa came up to the pair and added their weight to the huddle. They started springing up and down like children, back-slapping and hugging.

The Chett looked on with an amused smile. "Well, that answers my question." He cleaned and sheathed his knife and waited patiently until the celebration ended. When the four friends finally parted from each other, he said: "Migam.

Lynan. Whatever your name is. You still have three pots to deliver."

Lynan wiped his cheeks and nodded. "Yes, of course." He looked up in sudden remorse. "I haven't thanked you for defending me! I'm sorry, sir—"

The Chett waved aside his apology. "I am grateful for the opportunity of sticking one of Rendle's mercenaries. Besides, Gudon would never have forgiven me if I let any harm come to you."

"Rendle!" Kumul exclaimed in surprise. "He's the bastard behind all of this?"

The Chett regarded Kumul with something like respect. "Indeed. I recognized him as soon as he arrived with his company."

"Was Jes Prado with him?"

It was the Chett's turn to look surprised. "Prado is riding with him? All the gods of earth!"

"You know Gudon?" Lynan asked.

"He's waiting for you at my house."

"So you are Kayakun," Lynan said with something like relief.

The Chett bowed deeply. "Your Majesty."

"Who is Gudon, Lynan?" Kumul asked, frowning.

Lynan laughed. "I am sorry. This must be confusing for you."

"To say the least."

"Gudon was the pilot of the barge Prado stole. It was he who saved me from the man, and suffered great harm because of it. And Kayakun is Gudon's contact here at the sooq."

"Contact?" Kumul looked puzzled. "How does a barge pilot have a contact in the Strangers' Sooq?"

"Gudon is a Chett as well."

"Ah," Kumul said. He still looked puzzled but asked no more questions.

Suddenly, Jenrosa gasped and reached out to touch the scar on Lynan's jaw. "Lynan, what happened to you?"

"A present from Jes Prado," he said.

"I'll fillet the bastard," Kumul said lowly.

"Come," Kayakun said. "We must leave here. I will arrange for some of my people to clean up the alley. Captain Rendle will never know what happened to his men."

Lynan picked up the pots. Kumul offered to take them, but Lynan refused. "It takes training to do this job properly," he said, smiling.

Kayakun stopped at the mouth of the alley to make sure no one was keeping an eye out for them, then led the way onto the street. They had to go only a short distance before they reached one of the larger houses in the town. Instead of going through the front entrance, Kayakun took them to the back door, a solid piece of spray tree crisscrossed with iron bars. They entered a large kitchen. An iron stove along one wall warmed the room, and a long wooden table took up most of the space. Bustling servants came into the room. One took the pots from Lynan, another gathered their coats and cloaks, a third took Lynan's tunic with Gatheras's insignia and gave him a Chett shirt. Then Gudon appeared. He showed surprise at the unexpected crowd but quickly embraced Lynan.

"Truth, little master, did I not say you would be all right?"

"Truth," Lynan admitted, then introduced Gudon to his companions.

"We have to thank you for looking after our friend the last few days," Kumul said.

"It was my duty," Gudon said simply.

For a moment the two men carefully regarded each other. Kayakun invited them all to sit down. Servants brought clay mugs of spiced wine. Kayakun instructed them to take care of the bodies of the mercenaries in the alley. They left promptly.

"Bodies?" Gudon asked.

Kayakun quickly explained how they were followed by five mercenaries, their short conversation and the sudden appearance of Lynan's friends.

"We were sitting in the tavern wondering how to make contact with Lynan," Kumul explained, "when he walked by with Kayakun. Then we saw the mercenaries following them."

Kayakun described the brief battle, taking obvious delight in the telling.

"That will leave Captain Rendle a neat puzzle," Gudon remarked.

"So what happens next?" Kumul asked. He had vague notions about escaping at night from the sooq and heading west into the Oceans of Grass until they encountered a tribe with which they could find refuge. He hoped Lynan's new friends could give them directions or advice about where to go.

"There is little we can do while the mercenaries are camped outside the sooq," Gudon admitted. "But they cannot wait here forever. They must know that word of their arrival is already spreading to the tribes roaming nearby, and that a Chett war party will arrive to kill them. We remember Captain Rendle and what he and others like him did to our people before the Slave War."

"How long before such a war party arrives?"

"We cannot be sure," Gudon said hesitantly.

"We cannot stay here," Kumul said. "Even if Rendle leaves, he will leave agents behind, or inform those who wish Lynan harm. He may already have done so. It isn't safe for us here."

"He wouldn't ransack the sooq, would he?" Jenrosa asked.

Kayakun shook his head. "Each of these houses is like a small fort. His force is not equipped for fighting in the confined space of streets and alleys, any more than we here are equipped to got out and meet him in the field."

"Stalemate," Ager said.

"Unless Rendle receives reinforcements," Kayakun said. "There could be an army on its way here now from the east."

There was an awkward silence. Ager cleared his throat. "Just how much do you know about Lynan and the situation in Kendra?"

"Everything," Gudon said.

"You swear allegiance to the crown of Grenda Lear, and yet you are prepared to help Lynan? That would be counted as treason among some."

"And yet *you* travel with him and protect him," Gudon said.

"That is not an answer," Ager insisted.

Gudon sighed. "I cannot explain all here and now, but I tell you that we Chett will never forget what Elynd Chisal did for us. Prince Lynan is his son, and will always be welcome among us even though every other people in the kingdom turn their backs on him."

Gudon and Ager locked eyes for a second, then Ager nodded stiffly. "Good enough."

"We are still left with the question of what to do after Rendle leaves the sooq—if he leaves," Kumul reminded them.

"There is a way you can all be safe, and none of your enemies may find you," Gudon said. "I will guide you myself."

"Where is this place?"

"I did not say it is a place."

"We have little time for riddles," Kumul said darkly.

"I am not speaking in riddles, friend of Lynan, but you

will have to wait and see. I may say no more about it. You
will have to trust me."

There was another unwelcome silence, then Lynan said:
"I trust you, Gudon. I will come with you."

Gudon regarded him solemnly. "I knew you would, little
master." He glanced at Lynan's friends. "But what of your
companions?"

Before either Ager or Kumul could reply, Jenrosa said:
"If Lynan trusts you, so do I." She glared at the other two.
"And so do they."

"Well, that settles that," Ager said.

Kayakun slapped his hands together. "How good we are
all friends, especially in this troubling time. Now I suggest—"

Before he could suggest anything, one of his servants
reappeared and whispered something into his ear. His face
became serious. His servant made to leave, but Kayakun
called him back. "Bring food for our guests." The servant
bowed and left.

Kumul's stomach growled at the mention of food. He
looked apologetically at their host. "I have not eaten properly for a long time. None of us have."

"That will be taken care of," Kayakun assured him. "But
now something even more important than food has come up.
My servant reports that Rendle and his company are moving
out, and they heard from some of the merchants that his men
were talking about heading north, to Haxus." He turned to
Gudon. "As soon as they have left, you must go tonight, in
case Rendle changes his mind."

Rendle followed his men out of the sooq. At the first rise
he halted with Eder and Prado and looked back. "How sure
are you that the boy you saw was Prince Lynan?" he asked
Prado.

"Your five men never returned. That should answer your question."

"One day I will come back to this place," Rendle said. "I will come back with a thousand troops and raze it to the ground."

Prado sneered. "You really think the Chetts will let you live that long?"

Rendle ignored him.

"I had best go," Eder suggested.

"You have your men ready?"

"Yes, exactly as you instructed. Twenty-five riders."

"When you have finished your business, come straight to Kolbee."

Eder nodded and left.

"All you need now is for Lynan and his friends to do exactly as you want," Prado said mockingly.

Rendle caught Prado's gaze and held it until the other flinched and looked away. "Lynan will flee the sooq. Whatever friends he has left know there is no true safety for him down there. Every day Lynan stays increases his chances of being assassinated, or stolen away again. Only out there on the Oceans of Grass will he truly be safe." Rendle smiled tightly. "At least, that is what they think, and that mistake will be their undoing."

27

L YNAN felt whole for the first time since being taken by Jes Prado. Around him were his friends, including Gudon. They were all fed, all mounted on fresh horses—six mares, all sisters—and all equipped with saddle packs filled with food and water, as well as a felt gorytos for Gudon, holding a reflex bow and a quiver of arrows. Lynan had his sword back, carried all the way to the Strangers' Sooq for him by Ager. Well, not his sword, he reminded himself, remembering how he had won it in the encounter at the ford with Kumul, but a good weapon at least. And best of all he was rid of his clothes, worn thin and encrusted with grime, dirt, blood, and sweat. Kayakun had dressed them all in Chett garb, with linen trousers and shirts, heavy ponchos and wide-brimmed sun hats made from boiled leather. The only garment he had kept, stored in one of his saddlebags, was the green coat given him by the forester Roheth and carried all this way by Ager. Lynan had to admit they must have looked a strange sight getting ready to ride out of the Strangers Sooq in the middle of the night, with Kumul's poncho barely covering his shoulders and Ager's looking as lopsided as a drooping flower.

The moon overhead was nearly full and cast enough light

to read by, so when Lynan took Kayakun's hand and thanked him for all his help, he could easily see the lines of concern creasing the Chett's face. Kayakun gave the full bow the Chetts seemed so fond of. "Travel well, your Majesty."

Kayakun said brief farewells to the rest of the group, lingering only with Gudon, who leaned over his saddle so they could talk privately.

When they were finished, Gudon turned in his saddle to face the others. "We go now, my friends. Quickly as we can for the first hour. The farther away we are from the sooq, the safer we will be." He waved to Kayakun and spurred his horse to a trot, the others following close behind.

As they left the sooq, Gudon picked up the pace. The horses fell into a ground-eating canter, their manes fluttering like pennants.

Lynan felt he was entering a dream world. If the Oceans of Grass had captured his imagination under the light of the sun, under the light of the moon they captured his soul. It no longer seemed like a vast plain covered in grass, but a real ocean with real waves. It seemed to him they rode godlike across water, and underneath he sensed the heartbeats of great creatures, solitary and somnolent, never disturbed by the goings-on of lesser creatures. Above him, the dark sky seemed like smoked glass embedded with glittering gems. Like the ocean, the plains had surges and troughs. Gentle hills rose and disappeared as they rode by.

At last, Gudon reined back the pace and the mares happily continued at a quick walk. As both riders and mounts recaptured their breath, Lynan started to hear the sounds of the plain. There were so many crickets chirruping that the sound became a single melody; above them, he could hear the occasional hooting of an owl and the flapping, skittering wings of bats. And then the call of a kestrel. For a moment that seemed perfectly normal. Kestrels flew above all the world's oceans.

He pulled up his horse. For a moment the others rode on, unaware he had stopped; when they noticed he was no longer with them, they halted.

"What is it?" Gudon called back to Lynan.

Lynan motioned for them all to keep silent.

And there it was again. The call of a kestrel. He had not imagined it.

"I have never heard that sound before," Gudon said. Using his left leg to support his weight, he stood in the stirrups to survey the sky and land around them.

"And you never will away from the sea," Jenrosa added.

Lynan caught up with them. "Rendle?" he asked.

Gudon ignored the question and kneed his horse closer to Jenrosa. "Lynan tells me you are a magicker."

"A student magicker."

He put his hand in one of his saddlebags and retrieved what looked like slivers of diamond. "Can you cast?"

"I know the theory," Jenrosa said warily.

He gave the slivers to Jenrosa. "These will help, but hurry. We have not much time."

The urgency in his voice discouraged any more questions. She held up her palm to see better what Gudon had given her. Silvery translucent wafers shone softly with moonlight. She dredged from her memory the incantation for casting; it was one of the more ludicrous series of phrases, but she closed her hand around the wafers, shut her eyes, and recited the lines. Her hand tingled, but there was no finish, that relief that flooded through her when a magic was performed properly. She breathed deeply and tried again, but with no more success. She opened her eyes and found Gudon staring straight into them.

"I'm sorry, I—"

"Wait," he ordered. He drew his short, bone knife from its sleeve behind his neck and used it to cut a long line in the palm of his hand. He placed his hand over her fist. "Now, try again."

Jenrosa nodded, closed her eyes and started the incantation a third time. She felt the Chett's warm blood creep over her fingers. As she recited the words they seemed to vibrate in her mind, grow in size. She opened her mouth and the words poured out like a river of water. She felt the wafers in her hand writhe and move, and would have let them go if Gudon's own hand was not wrapped tightly around hers.

For the others, watching, nothing at all seemed to happen at first, but as the incantation grew in power and Jenrosa's voice grew stronger, the air above her seemed to distort and waver. For an instant, Lynan thought he saw the shape of a huge wolf twist in the sky, but then the image was gone as quickly as it had formed and he convinced himself it was his imagination.

Jenrosa finished, the last word almost a shout, and a wave of exultation and exhaustion washed through her. She slumped in the saddle. Gudon held her up and forced open her palm. The wafers were all gone.

"Good. The cast was made. Help will come." He looked up again to survey the terrain around them. "I only hope it will come in time." He lifted Jenrosa's head. "Are you well enough to ride?"

She nodded wearily, but to prove her point, she pulled away from him and sat erect in her saddle.

"Over there!" Kumul cried, pointing north. Between two low hillocks about halfway to the horizon they saw dark shapes flitter along the grass.

"We cannot outrun them," Ager said darkly. "Rendle's company are mounted on good cavalry stallions. They will chase our mares from here to the other side of Theare or drop dead in the attempt."

"We must try!" Gudon cried. "These horses were born

and bred on the Oceans of Grass, and there are no more sure-footed creatures on this world." He flicked the reins, and his horse immediately broke into a gallop. Without urging from their riders, the other mares followed.

The wind blew in Lynan's face, stinging his skin and making his eyes water, but his heart was filled not with fear but exhilaration. His excitement was sensed by his mount and she seemed to fly across the grass. Time seemed to stand still, and it was the world that passed under the mares' hoofs, turning on its axis with their speed. Whenever Lynan spied the enemy, they seemed no nearer.

But the enemy was equally relentless in the hunt. Eventually time started again, the mares slowed, and the black figures pursuing them began to close. The moon, which had seemed so high and bright, now hung near the horizon and the night grew darker and colder. With his crooked fate once more catching up with him, Lynan's exhilaration ebbed, replaced by a rising dread.

Gudon had been leading them west the whole time. Directly ahead in the distance Lynan could see a hill that rose higher above the plains than any other, and knew that the Chett must be taking them there for a last stand. He looked northward but saw no sign of the enemy. Then something made him look behind him, and there they were, slapping their horse's flanks with the flats of their swords. He counted five of them, then ten, then more. Their war cries, filled with a terrible blood lust, reached his ears and made his skin crawl. He looked ahead again and realized they would never reach that hill, would never have a last stand. They would be struck from behind like mice fleeing a cat.

Gudon cut sideways so he could shout instructions to Jenrosa, but the wind took his words away and Lynan could not hear him. He saw Jenrosa nod, rein back enough for Lynan to draw beside her. She looped the reins around her wrist and then grasped the manes of both their horses. She quickly uttered six words. The effect was instantaneous. Their mares gained fresh energy and seemed to leap forward. They quickly overtook the other three.

"Now the others!" Lynan shouted to Jenrosa, but she did not seem to hear him. "Jenrosa, help the others!"

She looked at him, and the grief she saw in her eyes turned his heart to ice. He looked over his shoulder once more and saw Gudon, Kumul, and Ager turn their horses. For a moment they paused and he knew with utter certainty they were looking at him for one last time, then Gudon drew out his bow and fitted an arrow and the three of them turned their mounts around and charged toward the enemy, their war cries so loud the stars in the sky seemed to shake.

"No!" Lynan cried. "No!" He pulled back hard on the reins and the mare screamed as the bit jagged in her mouth. As she broke from her gallop, he started turning her around.

"No, Lynan!" Jenrosa shouted at him and grabbed for his reins. Tears filled her eyes. "There is no other way! They've given you your last chance! Don't let them die in vain!"

Lynan turned on her with all his anger. "And what about you? What is your sacrifice for Prince Lynan?"

She pointed to the hill. "There is where I make my stand. What little magic I have I will use to protect you as you ride farther west. Gudon says help is on its way, and if we can slow the enemy long enough, you will reach it before they reach you."

His anger bled away. "I don't want you to die for me!" he cried. "I don't want anyone to die for me anymore!"

"What makes you think the choice is yours?" she asked, her voice almost scornful. "None of us had any hand in this destiny, but Gudon and Kumul and Ager won't fly from it, and neither will I." She grabbed him by his shirt and pulled his face next to hers. "And if you had one tenth the courage of your father, neither would you!"

Lynan pulled away. "I don't choose this destiny!" he

shouted back at her, and kicked his horse into a gallop, back toward the enemy.

"Oh, fuck," Jenrosa breathed and drew her sword from its saddle sheath. In her present state of mind it would probably do as much good as any magic she might raise. Her friends were going to die, and she knew with a strange satisfaction that she did not want to live without them. She waved the sword experimentally above her head. It whistled in the air. *That's a good sign,* she thought, and spoke a word in her mare's ear. The horse shook her head, whinnied, and broke into a gallop, doing its damnedest to catch her sister.

Lynan had by now drawn his own sword. He leaned hard over the saddle, the blade parallel with the horse's head, and prayed to God his courage would hold. He saw his three friends engaged in a confusing melee with at least five of the enemy, their weapons rising and falling, their horses wheeling around each other. Another three or four of the enemy lay dead around them, all with arrows sticking from throats or eyes. More of the mercenaries were joining in as they caught up with the fight, but they were too disorganized for their greater numbers to truly tell. His friends used the enemy as shields, and their nimble mares let them maneuver more easily in the mass of stamping, champing horses.

Lynan shouted no war cry but hewed straight in. His first target was a mercenary circling the melee searching for a way to get in, and Lynan's swinging sword caught him on the side of the head, taking off his helmet together with an ear. As he passed Lynan swung the blade back and felt it sink into the man's face. He jerked it free and straightened his arm, pointing the sword directly to his second target, a mercenary who had already lost his helmet. He kept the hilt in line with his face, just as Kumul had taught him, and bore down on the man. Six inches of steel slid through the mercenary's neck and spine. The collision jarred Lynan's arm, and as he pulled the blade free from the falling enemy, he cursed himself for not bending his elbow before the sword point struck home. He had not remembered all of Kumul's lessons.

By now more of the enemy had ridden up and, seeing Lynan, were determined to disarm and capture him. Lynan saw only one way out. Or, rather, in. There was a gap in the central mass of struggling horses and men, and he spurred his mare through it. He caught a glimpse of Kumul's horrified face when the giant saw him, but had no time to shout a greeting. A sword seemed to come from nowhere, probably aiming for Kumul. The constable was too fast, however, and easily deflected the blow. Lynan was not fast enough, and the flat of the blade whacked him in the ear. He shouted in pain, riposted, and felt the blade strike something solid.

Another mercenary was going for Kumul, swinging a short mace above his head. Lynan twisted his horse around and lunged, sending the tip of his sword through the enemy's armpit. The man screamed and fell, but quickly scrabbled to his feet. As Lynan was about to swipe at his face the man was knocked down by a horse. He screamed one last time as a pair of hoofs trampled his chest and head.

Lynan found himself squeezed between two mercenaries, his sword arm jammed against his side. The mercenary on his right raised his own sword and used its pommel to strike against Lynan's skull. Lynan heaved sideways, unbalancing the man, and as he righted himself, he whipped his head forward, breaking the man's nose with his forehead. The mercenary pulled back on his horse's reins and was swallowed up in the melee. His sword arm free, Lynan now struck at the enemy on his left but missed. His opponent, made aware of the threat, tried to punch Lynan away, but then Ager appeared beside him. The crookback's short sword made a single thrust and the man slumped over his saddle.

"What the fuck are you doing here?" Ager demanded angrily, but Lynan's horse was carried forward in a sudden

surge and he had no time to reply. He swung his sword to
left and right, hitting leather armor and steel helmets, but
making no effective strikes. Suddenly the area around him
cleared and he found himself outside of the melee.

Two mercenaries, one with a face like a bear's backside
and the other with a scar running along his nose, saw him
isolated and charged. Lynan wheeled his mount in the opposite direction, looking desperately for a way back in to the
squabbling confusion and some kind of anonymity. Then
someone rushed past him, holding a sword in a most unusual
fashion. He heard a blade smack into flesh, and wheeled
around again. Jenrosa's mare had kept on going, taking her
well away from the man whose face she had bruised, while
his companion—scarface—clumsily swiped at her as she
galloped by.

Lynan charged now. He drove his knee into the thigh of
the man Jenrosa had attacked to keep him off balance, and
at the same time brought the edge of his sword directly into
the middle of the second mercenary's face, right in line with
his scar. The man had no time to scream. His blood sprayed
Lynan as his horse carried him away from the battle. Lynan
wheeled a third time, and rising slightly in his saddle, used
all his strength to swing his blade into the neck of bear face,
scooping out a wedge of muscle and tendon. The mercenary
automatically opened his mouth to scream, but the air whistled uselessly through the gash in his throat. His horse
reared, stumbled, and fell on top of him.

Jenrosa had gotten her horse under control and was looking for more likely targets. Lynan had no time to worry
about her. He had seen another group of five mercenaries
riding hard toward the fight. He knew that with their arrival
the weight in numbers finally would be too great for his
friends. He did not think, he just reacted. He galloped toward them, sword held out in front again. He chose the man
on the left, but instead of charging in turn, the mercenaries

parted, and Lynan found himself riding between them, his sword swinging at nothing but air. He wheeled around and saw the five were circling him.

One of them shouted out: "We wish you no harm, Prince Lynan. Throw down the sword and surrender!"

In response Lynan charged again, but once more they moved out of his way, then closed in around him as he pulled back.

"Then we'll have to do this the hard way," the same mercenary said, and nodded to his fellows.

They all rode in at the same time, holding their swords so they could use the flats of their blades. Lynan concentrated on one of them and swung for his head but missed. Then the others struck. Lynan felt steel slap into his back and both his arms, and then his right hand. His sword dropped from his numbed fingers. He tried to turn, to grab at one of the mercenary's swords, but they eluded him, wheeling in turn to bring the flats down again, this time on his thighs and shoulders. All his muscles were locking in shock. He felt one foot come loose from his stirrup and started to fall. He grabbed for one of the enemy's saddles and dragged himself free from the other stirrup. The mercenary whose saddle he held growled at him and brought the pommel of his sword down on Lynan's hands.

Lynan screamed in pain and let go. He fell, hit the ground, and tumbled. He tried to scrabble to his feet, but the blades came again, belting him into submission, their horses crowding around him and barring any escape. He felt himself sliding to the ground again, drowning in a series of flashing blows. Then the attack finished, and a pair of rough hands grabbed him by the poncho; a second pair knocked his hat off his head and grabbed his hair. His whole body felt as if it had been trampled. He tried breathing in, but the air caught in his throat as pain spasmed through his chest.

He heard a high and wild scream but did not know or care where it came from or what it might mean.

To start with, Kumul was actually enjoying himself. The knowledge that he was going to die freed him to revel in his yearning to kill Lynan's enemies, to give the boy he had loved as a son for over fifteen years the only chance he had to escape. He felt invincible. His sword passed through limbs and necks like a scythe through wheat, and when he caught a glimpse of Ager carrying out mayhem of his own, he could not help shouting his joy.

The mercenaries crowded behind him to attack without being attacked in turn, but the giant seemed to have eyes in the back of his head. He countered every assault, and every time he swung his sword, it seemed to end in the scream of yet another of their fellows. As more and more of the mercenaries joined in the fray, it simply became more confusing. There were nine of them now, crowding in around the giant and the crookback and the wild Chett, but they just seemed to get in each other's way. And then a fourth enemy appeared, small and agile with a terrible sword. They had no time to recognize the prince, but then suddenly he was gone as quickly as he had come.

For Kumul, though, Lynan's appearance had been a terrible shock. Suddenly, the joy of battle was replaced by a terrible fear for his charge's safety. He saw Lynan get squeezed out of the melee and tried to join him, but now the mercenaries' numbers were too great, and he could do little more than defend himself.

Eventually, even his great strength started to ebb. He tried to break out of the mass to give himself more room to use his size more effectively, but someone always got in the way. Ager must have sensed what Kumul was trying to do, for he tried to plough a passage through the enemy using the weight of his mare, but even their combined efforts were failing.

Then Gudon shrugged off an attacker and drove into the swirling maelstrom. The enemies in front of Kumul wavered. He took his chance and charged. Just as he broke through, he saw Ager go down beneath a blow to his head. He wheeled around again, but then from the corner of his eye saw Lynan surrounded by five mercenaries. He hesitated, and in that moment two of the enemy rushed at him. Gudon moved quickly to take down the first, but the second got through and Kumul wasted precious seconds disposing of him. He quickly glanced around him. Ager was still in his saddle and, despite blood streaming down the inside of his hat from a savage cut to his crown, his sword was still in action.

Gudon swung by Kumul, shouting, "Go! Save Lynan!" then disappeared again. More mercenaries were peeling off from the main battle to take on the giant, but Kumul wheeled his horse around and charged the group circling Lynan. He saw with despair that the prince was unhorsed, and that the swords of the enemy were rising and falling like the arms of a windmill. He heard a scream of hate and fury, and suddenly another rider entered the fray around Lynan. He recognized Jenrosa, using her sword like a whip, thrashing from one side to the other. Her blows did little damage, but temporarily scattered the mercenaries.

The giant had time to see Lynan collapse to the ground, and then he was within striking distance of the first enemy. He brought his sword down in a crashing blow that took off the man's arm. Kumul pushed past him to get to the next mercenary. He did not have time to raise his arm for another swing, so drove his sword's hilt into an eye. The man fell away from him, crying in pain and shock. Kumul saw Jenrosa get off her horse and try to lift Lynan on to her saddle, but she was not strong enough.

Fearing the worst, he circled behind her and reached down for Lynan, grabbed him by the back of his poncho and with one mighty heave lifted the prince across the neck of Jenrosa's horse. Jenrosa leaped back into her saddle, but before she could ride away the surviving mercenaries who had tried to take Lynan reformed and attacked again, two taking on Kumul and the third going for Jenrosa. Kumul killed one easily, but the other knew what he was doing, merely parrying Kumul's assault and not trying to close in for his own attack.

Jenrosa tried to defend herself as best she could against her opponent, but the mercenary easily got by her guard and stabbed her in the thigh. She stifled her cry and wheeled around, trying to keep her horse's head between them, but the maneuver made her lose her grip on Lynan and he slipped to the ground. The mercenary gave a shout of triumph and pressed home his attack, forcing Jenrosa away from the prince. Even though she parried as best she could, she knew she was about to die. Strangely, she did not feel afraid, only angry that she had failed to save Lynan.

Kumul saw her predicament and could do nothing to help. Every time he turned, his opponent, the most skillful he had ever met, was there in front of him again, blocking his way and blocking his every attack. In desperation, Kumul flicked his sword in the air, caught it underhand, and threw it like a spear. The mercenary recoiled in shock and batted the sword away, but Kumul had the second he needed. He punched the mercenary in the face. The man's eyes crossed and his jaw opened. Even as he started to slide backward off his horse, Kumul reached for his knife and drove it into the bottom of the mercenary's throat, stapling his jaws. Blood spat out between the man's teeth. Kumul pushed him aside and slid half out of his saddle to retrieve his sword. He propped himself back up and looked for Jenrosa, then saw he would be too late to help her. Jenrosa had been dismounted. She was on one knee, and her opponent was raising his sword for a killing stroke.

And then someone behind the rider reached up, grabbed him by his breeches, and hauled him off. The pair collapsed to the ground. Kumul saw the mercenary getting to his feet, and Lynan, too weakened by his last effort to get out of the way, half crouching on the ground. The enemy gave a terrible shout of rage, lifted his sword, and brought it down. Even as the edge of the blade struck Lynan on the back, the point of Kumul's sword appeared magically in the mercenary's chest. The force of Kumul's charge lifted the man into the air, wriggling on the blade like a speared fish. Blood blossomed on his chest and spilled out of his mouth. Kumul whipped the sword down, dropping the mercenary on the ground, then jumped off his horse and ran to Lynan.

Jenrosa was already there, screaming and screaming, blood all over her as she cradled Lynan's body in her lap. Kumul knelt down beside them, his heart beating so hard he thought it might explode. Lynan was deathly white, but no blood seeped between his lips. He quickly took the prince from Jenrosa's arms and turned him over. The cut was deep, but the flesh was red, and he saw no bone or fat. He knew, though, that if they could not stop the bleeding, Lynan would certainly die.

And then he remembered the others. He saw Ager and Gudon, their horses side by side, their arms slowing with exhaustion but still managing to parry every blow, surrounded by eight mercenaries closing in with the scent of victory in their noses.

"Press your hands against his wound," he ordered Jenrosa. "I'll be back."

He ran to his horse and mounted, and with one last effort of will managed to get the mare to work up to a gallop. The horse got half the distance and suddenly collapsed underneath him. He fell to the ground, somersaulted, and was on his feet again. He started running, desperately hoping he could get there in time, but he felt as if he was running in sand.

Then one of the mercenaries pulled back from the melee around Ager and Gudon, and then a second. They turned their horses around and fled. Soon they were joined by a third, and one by one the others peeled off and turned tail. Kumul stopped in wonder, then something long and dark and feathered pierced the back of the last man and he fell from his saddle. Kumul looked at Gudon, but his bow was still in its gorytos.

Suddenly a group of new riders appeared, bows and arrows in their hands, reins held in their mouths, in hot pursuit of the mercenaries. They loosed a flight of arrows, and then another flight and another until all the fleeing mercenaries had been toppled from their mounts, each impaled by a black shaft.

Lynan swam in a sea of agony. Every time he took a breath, he felt his chest and back ripple with pain. He knew his eyes were open because he could see stars, and sometimes the blur of a face. He heard sounds, too, cries and shouts, the stamping of hoofs. Later, hands gently moved him one way, and then the other. More faces appeared. He thought he heard Jenrosa shouting at him, then Kumul. Why were they so angry with him? He felt someone attempt to lift him. He tried to tell them to go away. He hurt too much. Why could they not leave him alone? He was sure if he could just have some peace and quiet, he would fall asleep and everything would be all right. Then he heard Pirem's voice. No, that could not be right. Pirem was back in Kendra. Then where was he? He was lifted again and he felt himself carried away by new waves of pain.

The ocean. What was it about the ocean? He had to remember. It was important. He did not want to drown. He just wanted to sleep.

And then all was still again, although he could still sense movement. Figures passed him, and the legs of horses. He looked up into the sky and saw that the stars were going out. He wanted to close his eyes, and discovered that they were already closed.

I am asleep, he thought. *At last, I am asleep.*

28

AREAVA blinked in the sudden rush of light as she moved from the chapel and saw a sea of faces before her. There was a pause, a moment's stillness, and then the cheering started, first from her nobles and officers and the Royal Guards, and then moving back along the entire crowd like a wave rippling along a pond. It became tumultuous, joyous, and it carried her heart up into the sky. Her people, her subjects, her kingdom.

Kestrels danced in the air, and the kestrel pennant of the Rosethemes fluttered from every flagpole in the palace and the city. She raised the two Keys in her possession and they glinted in the bright sunlight, the Key of the Scepter which gave her the right to rule, and the Key of the Sword, which gave her the right to defend her kingdom come what may and with whatever means at her disposal.

Olio took her hand, and Dejanus and Orkid took their position behind her. She walked slowly down the steps to the forecourt, preceded by the court sergeant holding King Thebald's ornate Sword of State. The cheering continued, and now she could hear the clapping, the singing, and the blessings coming from her people. Nobles and ambassadors, subject monarchs and guild leaders, priests and malefici, joined in the procession as it moved past them. She left the palace and started the long walk through the capital, the avenue crammed with people kept back by the Royal Guards. As she passed, guards peeled away and used back streets to get to their new positions farther down in the city. She tried to keep a stately pace, but she was so filled with her own joy she wanted to pick up her skirts and run.

Children slipped through the guards and threw flowers at her. She laughed with them. Old women and men reached for her hand, and she gave it to them. Soldiers and peasants and brewers and potters and cloth makers and magickers all called her name, and she smiled at them, each and every one.

When she reached the old quarter near the harbor, people were hanging from second-story windows and looking almost directly down on the queen. They released ribbons in the gold-and-black Rosetheme colors. They drifted, fluttered and whirled down like windblown thistle, covering her hair and dress. She laughed and waved back at them, kissed their ribbons, blessed them in turn. She was so happy tears came to her eyes.

At last the procession reached the harbor itself. A squadron of her warships, their decks polished so highly they shone, their hulls freshly painted, and the kestrel pennant whipping from their masts, waited there. When Areava appeared, the crews, lined along the decks and standing on every mast, cheered so loud the windows in nearby buildings rattled. Seagulls escaped into the sky. She made her way, alone, to a dais built up in front of the ships and on which was perched a solitary chair, plain and unadorned. She reached the chair and turned around. This was the climax of her coronation, and when the cheering finally died, every person was on their knee, their heads bowed almost to the ground.

Everything was still. Time waited.

"You are my people," Areava declared in her strongest voice, the words ringing across the water. "And I will always be your queen. Nothing shall come between us. I live to serve this mighty kingdom of Grenda Lear, all its inhabitants, and its destiny."

She sat down, and the cheering started all over again. Olio climbed the dais, knelt before his sister and laid his forehead on her knee. "Indeed, sister, you are our queen, and none would have it otherwise."

She leaned over and kissed his head. "We have come through much since the deaths of our mother and two brothers, sweet Olio, but now things are as they should be." He looked up into her eyes and saw happiness and solemnity there. "It seems to me that the world, once again, is aright."

Jes Prado teetered from the tent, a leather bottle in one hand, and crisscrossed his way across the camp. A guard watched his progress with cruel amusement. He managed to reach the middens without accident, but as he fumbled with his belt, he lost his balance and tipped forward into the piss trench. There was a loud squelching sound and the mercenary disappeared from sight. The guard laughed hard and long, only stopping when he saw his sergeant leave his tent to start his inspection round. He forgot about the drunk Prado and straightened his jerkin.

Prado, now out of sight, threw away the bottle and made his way on hands and knees from the piss trench to the horse park. He chose the quietest stallion and untethered him from his post, then quietly, cautiously, led him into the darkness. When he could no longer hear the sounds of the camp, he mounted, and using his knees against the stallion's ribs and his hands in his mane urged him along the dangerous road back to Hume.

He had waited to escape for as long as possible, but had risked being caught this night because Rendle's increasingly unpredictable anger terrified him. Ever since reaching the border of Haxus, Rendle had been waiting for word from Eder, but none ever came. He refused to accept that his trusted lieutenant had failed him, and although the news about Lynan's existence and approximate whereabouts would win him favor in King Salokan's eyes, he was furious that the young prince had once again slipped through his fingers.

Prado knew that his own life was now worth nothing to Rendle, and if he did not escape would soon meet a convenient accident. Besides, if Rendle could sell his information to Salokan, then Prado could sell it to Areava.

He looked up into the sky, bright and remote, and wished he was a bird and could fly all the way home. He sighed. He was only a man, a lonely man cut off from friends and allies, and the road ahead would be as dangerous going back as it had been getting here. But he would manage it. He had news for the new queen. He looked back at Rendle's camp for the last time.

And a score to settle he thought. *Watch for me, Captain Rendle. I will come back for you one day, and cut off your head.*

Jenrosa entered the hide hut and immediately felt ill with the heat. A central fire, surrounded by white stone and fed by dung, burned brightly. Next to it lay a heap of woolen hides, and on top of the heap lay Lynan, unconscious and shivering. His fever had lasted five days so far and gave no sign of easing. His skin was yellow and his face—once so full and boyish—was scarred and gaunt with pain. Kumul was sitting next to him. At first, she thought he was praying, but then she heard the name of Elynd Chisal. She moved a step closer and listened.

"So when your father was murdered, you see, I took you as my son. Nothing formal, of course. I mean, a soldier doesn't tell the queen how to look after her own child, but I was going to make sure you were brought up right, just like the general would have wanted." Kumul's words thickened and the giant man stopped to clear his throat. He ran a hand through his short, graying hair. "But here you are, you see, all in a heap, and the Chetts don't have any medicine or magic to heal you because you're wounded so bad. So what I'm saying is that you have to do this by yourself. I can't help you anymore. No one can. But I'm not letting go, understand. I'm not going to let you just die, lad. So I'm going to talk to you. You hear my words and follow them back."

Jenrosa crouched down next to Kumul, gingerly moving her bandaged leg so it rested straight. Kumul's eyes were red, and he held Lynan's right hand in both of his. Jenrosa lay her own hands on Kumul's.

"There's nothing for it," he said hoarsely.

Jenrosa touched Lynan's forehead. It was damp and cold, despite the heat. "You should get some rest. I will stay with him."

"You are a magicker . . ." he started hopefully, looking into her eyes.

She saw her own pain and grief reflected there. She shook her head. "I really was only a student, Kumul. I know some tricks, some simple spells and incantations, but what Lynan needs is beyond my power, or beyond the power of any magicker I know of."

He shook his head. "I'm not going to let him die," he said fiercely.

She rested her head against Lynan's chest. His heartbeat was slow and faint. At that moment, if she could have given her life for his, she would have done so.

It would be a fair exchange, she thought, hoping a god somewhere was listening. *My life means something to me now. It would be a sacrifice.*

But Lynan needed something stronger than her life, she

told herself. *His ghost has traveled so it can probably see the dead. If only he hadn't lost so much blood.*

She blinked. Blood. The source of all life. She was chasing down a dim memory and when she caught it she gasped at the implications. Her eyes opened wide with sudden fear. Did she dare? It might kill him, and yet . . .

She looked at his pale body again, the wasting flesh, and understood she had no choice. She struggled to her feet and limped out of the tent. With a puzzled frown, Kumul watched her go. Gudon was sitting with Ager on the grass outside of the hut. They looked up at her, their eyes afraid.

"He's not. . . ?" Ager asked, but could not finish the question.

"No, but he will be soon if we don't do something." She looked around, but could not see what she needed. "Where are Lynan's saddlebags?"

"What?"

"For God's sake, Ager! His saddlebags! Where are Lynan's saddlebags?"

"In our hut," he replied. "What do you want them for?"

Jenrosa ignored the question and turned to Gudon. "Get them for me, and some of your potion."

"The haethu will no longer work," Gudon objected. "His wounds are too great—"

"Just get them!" she shouted into his face, and limped back to the tent.

A moment later Ager and Gudon entered the tent. Gudon gave her the saddlebags and a small flask of haethu. She searched through one saddlebag, chucking its contents onto the floor, but did not find what she was looking for.

"Oh, damn, damn, damn!" she cried, and opened the second saddlebag, again discarding its contents like a thief searching for coins. Then she pulled out the forester's coat. She searched its pockets and pulled out a soiled piece of green cloth. "Thank God!"

The others looked at her mystified.

"What are you doing?" Kumul asked.

They watched her open the stop to the haethu flask, then use a knife to scrape something dark stuck to the cloth into its mouth.

"What is it?" Gudon asked. "What are you doing?"

"Saving Lynan's life." She looked up at them and they could see how desperate, and how afraid, she was. "Blood for blood, " she said.

She put her thumb over the mouth and shook the flask vigorously. The contents turned a deep ruby red. She edged over to Lynan, parted his lips, and slowly let the contents of the flask trickle down his throat.

When the flask was empty, she. sat back, and the others watched expectantly.

"If this works, it may take a while," Jenrosa told them. Even as she finished the sentence, Lynan made a strange whining sound. His muscles went rigid, his back arched. His mouth opened and he screamed. Jenrosa and the others looked on in shock.

Lynan collapsed back on the hides, still again.

"Oh, please, God, don't let me have killed him," Jenrosa whimpered.

Ager leaned over and put his ear against Lynan's chest. "He is still alive." His eyes widened. "The heart is beating stronger!" He stared at Jenrosa. "What have you done?"

"I'm not sure."

"Saved his life!" Kumul said enthusiastically, and picked the magicker up in his arms and swung her around. When he put her down he kissed her, suddenly and unexpectedly. For a moment their eyes met and they both blushed. "You have saved his life," Kumul repeated.

Or taken his soul, Jenrosa thought to herself, her feelings more confused than they had ever been before.

29

AREAVA found solitude in her chambers. She had chased out her ladies-in-waiting and their chattering formality, her secretary and his obsequious formality, and the guards and their solemn formality. She was by herself and awake, completely and blissfully, for the first time since . . . she could not remember for how long. Her lover was with the ambassador from Aman, giving him letters for his father, King Marin. Olio had disappeared from the palace again; she decided she would have to look into that; she did not want anything happening to him.

Most of the guests from the provinces who had come for the coronation had now departed Kendra, and life in the city, after days of celebrations, was returning to normal. The members of the Twenty Houses, all her uncles and aunts and cousins to the sixth degree, had behaved themselves admirably during the coronation, and even took her announced engagement to Sendarus with equanimity. The provincials had been overjoyed at the news, of course. One of their own, in a manner of speaking, was marrying into the royal family. They probably all left the capital thinking if King Marin could pull off such a coup, maybe their children or grandchildren could marry into the next generation of

Rosethemes. The thought amused and excited her. It was about time Grenda Lear became a kingdom in fact as well as in name, rather than simply the means of benefiting a select few in Kendra.

She patted her belly. She was sure she was not pregnant yet but was confident she would be sometime in the next year. She wanted a daughter. She would be happy with a son, but most of all she wanted a daughter. What would she call her? Usharna, of course. And if it was a boy? Berayma? Olio? Sendarus or Marin? She grimaced. Never, never, Lynan. That name would be expunged from the royal family for all time.

She went out on her balcony. The white stone of the palace turned gold in the setting sun. *A beacon for the most distant ships,* she thought. *A symbol for the most distant lands.* An onshore breeze picked up the Rosetheme pennant on every flagpole and the black kestrel on each one seemed to take flight.

She heard a scuffle in the corridor outside. The guards had detained someone. Then she heard Harnan's voice explaining that the queen was busy with other duties and could see no one. A man's voice spoke out: he had urgent news. His name was Prado and he had urgent news.

Probably about Haxus, Areava thought, and smiled to herself. Harnan had been right all those weeks ago. The work never finished, not really. And then she remembered Olio's words as well, and felt proud that perhaps she was becoming more and more like her mother.

She walked with confidence to the great door of her chamber and pushed it open. Harnan looked up surprised. Next to him, still held by a guard, was the scruffiest, dirtiest man Areava had ever seen. His eyes met hers and she read something in them, but something she could not yet decipher.

She smiled at Harnan. "I am queen to all my people, good Secretary. I will be pleased to listen to this man's news."

"Mainly children this week, Your Highness," Father Lukaz said.

Olio parted the curtain with one finger and looked out over the ward. All seven beds were occupied, only two with adults in them.

"Your Highness," said the magicker behind him, "none of them is seriously ill. These do not need your attention." He was under strict instructions from Edaytor Fanhow not to let Prince Olio exhaust himself on cases that were not a matter of life and death.

Olio tried to rub the tiredness from his eyes. "I cannot let the children suffer," he said. "We will wait until they are asleep and then I will treat them."

Father Lukaz and the magicker exchanged worried glances, then the priest led the prince back to the kitchen. He put fresh bread and wine on the table, and a platter of ham, cheese, and onions. Olio looked at the food but decided he was not hungry. The wine would help, though. He filled a goblet and drank it quickly. The alcohol burned in his thin frame, and he felt better. He could feel the Key of Healing resting warm against his chest.

Soon, he promised it. *The children are still awake. We can do our duty soon.*

Gudon held him by the hand and led him from the tent. Lynan closed his eyes against the bright light until someone placed one of the broad-rimmed Chett hats on his head. The light still hurt a little, but if he squinted, the pain was bearable. There was a cooking fire nearby and he had to fight the temptation to flee the yellow flames. It was something he would have to get used to.

He looked around him. He saw Kumul, Jenrosa, and Ager

with his bandaged head, standing nearby, smiling and concerned, and he felt so much affection for them it almost
brought him to tears. Then he saw the Chetts. Hundreds of
them, all bowing to him, their heads tilted up so they could
see him. There was one Chett, however, who did not bow so
low. She regarded him with a strange mixture of fear and
what he thought might be hope. She smiled slightly, bowed
a little deeper, and Lynan nodded to her. Gudon had told him
her name, but he could not remember it. Indeed, he could remember little of anything since waking from his terrible
dream.

Gudon let go of his hand. Lynan held it up for a moment,
wondering at its hard paleness, like ivory. He walked forward a dozen paces, taking it slowly, getting used to the heat
of the sun high overhead. He surveyed the land around him,
and found the sight of the plains filled him with a joy he
could not explain. *I am home,* he thought, and then: *It is
time.*

"My name is Lynan Rosetheme," he said, his voice weak,
but in the still air his words carried to everyone. "I am the
son of Queen Usharna Rosetheme and General Elynd
Chisal. I possess the Key of Union. I am come to you."

All at once the Chetts started calling his name. The
sound—a great ululation—rose into the sky and spread
across the Oceans of Grass. Its faintest echoes reached every
city and town and village on the continent of Theare, and
reached the ear of every king and every queen of Grenda
Lear, and to them it sounded at the same time like the whisper of a lover's promise and the hissing of an enemy's curse.

Lynan was alive.